"I KNOW THAT KID. . . ."

The Quinns searched everywhere for their missing son. The son the cops couldn't find. And then a voice calls out to them. The woman in the car next to them recognizes the picture of the little boy. But she's racing down the highway. The Quinns try to catch her, but she gets lost in the traffic . . . and the only clue they have disappears. . . .

WHO HAS TAKEN THEIR SON?
AND WHY?

PRAISE FOR
BLIND SPOT

Adam Barrow

BLIND SPOT

A SIGNET BOOK

SIGNET
Published by the Penguin Group
Penguin Putnam Inc., 375 Hudson Street,
New York, New York 10014, U.S.A.
Penguin Books, Ltd, 27 Wrights Lane,
London W8 5TZ, England
Penguin Books Australia Ltd, Ringwood,
Victoria, Australia
Penguin Books Canada Ltd, 10 Alcorn Avenue,
Toronto, Ontario, Canada M4V 3B2
Penguin Books (N.Z.) Ltd, 182–190 Wairau Road,
Auckland 10, New Zealand

Penguin Books Ltd, Registered Offices:
Harmondsworth, Middlesex, England

Published by Signet, an imprint of Dutton Signet,
a member of Penguin Putnam Inc. Previously published in a Dutton edition.

First Signet Printing, January, 1998
10 9 8 7 6 5 4 3 2 1

PUBLISHER'S NOTE
This is a work of fiction. Names, characters, places, and incidents either are the
product of the author's imagination or are used fictitiously, and any resemblance to
actual persons, living or dead, events, or locales is entirely coincidental.

Battle not with monsters lest you become a monster.
And if you gaze for long into the abyss,
the abyss gazes also into you.

—Friedrich Nietzsche

Once again, for Judith

PART
ONE

PART

ONE

"You're sure this is all right, now?"

"Absolutely."

"You don't mind?"

"Listen, hon, we'll have a good time."

"It's a shame about the aquarium."

He glanced over at the line snaking down the marble steps and trailing away from the great colonnaded building. The diversity of peoples, their fidelity to stereotype, piqued his professional interest: brash, noisy blacks; swaggery, sinister Hispanics; earnest, chocolate-skinned India Indians, many of the women sweltering resignedly in traditional saris; intense, camera-toting orientals; rowdy adolescents; querulous seniors; here and there a few mincing homosexuals; middle-class whites, aloof, distant, but a little apprehensive-looking too (not, he supposed, unlike themselves); troops of squealing field trip school kids, some not much older than Jeff—and all of them leagued by the single leveling commonality of an oppressive, muggy, almost equatorial heat. He shrugged, said, "No way we could know."

"He'd have so liked to see the fish. He's talked about it all week."

"Once we're inside the planetarium he'll forget all about it. What's more exciting than a trip to the stars?"

The object of all this whispered concern stood a couple of feet to their left, gazing orb-eyed up, up, at the heroic figure of a saber-brandishing horseman, frozen in space and stone and time, leading the charge of a phantom army.

"Who's that?" the child asked.

"His name was Thaddeus Kosciuszko," his father said, enunciating clearly, deliberately, but by no means condescendingly. It was Marshall Quinn's conviction that children responded best to adult speech patterns, and for the most part that's the way he addressed his son. "He fought in the American Revolutionary War," he went on, simplifying the statue's inscription but not by much. "Helped make this country what it is today," he added with only a pinch of irony.

"Why's his name funny?"

"He was from another country. Poland."

"Got a knife."

"That's what you call a sword."

"Sword?"

"A long knife."

They were all three of them munching Chicago Dogs, the bulgy tubes of meat slathered with condiments and spilling over with relish, eating with that peculiar contortive tilt of the head hotdogs inspire. Periodically Lori Quinn stooped down and swiped the drippings from the boy's chin with a napkin. When they were finished, Marshall checked his watch.

"Okay. It's a quarter to three. Show lasts about an hour, according to the program guide. Why don't we meet right here, under the watchful eye of Thaddeus? Four-fifteen, say? That give you enough time?"

"Plenty. I just want to walk through the exhibit again. Maybe browse the bookstore awhile."

The exhibit she referred to was a special collection of ancient Egyptian artifacts housed in the museum's basement level. After the initial disappointment of the impossible aquarium lines, they had spent the better part of the day wandering through the museum, starting on the second floor and working their way down, Jeff skipping excitedly from one display to the next, plants to birds to extinct wild beasts, wearing them out with his incessant chattery questions, a child's inexhaustible curiosity and wondrous energy, seemingly oblivious to the heat and the jostling crowds. Until they began their descent into ancient Egypt. Then he wilted and, bored, turned fractious, fretful. Marshall's reasoned appeals ("Come on, Jeff, Mom wants to see these things. It's only fair. Didn't we look at all the dinosaurs?") pacified him not in the slightest, and so after their snack break he volunteered to take him to the sky show. It was, after all, her outing too. Rare occasion, for them, a trip into the roaring city. For them, an adventure.

"Enjoy yourself," he said. "And don't worry about us."

"You're sure you can handle him, Marsh?"

"Of course I can."

"Watch him carefully. Don't let him go anywhere near the water."

"How about a fountain? If he's thirsty."

"Will you be serious?"

"Only if you'll get moving. We don't want to miss the moon and the planets." He stepped over and tapped Jeff, still fascinated by the gigantic horseman, on the shoulder. "We're going now. Wave goodbye to Mom."

The boy lifted a tiny arm, shook it vigorously. "Bye, Mom."

"Bye, Jeffie. Be good now and mind Daddy."

"Tell her see you later," Marshall prompted.

"See later."

"See *you* later," he said, softening the correction with a fond smile. "Don't forget your pronouns."

"What's a pronow?"

"You are. Come on."

Hands linked, they set out down one of the walks flanking a long, grassy boulevard. No one watching could have mistaken them for anything other than father and son, the child a replica in miniature of the man. Both of them had shocks of light brown hair, both smooth pink faces (the father's leaner, of course, but remarkably youthful and unlined for his accumulated thirty-two years), clear blue eyes, noble Anglo-Saxon noses, thin mouths, strong jaws, slender, small-boned frames (the son's, at a month or so past three, still padded with baby fat; the father's flat in the chest and waist, narrow at the hips, build of a recreational jogger, which in fact he was). On both the individual features were nondescript, unmemorable, yet seemed to come together somehow to achieve the effect of handsomeness.

Midway they came upon another statue, this handsome pair, and paused for an inspection. Some martyred Bohemian statesman, unknown to Marshall. He tried to explain the concept of martyrdom without much success. Next came Copernicus, where he was on slightly firmer historical ground. At last they arrived at the planetarium and joined a short line outside a square, glass-walled building fronting the domed structure.

They waited. Sunlight splashed off the pavement. Traffic scooted up and down the boulevard's parallel streets. Horns tooted. Vendors hawked. A trace of a sultry breeze lifted off the lake. Powerboats skimmed the surface of the green water. Overhead, gulls dipped and soared through a shimmery white sky.

Marshall felt drained, battered by the heat and clamor and confusion. Under his loose-fitting shirt, sweat streamed south along the ridges and valleys of his ribs and spine, pooled in the band of his shorts. His stomach churned. No more Chicago Dogs. One was more than plenty. At his side, Jeff twisted and squirmed. "When's the stars?" he demanded.

"Soon."

"I'm hot."

"So am I. Be patient."

A throng of people came pouring out the several

glass doors. The line inched forward. And then they were inside, delivered into the clement wrap of cool, conditioned air, hurried along by teenage ushers through a lobby, down a flight of stairs illuminated by blue fluorescent lights in futuristic configurations, over to a ticket window where they were handed plastic eyeglasses in exchange for bills, and finally, mercifully, into a dimly lit auditorium. Swarms of kids, more of the field trippers, filed through banks of seats sloping toward three screens, the center one draped, the other two uncovered and angled off sharply to either side. Marshall gripped Jeff's hand and led him down an aisle to a couple of empty spots near the front.

In a moment the drapes slid back, and a paunchy fellow, hugely grinning, strode out onto the stage and in that fraudulent chirpy voice adults often inflict on children (sort of voice Marshall Quinn despised) welcomed them all to the Adler Planetarium and announced the show was about to begin. Two parts, he explained, prominently displaying the appropriate number of fingers: the first a brief introduction to the heavens right here in this auditorium, and after that the center screen would magically open, revealing an escalator to whisk them to the planetarium proper for the main event—dramatic pause—*Meteor Mouse*! They were instructed to wear their glasses throughout the first segment, for the full 3-D effect, and reminded, twice, to return them to the ushers before ascending the escalator. After a couple of limp stabs at wit, he bawled, "Okay, kids! Everybody ready?"

Chorus of affirmative shrieks.

"Then le-e-e-t's go star hopping!"

Marshall smothered a sigh. Reminded himself this was his idea. He helped Jeff adjust the glasses, put on his own. The lights faded. Center screen a silhouette of the city skyline materialized on a horizon framed in pale blue, while a creamy female overvoice invited them on a trip through the cosmos, commencing at their present astronomical address—Chicago, North America, Earth—and proceeding outward through the solar system (the tiny ball of Earth gradually receding as she spoke, field of blue darkening, blackening) and galaxies whirling with stars. The three screens, working in concert, created a feel of spectacular velocity, a dazzling, almost vertiginous effect. Delighted oohs and aahs rose through the auditorium. And as the voyage continued on into the vast immensities of space, the voice encouraged them to search for patterns, design.

Abruptly it was over, the limits of the universe prudently left unexplored at the boundaries of theology. The lights came on, and the center screen, even as promised, parted. Marshall stood, stretched, looked down at his son, whose eyes were comically veiled by the glasses. A diminutive celebrity. "Did you like that?" he asked him.

"Where's the mouse?"

"Coming right up. Next feature."

He steered him toward the line forming at the foot of the escalator. Obediently, they handed over their glasses to a vigilant usher. Up they went. Emerged into another auditorium, this one large, circular, its seats arranged in ascending blocks split by narrow aisles and banked around a metallic device that looked, curiously, like some giant robotic bug, identical bulbous heads freakishly sprouting from either end. "What's that thing?" Jeff asked, jabbing a finger at it as they settled into seats near the middle of an otherwise empty file.

"I think it's the projector."

"What's a jector?"

"*Pro*jector. It's a machine that, well, casts an image—a picture—on a screen," Marshall said, grasping after a vocabulary to capture an explanation, conscious of his woeful ignorance of technology. "Like at the movies."

"Looks like Robocop."

"There's a resemblance."

The auditorium was filling but slowly. Painfully slow. Kids rolled off the escalator like finished products of an assembly line, darted about wildly. Their adult guides, harried, spent, chased after them scolding and corraling. Jeff, catching the fever, wiggled restlessly. Marshall reached into a pocket, produced a small bag of candy. "Well, look at this, would you?" he said, dangling it as though he had just made a most marvelous discovery. "Gummi Bears. Imagine that."

The boy's eyes widened. A grin scampered across his face.

"What do you think, Jeff? Should we eat them?"

"Mom said no."

Marshall glanced around slyly. "But Mom's not here. You see her?"

"No."

"So what do you think?"

"Eat 'em."

"I think you're absolutely right."

Marshall popped a candy in his mouth, handed Jeff the bag, and leaned over and whispered in conspiratorial tones, "This will be our little secret, okay?"

" 'Kay," the boy said around a mouthful of bear.

The lights dimmed. A great vault of daylight sky opened above them. Another female voice introduced herself as Cosmic Cat, temporary stand-in for Meteor Mouse, who was unaccountably delayed but would be along any minute now. The sky deepened into night. Clusters of stars winked on, salted the heavens. Among them an unmistakable feline figure appeared, directing the viewers' attention to assorted constellations—the Dippers, Leo the Lion, the Archer Sagittarius, Draco the Dragon—in a voice unbearably cute and punctuated by a particularly grating "meeow." Presently the tardy mouse arrived, and to the boundless mirth of the juvenile audience the two figures bickered tirelessly, like a pair of quarrelsome celestial house pets.

Marshall heard a small rustling in the row directly behind them. Latecomer, no doubt, groping for a seat. He eased back in his own. It was slanted as a recliner, cushioned, remarkably comfortable. The chill air soothed him. His limbs slackened. He indulged a mighty yawn. Shuttered his eyes. Tuned out the rackety voices. And promptly fell asleep.

Later—impossible to say how long—he was

jolted into wakefulness by a majestic crescendo of finale music. The lights were on. Children streamed through the many exits, emptying the auditorium. A lingering trace of an odor, faintly sweetish, rose from the seat next to him, which also was empty, his son gone.

At about six p.m. that same day, Odell DeCruz was about to exit his Brookfield apartment when the rattle of the phone brought him up just short of the door. He went into the kitchen, picked up the cellular and, assuming it to be a business call, said, "Dingo," the name by which he was commonly known to all his associates.

"Dingo?" a snarly voice gave it back to him.

"That's right."

"Sal."

"Sal. What can I do for you?"

"You in a talkin' position?"

"I am," Dingo confirmed, strolling into the empty living room, receiver fused to his ear.

"Remember that piece merchandise you was askin' about, couple months back?"

"Help me out, Sal. We've discussed all kinds of merchandise."

"Crumbsnatcher."

It took Dingo a moment to translate the street rap in his head. For himself, he preferred a precise, explicit, almost formal diction. It was a way of distancing one's self. Also an elevating discipline. "Oh, yes," he said. "I believe I do recall that one."

"Think maybe I got somethin' for ya."

"Splendid, Sal." It was a word he'd picked up recently, *splendid,* made it his own. He liked the liquid peal of it, the way it came oiling off the tongue.

An exasperated sigh rode down the wire. "That mean we're doin' some business? That splendid?"

"Well, I'd want to speak with my contact first, of course. Get back to you."

"Unh-unh. I gotta put a wrap on it tonight."

"Awfully short notice, Sal."

"Yeah, well, it's a seller's market out there. And this ain't the kinda merchandise y'can store too long."

Dingo hesitated. He didn't much like being stampeded into a transaction, particularly when the product came sight unseen. On the other hand, this one held the potential for a small but tidy profit, depending on how the haggling went. Enough, possibly, to replace the wooden coffee table he was gazing at right now with an elegant marble and glass one he'd come across in the pages of an interior design magazine. Spruce up the already well-appointed (by his tastes, for in this, as in all things, he was entirely self-taught) room not a little.

"So what's it gonna be, Dinger?"

"That's Ding*o*," he said, sudden wintry edge to his otherwise studiedly silken voice.

"Same question. An' I ain't got all night here."

"We'll take it," Dingo said crisply. Even if he didn't care for them, instant decisions were nothing new to him. Sometimes they secured a handsome return, other times not. Went with the territory.

Sal recited a west side address, instructed him to

be there "nine bells sharp. Get a look at what you're
buyin'. Arrange the swap."

Dingo copied the address in the pocket-sized
ledger he habitually carried, frowning as he wrote.
Not one of your better neighborhoods. Price, of
course, was not mentioned. That would come later.
Part of the waltz. It didn't matter. Though he was
without experience in this sort of merchandise, had
never trafficked in it before, he had an idea of its
general range, value, markup, and negotiating cushion. He rung off with a promise to meet Sal at the
specified hour, and immediately pecked out a number, long since committed to memory, ambling into
the bedroom and studying himself in the full-length
mirror on the door as he did.

He was not displeased with what he saw: sober
young man, trim, rigidly—some might say stiffly—
erect (perhaps in compensation for a slightly shorter
than average height: If there was one thing Dingo regretted about his physical self, it was that his growth
had stalled out at four inches short of six feet), nattily
outfitted in a pastel blue linen suit, double-breasted,
the trousers knife-creased, set off by burgundy silk tie
and matching tasselled loafers. Good clothes, expen-
sive. Made a statement. He was about to extend this
somewhat preening self-inspection to the lineaments
of his face when, after about a dozen rings, a breathless voice demanded rudely, "Yeah?"

"Dingo calling, Jimmie."

That's as much as it took to restore a civil note,
jocular but respectful, to the voice. "Hey, Dingo.
Sorry took me so long get on the horn. Just comin'

outta the shower. Matter fact, I'm standin' here in the bareass right now."

An image, monumentally disgusting, took shape behind Dingo's eyes. He did what he could to blot it, said, "Perfectly all right, Jimmie. We connected."

"So how ya been?"

"Good. Doing well by doing good." He chuckled softly, got a responsive snicker.

"Doin' good, that's what cracks the nut every time," the Jimmie voice allowed. "So what's up?"

"Do you remember an inquiry, from one of your co-workers, about a child?"

"Sure do."

"Well, it seems we might be able to help him out."

Line full of dead air. "Anything wrong, Jimmie?" he asked into it.

"Y'mean, like now?"

"Very soon, I expect. No more than a few days."

"Jeez, I dunno, Dingo. That was awhile ago, guy asked. Back in January, I remember."

"January, June—it matters not. Money's good anytime, Jimmie. Spends the same."

"Well, yeah. But I'd hafta check with the fella, see he's still interested. See, he come on real casual like, said it was a friend he was askin' for."

"Not our problem," Dingo said, putting some of that January into it. "I've made a verbal commitment. With the wops. And as you know, with them that's as good as a deal."

"Yeah, I heard."

"So what I want you to do is phone this person tonight, tell him where we are with it and—"

"Do better'n that," the voice broke in. "Gonna see him, couple hours. Retirement party, one a the plant grunts hangin' it up. I can talk to him there. Face on face."

"Splendid, Jimmie. Meanwhile, I'll be checking the merchandise. If it measures up and if the terms are satisfactory, I'll call you later tonight with the details. Where can you be reached?"

"It's a VFW. Down in Lockport."

"Number?"

"Hol' on. Get it for ya."

Sounds of footsteps receding. Dingo got out his ledger book, skimmed its pages idly, tapping a loafer on the carpet and wondering how far off the day was when he'd be working with people of class, polish. Returning footsteps. A number read to him. He copied it down under the west side address. Meticulous man. "And the figure we're talking about," he said, "is 20K, correct?"

"That's what he tol' me his friend got to spend."

"Should be some bargaining space inside that amount. A little finder's fee."

"How much you lookin' to clear, Dingo?"

"Hard to say. In any case, you tell him to alert his friend. It'll be a cash transaction. Funneled through us."

"I'll tell 'im."

Dingo caught an edge of uncertainty there. Didn't cheer him. So he said, "Make it plain there's no room for skating here. No reneging if the deal goes through. He approached us, we're delivering."

"Do my best."

Dingo didn't like hearing that expression either, its undercurrent of pleading, apology in advance. Loser speak. "As long as your best results in a close," he said. "You do understand that, Jimmie?"

"Yeah, I got ya."

Dingo said, "Excellent," giving *splendid* a rest. "Oh, one other matter. Looking at the accounts book here, I see we've got one that's seriously overdue. Somebody named Caulkins."

"Ol' Lester. He's a little light up top. Y'know, brains scrambled. But he's okay, he'll come through."

"Let's give him a nudge anyway."

"Do that tonight. He'll be down the party. It's a not to worry, Dingo. Lester, he's a good ol' boy."

"No doubt. But you talk to him. I'll be in touch."

Dingo carried the phone into the kitchen, recradled it, went back to the living room, and sank onto his cushy, velveteen-covered couch. He lit a cigarette, expelled languid streams of smoke at the ceiling. Reviewed his evening plans. Originally he'd intended to dine at one of the finer local establishments, in solitary (for he had no friends, wanted none) celebration of the benchmark day: Friday, June 3, his thirtieth birthday. He'd planned to linger over a martini or two (even though he didn't much care for them), enjoy a fine dinner, reflect on the progress of his life to date, consider the lucrative possibilities of the decade that seemed to stretch out limitlessly ahead of him. Have to shelve all that now. Business comes first. But if he came away with a dime (*thousand,* he reminded himself: speak correctly, even in your thoughts) or so for his trouble tonight, he'd celebrate another time, maybe treat himself to a little getaway, hire a working girl to come along. Figured he had it coming, working man like himself.

While Dingo was consoling himself with visions of a brighter tomorrow, some twenty miles to the south and west Lester Caulkins was at that same moment regaling a group of his fellow workers with another in his endless accounts of antic misadventure. They were gathered at the Lockport, Illinois, VFW post, a macho knot of burly men standing hunched over the bar, popping back shots or pulling beer straight from bottles, dragging on smokes, sweating a little, all of them looking just a trifle uncomfortable in their dress-up slacks and sports shirts.

"So I talks Doug the Rug from over the Box Shop there into comin' with," Lester was saying, "an' we wheels over this spook bar off Cermak, other side Pulaski, which shoulda tol' me somethin' right there. We struts in bigger'n shit, me'n Doug, an' right off I see it's superdumb, what we're doin' here."

Somebody in his audience said, "You never was exactly famous for smart, Lester." Ordinarily he would have been addressed by his plant tag, "Cock," a mangling of the already trimmed "Caulk," but since there were women present (though none at the bar or for that matter anywhere in earshot) and since this was, after all, something of a formal occasion, a certain propriety prevailed.

Lester's chunky, boyish face enlarged in broad

grin. "Hey, listen, that ain't what the lady at the license office said, last week I was gettin' my plates renewed. I tell ya that one?"

"Maybe you oughta finish this one first," drawled the honoree of the evening, one Arlo Harpstead. Because his tag was an innocuous "Harp," that's what everyone here called him tonight, including a man with an extraordinarily voluminous swell of belly, big as a feedsack but solid underneath as a battering ram, who seconded the suggestion with an amused "Harp's right, Lester. Spit it out. Della'n me gotta be in by midnight."

That got a laugh all around.

Thus encouraged, Lester pushed on with his tale.

"So here we are, see, room fulla bluegummers, only white faces in the whole joint. Doug, he's yankin' on my sleeve, sayin' c'mon, we gotta bugass outta here, but I figures we come this far, what the hay, huh? So we sorta moseys over the bar, easy like, like we ain't lookin' for no grief, an' I sez the bartender—mean-lookin' spade, I tellya, an' big!—holy shit, you shoulda seen!—make The Fridge—remember him?—Bears there?—make him look like one a them pygmys they got over to Africa—I mean, we're talkin' King Kong big here—"

Standing next to the man sporting the belly was another who might as easily have fit Lester's description. Tall, square, thick-necked, keg-chested, shoulders with a powerful slope to them, wide waist and hips, trunks of thighs, he projected an impression of enormous contained strength. This large man elevated a shovel-sized hand in a stop signal gesture, and in a voice surprisingly gentle said, "What'd you say to him, Lester?"

Lester, his retrieval system never too quick in the best of circumstances and decelerated now even more by two hours of nonstop drinking, looked at him blankly. "Who?"

"The bartender you're tellin' us about. Remember?"

"Oh, yeah, that one. What I sez is I asks him, real mannerly, nothin' wiseass, he seen Miss Shineequa Washington around, and he goes—"

"I can remember when she first come to work," Harp cut in on him, "her name was Lois. You remember that, Waz?"

Waz, the bellied one, shook his head baffledly. "Where they get them names, jigs?"

"Bowl alphabet soup," somebody suggested.

"When'd she hire on?" Waz wondered aloud. He turned to the large man beside him. "You know, Buck?"

Buck shrugged. "Y'got me. Eighty-four, five, somewhere in there."

"It was '88," Harp said confidently, and nobody contested it. Forty-four years on the job and an impeccable memory for plant lore had established him as indisputable custodian of all the significant facts, any worth knowing. " 'Bout the time your blacks comin' out with that crazy jungle music. She was always playin' it on her portable, breaks."

"Real loud too," someone else remembered. "Way they do."

"Had a cute little rump on her back when she was

Lois," Harp said after first glancing over his shoulder to be certain his wife was out of range. "One a them high ones they get. Like a porch."

"Ride 'em high, huh, Harp?"

"Wouldn't know 'bout that. Ask Lester. He's the one nosein' around that black butt, tryin' to jump it."

All eyes returned to Lester, momentarily forgotten in the wandering excursus. He snapped a recollective finger. "Talkin' music makes me think, part I was gonna tell ya. See, this bar had a band, call 'emselves The Confederate Niggers, all duded out in army uniforms, gray ones, South. They was playin' all them South songs, y'know, 'Dixie,' 'O'l Man River,' that Black Joe one, only in hip-hop. Rappin' the words. I'm tellin' ya, it was somethin' to hear." He paused, evidently trying to recapture the moment. "Went sorta like this," he said, stepping back from the bar and offering a chanted, swaying, finger-popping rendition: "Massa inna col' col' muthafuckin' ground."

"Watch the language," Harp said, scowling. "My grandkids around here someplace."

"I was in a place on Rush Street once," somebody remarked, "had same kinda thing. Only it was Jews. Went by Ikey Finkelstein—somethin' like that, Jew name—and His Texas Sheenies. Did all country, only in New York accent, y'know. How they talk. 'Cept it was singin', course."

The one called Buck rolled his eyes heavenward, or as near heaven as the smoke-fogged ceiling allowed. "Jesus, Lester. What happened to the story?"

"Which one?"

"Back in the bar there."

"Where 'bouts was I?"

"You was askin' the bartender he seen Shinee-keefoo," Waz reminded him, "or whatever her name is now."

"An' whose ass now-days blown up big as a whale," somebody interjected, "an' ol' Lester still can't mount it."

Everyone chortled, even Lester, pleased to be center stage again. His story resumed: " 'What you boys doin' in here?'—this is him now, bartender, goin' to us—'You lookin' to hit on a sister? That it? Split some dark oak?' I tells him Shineequa'n me works same plant, she asks me meet her here. Which is a true fact, only now I'm thinkin' maybe she bendin' me over, tellin' me meet her this place."

"You always was a deep thinker, Lester."

A new voice, this one, tinny edge to it, coming off a wiry little fellow, blade thin, just now arrived and swaggering through the press of bodies deferentially parting at his advance. Lester swung around, churned a pudgy fist in salute. "Hey, Jimmie Jack, how they hangin'?"

"Hangin' hard, Lester. Like always."

"Yeah, like a case a the permanent stone balls," Buck muttered, but under his breath. He picked up his beer and pushed away from the bar.

Waz looked at him puzzledly. "Where ya goin'?"

"Over by the girls."

"Can't leave now," he protested. "Lester's just gettin' to the good part."

"You can fill me in how it comes out," Buck said, marching off.

"Which story's this?" Jimmie wanted to know.

"Time I was in that spookadoo bar, askin' for Shineequa," Lester said.

"Already heard it."

"Let 'im finish, f'chrissake," Harp said.

When he smiled, as he did often and easily and was doing now, James John (familiarly known as Jimmie Jack, or simply Jimmie) Jacoby's upper front teeth protruded slightly, and with his recessive chin, pitted cheeks, snub nose, squinty eyes (which seemed to squint even here, in the subdued indoor light), low shelf of brow and knobby skull only partially covered by lank, mouse-colored hair, his features, normally unhandsome anyway, took on the feral aspect of a toothy sniffing predatory rodent. He brushed a hand through the air, show of indifference. "It's your party, Harp."

Harp merely grunted, signaled for Lester to proceed.

"Forget where I was at," Lester confessed sheepishly.

"Eight ball behind the bar startin' to lean on you," Waz prompted him.

"Oh. Right. Bartender. Well, rest of it y'can pretty much figure. Him'n bunch his bro buddies boost me'n Doug right off our feet—I mean, we was doin' the ozone boogie there—an' heaves us out the back door, alley, where they tune us up good. Me, I end up facedown a trash can, chewin' on cold ribs, got a zipper in my arm off a broke bottle or a shank, never did find out which, an' hafta turn in the hospital, get it stitched up an' one a them shots they give ya, the lockjaw."

"Look like it didn't take, though," somebody said, and they all hooted.

Even Lester, who, beaming with pleasure at his audience response, went on: "Listen, think that's bad, y'oughta seen what they done to Doug. Just torched his rug is all, an' stuffed it down his pants, backside, give 'im a real case the red ass."

Now everybody whooped.

When the laughter dwindled some, Jimmie said, "I told Lester he shoulda come see me. Open that zip up again, make it look like it happen at work." His elastic smile widened. At nobody in particular, he winked slyly. "Good for a Caddie in the plant there."

" 'Less they find ya out," Harp said. "Then it's good for a walkin' ticket."

"Do it right, nobody find you out."

"No, thanks," Lester said. "Once plenty. I ain't big on blood. 'Specially my own."

"Little blood, lotta bucks," Jimmie opined philosophically.

"No way. Ain't pushin' my luck."

"Only luck you ever had, Lester, is the lame kind."

With the entertainment apparently over, most of the men drifted away, Waz and Harp among them. And when the crowd at the bar was sufficiently thinned, Jimmie leaned over to Lester and murmured, "Speakin' of which, luck, like we was minute ago, there's somethin' I gotta run by you.

Whyn't you meet me back in the pisser? Smoke a
bone, talk a little."

The Quinns were sitting in a cramped, windowless
cubicle on the first floor of a Chicago P.D. precinct
station, which one they had no idea. Somewhere in
the vast and tumultuous and suddenly fearsome city.
Down the hall a riot of furious activity rose from the
entrance: chorus of strident, squawky voices, interminable jangle of phones, the occasional peal of
coarse laughter, occasional trumpeted obscenity or
curse or plaintive wail.

For well over an hour they'd been waiting, and for
Marshall the three hours before that had flashed by
in a dizzying blur. A clash of disjointed images
crowded his head. There was himself (seen now
rather like a bumbling player in a surreal film, some
grotesquely warped fantasy) frantically combing the
emptying auditorium, calling his son's name in a
voice hollow as an echo off a mountain lake. There
he was tracking down a planetarium security person,
baby-faced kid assuring him nothing to be alarmed
about, sir, these things happen all the time, the boy's
probably wandering one of our many corridors, got
turned around, we'll find him. . . . His son's fate in
the hands of an insouciant infant. Now see Marshall
sprinting down the boulevard, weaving in and out of
the crowds like some accomplished broken-field
runner, catching sight of Lori waiting perplexedly in
the lengthening shadow of the redoubtable charging
Thaddeus. Watch her face crumple at the news,
agony of fright. See them both standing in the park-

ing lot outside the museum, mouths—his, anyway—going mile-a-minute, arms flagging, gesturing wildly at a pair of uniformed police officers phlegmatically taking notes while the dome light of their squad car pulsed like an accelerated heartbeat and a circle of curious onlookers, faces flushed with that glow of importance witnesses to catastrophe will get, widened around them. Follow the Quinns on a back-seat ride in that squad car through some mean, maimed city streets; into a dingy building, its air hot, sluggish, thick; past a block of counter behind which more cops, some uniformed, some not, scurry; through a poorly lit hallway to the cubicle—two metal folding chairs, a rickety wooden table and nothing else—they occupy now; handed forms to complete, which he dutifully does; instructed to wait right here, somebody be with you soon.

Soon? By whose measure, soon? Not his.

He studied the worn black linoleum at his feet. Stole a glance at his wife. All the implicit accusations ("Asleep!—but *how*?—how *could* you?") and recriminations ("I don't *know* how—it was dark in there, cool, out of the heat—anybody would have—*you* would have") were over now, and she rocked back and forth in her chair, eyes squeezed shut, moaning softly, as if to ward off everything she was experiencing, this alien assault on her senses. Her abundant ash blond hair was sadly disheveled, her face, a perfect heart shape, streaked with tears, white as bone dust. She seemed to have arrived at some plateau of infinite dread, a terror abstract and unalloyed. "God *damn* it," he muttered. "What's going on? Where are they?" She said nothing, and no one came.

Till eventually a uniformed figure appeared in the doorway, filling it, a flattened metal chair tucked under one arm, couple of police report forms in the hand of the other. "I'm Sergeant Glenn Wilcox," he said by way of identification. "You're the Marshalls?"

"Quinn," said Marshall, rising. "Marshall's my first name. This is my wife, Lori."

He unfolded the chair, examined one of the forms with a myopic squint, said, "Yeah, right, Quinn. Sorry about that." He stuck out a liver-spotted paw for Marshall to grip, then bent over and offered it to Lori, who, eyes open now but still glassy with shock, touched it gingerly.

At a nod from Wilcox the two men sat. He laid the forms out on the table, studied them a moment, while Marshall studied him. A big man, fifty or better by Marshall's estimate, thick-set, substantial gut, baggy seen-it-all face, and an aura of immense weariness about him, almost a lassitude, cheering not at all. Finally he lifted pouchy eyes and said, "Also sorry about what's happened here," his voice, in contrast with the charitable words, a growly bass rumble.

"We appreciate that," Marshall said, struggling to hold his own voice level but acutely conscious of the tremor in it. "But we'd like to know what's being done to find our son."

"Everything we can. Got his description on the wire, and our people checkin' all the neighborhoods around the museum."

"Any word yet?"

"Not yet, Mr. Quinn."

Marshall cleared his throat, hoping it would steady his speech some, erase the quaver. "Are you the officer, uh, assigned to the investigation? In charge, I mean?" Hoping equally he had the terminology right. What did he know about this angry, fractured world they'd been thrust into, abruptly and without warning? He knew nothing. What he'd seen on television, that's as much as he knew.

"No. I work the desk out front."

"Who, then?"

"A detective probably. Be along any minute now."

"Will he find Jeff?" It was Lori speaking, a peculiar matter-of-factness to the question, like some mildly interested third party, one of those spectators in the parking lot back there.

"He'll sure try, ma'am," Wilcox said, his *ma'am* a kind of quaint anomaly of address for this slender, fragile girl, not yet thirty, young enough to be a daughter or a niece. He arched a shaggy brow. Watched her narrowly. "You all right, Mrs. Quinn? Want some coffee?"

"No, thank you."

"Doughnut? We got doughnuts."

She shook her head slowly, stared at the hands clasped tightly in her lap. The rocking motion had stopped now, but her gaze was empty, lost.

"Mr. Quinn?"

"No, nothing."

"Sure? Been a long day for you folks."

"Look," Marshall said, firm as he could pitch it. "I

don't understand the delay. It's been—what—four hours. Closer to five. And nobody's told us anything, talked to us."

"I'm talking to you, Mr. Quinn."

"Then for God's sake tell us something. Tell us what's happening."

Wilcox gathered a fleshy underfold of secondary chin in his fingers. He seemed to consider it necessary to sigh. "See, what you don't understand is how things work here. Procedures. Like I told you, our people looking for your boy right now. We don't turn him up tonight—I'm not saying that's gonna happen, but we don't—then the detectives outta Four, they'll step in."

"Four?"

"City's divided up into five areas. We're in Four."

"This detective you say is coming, he's in this building?"

"No, he works outta Area Four headquarters. Over on Harrison."

"Then where are we?"

"You're in District One precinct station. Right off South State."

Precincts, districts, areas—it was like some labyrinthine maze fiendishly constructed to baffle and torment experimental rats. And he got to be the hapless rat. Which was maybe only right and fitting, given what he'd done. "Then this detective," Marshall asked, all the firm, what there was of it, gone now, replaced by pleading, "he'll be the one in charge?"

"Correct," Wilcox said patiently, tone of a patient tutor instructing a somewhat backward child. "That is, if we got no luck locating your boy tonight. Which could still happen. It don't, then it'll be an aggravated kidnapping."

A quick little spasm, brief as a palsied twitch, seized Lori's thin shoulders and was instantly gone. She said not a word, and her eyes never left her lap.

"What we call a heater case," a clipped voice at the cubicle's entrance pronounced. "Right, Glenn?"

Wilcox turned slightly. "Hey, Palmer. You made it."

"Did at that."

" 'Bout time."

"Got held up."

"These here are the Quinns," Wilcox said, wagging a thumb in Marshall's direction. "Palmer Thornton," wagging it back. "Detective I was telling you about. From over to Four."

Marshall stood, extended a hand. The detective reached over and gave it a small squeeze. Lori didn't look up, didn't move. "Detective Thornton," Marshall started to say (he assumed you addressed them by title), "what we'd like to know is—"

That's as far as he got. Thornton made a curt dismissive gesture. "Be right with you. Need a word with the sergeant first. Glenn, you wanta step out here minute, bring the paperwork along with you?"

Wilcox heaved himself up out of the chair and followed the detective into the hallway, the two of them suddenly gone, leaving Marshall standing there stunned, his frustration and anger and fear mounting, equal parts, mouth still moving in desperate wordless twists. Feeling something of a timid milksop.

Something of a fool. His skimpy impression of this
Thornton, this detective charged with finding their
son, was fortifying not in the least: a tall, sturdy
man, youngish, this side of forty by an easy five
years, maybe more; conspicuously well built under
the shortsleeve white shirt and tie, bodybuilder's ex-
aggerated shoulders and lumpy arms; good-looking
in a sleek slick arrogant way, but very studiedly the
wised-up street cop, reaching after a cinematic conception of himself, working too hard at it for Marshall's tastes. Unless he was mistaken. Unless that's
the face, callous and remote, they all of them,
Wilcox included, showed an innocent, uninitiated
world of cowed and helpless citizens, while behind it
lurked a stony resolve to solve the murder, recover
the child, see justice done. He hoped it was the latter.
To Lori he said weakly, "I'm sure they'll be right
back. Let us know what's going on." She made no
reply.

He crept over to the entrance, listened a moment
but could hear nothing. Cautiously, he peered around
it. They were standing several feet down the hall,
speaking animatedly but sotto voce. Thornton
glanced up from the forms in his hand, saw him,
smiled thinly, beckoned. Marshall approached them.
This time he said nothing. Put the burden on them
for a change. That's what they're paid for.

But the opening line, delivered by the detective,
was about the last thing he expected: "Says here
you're a professor, Mr. Quinn."

"That's right," Marshall said stiffly.

"What do you teach?"

"Sociology."

"That's at that college out in Naperville, right?"

"Yes. North Central." Marshall sensed it was neither necessary nor useful to mention the college was small, private, church-affiliated. Not in this company. Anyway, he had no idea where this avenue of chummy talk was leading.

"I'm workin' on my master's," Thornton said. "Criminal justice."

"Good for you."

"Nights. Class at a time. Slow goin'."

Marshall pulled in a deep breath, released it slowly. Buying an instant of time to collect his words, phrase them properly. "You know," he said, staring at him steady as he could, "that's very commendable, your pursuing an advanced degree. But as you might guess, I really don't give a good god damn right now and—"

Thornton put up staying palms. "Hey, easy, Mr. Quinn. We're just chattin' here."

"I'm not *interested* in any more chatting. I want— no, that's not it—I *insist* you tell me what's being done to find my son." But he'd lost the momentum of indignant outrage, and he knew it. It was his voice again, rising in shaky whine, perilously close to spineless cheep, gave him away, for all the blustery words. He felt a sharp stinging sensation in his eyes. He looked away. Determined not to weep, not here, not in front of them.

Sergeant and detective exchanged glances. Thornton arranged his face in an attitude intended perhaps to convey sympathy, but with a certain measure of scorn in it too. "Listen," he said, "we know how you got to feel. What I understand Sergeant Wilcox here already told you, that's what we're doin'. Which is all we can, this point in time."

"But what am I—we—supposed to do? There must be *some*thing."

"Nothin' you can do here, Mr. Quinn. It's Glenn's thought, mine too, you and Mrs. Quinn oughta go on home."

"Home?" Marshall repeated, wonderstruck.

"Yeah, home. We get any news tonight, we'll ring you right up. We got your number."

"She's lookin' pretty upset," Wilcox put in. "Your wife, I mean. Our thinkin' was you should get her outta this environment."

"Maybe get hold your doctor," Thornton suggested. "Have him give her something, sleep."

"You got a family doctor out there, Naperville?" Wilcox asked him.

"Yes."

"You don't want her tweakin' on you," Thornton said.

"Tweaking?"

"What he means," Wilcox explained gently, "is, y'know, breakin' down. Gettin' hysterical."

"Can happen," Thornton said. "Seen it before."

Marshall hesitated. About Lori, they might be right. He'd never seen her like this, never. Ordinarily she was composed, capable, serenely efficient, equal to any small domestic distress, the many facets of her busy life—wife, mother, substitute teacher, homemaker, hobbyist, club member, church volunteer, activist in a variety of worthy causes—all in harmonious balance, all in admirable control. But then there was nothing ordinary about anything that was happening here. So maybe it made a kind of sense, what they were recommending. "I could take her home," he said, "get some friends to stay with her. Then come back."

Wilcox frowned. "Be better you stayed with her. Anyhow, you lookin' kinda beat up yourself. An' like the detective said, nothin' you can do here. Be easier on you both, waitin' at home."

"Any news, you'd call me?"

"You're top of our list."

"But if you shouldn't find him tonight? Then what?"

Wilcox let Thornton field that one. "Be a whole different ball game," the detective said. "We'll put a team together, widen the scope of our investigation."

"What does that mean, exactly?"

"Worry 'bout that, time comes. We don't get anything tonight, I'll be out to your place, Naperville there, tomorrow. Tell you all about it."

"So what do you think?" Wilcox asked him. "You wanta go get your wife? Get started?"

"All right," Marshall said, feeling part desolate, another part curiously relieved, rather like an ailing patient must feel, he supposed, frail and tottery, yielding himself over to the ministrations of wise physicians.

"You folks got a car?"

"We took the train."

"Could catch a cab over the station," Thornton suggested.

"Nah, that's okay," Wilcox said. "I'll get a vehicle, give 'em a lift."

Thornton shrugged and sauntered away, not another word to Marshall, who said anxiously, like that cringing patient he'd become, "Where's he going?"

"Gonna catch up on where we're at so far. Whyn't you bring Mrs. Quinn out front now? Wait for me there."

Without comment or protest, Lori agreed to the proposal to return home, presented by Marshall as though it were an integral part of some carefully crafted master plan. And so they waited, as instructed, opposite the counter in the precinct entry, standing against a wall by a bank of phones. She was silent, her features blanched, expressionless, utterly unreadable. Calamity's trance. And he, wirestrung yet, but overtaken by fatigue and a fuddled sense of dislocation, could summon up nothing to say. Emptied of solace, run out of sustaining words. Bankrupt of will.

Behind the counter, cops charged back and forth, their voices elevated in permanent fortissimo, enduring howl. All of them had sagging, meaty faces that betrayed too much lingering over sugary pastries and coffee. One slurped noisily from a mug bearing the legend "I don't give a shit." Another, responding to a barked query, bawled back, "Already tol' ya his name's José, dickeye, an' he got a brother name a Hose B," bursting into pleasured smirk at his excellent bon mot. Signs on the walls forbade smoking, advised lawyers they could see prisoners (a couple of whom, surly blacks, were being hustled, handcuffed, through a swinging plywood gate and down a dark corridor) only after they were processed, and warned that an escape alarm system secured all exits. An incongruous tire leaned against a shelf stacked high with report forms. The phones never let up. Altogether, a spectacle of dissonant, sordid ugliness, life's seedy underside, its cast wearing their seediness and cynicism like body armor, reveling in it, the way souls consigned to the innermost circles of hell must flaunt their hopeless roaring defiance; and watching the unfolding scene, taking it all in, Marshall had to wonder what terrible sin of his own had brought the two of them here to share in the ruin and despair.

No time to pursue such morbid thoughts, for just then Wilcox stuck his head through the door and in a bellow to match the din called, "All set, Mr. Quinn, let's roll." He ushered them into the backseat of a car whose logo, presumably innocent of irony, proclaimed: Chicago Police—We Serve and Protect.

They rode in silence. Pulled up at the Jackson Street entrance to Union Station. Marshall and Lori climbed out. She stood there dazedly while he stooped to the window, offered his thanks.

"Nothin'. You folks find your train okay?"

He said they could and, unable to leave it alone, added, "You'll phone us if you hear anything? Anything at all?"

"Well, I'm goin' off duty, but Detective Thornton, he'll keep you posted."

"Thornton?" he said, unable now to contain the dismay in his voice.

And Wilcox, catching it, said wearily, "Y'know, Mr. Quinn, thing like this happen, people sometimes feel like they gotta find a villain. Thornton, okay, he can be a hotdog. Pain in the butt sometimes. But he's good."

"I'm sure he is. It's just that he didn't seem too, well—" He faltered, searching for the right word, settled finally on the inoffensive "engaged."

"You don't wanta mix us up with the bad guys," Wilcox advised him. "They're out here." The *here* indicated with a sweep of an arm across the interior windshield.

"But will you find him?"

"Do our best."

Punctually at nine p.m. Dingo emerged from an elevator on the fifth floor of a crumbling apartment building, glanced about warily and, once satisfied, started down a narrow cinder-block hallway reeking of urine and some ineffective cleansing agent and illuminated scarcely at all by a couple of bare bulbs at either end. He checked the numbers on the doors. From behind them came muffled sounds of televisions, squabbling voices, wailing babies. Midway along the hall he found the number he was looking for. He paused, adjusted the knot in his tie, smoothed the crease in his trousers, patted the butterfly knife— his weapon of choice—tucked into the belt under his suit coat. It was a cautionary habit picked up years ago, Illinois Youth Center Correctional Facility.

Doing business, it's always best to come strapped with something. You never know. Particularly with the wops.

He drew himself up to his full height. Knocked. A gravelly voice on the other side demanded, "Yeah, whozit?"

"Dingo," he said, the name also acquired at the Facility and stuck like glue over all these years.

Click of a dead bolt. The door cracked open just enough for a pair of dark, foxy eyes to appear in the notch.

"It's really me, Sal. You can open up." Wops loved their little games.

The door swung back, and Sal motioned him into a small, cluttered room furnished, no doubt, by the Goodwill, castoffs at that, its carpet soiled, scarred plaster walls done a seasick green. Nasty room. Nastier yet was the garlic-heavy odor of some recent dago feast chilling in the galley kitchen to his immediate left, and assaulting him head-on off Sal's sour breath as he pushed his face up close and said, "You know Vincent?"

Dingo followed an over-there toss of the head to another man stretched out on a couch behind him, reading a comic book. Big man, filled a couch. Dingo recognized him from some distant transaction. "I believe we met once," he said.

Vincent lowered the comic, ran his eyes over him, flicked a greeting finger off a brow and went back to reading.

End of amenities. The thing about your wops is they're always wearing it, always performing. Even

these two, couple of third-stringers, not enough is-
land of Sicily in them to be anything other than
loosely connected, fated by blood to be forever on
the fringe of the heavy action. Which also meant
they could be outlawing here. Which made it all the
more risky. Two of them, one of him. Step lightly.

"So, Dingo, you ready do some dealin'?"

Sal speaking, still in his face, or as near as he
could get, given the fact he cleared five feet by no
more than an inch or two. It was one of the few
things—possibly the only thing—Dingo found to
like about him, looking down into those froggy,
bulgy eyes, examining the scalp under the oily wisps
of soot-colored hair, down being the only way to
look at this squat little greaseball. Somewhat mock-
ingly he said, "That's what I came for, Sal."

"Little outta your line, ain't it?"

"Whatever sells," Dingo said and, giving it just a
shred of a beat, added, "Of course, I'll want to see
the merchandise first."

"No prol'um. Even got a selection for ya.
C'mon."

Sal led him to a doorway opening onto a tiny
room dominated by a single bed. A nightlight
plugged into a wall socket revealed three boys, fair
of skin and hair, slight of bone, naked but for their
undershorts and laid out crossways on a filthy mat-
tress, sleeping peaceful as cherubs. The oldest
looked to be—what?—no more than six or seven,
near as Dingo could tell, the youngest maybe half
that, the other somewhere in between.

"There y'are," Sal said proudly. "Not a pick-aninny in the lot."

"Where do you find them?" Dingo asked, genuinely curious. He took a professional interest in such matters. A businessman always had to be alert to new avenues of opportunity.

"These ones here?"

"Generally."

"Why you ask? Thinkin' a branchin' out?"

"Curiosity, Sal. That's all."

"Oh, your zoos are good, ball parks, schools, beach in the summer, some a them museums downtown. Places like that."

"How do you go about securing them?"

"Snatch 'em, y'mean?"

"Yes."

"Depends. Sweet talk do it sometimes, sometimes takes little happy gas in a hankie, which is trickier. These you lookin' at here, that's what it took, all three. Lemme tell ya, it ain't easy. Ain't like regular boostin'. With your ankle biters y'gotta be quick."

"I'm sure. They're awfully, uh, young, aren't they?"

"You can talk normal," Sal assured him, for Dingo had been speaking in hushed tones. "We got 'em on some, y'know, Nytol. Own special brand."

"That's a comfort."

"You think young?" Sal pointed at the oldest boy. "See that one there, he's almost over the hill. We got a sayin', this game: fucked before eight, or it's too late."

"What about that one?" Dingo asked, indicating the youngest.

"Yeah, well, he's maybe little on the tender side. Figured he'd be just about right, what you got in mind. Fresh, too. Just picked him up today."

"How much?"

"Twenty long takes him home."

"I'll give you ten."

Sal snorted contemptuously. "I was born at night, Dingo, but not last night."

"Ten. He's too young for your other . . . trade."

"Be surprise. Some them chicken hawks out there like 'em real pink. Fresh outta the cradle. Get an easy twenty off them people put out *Hot Tots*. 'Nother couple years he'll be ready for the squirm flicks."

"All right, fifteen, then."

"Eighteen. Nothin' less."

"Seventeen five."

Sal's lips, pink as worms, shaped a sneer. "You tryin' job me here?"

"Seventeen five. That's my best offer."

"Gotta be some Hebe in you, Dingo. Okay, deal. Let's go out the other room, finalize."

Dingo followed him, positioned himself carefully along a wall facing the couch where Vincent still lay, still absorbed, it appeared, in his comic book. Sal stood between them, scribbling something on a scrap of paper. He handed it to Dingo, said, "What you got there's an address, drop house out to Elgin. How it works is we got a cunt out there, plays the sad mother. We dummy up the papers on the kid, birth certificate, that kinda shit, make it look like what y'call a brokered adoption. Us the brokers. You have your clients there Sunday morning, they got 'emselves a kid."

"They'll be there," Dingo assured him. He pocketed the address, took a step toward the door. "Pleasure doing business with you boys."

Sal moved into his path. " 'Cept it ain't quite done," he said. "We gotta see some earnest money."

"Earnest money," Dingo repeated after him, thinking. So now it comes, crunch time. Treachery the only constant in this shifting, shifty business. He smiled, melancholy speck of a smile. His eyes were absent of any emotion other than an infinite sorrow at a world that never quite measured up to his expectations, his expression grieved. Indeed, with his long hollow chiseled features, his rigid posture, refined bearing, precision speech, tasteful clothes, he might have been mistaken for a Calvinist minister on his way to preside over a vesper service.

"That's right," Sal said. "Half down. Now."

"Surely you don't think I'd be carrying that kind of money. In here?"

"Then you better trot on home an' find it. 'Cuz that's the rules, this game. Half now, half on delivery."

Dingo laid the tips of his outstretched fingers together, peered over them at Sal, and beyond him to Vincent, who was just then setting the comic on the floor and curling himself upright on the couch, apparently listening after all. "No," Dingo said mildly. "Once the transaction's completed you'll be paid in full. Meantime, you've got the child. Pretty solid collateral, I'd say."

"That's what you'd say, is it?"

"Yes."

Sal itched his scalp, exciting a shower of moist dandruff that went floating onto his fatty shoulders. "See, Dingo, what your prol'um is, you don't listen good. I'm tellin' ya how it works. Rules. Y'got rules, y'gotta have a force man, make 'em stick."

"That would be Vincent."

"That's the idea. Now, you wanna talk to him?"

"Not especially."

"So what's it gonna be? That half I'm sayin' here."

Dingo collapsed the fingers steeple, pressed his palms together in a gesture oddly reminiscent of praying hands. "No," he said, mild yet, but firm.

Sal signaled his partner. "He's little slow tonight, Vincent. You explain it to him?"

"Yeah, I can do that," Vincent said, lumbering to his feet and crossing the room.

Dingo didn't move. His sorrowed gaze remained locked on Sal, hands still fixed in prayerful attitude. "There's no need for this, Sal," he said.

"Tell it to Vincent."

Now he was looking up into a flattened, fissured face looming over him, full red mouth opened in shark grin, exposing yellowed snaggle teeth and expelling a breath equally as foul as Sal's, maybe worse. Positive genius for ugliness, your wops. Vincent took the lapel of his coat and rubbed the fabric between thumb and forefinger. "Nice threads," he said. "Where'd you pick 'em up at? Kmarts? Blue light special on blue suits?"

A peculiar glint came into Dingo's eyes, a lucency, like two slivers of green bottle glass shimmering under a harsh sun. "No," he said. "And that's Kmart, by the way, no *s* on the end." His palms suddenly parted and he thrust his arms upward and seized Vincent's ears and yanked, simultaneously and with a flamenco dancer's staccato grace spiking the heel of a tasseled loafer into an instep, shattering bone by the welcome sound of it, an assessment confirmed a nanosecond later by Vincent's astonished squawk and comic one-legged hop, hands clutching at ears dangling by stringy cords of gristle. Dingo spun around and drove little Sal into a wall. He whisked out his knife, flipped the blade, and laid it across Sal's throat. Sadly, very softly, he said, "Why can't we do business in a civilized manner, Sal?"

"You're fuckin' whackadoo, Dinger, know that?"

He applied a small pressure to the blade, drawing a thin line of blood. *Dingo* he could tolerate, but not *Dinger,* jailhouse jargon for lunatic. Entirely uncalled for, to his thinking. "That wasn't the question, Sal."

"Awright, awright. Do it your way."

"Sunday morning, then? Full payment on delivery?"

"Yeah yeah yeah. But you better come with that loot or you gonna be lookin' over your shoulder rest a your days."

"Have I ever failed you, Sal?"

He took a cautious step back. Glanced at the

lumpish figure crumpled on the floor now, groaning. Nothing to fear from Vincent anymore. Or from Sal, swiping the blood from his neck, glowering at him. He started for the door.

"What about Vincent?" Sal called after him.

"What about him?"

"What you done to him."

"Occupational hazard," Dingo said over his shoulder. "Check your medical plan. He's probably covered."

And with that he was gone.

Back at the apartment, Dingo went directly to the phone and dialed the number given by his confederate.

"Lockport VFW," boomed the answering voice, swept along on a blast of music and boorish laughter.

"I'd like to speak with James Jacoby, please."

"Who'zat?"

Dingo sighed. "Jimmie."

"Jimmie Jack?"

"Yes."

"Hol' on."

It took awhile but eventually another voice, just as coarse but with a touch of expectancy in it, announced, "Jimmie Jack talkin'."

"Dingo, Jimmie."

"Hey, Dingo. Figured it'd be you."

"How's the party?" he inquired conversationally, stringing it out a little, making him wait.

"Good party. Real hoot."

"Pleased to hear it."

"So whadda *you* hear?"

"Most agreeable news, Jimmie. Merchandise meets all the specs. Arrangements sealed. Price settled on."

"What'd it come in at?"

"Eighteen."

"That the best y'could do?" Disgruntled edge to the voice now, surly even.

"Margin's slim, this sort of product," Dingo said. "I was lucky to get that. Required some, well, wrangling."

"I was hopin' we'd maybe do little better."

"I'd call one large for each of us rather a nice profit for an evening's work. Never pays to get greedy, Jimmie."

Jimmie had no comment on this sound advice. "So what's the poop," he said, "them arrangements you was sayin'?"

He spelled them out for him: time, location, transfer of cash details, concluding with the directive to pass along these instructions to his contact man immediately.

"Fella's here tonight. I'll talk to him."

Dingo detected some of that skittish waffling he'd heard before, their earlier conversation. Not gladdening. "More than just talk," he said, chilliest of tones. "What I want is . . ." He trailed off, looking for just the exact word, fixing finally on "execution" and not at all unhappy with it, its double-edged meaning. "Deal's been struck," he went on. "My good name's at stake here. Yours too. Follow?"

"Yeah, I follow."

"Splendid."

"Get back to ya."

Dingo put up the phone, poured himself a brandy, and took it into the living room. He switched on the stereo, settled into a chair, feet up on an ottoman. The dulcet strains of some classical piece, he didn't know which, filled the room, mellowed him, inspired a pensive mood.

He reflected on the events of the evening, most notably the pointless little scuffle in that grimy apartment. A bit out of proportion to the disagreement, perhaps, but then it's always best to establish one's authority, one's presence, forcefully and early on and absolutely without fear. Another hard lesson painfully picked up over the course of his entirely unjustified eight-year stay at the Facility. Eight years wrongfully lifted out of his life, swindling him of his youth. Set him seething even yet, thinking about it.

They said he'd killed his parents, cold-bloodedly and without remorse, but he knew that couldn't be right. He knew better. They'd died in a fire, Mom and Dad, consumed by flames on a night he'd been innocently off at the movies. Or maybe it was a Scout meeting. Or maybe he *had* been in the house, watching television, and escaped only by a stroke of luck. Hard to remember anymore. So long ago.

Still, they said he did it. Claimed to have the proofs. Stuck him away in the Facility, a terrified thirteen-year-old white boy, nice upbringing, decent, hardworking (till they died) parents, a diligent student (even played French horn in the school band), Star Scout. Buried him alive.

No good thinking that way, puzzling over it, picking it like a raw scab. Road to madness. So instead he sipped his brandy and wished himself a happy birthday and turned his thoughts to the handsome coffee table he'd be getting soon, a gift to himself, affordable now with those extra five bills tacked onto his thousand.

Norma Buckley was an attentive wife, something of a throwback to another time. Alert to her husband's every need, she kept watch as he methodically vanished a plate of steamy food, picking at her own, and the moment he was finished she inquired if he wanted anything more from the lavish buffet spread out over a table at the back of the hall. The volume of the music was such it was necessary to lift her reedy voice a level or two, though by no stretch could it be called a shout. As always, she addressed him by given name, Dale.

He cupped a hand behind an ear. "What's that?"

"Have you had enough to eat?"

Buck leaned back, thumped his firm, if swollen, midsection, sighed contentedly, deliberated. "Little more that chicken be good."

She reached for his styrofoam plate, removed the plastic fork and knife, and rose from her chair.

Across the table the Wazinskis, Mike and Della, took in this familiar little domestic scene amusedly. Waz (who had been known as such for so long and by so many people he oftentimes failed to respond to his own proper name) shook his head in elaborate show of awe. A teasing grin lit his broad, bluejowled face. "Boy, you sure got this one trained right, Buck."

"She's a keeper, all right," Buck deadpanned. It was a running joke between them.

"I ask Della here do that, she serve me up a five-finger sandwich."

Della there made a fierce face and a balled fist and delivered a punch, playful but solid, to his thick bicep. "Like this, you mean?"

Everybody laughed, Norma a little less than the other three, more of a good-sport titter escaping from behind a widening of the mouth. She was in the habit of smiling and laughing at all the places in a conversation you're expected to, but there was a certain forlorn distance in her manner, a wistfulness, as though she carried with her a durable, aching sadness. "Be right back," she said and started away, purposeful of step, an uncommonly tall woman, willowy, with straight darkish hair flecked here and there with silver and flowing over frail shoulders habitually set in the slightest of stoops, perhaps to minimize a height not all that far off her husband's. She threaded through a crowd gathered to cheer on a flock of boisterous children romping across the dance floor, jiggling to the beat, clowning for the delighted grown-ups. She paused, not long, watched their antics. Her face, angular, narrow-margined, near to gaunt, tightened. A cloud of hurt passed over her troubled gray eyes, and the smile she mustered was closer to a twitch. She moved on to the buffet, heaped chicken on the plate, said some praiseful words to the servers, and returned to the table.

"I tell ya," Waz was telling them all, "Harp really knows how to put on a feed."

"Good chow," Buck agreed, gazing first at the plate of it set in front of him, then at his wife, fondly, adding, "Thanks, honey."

"Enjoy," she said.

Waz wondered who "put it all together." His voice, amplified and roughened by two decades of bellowing over the roar of machines, was more than equal to the bedlam in here.

"Hired a caterer maybe," Della said.

"No," Norma corrected her gently, "it was his children. They arranged the whole thing."

"How do you know?"

"Irene, his wife, she told me. They have four children, two daughters and two sons. Seven grandchildren. A lovely family."

For an awkward moment nobody said anything. Buck stared at his food, Waz into a plastic cup filled with beer. Della looked away. The moment lengthened, relieved at last when the d.j. throttled the music just enough to announce, "This next one's for the guest of honor," and at the opening bars of "Take This Job and Shove It" the audience howled appreciatively, joining in on the jeered refrain. As soon as the tune ran down, Harp was escorted to the mike and presented a series of gag gifts: a deck of cards ("brush up on your solitaire"); shuffleboard pole ("keep yourself in shape"); seniors discount card for a local eatery, along with a bottle of Gas-X; cane; and a melon, honeydew ("get yourself ready for all the 'honey, do this, honey, do that' comin' up").

Then "As Time Goes By" was played and Harp's wife dragged him, protesting, onto the dance floor and they swayed, Harp a bit stiffly, to the sweet, sad melody, drawing a big round of audience applause and loving hugs from their assembled grandchildren when it was done.

Over at the table Buck allowed, "Gonna miss old Harp."

"Say that again," Waz concurred.

"Best millwrght at the plant."

"Next to yourself, 'course," Waz joshed him.

"No," Buck said soberly, "he's better'n me. Time's we worked together, I swear he knew what I was thinkin' before I did myself."

Della, visibly bored by the drift toward shop talk, turned the conversation another direction. "What are you up to this weekend?" she asked Norma.

"Oh, I'll be putting in the garden."

"You don't make Buck do that?"

"He's paneling the basement."

"He's been doin' that basement six months now," Waz snorted. "Think maybe he's shuckin' you, Norma."

Buck chuckled tolerantly. Norma smiled.

"Don't pay any attention to him," Della said. "Get him to do anything around the house, that's worse than yanking teeth."

Waz stretched his lips back, simulating a toothless grin. "Yeah," he said, "an' look what it got me."

Della made a quick little shooing motion with her hands, the gesture lifted from a bag of coquettish mannerisms and knowing expressions that hinted at a history of worldly feminine mischief. She was a small woman, almost pocket-sized alongside her hulking husband, round and amply bosomed, shapely once but running now to plump. Her hair was sheared fashionably short, very near a brush cut, and bleached a startling platinum, setting off milky blue eyes, heavily shadowed, rosy cheeks heavily rouged, and full, pouty lips vividly lacquered red as ripe strawberries. Archly dismissing Waz's effort at comedy, she said to Norma, "You going to have flowers this year?"

"Oh, yes. I always have flowers."

"I don't know how you do it. Where you find the time."

"Well," Norma said ruefully, eyes downcast, fixed on her lap, "time's one thing I've got lots of."

Which once again effectively silenced the talk.

Fortunately for them all, Harp just then came striding up to the table, Lester in tow. With mock exasperation Harp said, "Anybody here explain to this bucket head the geography, state of Wisconsin?"

"Give 'er a go," Waz volunteered. "What's the prol'um?"

"Prol'ums this. I'm tellin' him how me'n Irene gonna take the Airstream up by La Crosse next week, that piece property we got up there. He sez, 'Oh, I know that part a the country, spent some time up in Green Bay once.' "

"Green Bay's over by the lake," Waz said.

"*I* know that. Tell him."

Lester was by now slumped in a chair, fingers linked like trussing wire under a spongy arc of tummy. A couple of buttons on his brilliant orange shirt had come undone, displaying terraced mounds of hairless, white-marbled meat. His eyes were owlish, smeary, blank. Waz turned to him and said patiently, "Green Bay's east. La Crosse, that's clear over the other side the state."

"They got a big river by Green Bay?" Lester wanted to know, sloshing out the question.

"That's Lake Michigan, brain-dead," Harp said. "River you're thinkin' of's Mississippi. An' that's by La Crosse."

"Then that's where I was at."

"Where?"

"That place you said."

"La Crosse?"

"Over by the river. Where they make the over-alls."

"Overalls?" Waz said. "Fuck's overalls got to do with anything?"

Norma flinched. She mumbled something inaudible to everyone but Buck, who said, "C'mon, Waz, watch the words, huh?"

"Oh. Yeah. Sorry."

"Maybe he means Oshkosh," Della suggested. "Where they make those overalls. Oshkosh B'Gosh. Except I don't think there's any river there."

Lester leaned over, peered at her. "Hey, Della, you join up the army?"

Della looked baffled.

"Wha' happen your hair? Look like somebody give you a buzz job."

"God, he *is* brain-dead," Della sniffed peevishly.

Waz patted her knee. "Don't mind him. Little swacked, is all."

Harp threw up his hands. "Overalls, army, haircuts—I thought we was talkin' about La Crosse here."

"That's where I musta been," Lester said. "Reason I remember is I was drivin' my Chevette—this was a few years back, had a Chevette then. All I could afford." He broke off there, gazed at them expectantly, as though a lucid explanation had just been offered, untangling all.

"So?" Buck said.

"What?"

"What's the Chevette got to do with it?"

"With what?"

"You rememberin' it was La Crosse."

"Oh. That. Well, see, there's some bikers on the road, zippin' in an' out the cars. Pretty soon we all just comes to a deadass stop, nobody movin' at all. I looks out the windshield, couple bikes in front a me. Look left, right, same thing. Rearview, all y'can see is bikes. Hogs, Fat Boys, Specials, Glides—everywhere bikes. I'm thinkin' holy shit, I'm surrounded by 'em, bikers. It's like that show where the birds come after the people. *Psycho*."

"That ain't *Psycho*," Waz declared. "*Psycho*'s the one where the broad got slashed in the shower."

"He's thinkin' a *Birds*," Buck said.

"That's what I just said," Lester protested. "I just said that."

"What I'm sayin' is that's the name a the picture. *Birds*."

"Whatever. Anyways, I hit the locks on the doors, roll up the windows, even though it's hotter'n pistol—August, I remember right—an' your Chevettes ain't got no air, course—but these bikers they got me boxed an' they lookin' real mean an'—"

"They can be badass, all right, bikers," Waz interjected.

"Not all of 'em," Buck dissented. "There's them Bikers for Jesus. Hear they're okay."

Harp thwacked his brow with an open palm. "You boys a big help, gettin' this La Crosse matter cleared up."

Lester looked at him perplexedly. "But that's what I'm sayin', Harp. When I gets to this town, I asks around and folks tell me all them bikers comin' for a big rally, the Harley plant, some anniversary, forget which one. An' Harley's in La Crosse, right?"

"*Milwaukee!*" Harp exploded at him. "You was in *Milwaukee!*"

"Milwaukee a city, like?"

"Yeah," Buck drawled. "It's a city."

Lester shrugged. "Okay. Guess it was Milwaukee, then."

"Y'know, Lester," Harp said, cooler now, resigned, "tryin' to follow your line a thought, be easier nailin' spaghetti to the wall."

Lester, cheeks puffed in dippy grin, beamed like a man just been paid a most generous compliment. A ghost of a scar, dead white, ascended off his upper lip, inflicted years ago, plant legend had it, by the rash acceptance of a dare, the details of which were murky, something about a firecracker lit in his mouth and ejected a split second too late. Buck, with a nod at him, said, "See what you're gonna miss, Harp, quittin' on us?"

"Yeah, miss it like a case a the—the—" He groped, reddening, after an acceptable alternative to the conventional *clap*, which certainly wouldn't do in the company of ladies. None came to him, so he put a benign hand on Lester's head, tousled the hair, pale and fine as corn silk, and said, "Miss this genius." And to change the subject he asked, "Everybody havin' a good time?"

"It's just a wonderful party," Norma answered for them all.

"Glad you're enjoyin' yourselves."

"All your friends here," she went on, "family."

"Lot a people showed up, all right," Harp said proudly. With a sweeping glance he took in the crowded hall. "All the old gang."

Among those milling crowds Jimmie Jack could be seen circulating, gripping palms, clutching biceps, slapping backs, exchanging warm words. Working the room. Also, and quite unmistakably, working his way toward their table where, once arrived, he nodded greetings all around, laid a comradely cuffing punch on Harp's shoulder, and said, "Sensational wingding, Harpo. Real hoo-ha."

Harp responded with a chilly thanks.

"Free booze, free eats—gonna set you back little."

"I can handle it."

"You can't, put it on Lester's tab here."

Lester, too blitzed to speak, merely snickered. No one else had anything to say.

"So how's it feel, bein' a man a leisure?"

"Feels good," Harp said.

"Bet it does, at that. You be sure'n stop by sometimes, say hello all your workin' stiff buddies still in the slammer."

"I'll do that."

The pleasantries exhausted, Jimmie started to saunter away, paused and, as though in afterthought, said, "Oh, yeah, Wazzer. Got a minute?"

Waz looked at him warily. "For what?"

"Step over my office an' I'll buy you drink on Harp. Fill you in."

Waz got to his feet and followed him to the bar.

"What's that all about?" Della asked Buck.

"Beats me."

"Now, there's one I ain't gonna miss," Harp muttered.

Buck shook his head, vigorous assent. "That's a goddamn true fact."

Norma winced. Della sulked. Lester mumbled something largely unintelligible, "ain't so bad" in it somewhere.

And over at an otherwise unoccupied end of the bar the two men were huddled, Jimmie commencing in confidential whisper, "Got the good news bean drop on ya, Wazo, gonna make your night. Here's the buzz."

And a few moments later Waz took Buck aside and whispered much the same message in his friend's ear; and Buck's open, weathered face worked through a battery of expressions—astonishment, doubt, suspicion, anxiety, hope—and he said grimly, "This the straight goods?" And when Waz confirmed it, Buck's expression settled into an exultant joy and he stammered, "Jesus, Waz, I can't hardly believe it—this is just great—wanta thank you—all you done—wait'll I tell Norma."

And at the same moment, in the placid community of Naperville, situated no more than fifteen miles to the north, Marshall Quinn was doing his best to comfort his anguished wife, her ominous, mystifying mood of the past several hours broken, abruptly and the instant they stepped through the door of their home, by great shuddering sobs, face dissolving suddenly into tragic mask of wild sorrow and unspeakable loss. The doctor, same one who serviced the campus and enough of an acquaintance to summon at this late hour, was departed now, stumbling over a few commiserative words on his way out, empty words, and Lori was sinking slowly into a sedated sleep, moaning wretchedly, "He's gone . . . Jeffie's gone. . . ."

Marshall sat in a chair pulled up by the bed. He stroked her hot brow. Held her hand. Made soft cooing sounds. Her voice went slurry. Gradually her fevered tossing slowed, stopped. He looked out the window at a black sky riddled with stars and a moon round and yellow and veined as a jaundiced, bloodshot eye. Everything seemed distorted, a buckled, misshapen world born out of a single lancing stab of psychic pain and reassembled in queerly warped designs and patterns. It occurred to him the sounds he had been uttering were something more than that,

were in fact words: "I'll find him—I promise you—
I'll find him," crooned over and over again, as
though the act of repetition might invest the histri-
onic and altogether feeble pledge with a measure of
sinew and force he felt not at all.

PART
TWO

The man driving down the East-West Tollway late one Sunday morning was surely Marshall Quinn, though it would have required something more than a cursory glance to establish that fact. This Marshall Quinn looked nowhere near as breezy and self-possessed as the one who had embarked on a make-believe journey through the stars ten weeks and two days (by his exact count) ago, and returned out of sleep dark to a real Earth wrapped in its own senseless and unrelieved darkness. Nor so young. This Marshall's face was haggard, scored with fatigue, its brows irritably pinched, eyes hostile—face of a man who measures everything and everyone through a lens of sullen, prepared bitterness no longer crimped by the optical illusions of eternal hope and foreordained happy endings.

Nevertheless, when he spoke to his wife—which was much less frequent lately—but when he did, his voice, in contrast with a mouth set in a grim, combative line, was surprisingly gentle. Patiently, automatically, as though the words had been committed to memory and were being recited to himself, he ex-

plained the day's agenda: "What we're going to try
to do is cover an area west and a little south of the
museum. I've got it all blocked off on the map. I
think we can get a good share of it done today, if we
hustle. And if this damnable traffic would ease up a
little."

She had nothing to say to this, and the damnable
traffic rolled on, clotting the highway, barreling
along at breakneck speeds. A blistering sun poured
down on them, glanced off the hood and pierced the
windshield. Sinuous waves of heat danced off the
concrete. The city skyline rose like a file of tomb-
stones framed against the horizon. He looked over at
her, tried again. "Are you sure you're up to this?"

She nodded dully. Her despair, so bleak and
numbing and final it bordered on catatonia, seemed
to lend her features a kind of somber, waxen beauty,
the way a total surrender to disaster will erase the
deepest furrows of dread. To Marshall she seemed,
astonishingly, lovelier than ever, a peculiarly en-
hanced likeness of the woman he remembered dimly
from that time before the trauma began, this one
etched in the most delicate of glass.

"You know," he felt compelled to say, "that we'll
have to be around Soldier Field. And there's a game
this afternoon."

Some small animation came into her vacant face,
a look not quite fearful but heavy with misgiving.
"Game?"

"Yes."

"There'll be crowds?"

"That's the point," Marshall said, with an effort

holding his voice as even as he was able. "The more people we talk to, the more who see the leaflets, the better our chances."

The leaflets he was referring to were piled high in the back of their boxy Volvo wagon. Under a stark block-lettered legend that implored HAVE YOU SEEN ME?, they bore a recent photo of a smiling Jeffrey Quinn, a catalog of descriptive details, and a number to call. One of them, blown up to poster size, was secured to a window of the backseat, driver's side.

"It's no use," she said, more sluggish than desolate, listless more than tragic. "You know it's no use."

Because she was probably right, it took another effort, greater than the last for Marshall to swallow the anger rising in his throat. He did, though, saying only, "That may be. But somebody has to do something."

About that, at least, he was the one certainly right. They had long since been forgotten by the vaunted media. After a brief rush of attention (local television anchormen reporting Jeff's abduction in tones fraudulently mournful, their expressions studiedly doleful; prominent coverage in the metro sections of the *Tribune* and *Sun-Times*), the story, gloomy and unresolved, lost some of its sensational luster, gradually dwindled to afterthought mention on the six o'clock news, slipped to the newspapers' back pages (next to obituaries), then vanished altogether, both places, ousted by fresh disasters, of which there was an ongoing and abundant supply. Enough to titillate everyone.

The police were ineffective, all their efforts to date come to nothing. After the promised visit by Detective Thornton the day following the debacle, and after weeks of sporadic, confounding (and increasingly fewer) meetings with him and his "team" (which consisted, near as Marshall could tell, of another officer expertly schooled in the same intimidating detachment), they'd heard not a word. Lately his calls to Thornton went mostly unreturned, and when they were, all he got (and that dispatched on burdened sigh) was a vague "Workin' on it, Mr. Quinn, followin' up some leads. Like I told you, it's front burner with us. Soon's we get something solid, I'll be in touch."

Front burner. Sure. Worse than powerless, the police. If he could have scraped together the money, he'd have hired a private investigator, but their astronomical fees, as disclosed through a few timid phone inquiries, quickly disabused him of that good notion.

Worst of all was the procession of social workers and so-called mental health counselors and support-group zealots and pastors and colleagues and acquaintances and assorted hothouse healers that appeared uninvited at their door, professional and amateur misery mongers who seemed, all of them, to possess a certain lip-licking eagerness to supply a sympathetic ear and pass along proven prescriptions for "coping skills," as if some earnest twelve-step program could dispel the ache of loss, restore emotional balance, instruct them in the virtues of resignation. What Marshall had learned, these ten plus weeks, was not acceptance but the hard lesson that everyone—be they aloof or solicitous, pitying or practicedly neutral—was powerless, no one capable of help.

Which left only themselves. More accurately, given her tranced retreat into some anguished, cloistered chamber in her head, only him.

So what he'd done was prepare the leaflets, had them printed by the thousands, and engineered a plan, independent of police and any do-good agencies, to distribute them street by methodically mapped-out Chicago street, nothing scattershot about it. Blanket the city, if need be, till his son's image was graven in the consciousness of every last one of its citizens, till one of them came forward and said, "I know where he is, come with me, I'll take you to him." Persuaded that he, small-town waif transplanted to suburban innocent, could make it happen, if only because, by the testimony of his own hollow words, *some*thing had to be done and the someone elected to do it had to be himself, criminally negligent author of all their grief.

That was the substance of his estimable plan. But in the week or so they'd been at it (his doomsayer wife paradoxically insisting on tagging along, doubtless out of fear of the awful silence of an empty house, a terror deeper even than crowds), what he'd discovered was still another bitter truth: the passionless distance of strangers, an indifference to any pain not their own that oftentimes shaded over from the annoyed rebuff into stony resistance, now and again even into gratuitous mockery. Thinking about it only fueled the smoldering fire of his impotent anger, set his hands to trembling on the wheel. Better not to. Better to—

"Marsh! Look out!"

Lori, yanking him back from all these wandering reflections with a warning cry. For just then a car, materializing out of nowhere, out of some treacherous blind spot in the mirror, swerved into their lane, abruptly and without signal, and only by jamming the brakes was he able to escape a collision, and then only by the narrowest of margins. Heart clubbing, rage unbottled now and focused, finally, on something tangible, visible, he called out, "God damn crazy reckless son of a bitch! Asshole!"

Lori looked at him curiously. Quietly and without a trace of reproach, she said, "You're cursing, Marsh. You never used to curse."

"Did you see what that bastard did? Cut me off like that?"

"I saw it."

"Could have killed us."

"He didn't, though. Nothing happened."

"I ought to ram him. Climb right up his rear end."

"That would be all we'd need. A car wreck."

Yet another in that mounting tally of harsh truths, self-evident, it seemed, to everyone but himself, her even. Still fuming, he punched the accelerator, made no reply. The next few miles they rode in silence.

A sign alerted them to a toll plaza just ahead. He fished through his pockets for some coins. Swung into a line of cars backed up at one of the several exact-change booths. In the lane to his immediate left, three cars up, was the same one that had very nearly done them in. It was a large, square vehicle, looked to his untrained eye like a Buick or Mercury or Chevy maybe, older model, faded bronze color, splotched with rust, badly in need of a wash. Man behind the wheel, woman in the passenger seat. Marshall longed to get his Volvo up beside them, let them know by look or, if necessary, crude gesture what he thought of their lunatic driving. Too much to hope for.

And yet, miraculously, that's exactly what happened. Their line stalled, his slowly advanced, and when the two vehicles were parallel he presented them with a fierce, scowling face. Neither occupant took the slightest notice of him. The man drummed the wheel impatiently, pinch of a cigarette dangling from his lips; the woman, dumpy blonde with a butch hairdo, appeared to be yammering tirelessly. Marshall muttered "Assholes" again, but softly this time, and under his breath. And as if that barely articulated obscenity somehow reached her above the roar of the traffic and across the gap between them, penetrating closed windows, both cars, the woman turned and inspected them with about the same level of curiosity one inspects the progress of a pesky bug climbing up a pane of glass, and was about to turn away when her eyes fell on the poster in the Volvo's window and they steepened and her jaw fell open and she mouthed—not to Marshall but to her astonished-seeming self—the unmistakable words: "I know that kid."

Still gaping at the poster, she elbow-jabbed the driver, an urgent demand on his attention. Exasperatedly he turned, squinted. His face darkened, and he looked away quickly.

Marshall was dumbstruck, paralytic. And as in some bizarre dream where events, jeering at logic, occur capriciously and perversely and outside one's control, their line began to move and his didn't, and they edged out ahead, first a single car length, then another. The woman's mouth was going rat-a-tat now, hands flying, miming some agitated show of incredulous confusion. Her head swiveled between gradually receding Volvo and driver, who pointedly ignored her, pulled their car into the bay, flung coins into the chute and, the instant the gate lifted, took off squealing, not a look back.

And Marshall, with the sudden wild panic of a drowning victim going under for the last time, commanded his leaden nerve ends to act! Act! He fumbled with the window and stuck his head out and called after them, "What?—what?—what?—you know him?—where is he?—wait!"

His voice was swallowed up in the whoosh of vehicles bolting through the gates.

And Lori, startled out of her private reverie, exclaimed, "What is it? Jeff? Is it Jeffie?"

Marshall could see the car merging into the streams of traffic on the other side of the toll booths. The one directly in front of him was by now idled opposite the change chute. Its driver appeared to be an elderly matronly lady, somebody's kindly grandmother. Slowly, infuriatingly slow, an arthritic claw came through the window and released some coins. One of them missed the chute. The door swung open and she shuffled out and stooped over in that lock-kneed, ass-aloft posture of stiffening age and recovered the errant coin.

Marshall laid on the horn. "Move it!" he bawled.

Lori was frantically tugging his sleeve. "Tell me, Marsh. What did you see? *Tell* me!"

"Goddammit, move!"

Taking her time, the sweet granny dropped the coin in the chute. She paused long enough to glare at him defiantly and to elevate a gnarled middle finger, then climbed back into her car and sped away. He swung the Volvo into the bay, threw in his own coins, and in the split second it took for the gate to rise he pounded the wheel furiously, muttering, "Up, damn it! Up up up!" He stomped on the pedal, and the car lurched forward, picking up speed.

"What is it? What's happened?"

Lori shrilling at him. Swarms of vehicles zooming around him. Sun blinding him. Had to concentrate, center himself, think, remember. "Notepad in the glove compartment," he said. "Get it."

"Was it Jeff? Did you see—"

"Just get it."

"But I don't—"

"Get the goddam pad!"

She got it.

"You want to help? You want to find him? Write this down. Illinois plate, letters AZ or AS in it, Z or S, one or the other, Buick or a Mercury, four-door, I think, about an '88, '89—Christ, I don't know, somewhere in there, bronze color, lot of rust on it. Man and a woman, forty, say, maybe a little older, hard to tell, woman had blond hair, cut short, man I couldn't see much of, big, I remember, heavy . . ."

He trailed off, run out of remembering. Lori scribbled silently. She looked chastened, hurt, bewildered. And not a little frightened at his driving. But he was oblivious to it, eyes fastened on the road, jaws clenched, yellow-knuckling the wheel, weaving in and out of lanes dangerously, blazing down the highway in a maddened, futile effort at catch-up. In a sensible Volvo station wagon. Rolling representation of everything he was: cautious, timid, sheltered, unseasoned in conflict, unschooled in strife.

Might as well be chasing the wind. The Buick or Mercury or whatever the fuck it was, nowhere in sight. Swept up in the glut of traffic. Vanished utterly. Like those heat waves in the near distance will vanish at your approach. Like some hallucination appeared magically, and as mysteriously gone. The car, the woman with her soundless declaration dangling a flimsy thread of hope, the whole encounter, all of it a fragment of his fevered imagination, something he had willed into being. A sop to his incapacity and his helpless grief.

Except it was no hallucination, and he knew it. No. Rather his own craven failure to act—freezing there like a stricken fawn in that critical sliver of a moment—had forfeited the single opportunity gifted to him. That and his wicked luck.

He turned off at the next exit ramp. Pulled into the parking lot of a strip mall. Killed the engine. He sat stiffly, stiff as that irascible old granny back there, as if he were holding himself in. His face

worked through shifting attitudes of defeat and
stunned disbelief and self-loathing, but when he
spoke it was in the voice of a man more bemused
than enraged. "I lost them. Jesus God, I can't believe it. I *lost* them."

The bronze, rust-cankered Mercury chugged
down Maple Avenue, deliberately slow now,
though for no apparent reason since the suburban
Sunday traffic was relatively light. Sweat beaded
on the driver's forehead and over his lip, and
moons of it dampened the pits of his T-shirt. His
complexion, normally ruddy as boiled beef, was
gone pallid, gray. His dark eyes flicked nervously
at the rearview mirror. He lit a steadying cigarette.
And to revive a conversation silenced back on the
tollway with a sharp barked command, he said, for
something to say, "Hot out."

Got only more of the silence.

So he came at it another angle. "We decide to
keep this heap, I'm gonna have to work on the air
condition."

"Don't try to change the subject, Waz."

"Look, Della, I'm tellin' you—"

"And I'm telling you, kid on that poster looked
just like Davie. Like in *exactly* like. Dead ringer."

She was pressed up against the door, staring
stonily through the windshield, letting him know by
word and tone and sulky set of her dimpled chin he
wasn't going to get off that easy. Talking about
weather and cars and air conditioners, for chrissake.
Like it never even happened.

"How the hell you know that?" he said, steaming up again. "We couldn't of been there half a minute, tops. Less'n that. You didn't get no good look at it."

"Know what I seen."

"You been watchin' too much tube. Goddam soap operas gettin' to you."

"That might be," she said pettishly. "Still know what I seen."

"Okay. Good. You see whatever fuck you wanta see. But I don't want you go sayin' nothin' to Buck or Norma. Either of 'em. Okay?"

"You better just tell me what's going on, Waz."

"Ain't *nothin'* goin' on," he sputtered on a mighty, spittle-winged exhalation, stubbing out the half-smoked cigarette in a choleric fit of temper. "Which is what I'm tellin' you right now. Which is how it is and that's all it is. You understand what I'm sayin' here?"

Della gave him a wary sidelong glance. "I understand," she said, even though she didn't. What she understood better was that hair-trigger temper of his, and the note of finality in his voice.

"So let's just stuff a sock in it, huh?"

They had turned off Maple now and were coming down a quiet street lined with trees and homes modest but well tended. A frame two-story with a manicured lawn and an abundance of shrubbery occupied a corner lot just ahead. Before Waz arrived at it he brought the car almost to a crawl and said again, emphatically, one last time, "Okay?"

She nodded.

"Wanna hear you say it."

"Awright, awright. You happy now?"

"Not a word."

"What'd I just say?"

"Okay."

A winged eagle was painted into the wall over the garage door, and above it the straightforward announcement: THE BUCKLEYS. A Pontiac of about the same vintage as the Mercury was parked in the drive, blue-jeaned male buttocks protruding from under its raised hood. Waz swung in next to it, hopped out, and with a labored heartiness called, "Yo, Buck, this GM junker givin' you grief again?"

Buck slid out from beneath the hood, grinned, drawled, "This junker still be clickin' off the miles when they tryin' to peddle your Merc there for parts."

Waz's knob-knuckled hand was outthrust in greeting, and seeing it, Buck looked at his own grease-smeared palm, hesitated. Waz grabbed it anyway and they shook vigorously, the clasp turning quickly into another of their habitual little contests of strength, each trying to outmuscle the other. Della, who had stepped out her side of the car and fallen in behind Waz, had to smile in spite of herself, as if she were watching a couple of unruly kids. Eventually Waz released his grip, admitting grudgingly, "Okay, you win."

"Always do," Buck said, and then, acknowledging Della, he held out grimy arms and beckoned her. "Della, honey, you come on over here. I'll protect you from this ape."

"God knows I need it." She slipped inside the extended arms and gave him a cautious hug.

"Where you two been? Lookin' for you 'bout an hour ago."

"Uh, traffic on the East-West kinda thick," Waz said vaguely. He didn't dare look at Della, but he heard her make one of her little sniffing sounds.

"East-West? What you doin' up there?"

"Went over to Aurora. Check out a Honda Diaz tryin' to con me into buyin'."

"Diaz?"

"Y'know, Vic the spic."

"Machine shop Vic?"

"That's the one."

"He's okay. Knows his cars."

"So do I."

"So you gonna buy?"

"No way. Stay with the Merc, pro'ly."

"Big mistake."

"Least I know what I'm drivin'. An' it ain't rice."

"Yeah, well," Buck said thoughtfully, "something to that too."

"Damn straight, somethin' to it. Gooks cop any more our jobs, we'll all be feedin' on your basic fish-eye burgers."

Della, satisfied her filmy pink blouse was unstained from the quick embrace, tapped a heel on the asphalt. "You two planning to spend the day out here solving the world trade problems?"

Buck winked at his buddy. "I dunno, either that or go inside. What you think, Waz?"

Waz winked back, shrugged. "Six a one to me."

"Let's try inside awhile."

He dropped the Pontiac's hood and led them up the steps and onto a roofed porch strung with hanging flower baskets and through the door into an immaculately ordered living room furnished with sofa, pair of matching chairs, La-Z-Boy, and sturdy wooden coffee and end tables. A big console TV dominated one wall, a bookcase the other, one shelf of which held a set of Comptons encyclopedias, some well-thumbed volumes on auto and home repair, a stack of photo albums and a few paperbacks, another a row of polished bowling trophies, and the rest a variety of collectibles: ceramic figurines, commemorative plates, carnival glass, couple of antique Jim Beam bottles. A framed painting of a brooding Jesus hung above the entrance to the kitchen. "Norma's around somewhere," Buck said. "Been cleanin' the place up."

"What's to clean?" Della remarked.

"Well, can get a little messy. With the boy now, y'know."

"You want messy, try teenagers."

"Can't wait."

A door closed on the second floor, and there was a sound of footsteps on the stairs behind them. "That's her now," Buck said.

Seeing them, Norma's face ignited in a smile, genuine flush of pleasure in it. "Dell, Waz—you made it!" She crossed the room and the two women embraced, Della elevating onto tiptoes and reaching upward to accommodate her friend's height. "We were getting worried," Norma said to her.

"Talk to him about that," Della said, indicating Waz.

"Hey, Norma. How's she goin'?"

Norma disengaged herself and stepped over and gave him a warm hug. "Going great, Waz. But what I want to know is why you two been such strangers."

"You know how it goes. No rest, you're wicked."

"We wanted to give you some time to get settled," Della explained. "Y'know, used to things. How's he doing anyway, Davie?"

Now Norma's face took on a look of pure motherly bliss. "Wonderful, Dell. Just wonderful. He's such a sweet kid."

Della looked around expectantly. "Where's he at?"

"Oh, he's asleep yet. I was just up checking on him. Dale took him down to the park this morning and got him all worn out."

She beamed at Buck, who stood there sporting a proud father grin.

"Which park's that?" Waz wanted to know. "Hummer?"

"No, that one over on Fifty-fifth," Buck said. "They put in a little merry-go-round, just for the summer."

Waz had a crooked smile stuck on his face. "Merry-go-round," he said absently. "That's nice."

"Kid loves it."

"Yeah, that's good too. Listen, Buck, you offerin' beer, or we got to drink outta the garden hose?"

"You know where it's at. Help yourself." He started up the stairs, adding by way of over-the-shoulder explanation, "Gonna shower. Switch on the TV there, Waz. Game'll be on in a minute."

"Some host," Norma said, mock disgust. She tried to steer them toward chairs. "Sit, sit. I'll get it."

Waz waved her back. "You heard him. I'm doin' the honors. Norma? Dell? What're you drinkin'?"

"Too early for me," Della said.

"Nothing for me either, thanks."

"Couple wimp ladies," Waz said, still smiling, let them know it was all in good fun.

They settled onto the couch, and he went into the kitchen, got a can of Bud out of the fridge, popped it, and took a long, gurgly swallow. He lit a cigarette. Listened carefully to the voices trailing in from the living room.

"So how's Heather? Little Mike?" Norma, asking about their kids.

Della responding. "Both doing real good. Well, good as you can expect, teen years."

"Seems like an age since I saw them last."

"Heather's trying out for cheerleader this year. And 'little' Mike, he's not so little anymore. Size of his old man, and just as ornery."

"It's hard to believe they're in high school already."

"They grow up fast."

Waz kept on listening. So far, so good.

Till Della had to put in, "You'll find that out with Davie."

"I know. These are the precious years."

"Sure glad everything worked out."

"Thanks, Dell. So am I."

"He playing with the neighborhood kids? Got any little friends yet?"

"Not yet. He's awfully shy. It takes time."

Della's voice lowering now, almost a whisper. He had to lean over toward the door to catch the words. "How about—you don't mind my asking—uh, before? He seem to remember anything from before?"

God *damn* her. Couldn't leave it alone. Norma's reply he missed altogether. Too low to hear. His stuck-on smile had long since come undone, and in its place was the pained expression of a deeply troubled man.

Wilcox was gazing at the yellow legal pad laid out on the table in front of him. He massaged his temples, kneaded them, actually, as though the circular motions, wide and deep, might erase a serious migraine. He led a crowded life, full of faces, all of them distressed to one degree or another, most of them blurred, forgettable. These two he remembered, but not very clearly. Took awhile into the agitated, disjointed account for it to come back to him. Now he studied the skimpy notes recorded off that account and said, "All this happened—when again?"

"Like I said, about an hour ago. Ninety minutes. No more than that."

"And where abouts?"

"On the East-West Tollway. At a toll plaza near the 355 junction, I think."

"You think?"

"Could have been farther. Closer to the Tri-State

maybe. I'm not exactly sure, but I could find it easy enough."

"I see. Tell me, Mr. Quinn, why'd you come here?"

Marshall was perched on the edge of his seat, staring at him anxiously. They were in the same cramped little cubicle, the air just as sluggish and thick as that first time. Lori, sitting to his left, just as dreamily remote as then; Wilcox, across the table, just as impassive. Neither of them seemed to grasp the significance of the extraordinary event back there on the highway. And since he did, it was with a certain chagrin—better make that humiliation—he felt obliged to admit, "I got turned around coming into the city. Lost, I suppose. Yes, lost. Couldn't find Harrison. We were driving down this side street, and I looked over and there was your precinct station. Anyway, Detective Thornton probably wouldn't have been there even if . . ." He had the uncomfortable sense of talking too much and too fast, explaining too much, serving up more answer than there was question. He broke off, let it go.

"Pro'ly not, it bein' Sunday."

"I thought possibly, well, you could help."

Wilcox sucked in a big, weary breath. "What we got here," he said, and his voice was patient, even, "couple letters off a plate, one of 'em a maybe, pretty slim description of a vehicle . . ." He paused, seemed to think it over. Lifted his gaze and fixed it on Marshall. Steady gaze, eyes touched with regret, face wearing the dolorous look of a man stuck with the delivery of bad news. "I gotta tell you, Mr. Quinn. It's not a whole lot to go on."

"But can't you run some sort of computer trace? At least isolate the possibilities?"

"Could do that, we had a partial plate ID. Run what y'call a variation scan. But two letters, one, that don't hardly qualify as partial."

"I'm pretty certain it was a Z, the second letter. Looked like a Z."

"Say it's a Z. You got any idea how many vehicles we'd be lookin' at? It's not like we got an exact description. Don't even know the make for sure, right?"

"I'm positive it was either a Buick or a Mercury," Marshall said, but his voice was picking up that tremor again, same as before, sounding anything but positive.

"Okay," Wilcox sighed. "This Buick or Mercury, AZ or AS in the plate, it could be from the city, out state, down state, anywhere. Could be a thousand vehicles come close to your description. More'n that, even. See what we're up against?"

"But it's a place to begin. Up to now there's been nothing. Nothing. Handful of air."

"That may be all you got here, Mr. Quinn. That air."

Wilcox was doodling on the yellow pad now, avoiding his eyes. "I don't understand what you mean," Marshall said.

"Mean it could be a, well, prank," he said, seemingly absorbed in the inventive squiggling produced by the ballpoint, independent of his hand. "Y'know, somebody makin' a little joke."

"A *joke*? You're saying it was all a joke back there on the highway?"

"Not sayin' it was. Sayin' it could of been."

"Nobody'd be that sick."

"Or that cruel," Lori put in, her first contribution to the dialogue, offered flat and uninflected, voice of someone in a mild stupor.

Both of them looked at her, Wilcox doubtfully and Marshall embarrassedly, as though irked by the inapt comment of a slightly disturbed child. Sort of comment that arrests a conversation, as it did this one, till Wilcox returned his attention to Marshall and said bluntly, "You don't wanna bet on it."

He felt a big pulse of helpless rage throbbing in him, coming up out of some tight, hollow place in his chest. Not so much at this man seated across from him as at the implication of his remark. A joke. Too staggering to get the mind around it. Too vicious. Too evil. "Sergeant," he said, all pretense of composure, self-possession, all gone now, dismissed by pleading, "we're talking about my son. Will you do the computer trace, scan, whatever it is? Will you do that for us?"

"What I can do is run it by Thornton. Be his call."

"But will *he* do it?"

"Not gonna lie to you, Mr. Quinn. I don't know. Help if we had more on the vehicle. There anything else you can give me?"

"No, no, there's nothing more . . ." Marshall's head moved slowly, side to side. He tugged his lower lip, ransacked his memory. "Wait a minute. Wait. There was a sticker. Back bumper."

"What kinda sticker?"

"One of those 'Buy American' things. Said 'Save U.S. Jobs—Buy American.' Had a flag unfurled. You know the kind I mean?" The image sharpened in his head. He didn't wait for a reply. "And there was some sort of symbol—couldn't make it out—in the corner, lower right-hand side."

"See them stickers on half the bumpers this town, now-days."

"But that symbol, couldn't it be a company logo or a union label? Something like that?"

"Might be," Wilcox said. He scribbled something on his yellow pad, looked up, suppressed another sigh. "That it?"

"That's all I can remember."

Wilcox put down the pen and got to his feet, signaling interview's end. "Well, guess that about covers everything."

"When will we hear something?"

"I'll get this over to Detective Thornton. Whyn't you give him a call, few days?"

"If he agrees to do it, how long would it take?"

"Hard to say, Mr. Quinn. Size job we're lookin' at, could be awhile. It's not like the movies, all that high technology at your instant service. C'mon, I'll walk you folks to your car."

The Volvo was parked near the corner of the street outside the station. Marshall got the door for Lori, then turned to Wilcox and mumbled something in the way of thanks. For what, he wasn't quite sure.

"Your wife, Mr. Quinn. She, uh, okay?"

"She's on medication," Marshall said, studying the sidewalk, unable to meet his eyes. "She's pretty depressed."

"I'm no doctor, but look to me like she could use some, well, professional help."

"Appreciate your concern. I'm seeing to it."

Wilcox glanced into the backseat of the wagon. "Them the leaflets you was tellin' me about?"

"Yes."

"She shouldn't be down here, y'know. You either. This is a badass neighborhood. Ain't no Naperville."

"I've got to do something," Marshall snapped, more than a touch of bitterness in it. "Nobody else is."

Wilcox dropped a cold, heavy glare on him. Squad room glare. "Look," he said, "you're a professor, right?"

"That's right."

"Okay, we don't come in your classroom, tell you how to teach. Don't go tellin' us how to do our work. We're doin' all we can. More'n you think."

Marshall lifted a hand and balled a fist. But it was an imploring gesture, utterly unthreatening, full of desperation. A squeezing at air. His handful of air. "I know you are. I'm sorry I said that. Sorry."

"Forget it," Wilcox said and, softening some, "You find your way back now?"

"I'll find it."

"Everybody knows your Snap-On's top a the line," Waz was declaring, winding down a long, rambling panegyric to the Snap-On label. "Cadillac a tools. You wanna go on the cheap, you get Craftsman."

Buck, patiently waiting his turn, playing at gadfly, merely drawled, "Nobody sayin' Craftsman the better tool. All's I'm sayin' is for your average job—not talkin' out to the plant, talkin' around the house, workin' on the car—they do just fine."

"Fine? You think fine? What happens one of 'em goes out on you, don't work right? Answer me that one."

"Run it over to Sears, show 'em your warranty. They'll stand behind it."

"Yeah, only it's *you* doin' the runnin'. Something go wrong with a Snap-On, whaddaya do?"

Cornered by this irresistible logic, Buck put up an acceding palm. "Okay, you call, they come out."

Waz jabbed a triumphant finger at him. "There you are! There's the difference. Along with your basic quality, 'course."

Where and how the Great Tools Debate began, neither of them, if pressed, could have said. Somewhere back in the wandering, beer-fueled dialogue of the past several hours. They were sprawled in adjacent chairs facing the television, their attention only partly engaged by the game unfolding on its screen. Waz, with the easy intimacy of long-term fellowship, had his shoes off and feet up on a coffee table. Slack-limbed and somewhat bleary-eyed, he appeared to have forgotten whatever it was had been troubling him earlier. He emptied a can of Bud, lit another in a chain of cigarettes, and fired twin jet streams through nostrils from which sprouted an extraordinary thickness of wiry black hair. "Yeah, comes to tools, Snap-On's your Cadillac line," he repeated, clearly enamored of the metaphor, speech a trifle slurred.

Buck, not quite willing to let it go, countered, "If you wanta buy a Cadillac when a Chevy do the same job."

Over on the couch the wives were chatting animatedly, Norma held a can of Diet Pepsi; Della sipped a gin and tonic, daintily but steadily. They ignored the game but the continuous ebb and flow of the tools debate was impossible to disregard altogether, and finally, rolling her eyes at the ceiling, Della said, "Honestly, sometimes I think those two were born to argue."

"They do have a good time, though," Norma allowed tolerantly.

"If ragging at each other's a good time."

"You know, I just love your outfit," Norma said, gently steering the talk in another direction.

Della's face opened in a gratified smile. "Thanks. Picked it up just last week. Know where?"

"Where?"

"A consignment shop, if you can believe that."

"Really!" Norma exclaimed dutifully.

"Really. Me and Lorraine—you remember my friend Lorraine?—works at the Hair Port there in Lisle?—we're out at Fox Valley browsing through this place, and Lorraine sees it and she goes, 'Dell, look at this, be just perfect for you.' I says, 'Oh, no, it's way too young for me,' but Lorraine, she makes

me try it on anyway, and once I did I just had to have
it."

The perfect outfit (in striking contrast to Norma's
plain cotton slacks and knit, floral print top) consisted of a pair of thigh-clinging pink Spandex shorts
peeking out from beneath a puffy mini-skirt, also
pink, and matching silk blouse cut low to reveal a
deep cleft between rubbery breasts that had a ten-
dency to jiggle whenever she spoke excitedly or gestured expansively, as she did now.

"Lorraine was right," Norma assured her. "It looks
great on you."

Della drained off the last of the gin in her glass.
"Waz seems to think so," she said, hint of a coy leer
in it.

Uncertain what to say to that, Norma offered another drink.

"Well, maybe just a splash."

She took the glass, glided across the room, and
picked up the spilling-over ashtray and Waz's empty
can. "Waz?" she asked him. "Another?"

"Always bust a Bud."

She turned to Buck. "Hon?"

"I'm still good," he said. "Gettin' hungry, though.
When we gonna eat?"

"Pretty soon now. I want to let Davie sleep just a
little while longer."

Buck nodded agreeably and gave her an affection-
ate backside pat, and she gave him back a fond smile
and disappeared through the door to the kitchen.

Della, never content to be on the fringes of a conversation, called over to the two men, "Who's winning?"

"You heard it," Waz said. "I made him own up to Snap-On bein' best."

"Talkin' about the football game, dumdum."

"Bears kickin' butt again," Buck told her.

"They ain't doin' that good," Waz grumbled.

"Face it, Waz. They're smearin' 'em."

"Aah, exhibition games, they don't mean jack shit."

"Win's a win."

"Know what they oughta do? Tellya what they oughta do. Bring back Ditka."

"Ditka? Ditka's a loser."

"Loser!" Waz thundered. "Mike Ditka a *loser*? He's the one brought this team back. Made 'em. Hadn't been for Ditka they'd be playin' sandlot ball right now. Even you gotta admit that, Buck."

"Yeah, well, he did okay," Buck conceded, but with a qualifying, "at first. Toward the end there he was showboatin'. Doin' more commercials on the television than coachin'. His prol'um is he forgot what they were payin' him for."

"Tell ya who forgot," Waz said, warming to this new avenue of controversy. "People the city of Chicago, they're the ones forgot what Mike Ditka done for 'em. Give ya a for instance. There's this bar up on Ogden, forget the name a the joint, use to serve a Ditkaburger, big special, plate a fries, side a slaw. Remember that place, Dell?"

"Fifty bars this end of Ogden, and I'm suppose to remember one with a hamburger?"

"It's like a made-over house. Right next to that Ford dealer."

"Tell the story," Buck urged him. "You gettin' bad as Lester."

"Anyway," Waz pushed on, voice rising indignantly, "last time I'm up there I looks at the menu, no Ditkaburger. So I asks the waitress where it's at, and y'know what she says?"

"What'd she say?"

"Says, 'Ditka? Who's he?' Wiseass, y'know, like he's a nobody now, ain't good enough for their menu, this dive."

"You shoulda ordered a Wannstedtburger instead," Buck suggested, grinning. "Pro'ly taste the same even if it don't carry the same sound to it."

"Yeah," Waz said sourly, "just like he—Wannstedt, I'm sayin'—don't carry same weight on the field."

Norma was back in the room now, dispensing drinks. Something happened on the screen, a long breakaway run, and Waz and Buck let out simultaneous whoops. And on the stairs a child appeared, hair tousled, clothes rumpled, clutching a teddy bear in one hand, rubbing the sleep from his eyes with the other. Norma rushed over and gathered him up in her arms, crooning, "Davie, you're up. You have a nice nap? You slept so *long*! Were you all tired out?"

The boy looked around the room timidly, said nothing. Jeffrey Quinn, in this incarnation, seemed smaller somehow, slighter, drawn in on himself, as though all the boundless energy and frisky curiosity of the child at the museum had seeped out of him.

Norma carried him over to the couch and cuddled him in her lap. She smoothed his hair tenderly, and on her face was a look of almost beatific joy.

"Hey, boy," Buck called, voice full of an awkward fatherly pride, " 'bout time you woke up."

Waz grinned weakly, the game forgotten now and all the trouble coming back into his eyes. He shot a worried glance at Della, whose expression was a shifting stew of wonder, perplexity, and a secret certain knowledge. She covered it with a carefully induced smile, and in a shrill soprano said, "Hi, Davie. You remember me?"

"You remember Mrs. Wazinski," Norma tried to prompt him. "Can you say hi?"

The boy shrank deeper into her arms, hugged the bear tighter. Over his head Norma silently mouthed the words, "He's still real shy."

But Della, not to be put off, edged in closer on the couch, said, "What's your teddy's name, honey?"

And in a small frightened voice, barely audible, the boy whispered the single word, "Jeffie."

Another football fan, Glenn Wilcox, got the score of the game late that afternoon and was, in his own quiet way, cheered at the news, seeing he had a double saw riding on the Bears. Made his otherwise routine day: half a dozen muggings, about the same number of boosted vehicles, your usual quota of D & D's, one rape, one flasher, couple of domestics. Routine except for that visit by the putz professor and his spaced missus, kept nagging him. Not that it was exactly sympathy he felt, or for sure any urgent obligation, not off that loopy, fuzzy story they got to tell. Too many years on the force for that (and only eighteen months and counting till retirement). That long, you learned to maintain a professional distance, never get personally involved. Still was hard to scrub the image of their eager citizen faces, playing at crime fighter, pair of suburb biscuits like that, with their leaflets and their heavy tollway clues. Kind of sad, you thought about it, which all afternoon he'd tried not to do, but for reasons unclear to him, couldn't get a handle on, it kept coming back to him. Maybe because, twice divorced himself, three kids, two of them boys, none of them give him so much as the time of day, as lost to him forever as the Quinn boy most likely was, all this time gone by— maybe because of that he could understand a little how they felt, some of their desperation. So even though he knew it was pointless, worse than useless, he went ahead anyway and picked up the phone and put in a call to Thornton over at Four, and when, after a lengthy hold, he got him on the line, he said, casual as he could pitch it, "Hey, Palmer. Glenn Wilcox."

"Glenn. How's by you?"

"Same old song. You?"

"Holdin' course. Loose but holdin'. What's up? And don't say what you're gonna."

Wilcox forced a chuckle. "Been awhile since that one got up, my age."

"Not that, what then?"

"You remember them people from out to Naperville, Quinns? Got their kid snatched?"

"Like I'm gonna forget. That weenie been crowdin' me two months running."

"Yeah, well, today's my turn in the barrel."

"No kiddin'. How's that?"

"They was in here all stoked over some big lead they turned up."

"How come you got volunteered?"

"Got lost. Ended up here."

Thornton snorted. "That gimp get lost in a phone booth."

"Don't I know. Anyway, long as they're here I figured I'd listen it out. Spare you."

"Owe you one. I'm up to my ass in backlog. So what's this serious lead?"

"Pro'ly nothin'."

"So try me anyhow."

Wilcox related the tale of the highway encounter, trimming it down, bare bones, since he knew Thornton, never a patient man, had a low flapjaw threshold. Soon as he's finished, Thornton said curtly, "Somebody jivin' 'em."

"That's what I told him, this professor. 'Course, he wants us run a scan."

"Off that? One letter, no make on the vehicle? No way. Nothin' to scan."

"Told him that too."

"Fuckin' amateurs."

"Well," Wilcox said, "just thought I'd let you know. He'll be buggin' you about it next week."

"Be Vern's prol'um. Tonight I'm vanished, *evapo*-rated. Two weeks vacation."

"Hey, good on you. Enjoy."

"I'll do that. Talk to ya, Glenn."

Wilcox put up the phone and poured himself a cup of the vile station house coffee. Burned going down, burned his gut. He drank it anyway. Unaccountably, a memory of his youngest boy came to him. Got to be—what?—fifteen now, last seen over a decade back, lived somewhere out in Utah with his bitch of a mother. Memory was blurry, like a dream memory, like he'd dreamed him into existence, then dreamed him away. Like his whole life gone by, fart in the wind.

No good thinking that way, so he turned his thoughts to the conversation with Thornton. Vacation. He wondered where he was off to this time. For sure someplace glitzy. Thornton was famous for his vacations. Vine had it he wasn't above shaking a few trees, fund them. Which was nothing to him, none of his business. Except that's why the rap on the street had the department motto as We Serve and Collect. And that's why poor dumb fucks like them Quinns sit home watching a phone that don't ring, waiting for word that don't come.

He remembered a badge he knew over at Four, whiz on the computer, made a name for himself working grand theft auto. More times than a few he'd helped him out, could call in a favor now, he wanted. Why not? Couldn't hurt. Pacify the parents. Be his good deed for the decade.

Shortly before eleven o'clock that night, a black Lincoln Town Car bumped its way down a deserted back road near a bugspeck village that went by the

improbable name of Sandwich. After a few miles the
driver pulled off the road at a stand of trees, cut the
engine, and waited in the latticework of shadows
cast by a lemony rind of moon. About a quarter of an
hour later, two thin fingers of light appeared in the
distance, fattened, seemed to merge, and in another
moment a Plymouth van swung in under the trees
and lurched to a stop alongside the Lincoln. Simultaneously the two drivers exited and stepped to the
rear of the vehicles, lifted trunk and tailgate, respec-
tively, while exchanging laconic greetings through
the simple pronouncement of the other's name.

"Dingo."

"Jimmie."

Without another word they set immediately to
work. One by one, keeping tally in his head, Dingo
removed several flat cardboard boxes from the trunk,
then a large square one and a number of smaller cartons, handed them over to Jimmie, who stacked them
carefully in the back of his van. When the transfer
was completed, they secured their vehicles and came
around either side of the Lincoln and got in the front
seat. Dingo unlocked the glove compartment and
took out his ledger. Leaving the compartment door
open to supply some small light, he read from a page
in the book: "Seven VCR's, one case of V.O., five of
Marlboros, and eleven Nikon cameras. Does that
match your count?"

"Says it in the book, it's gotta be right."

"You've got all the figures down?"

Jimmie leaned in close and scrutinized the numbers opposite each item on the page. Dingo recoiled

slightly, nostrils twitching. He reached into a pocket and produced a roll of breath mints. "Would you like a Cloret, Jimmie?"

Jimmie, still engrossed in the numbers, lips moving as he read, replied absently, "Huh?"

"Cloret?"

"Cloret? Nah, never use 'em."

"I noticed," Dingo muttered in stoic aside.

Evidently it went on by Jimmie, who glanced up and said, "Numbers look good. How 'bout that cat? You able to get ahold any?"

"I was. It's in the compartment there."

Jimmie removed a leather pouch and held it up in gleeful display. "This the one gonna stain our fingers sugar green."

"Maybe. But I'd be very careful how you dispose of it. That's not weed you're holding, or crank. It's got a jacket for deadly. Fatal, even."

"Negative in the sweat department," Jimmie assured him. "Dude I'm layin' it off on doin' his own dealin', gonna be a big-time rack-a-teer. So that puts plenty space between us and the serious heads."

"Still is risky. Merchandise, soft feed, that's one thing. This is another. Get nailed on this and you're looking at a heavy jolt."

Dingo was acutely conscious of backsliding into street, for all his disciplined efforts at linguistic betterment. Talking to Jimmie the words just spilled out, impossible to contain, though no less disagreeable to him. He resolved to work on it, hold firm to his fastidious and insular agenda.

"Ain't nobody gonna get nailed, Ding. You got my guaranfuckintee on that."

"I hope so," Dingo said quietly, leveling a bone-cold stare on him. "You wouldn't enjoy doing time, Jimmie. Someone like yourself. Nor would I. Once a lifetime is more than plenty."

Jimmie shifted uneasily in his seat. "Man, you got that one right, time," he said, and to wrap things up fast, get himself out from under that stare, added, "So, we all squared away for tonight here?"

"Not quite. Couple of other matters we need to consider."

Jimmie managed a slack grin, thinking, Uh-oh, don't like the sound of that, not one little bit. So he was pleasantly relieved when Dingo thrust a wrist under the light and said, "You didn't notice my new watch."

"Holy shit! That a Rolie?"

Dingo smiled. Small, enigmatic smile. He took off the watch and handed it to him. "Would you like it?"

Jimmie hesitated, wondered if it was some kind of gag, give you a shock or squirt water in your face. Didn't figure, Dingo giving anybody anything for nothin'.

"Take it," Dingo urged him.

"You're givin' *me* a Rolie?"

"As a matter of fact, it's not a Rolex. But you'd never know it, would you?"

"It's a fake?"

"Very authentic-looking fake, I'd say. And it happens I've got a source in Gary could supply us. Think you could move them at your plant?"

"Fuckin' A. Watches always a big item in there. What kinda dollar we be talkin'?"

"To make it worth our while you'd have to deal in quantity. In lots of a hundred I can get them for fifty each. Expect you could get, oh, two-fifty."

Jimmie did the mental arithmetic, whistled softly. "Be a nice take for us."

"Question is, can you move a hundred?"

"Oughta be able do that, easy."

"Ought to," Dingo said, smile suddenly departed, chilly stare back in its place, "or will?"

"Will," Jimmie repeated for him. "Maybe do better'n that, even."

"That's what I like to hear, Jimmie. Because of course I wouldn't want to commit to a delivery unless you were absolutely sure."

"Time-wise what're we lookin' at?" Jimmie asked, and then, hearing his choice of words, snickered, "That ain't a little joke I'm makin' there."

Dingo, unamused, said, "Two weeks. I'll go ahead with the arrangements on my end, you keep me informed of your progress."

"You got 'er, Dingo."

"Splendid. Now, take this one along with you. Use it as a demonstrator model. Should help you place your orders."

Obediently, Jimmie slipped the watch around a bony wrist. "That it, then?"

"No. You remember I said a couple of matters."

"What's the other one?"

"The Caulkins account. Seems it's still in deep arrears."

"Huh?"

It was a word he'd come across in a book on business management, *arrears,* had a nice substantial ring to it. The book was an endless source for words like that, and he was trying to get through a chapter a day. You're in business, you want to sound like a businessman. "Delinquent," he explained. "Past due. Late. I believe we spoke about this some time back. A couple of months ago, at least. Remember?"

"Yeah, I remember that. But he's been makin' some payments on it."

"Be a reach to call those puny sums payments, Jimmie. Looks to me like you've got a stiffer." Dingo regretted having to put it this way, but sometimes, given your audience, that's what you had to do, make your point.

"Lester a stiffer? Nah, no way. He's maybe pullin' with one oar, but he's basically a harmless shithead. He'll come up with it."

"I want that account brought into balance, Jimmie."

"Lemme see what I can do."

"Do that. You've got a week."

"Week!" Jimmie squawked. "Jesus, Dingo, I remember right, it's some pretty large cush he owes. Ain't like he's goin' noplace. An' I gotta do business with them boys, y'know."

"This *is* business. A week."

In the pale compartment light the skin on Dingo's face appeared sallow, yellowish, and drawn tight over the bones as the skin on an onion. His mouth was set in a thin line, turned up slightly at one cor-

ner. A smile?—not a smile?—no way Jimmie could
tell for sure, but looking at it he was sure of one
thing, fucker was cuttin' with a dull tool and you
never wanta dick with a looper. So he edged over toward the door, saying, "Okay, I'll try."

"Try hard, Jimmie. I'll be in touch."

In the second floor bedroom of their Westmont
home, the Buckleys lay contentedly side by side.
The light from his post-coital cigarette made a tiny
hole in the dark. She gazed at the ceiling, working
up her courage. Finally she said, "Dale, could I ask a
big favor?"

"I dunno. Once a night 'bout all I'm good for anymore."

She gave him a playful little swat. "Not *that*!"

"What, then?"

"Now that we've got Davie, would you mind ter-
ribly not smoking in the house?"

"Why you want that?"

"Well, you read about all that secondhand smoke
being bad for people. Especially children."

Buck thought about it a moment. "Sure, I can do
that," he said, and he butted the cigarette in the ashtray on the nightstand. "Take it outside when I got
to. Be kinda tough in winter, though."

"You could use the garage."

"Yeah, that'd do."

She snuggled up next to him. "Thanks so much,
hon. I know it's a lot to ask."

"It's nothin'."

"Isn't it wonderful, having him?"

"He's a good kid, all right. Awful quiet, though. Almost like, y'know, sad. 'Bout the only thing makes him smile, for me anyways, is that merry-go-round, down the park."

"He's getting used to us. Takes awhile. But it feels like we're a real family again, now he's here."

"Yeah, it does."

"Maybe," she ventured cautiously, "we could go back up to the Dells sometime. The three of us."

"Dells," Buck said, stalling. He knew where this line of talk was leading, and he had no desire to follow it too far.

"For a little vacation. Like we did before."

"Not so sure that's such a good idea, Norma."

"Why not?"

"You know why."

"Sara, you mean."

"That's right," he said, unable even yet to utter her name.

"Remember how much she liked it? All the fun we had up there?"

Only too well, he thought, but he kept silent. Too many blighted memories here. Too many ghosts.

"I wonder how he'd have gotten along with her, Davie."

"C'mon," Buck said gently, "no good thinkin' about things like that."

"I know. But wouldn't they have been a pair? Sara always chattering, always so, well, sunny. She'd have brought him out in no time at all."

"She's gone, Norma. Can't bring her back."

"I know, I know," she said, and began to weep softly.

Buck put his arms around her, drew her closer. "Been six years now. Can't change the past."

"Six," she repeated, the mingled colorations of wonder and disbelief and denial in her pitch, as though the simple articulation of that number erased the time and the sorrow and all the slow-ticking moments of loss it represented. "Seems like just yesterday she was dancing around the house, laughing, singing. Remember how she loved to sing?"

He remembered it, his daughter's high, clear voice filling a room. Also did he remember, vividly yet, across the widening distance of all those years gone by, the leukemic death sentence laid on her by a pitiless God, and the last terrible hours of her life, her withered body eaten away by the wildly multiplying outlaw cells, drifting in and out of a drugged sleep till even the drugs were powerless to shield her from pain, powerless as he was, her father-protector, unable to protect anyone anymore, stalking the white, neutral halls of a hospital, fists balling and unballing, raging against God and fate and drugs and doctors, unable any longer to endure the anguished screaming and to meet those hollow baffled terrified eyes wordlessly pleading for a help he couldn't give. He remembered, all right, but that's all he could bring himself to say: "I remember."

"Sometimes, when Davie says something to me, it's like it's her voice I'm hearing. Once, just the other day, I even started to call him by her name. Does that sound crazy, Dale?"

"Don't sound crazy. But you got to let it go."

"I'm trying. I will."

"We got the boy now. It's like you said, family again. Like a second chance at it. New start."

"Maybe that's how God wanted it to be."

"Maybe He did, at that," Buck said, believing not a word of it.

And no more than ten miles away, in the cramped little room of their Naperville home designated as his study, Marshall Quinn was, at that same hour, thinking not so much of God and fate and family (though occasionally such sterile reflections would intrude, puncture his rapt concentration) as of an elusive symbol on a banal sticker affixed to the bumper of a murky vehicle fleeting off, lost to the desperate reach of his fading, failed memory. Search it as he might, pinch and prod it however he would, it yielded up nothing. Yet if the psychologists were to be believed (he persuaded himself), nothing is ever lost, everything indelibly stamped on the plate of the subconscious, a lifetime's bundled experience waiting only for some sensory trigger to unseal it, piece by piece. The way the monotone hum of a fan will unaccountably spark some forgotten melody, say, or the shape of a cloud call back a ghost of an inconsequential face from the country of the past, and with it a rich catalog of particulars buried under the weight of the years.

And so he remained rooted to his chair and hunched over a battered wooden desk, forehead creased, chewing the tip of a ballpoint, staring fixedly at a dwindling pad of unruled white paper laid out in front of him. Crumpled scraps of it spilled from a wastebasket and littered the floor at his feet. At the top of the covering sheet was a rectangular diagram of a license plate with the letters AZ penned in and bracketed by question marks, and beneath it a sketch of a bumper sticker, complete with unfurled flag and "Buy American" legend. The remainder of the sheet was given over to a series of crude drawings, associative links designed to pluck an image of that confounding symbol from the shadowland of memory. Here were fashioned stick figure persons with big faces cast in a variety of expressions: stern, smiling, quizzical, blank; there miscellaneous clumsy renderings of birds and animals: hawks, eagles, lions, bears, wolves, in a variety of stances; elsewhere assorted machines of transport: cars, planes, boats, cycles, trucks, tractors—and all of them, persons, animals, machines, crossed out or angrily scribbled over. The deeper he probed, the more impenetrable the darkness, and the more it closed around him.

Eventually, all his meager artistic talents and all his inventive energies exhausted, he put down the gnawed pen, glared at it accusingly, as if it had somehow betrayed him, and cradled his head in his hands. And from out of a spirit bitter as a poisoned well the muttered words "Damn damn damn damn *God* damn *God* damn" rose to his lips, emerged almost as a rhythmic chant.

Apart from the harsh yellow light of a gooseneck lamp on the desk and a narrow slant of moonlight

from the brace of windows above it, the room was
otherwise dark. Two walls were lined with floor-to-
ceiling shelves packed with books and learned journals. Along a third, flanking the entrance, was a pair
of tables, one holding an inexpensive word proces-
sor, the other an ancient manual typewriter, valued
possession, Marshall had been told often enough, of
his late father. Late by close to three decades now,
gone before he'd ever known him, the way his son
was gone, an empty, aching void at either pole of his
life. The two vanished masters of his blood. Except
the one you could understand, adapt to, accept—
death with its punctual certainty; the other a kind of
rascally jest, beyond comprehending, scattering all
you knew—or thought you knew—of reason and co-
herence and order. And finality. For if Jeff was dead,
certifiably dead, there could be at least the mercy of
closure, and with it an enduring image of childish innocence, frozen forever in time, almost, as with a
never known father, a peculiar sorrowful blessing.
No blessing here, no mercy. And no terminus.

On a corner of the desk was a framed photo of the
Quinn family, a studio portrait, stiffly smiling threesome in their dress-up clothes. Gazing at it now,
Marshall could bring back all its trivial details, its
where and when, sights, sounds, smells, words spoken, even the face of the fussy photographer, the
tenor of his voice, his unctuous manner ("Could we
all just tilt our chins slightly to the left, please? Can
we get the boy to look directly into the camera? Big
smiles now, folks!"). Everything. Yet something so
simple, so elementary, as an inane symbol on a

bumper sticker remained stubbornly outside his grasp, taunting and fugitive as the moonbeam filtered through the window: seize at it and it's gone.

He switched off the lamp and got up heavily and crossed the room and shuffled down the hallway. At the open door to Jeff's room he paused, adjusting his vision to the dark. Soon he could make out the contours of a bed, a shelf piled high with kiddie books pored over nightly by father and son as prelude to sleep (did he imagine similar, time-twisted episodes from his own lost childhood, a father's sonorous voice lulling him into slumber?—he couldn't remember, couldn't be sure), a chest filled with miniature men and battery-powered toys that, activated, made curious clattery noises. At the foot of the bed was Jeff's hands-down favorite plaything, a weather balloon, round and squat as an outsize pumpkin, like one of those horticultural freaks displayed at county fairs. How readily his memory summoned the day he had first discovered it in some obscure scientific catalog, and the long-awaited day of its arrival in the mail (a Tuesday, it was, precisely ten days before the sky fell), the two of them laboriously inflating it with an old and rusted bicycle tire pump, its remarkable buoyancy, lighter even than the air that suspended it, Jeff's squeals of delight at sending it soaring with the simple tap of a hand over the tops of trees, over the roof of their two-story house, Lori's concern as they chased it recklessly, winddriven, down the street. And recalling it now, that playful little scene, all of it, he was overtaken by a helpless longing for another time, when the world he inhabited was as orderly as the theorems of geometry, or as statistically predictable as those great social forces he traced and measured and explained for a living. Not anymore, he reclined and measured the world by the indecipherable texture of his own dry misery, which came to him only in fragments, piecemeal—a photo, empty bed, shelf of unread books, collection of silenced toys, grounded weather balloon—explaining nothing at all.

He continued down the hall. Entered the bedroom. Got out of his clothes and slipped into bed, quietly as he could. Lori didn't stir. And lying there beside her, this stranger who was his wife, lost in a narcotized sleep, dreaming her anguished dreams, it occurred to Marshall that the past, which had always seemed so immutable, so real in the living and remembering it, seemed now like a possession—the antique typewriter, say—lifted furtively from another man's life.

PART
THREE

A group of Norse Aluminum employees, Buck, Waz, and Lester among them, was gathered near an entrance to the cast house at the south end of the plant, finishing off their lunch. From where they sat, lined up like a file of frazzled ducks against a soot-blackened wall, they could look down a wide rolling belt, wide enough to accommodate fourteen-ton ingots of raw aluminum and reaching deep into the plant's interior. A funnel of pale light cut through a window on the roof fifty feet above them and pierced a haze of rising dust thick as fog. In a pit some thirty yards off to their left, an enormous furnace belched flames and puffs of black smoke like some squat, swollen smudge pot. Still, it was a little cooler here by the doorway, relatively speaking, and somewhat removed from the echoing screech and boom of the machines, and so in the worst of the summer heat this is where they habitually chose to eat.

Lester was winding down a tale of sexual conquest grown large in the telling, though wholly fabricated simply as prelude to a punch line he'd heard somewhere: "So I got her all steamed up and moanin' now, way they do, and she goes, 'Gimme ten and make it hurt.'"

"Mighty tall order for you, ten," said the man seated next to him, one Albert Buttrum, commonly addressed as Butt, for obvious reasons, though just as frequently as Beans, for his unvarying lunch fare—a can of cold My-T-Fine pork and beans—and for the malodorous and often explosive results it inevitably produced.

"Hey, don't I know it," Lester agreed, tittering in advance of the line he'd been waiting to deliver, a spasm of childish delight.

"So what'd ya do?"

"What I done is bang her five times and kick her in the ass on my way out the door."

Everybody guffawed, but listlessly and without much mirth. The plant's ferocious inferno of noise and heat had wrung the sweat and the spirit out of them, staining their blue twill uniforms and reducing them to limp, sullen shells of themselves. All but Lester, sprightly as ever, for reasons everyone understood and tolerated, more or less, the way a hapless, worthless lovable hound is sometimes tolerated. Waz swallowed the last of a dried-out bologna sandwich, what he referred to as Della's horsecock special, washed it down with Mountain Dew, and said sourly, "You ever go five times one night, they be fittin' you out for a wheelchair."

"Might not be so bad," Lester said. "I hear your crips do real good, boinkin'-wise. Real ass bandits."

"How they gonna do that? Can't even get it up, most of 'em, is how I hear it."

"That's the point right there. Twats think they give good head 'cuz a that. So they always sniffin' around 'em."

Waz looked at him skeptically. "That's about the dumbest theory you come up with yet."

"Listen, ain't so dumb. I know a fella tested it once. Wanna hear how?"

"Yeah, how? Throw himself in front of a truck so he'd be a crip, check out your dipshit theory?"

"Sounds like somethin' Cock here'd do," Beans put in, alluding to Lester by his plant tag.

"You guys wanta hear this story or not?"

"Tell the fuckin' story," Waz grouched. Five minutes left on lunch break, nothing better to do.

"Okay," Lester commenced, "what he done, this fella, is rent himself a wheelchair, one a them places got all your crip gear, drugstore, I think it was. Or maybe was a, like, hospital supply. Forget. Anyway, once he got it, got use to zippin' around in it, he wheels into a bar—this was over to Lyons, I remember correct—and orders up a beer and waits. Now, what you got to picture in your mind here is a guy ain't exactly no looker. Matter a fact, way I remember—been, oh, five years or better since I seen him, least—it's like somebody beat on him with the ugly stick. We're talkin' big-time ugly here, downtown."

"Awright," Waz broke in irritably, "we got the picture. Get to the story part."

Lester looked at him, puzzled and just a little hurt. "Jesus, you in a foul mood today, Wazzer."

"You gonna tell it?"

"I'm tellin' it," he said and resumed the story. "So anyway, he's pretty quick got a gang a fluff around him, this fella. Part of it's the pity thing, 'course, but other part's them thinkin' they maybe got a world-class carpet muncher here. Don't matter which to him, he got the pick a the litter. He takes the one he wants back to his place and gets her all positioned on the kitchen table and wheels right up and goes divin'. Gives her a real mustache ride."

"So what's that prove?" Beans wanted to know. " 'Less you get your jollies off goin' down. Which I ain't never heard of. Not for no real man."

"See, that was his trouble," Lester said. "That's where it all gone wrong for him. He's sportin' a steeler 'bout to split his zipper, gets so jazzed he forgets he's supposed to be a gimp and hops up outta his chair and trys to climb her."

"What'd she do?"

"Well, now she just lookin' at another poor lumper tryin' to hose her, piss ugly one at that, so it ain't no big surprise she's pretty hacked off, particular him not bein' a genuine crip like he made out to be. So she shags her ass outta there, leaves him with a serious case a the granite nuts."

"Which kinda sinks your theory, don't it?" Waz said.

"How you figure that?"

"Said it yourself, dickweed. Guy goes to all that work, comes up stoners."

"Got her on the table there, didn't he?" Lester said heatedly, defending his proposition. "Got her stoked and spread. A Mr. Fugly like that, never gets no tail, nobody even give him a mercy fuck."

"Didn't that time neither, way you told it. Don't you ever listen to your own stories?"

"Still got himself that close," Lester insisted, the *that* indicated by a tiny space between extended thumb and forefinger.

"Close only counts in horseshoes and hand grenades," Beans remarked dryly.

"His prol'um was he just got too excited. Too, y'know, eager, is all. Couldn't wait it out till she got herself a wide-on won't quit, take any kind a meat, crip or not. That don't mean the theory don't hold up."

Nobody had the energy to argue, and so as a kind of dissonant coda to the issue Beans lifted a fat cheek and corked a thunderous tooter.

"Holy Christ, Beans," Waz groaned as its bouquet wafted his way, "you got to poison the air any worse'n it already is?"

"In here that ain't poison. It's perfume."

Lester took a small, plastic bag of colored capsules from his shirt pocket, shook two into the palm of a hand, and gulped them down on a wash of Dr. Pepper. Everybody watched him, nobody commented.

Buck, who had been listening quietly, contributing nothing to the discursive noontime conversation, now shook his head slowly and allowed, "Y'know, it's real educational, eatin' lunch with you boys. Just like bein' back in school again." He glanced at his watch, hauled himself to his feet, and stretched like a man rousing himself from a deep sleep. "Too bad time's up."

Following his lead, the rest of them stood, and in a group they started down the walkway along one side of the rolling belt. Waz fell in beside him, said, "How 'bout we scoot over the Greek's after shift, throw back a couple pops?"

"I don't think so," Buck said. "I gotta get home."

"C'mon. Friday night, you can do one."

"Nope, can't. I'm takin' Norma and the boy out to supper."

Waz thrust his face up close, whispered urgently, "See, that's the thing. We gotta talk."

"About what?"

" 'Bout your boy there."

Buck looked at him narrowly. "What about him?"

"Oh, nothin' heavy, nothin' get stressed over. Just, well, this thing come up, other day, wanna run it by you."

"What thing's that?"

They were approaching the wing of the plant that housed the machine shop and tool crib, Waz's assigned work station. "Tell ya 'bout it over a beer," he said. "Okay?"

Buck thought about it, but not long. He was more curious than worried, even though he didn't much like the evasive glide in his friend's eyes. He held up an index finger. "One."

"Terrific. Where you gonna be?"

"Workin' the hot mill."

"Meetcha there."

Lester, trudging along behind the others, evidently still intrigued by the aphrodisiac possibilities of paraplegia, called after them, "Think maybe I'll rent me a wheelchair myself, try it out on the lady at the license plate office, gimme all that grief that time. I ever tell you guys that one? It's real comical, what happened."

But with the remainder of the shift ahead of them, nobody was interested anymore, and nobody bothered to reply.

Marshall was gaping, chute-jawed, at a thick and very formidable-looking sheaf of papers, a computer printout, its pages linked fanfold fashion. The expression on his face was a compound of disbelief and sinking woe; Wilcox's, across the table from him, one of sympathy shot through with little lines of annoyance. "But couldn't your officers go through it?" Marshall said. "Weed out some of the . . ." His voice trailed into silence, empty of inspiration.

"What?" Wilcox asked, clearly rhetorically. "Weed out what?" He elevated the top sheet, opening the printout like some fragile accordion. Making a visual point. The unheard music of futility. "You got maybe thirty-four hundred vehicles here got AZ in the plates and come anywhere close, your description. What there was of it. Same numbers with the AS. Where they gonna start? You got any idea the man hours we'd be lookin' at? That's if we had 'em available. Which we don't."

Marshall stared at his hands. No disputing that.

"Only reason I got this, first place," Wilcox explained, "is because I tapped a favor. Wanted you to see it. See what we're up against. Also see there's people workin' on your case, 'spite a what you think."

"I appreciate that," Marshall said, and he did too, but not enough to restrain himself from adding, "Especially since Thornton's decided to go off on vacation."

Wilcox gave him a sideways glance, more of the annoyance in it now than the sympathy. "Even cops got a right to some time off."

No arguing that either, he supposed, though that didn't make it go down any easier. Following Wilcox's advice of last Sunday, he'd waited till yesterday to contact Thornton's office, got the stupefying news the man charged with finding his son was on vacation, for God's sake, be gone another ten days, and the even more deflating word that nobody had ever heard of his license plate lead, never mind taken any action on it. He'd slammed down the phone and, choking with rage, called Wilcox, who waited out the stormy tirade, then calmly instructed him to come in the next afternoon. "Got something here to show you." Fortunately for Marshall, Lori had an appointment with her doctor today—burden enough just finding his way through the maze of city streets without her to attend to as well. When he'd arrived at the precinct station, Wilcox, spotting him in the door, shambled out from behind the counter and led him down the hall to the now familiar cubicle. Offered him a chair. Remarked on the heat.

Asked how he was doing. Inquired after his wife. And then laid on the bad news.

Now he felt not quite shattered, but not quite whole either. His face seemed to twitch with desperation and strain. He said, "Give it to me, then, your list. I'll do it."

"*You'll* do it?"

"Yes. Me. Or I'll hire someone to help me," he added, recognizing the absurdity of this bold declaration even as he spoke it, given a checkbook already dipping perilously close to empty.

Wilcox sighed. He was an accomplished sigher, Wilcox was, investing those expirations with an assortment of dramatic pitches and tones more expressive than words. This one carried the weight of official responsibility in it, preface to a pronouncement, and he drew himself up and said in flat officialese, "I'm not authorized to release that kind of data."

"So what are you telling me, Sergeant? About the incident on the highway, I mean. I didn't just imagine it, you know."

"Not sayin' you did"—thin wheeze of regret now—"sayin' there's not enough to go on here. You got to face it, Mr. Quinn. It's a dead end. Was pro'ly somebody all twisted anyhow."

"So what do you suggest I do?"

The sigh took on a note of immense fatigue, and all its attendant vexation pooled in his eyes. "Look, your boy's been missing—what?—three months now?"

"Eleven weeks today."

"Okay, eleven weeks. All your flyers, posters,

scoutin' the neighborhoods, conductin' your own investigation, all that done what? Turned up what?"

The length of his pause seemed to suggest a demand for answer, so Marshall said that which was
undeniably true: "Nothing."

"There you are. Zip. Nada. You askin' me what to
do? Tell you what to do. Stay off these streets, you
and Mrs. Quinn both. 'Specially her. You got gangs
out there, four-corner hustlers, dealers, boosters—
any one of 'em open you up for the loose change in
your pocket. This is a world you don't know nothin'
about. Trust me on that. Let us handle it. We got our
procedures. Got our ways."

The baggy face went slack, as though the prolonged caution had drained all that was left of a
scanty vitality out of it. Marshall considered everything he'd heard. Ways. Procedures. What had begun
as a small misgiving eleven weeks ago, faint doubt
over the arcane skills and brisk efficiency—the commitment—of these guardians of the public weal, had
become now a bitter conviction. He was alone in
this, and for all the ersatz pity (or was it a veiled
contempt?) in that jaded face staring him down,
waiting for an assentive reply, there was nowhere to
turn, no resource apart from himself. He came up out
of his chair and said bravely, "I'm going to find him,
Sergeant. Whatever it takes, however it has to be
done, I'll find him."

Wilcox responded only with a stoic shrug and
downward cast of his remote, weary eyes.

Later, Marshall sat in the sun-yellowed grass outside the planetarium, drawn there as though by some

irresistible psychic tug. Locus of his private
calamity, eleven weeks past. Like the burned-out
cop, he was thoroughly depleted, emptied of forti-
tude and will. During those long weeks whatever remained of the already fractured rhythms of sleep had
been periodically (as recent as last night) broken by
a bizarre recurring dream. Transparent to interpretation, it confined him to a square box of an elevator in
some gigantic, multi-storied tower, trying frantically
and without success to get off at his appointed floor,
the number of which was unclear to his dreaming self.
If it was nine, the box glided smoothly to fourteen; if
sixty-three, it descended effortlessly to forty-four,
stopping there to take on processions of ebullient
faceless passengers who entered and exited freely, at
the confident touch of a numeral, insensible to his
plight, deaf to his petitions.

Reconstructing that decidedly ambiguous dream,
he was reminded of the low theatrics of his stalked
and quite unrestrained exit from the station, and of
all the sustaining delusions he'd clung to, slick mu-
tations in the relentless progress of tumorous growth
and change transforming him slowly but inexorably
into the man he had become, diseased by frustration
and impotence, cancered by self-loathing. He had
been innocent then, eleven weeks back, and innocence, he recognized now, was at bottom its own
kind of theatrics, of pretension, feeble stab at absolu-
tion. Innocence excused nothing.

The sun, in this waking life, was dipping off to the
west, a blaze of white, and the sky was white, and
the lake stretched out like a coil of polished sheet

metal, hard and glittery, reaching to the end of the world. His brave resolve came back to him, a stubborn rebuke, but with a hollow echo to it, and he wondered if he believed it anymore himself. Or if he ever had.

The five-stand hot mill was situated almost dead center along the rolling belt. It looked curiously like five locomotives stood on end, like a child's playful conception of train engines poised for flight. True to its name, each stand emitted blasts of visible heat in the form of dense, whirling clouds of steam. When a slab of aluminum came down the belt a spray of oil and water drenched it as it passed under the mill's blades, the contact producing a grinding screak of metal and an acrid stench that hung heavily in the air. A much smaller conveyer belt angled off laterally, firing a stream of jagged metal scraps into a dumpster set on the walkway. Between slabs the mill by itself generated a deafening roar. Because the plant's only windows were on the ceiling high above, and its only other source of illumination artificial, hard angles of light fell across the mill and cast long shadows over the grainy brick floor.

At the bleat of the shift whistle Buck came clambering down the ladder at the end of the catwalk linking the five stands and joined Waz, waiting for him by the dumpster. They started for the closest exit, a hundred yards away. "Get 'er ironed out yet?" Waz asked, alluding to whatever mechanical failure had occupied his friend's day.

"Got 'er runnin'," Buck said, "but it still ain't quite right. Sure could use Harp here."

"Old Harp's sittin' on the banks a the Mississippi reelin' in walleye or whatever it is they catch up there and soakin' up brew. Like we're gonna be doin', minute, least that brew part anyway."

Buck, wasted from eight hours of pretzeling himself into the hot mill's tightest corners and crevices, had all but forgotten the mysterious urgent invitation. Now that it came back to him, he said, "Only got time for one, remember."

"Even one go down good, 'long about now."

Halfway to the exit Lester caught up with them. His round face was fixed in a vacant Plutoish grin, and in his eyes there was a giveaway sheen. They walked stoop-shouldered, all three, and their uniforms were splotched with grease, sodden with sweat. Sweat limpened their hair, glistened their brows. Waz mopped his with a damp kerchief. "Jesus fuck," he grumbled, "gotta be hun'red twenty degrees in here."

"Yeah, well, air condition ain't all that high on management's priority list," Buck drawled. "Last I heard."

"So you better get to like it, Wazzer," Lester said impishly.

Waz regarded him with weary irritation, like some pesky buzzing fly, forever out of reach. "I do it, Cock, same as you. But I don't got to like it."

"What you need's some substance to abuse. Chill you out."

"Huh, chill like you, I s'pose," said a thoroughly

disgusted Waz. "Be on everything but skates. That what you recommendin' here?"

"Ain't so bad. Keep ya warm in winter, cool in summer. Make the day just rocket on by. Why, feel to me like I just punched in. Go another eight, I had to."

"Yeah, fry your brains too, poppin' all them doodies. No, thanks. I'd rather sweat."

"Oughta get yourself a cushy job," Lester suggested. He pointed at a string-thin fellow slouching against a wall by the exit up ahead, buttonholing a couple of departing workers. "Like Jimmie Jack there. Lookit him. He ain't sweatin'."

"Don't know the right people, way he does."

"It ain't who ya know, Wazzie. It's who ya blow."

"Blowin' maybe your style. Ain't mine."

"Ain't your luck. Mine either. I tell ya, he's so lucky, Jimmie, he sit on a wasp, he come up shittin' honey."

"Bee, numbnuts. You mean a bee. Wasps don't give honey."

"Whadda they give?"

"Stings."

"Okay, a bee, then."

As they approached the door, Jimmie pushed off the wall and sauntered toward them. His uniform was spotless, trousers still held a crease, and he was indeed unsweated. A pearl stud glittered in one ear, matched his wide, starched smile. He hailed them with a high-handed wave. "Yo, grunts, what's shakin'?"

"Shakin' ass outta here," Lester replied for all of them.

" 'Bout that time, huh."

"Hope to lay a loaf in your lunch bucket, it's time."

"Speakin' a which, time," Jimmie said, lifting a wrist, displaying his watch, "take a scope at this."

Lester and Waz stepped in for a closer look. Buck hung back. "Holy shit," Lester exclaimed. "That a Rolex?"

"Ain't no Timex."

"You pushin' 'em?"

"Might be I could rustle some up, you boys."

"How much?" Waz wanted to know.

"Deuce and a half put one on your arm. Go to a, like, jewelry store, set you back an easy ten long."

Buck, who normally avoided conflict and seldom initiated it, was just bushed enough, impatient enough, to remark acidly, " 'Stead of your bargain-basement store, huh. Back of an alley. Or somebody's truck."

He stood half a head taller, so Jimmie looked up at him carefully and the viper smile never left his pocked face. "Hey, man, lighten up. Get a vice. It's a deal I'm offerin' you here."

"Shove your deals," Buck said, and he spun on his heels and strode away.

Waz took off after him, but Lester remained. "What's chewin' on his ass?" Jimmie said.

Lester shrugged. He was still staring at the watch, shaking his head admiringly, properly dazzled. "There anything you can't get ahold of, Jimmie?"

"Name your commodity. Anything to order."

"Wouldn't mind havin' one a them Rolies my-self."

"I dunno. You do got some other paper out there yet, an' you know I gotta see some green on it by Sunday, no later. You ain't forgettin' that?"

"Oh, yeah. I'm workin' on it."

"Attaboy," Jimmie said, laying a spindly arm on his shoulder. "C'mon, let's slip over the Greek's. I'm bookin' my orders there."

In spite of its somewhat ostentatious name, the Norseman Lounge and Supper Club was in fact nothing more than a long, rectangular, badly lit, unpartitioned barn of a room with a line of graffiti-scarred wooden booths along one wall, bar on the other, and a couple of pool tables in the back by a portal offering an unwanted peek into a supremely dingy kitchen that served substantially more burger, slaw, and fries plates than anything approaching suppers. It was located about a quarter of a mile down the road from the entrance to the Norse Aluminum plant, within sight of the gigantic sign depicting a heroic Viking warrior bearing shield and spear that was the company's trademark, and from whence came the tavern-eatery's name. Since its clientele consisted almost exclusively of Norse employees, it was busiest during those hours immediately before and after the plant's thrice-daily shift changes, during which times, as now, it was jammed with rowdy men in soiled blue uniforms chugging beer and booze, raising a raucous din of whoops and shouts, and blueing the air with smoke.

Presiding behind the bar, mein dour host, was Nicholas Last Name an Unpronounceable Clash of Vowels and Hard Consonants, a squat swarthy surly man whose filthy apron girdled a middle of such corpulent bloat he was known, unsurprisingly, as Skinny Nick, or sometimes simply The Greek. Three waitresses scurried about frantically, or at least two of them, stout and uncommonly homely, did. The third, a tall, twentyish woman outfitted in black velvet killer heels, fishnet hose, pink hot pants, push-up bra, and with a tower of orange-tinted hair and lipstick the color of freshly drawn blood, was reputedly the owner's favored squeeze of the month, which perhaps accounted for her sultry lassitude and her notorious inability to get orders straight or make proper change. It was the former giving her trouble right now as she stopped by a booth near the back and inquired around a wad of gum, "What is it you fellas drinkin'?"

For answer, Waz pointed at the label on one of the many empty bottles on the table.

"Oh, yeah, Buds. So, you want a couple more?"

"Buck?"

Buck was pulling on a cigarette, gazing worriedly into some private middle distance.

Waz said his name a second time.

"Huh?"

"You do another?"

"Okay. One more."

"Don't s'pose you could clear off these dead soldiers," Waz suggested to the departing waitress.

"Get 'em when I come back," was her impudent reply, sashaying away, trim hips swaying.

Buck expelled a fretful gust of smoke and resumed their talk. "This is not what I want to hear,
Waz."

"Hey, don't I know. Like I said, though, it's pro'ly
nothin', but I figured I oughta tell you."

"Tell me again. When was it happened?"

"Day we come over to your place."

"Last Sunday."

"Right."

"And it was where?"

"Up on the East-West."

"This guy in the wagon. What'd he look like?"

"Shit, I dunno, Buck. Didn't get much of a look at
him. Was Della doin' all the gawkin'. She's the one
first saw the poster in the window."

"So you didn't actually see this poster yourself?"

Waz squirmed uncomfortably in his seat. "Well,
yeah, I seen it. Not real good, though."

"And?"

"What?"

"C'mon, Waz. You know what I'm askin' here."

"Tell ya the hones' truth, I don't know if it was
the same kid or not. For sure, I mean."

"What's Della think?"

"Della don't know dick. She seen too many soaps
on the TV."

"She been talkin' to anybody else?"

"No way. I told her put a lid on it."

Buck stubbed out his cigarette. For a moment he
was silent, eyes inward turning, sorting through
everything he'd heard, the whole distressing tale
gone over again and yet again these past three hours.

After its first telling he'd got on the horn and called Norma, fabricated a flimsy excuse to cancel their evening plans, which, as always, she'd accepted without complaint or question (though with maybe a tremor of disappointment in her voice). That was Norma. And thinking about her now, he leveled his gaze on his friend and said grimly, "I don't want her sayin' nothin' to Norma. You understand that, Waz?"

"Yeah, sure, I understand," Waz said, but he had to look away, unable to meet the alarm in those eyes. Still, he felt impelled to add, "But you know Della. Comes to tongue waggin', she got herself a black belt."

"She gonna be at the open house?"

"She's talkin' about it."

"Then I got to find a way keep Norma home. She can't hear none of this. You know how she feels about the boy."

"Listen," Waz said, defensive edge to his voice, "who knows better'n me. 'Bout *all* of it. Who was it helped you make the connection?"

"I ain't forgot. And I appreciate it."

Just then the waitress reappeared. She set two cans of Coors on the table and stood there, brows knit, trying to do the calculations in her head.

"Comes to three-seventy," Waz volunteered, presenting her with a five.

"Yeah, that's it." She counted out two ones and three dimes and handed them over to him.

Once she was gone, the collection of empties still unremoved, Waz remarked, to lighten things a little,

"Dumb twat. Tell ya, drinkin' here could get to be a thrifty habit, even if you don't always get what you order."

Buck, however, had no interest in the transaction and, following his interrupted train of thought, he nodded significantly in the direction of the bar, where Jimmie Jack, surrounded by a cluster of men, was holding court, grinning, gabbing, now and again jotting something in a small notebook. "Appreciate it," Buck repeated. "But anything gets done through that sleazeball, you got to worry about."

"Hey, I hear ya. 'Course, all's he done was get your money to the right people, bump you to the top a their list. That's what he *does*. Don't mean you got to like him."

"Trouble is, whatever he's into always got a downside to it. Take that place out to Elgin, where we picked up Davie at. I gotta tell you, Waz, didn't look right to me."

"How's that?"

"Well, for one thing there's this guy, says he's a lawyer. Dago, fulla slick talk. Smoke, most of it."

"So he's a dago. You gotta have a lawyer, make things legal. An' he gave you all the papers says it is, right?"

"Yeah, we got the papers," Buck said doubtfully. "But then there's the lady suppose to be the mother, she don't look like no mother type to me. Look like some washout hooker. Hangs back, lets the wop do all the talkin' for her. Don't seem real sad, like you'd think a mother'd be, givin' up a kid."

"So what if she ain't sad? Nothin' to you. There's

lots a broads like that, ain't gonna win mother of the year."

"Maybe so. But the boy, he's all sleepy, like they got him on somethin'."

"Pro'ly did. Make it easier on him, goin' with strangers, new place and all. Easier on everybody."

"Still, whole setup seemed, y'know, funny. But I don't say nothin'. Not gonna spoil things for Norma."

"Can see why," Waz said in a labored stab at commiseration. " 'Specially after all them adoptin' agencies you went to, got nothin' but spook kids, or ones somethin' wrong with 'em. Five-year wait for a regular white one."

Buck didn't seem to be listening. "Only now, what you're tellin' me here . . ." He shook his head slowly, bewilderedly.

"Was pro'ly nothin' to it anyway," Waz said again, weaker this time.

"Yeah. Maybe. Except our Jimmie Jackoff there, he ain't never been in the charity business."

"You want me to talk to him? See what I can find out?"

"Not yet. I got to have some time. Think this through."

"I could talk to him. Anything, y'know, slippery goin' on, we could get your money back for you."

Buck stuck another cigarette in his mouth. Lighting it, his hand trembled slightly. Anxiety scored his broad, furrowed face, and when he spoke his voice was husky, a confessional voice, pleading for understanding. "Ain't the money. Don'tcha see, got nothin' to *do* with money. It's Norma. All them years we been married, the one thing she wanted was a kid. Only thing. Only thing I couldn't seem to give her. All them years tryin', hopin'. Makes you wonder about yourself. Makes you crazy, Waz. Then along comes Sara, like it's a miracle, and then she's gone, never saw her fifth birthday."

"Know how y'feel," Waz mumbled. It wasn't much, all he could think to say.

Wrong thing. Buck made blades of his big hands and chopped the air vehemently. "You don't know! How you gonna know? You ever lost a kid? Listen to her screamin' in the night? Watch her coughin' up blood? Watch her die? You ever done that? You don't know."

"You're right," Waz said, humbled. "I don't."

Buck softened some. "Now we got Davie, got another chance . . . you understand what I'm sayin' here? Norma can't go through it again. Neither can I."

Waz stared into his lap, shaken by this uncharacteristic show of emotion. Run out of flimsy explanations. Out of words.

And Buck, equally embarrassed, looked down at his watch. "It's late," he said. "I gotta get movin'."

"Yeah, me too."

They slid out of the booth and pushed their way through the crowd. Neither of them so much as glanced at Jimmie Jack as they passed the bar.

If she was puzzled and maybe even a little hurt by the last-minute change in plans (so unlike Dale, always so reliable), Norma was careful not to let it show. Not around Davie. But because all day long she had prepared him for tonight's special occasion, she had to think of something, some compensatory treat. An inspiration came to her. An hour later they were dining, the two of them, on hot dogs, baked beans, coleslaw, deviled eggs, potato salad, a sweetish lemonade, the hastily put-together feast spread across the metal table on the patio, its awning shielding them from a sun sunk low in the sky but still fierce. Their own little picnic.

Norma chattered away, making the kind of airy, silly talk adults, alone with a child, will sometimes make. Now and again he responded, but mostly he ate quietly, spooning beans and tilting his head to accommodate the tube of meat and bun to his mouth. Until something seemed suddenly to occur to him, some faint connection, and his eyes seemed to turn inward and he laid the half-eaten hot dog on the paper plate in front of him and volunteered the odd and altogether irrelevant remark, "There was a horse."

"A horse?" Norma said curiously.

"Uh-huh."

"Which horse is that?"

"Horse," he repeated, a note of impatience in the small voice.

"What did the horse do?" she asked, indulging him, remembering Sara and how a child's talk could veer off in strange directions, sparked by some vagrant association.

"Man on it. Had a knife."

"Did you see it on the television?"

He shook his head vigorously.

"Where, then?"

"Was a park."

"Merry-go-round horses?"

"No. Big one."

"But there aren't any other horses in the park, Davie."

"I show you."

He leaped off his chair and scurried into the house. Returned clutching the pad of paper and box of crayons he used to entertain himself whenever she was occupied with some household chore. The picnic forgotten, he pushed his plate aside and, face puckered in concentration, began to draw. When he was finished, he presented it to her, a childish representation of a horse, head and legs wildly disproportionate to trunk. Straddling its back was a stick-figure man grasping what appeared to be a spear. "There," he said emphatically, as though his point had been proven. "Horse."

"It's very nice," Norma complimented him. "You're a good drawer, Davie."

"Was *real*," he insisted. "I *saw* it. By the stars."

"You saw the horse at night?"

Again he tossed his head negatively. "By the stars."

"Stars? I don't understand."

"Where the mouse is."

For reasons she couldn't name, this jumble of fantastic images, lifted certainly from dreams or picture books or the television screen, vaguely disturbed her.

There were other drawings, done earlier in the day, on the sheet, and so to divert his attention she chose one and with a display of motherly interest asked, "And what's this?"

Two figures, one tall, one short, blank circles for faces, stood next to a structure with irregular blocks of windows and rectangular door and tail of smoke rising from its roof, clearly intended as a house. The tall one held a round object easily twice the size of its head. "Sky ball," the boy said.

"What kind of ball?"

"Goes up to the sky," he explained, pointing at the one above them, pinking in the gradually falling light.

"Now that's quite a ball, goes that high."

"Here's where they cried," he said solemnly, indicating another of his creations, three small figures centered in a square, either upright and suspended in air or reclining against some flat surface, impossible, in single dimension, to tell.

"Cried?"

"Uh-huh."

"Who cried, Davie?"

"Kids."

"What kids?"

He turned over his hands, a gestured confusion.

"Where did it happen?"

"In the bed."

"What made them cry?" she asked, not really wanting to know.

"When the mean man came."

"Oh," was all Norma could think to say. She had

the slightly queasy sensation of peering over the cragged edge of a deep pit, a child herself, engaged in forbidden explorations and stumbling upon some dark, forbidden place. When Della had asked, just the other day, what Davie remembered of the past, she had murmured, eyes averted, Nothing, he remembers nothing. Which was the truth, or as much of the truth as she cared to uncover. And the way she wanted it to stay. She had no desire to probe the darkness of that time before he came to them. Whatever it might have held, however terrible (and terrible it must have been—why else would he be so skittish, so wary of the world?), it was behind them, over. He was their child now, hers and Dale's, as surely as if they had conceived and she had carried and birthed him, linked by an urgency of love as mysterious and inviolate as blood itself, maybe even more so, in small requital for all the suffering their blood child had endured.

Dale was right. Nothing served by following such thoughts too far. Rising, stiffly smiling, she said brightly, "Let's go have a look at the garden, shall we?"

Hands joined, they crossed the sun-hammered lawn and inspected the plot of baked soil and withered vegetation that was all that remained of the Buckley garden. "Dried up," he said, a child's blunt assessment of the hard and inescapable truth.

As artless omen, in this present context, it was not cheering, but Norma, drawing from her bottomless well of hope, declared, "Next year will be better."

Later, tucking him into bed, still mindful of that

shadowed context, not quite able to shake it, she felt compelled to say, "This bed is safe, Davie. There's no mean man anymore. Just Mom and Dad, who love you very much."

He looked at her solemnly. "You won't go away?"

"Of course I won't. Why would you think that?"

"My other mom did."

"I'm your mom now, Davie. And I'll never leave you or go away. I promise."

He made no reply. Merely watched her gravely, this grave little man, with eyes remote and clouded, whether from drowsiness or disbelief she couldn't be sure, and the vague anxiety she'd experienced earlier, at the earnest interpretation of his fanciful drawings, returned to her now like a muffled thrumming in a distant chamber of her head.

And so, after the patio table was cleared and the kitchen restored to order, Norma found herself gravitating naturally toward the neatly stacked photo albums on the living room shelf. Whenever the steady current of melancholy that coursed beneath her placid features chanced to surface (as now it did), she took solace in those frozen winks of time gone by. She carried the albums over to the couch and began thumbing through them. Several were devoted exclusively to Sara, and certain shots, randomly selected, she lingered over, trying to recover their exact instants, the widening universe outside these narrow clips of space and circumstance and time. Here was the infant Sara, a tiny rubbery bundle of distressed flesh, but where were the cooing, soothing voices that surely must have been in the air? There stood the wobbly toddler, but what sly mischief, achieved or contemplated, had inspired that impish grin? And here she was hunkered down on the seat of a Big Wheel, convulsed in mirth by something done or said, long forgotten, graduated now to bold, pliant-limbed adventuress showered with affection and delighted by the ripening possibilities of a bounteous new world, her perfect trust in that world beaming in the sunny gaze given back to the camera's eye. A trust misplaced, as things turned out.

She laid the Sara albums on the cushion beside her and began paging through others, their chronologies inverted, paging backward in time. Watching herself and Dale grow steadily, magically younger. Seeing again her parents, and his, the four of them gone now, snuffed out by malignancies, assorted versions of the same plague that lay in blood ambush of their granddaughter, whom none of them lived to see. Some of these older photos were Polaroids, colors paled by the passage of years, the way life had been leached from their departed subjects, smiling their benign, camera-conscious smiles, blissfully unaware of the private catastrophes ahead.

Norma, her griefs and remembered joys a curious enchanted alloy, felt the presence of a strange assembly in the empty room, as though it were peopled suddenly by the departed spirits of the dead, returned to summon from the sorrowed silence of her heart a simple truth: Life is a miraculous gift, all too fleeting and so all the more to be treasured while it remained; and the reminder of that truth kindled in her a wordless pledge to her husband, herself, but most of all to

the child sleeping soundly and, she hoped, dream-
lessly upstairs.

*   *   *

"Doctor will see you now, Mrs. Quinn," said the
beckoning nurse, voice a peculiar clash of neutrality
and uneasy pity that lately seemed to inform the
voices of everyone, acquaintance or stranger, who
addressed her. Lori put aside the magazine held
purely as shield against any unsolicited stabs at conversation, rose with the severe formality of a termi-
nal patient, and followed the starched white uniform
down a corridor, conscious, at the announcement of
her name, of every eye in the crowded waiting room
trailing her. The sly, prying, better thee than me nature of a small town.

For Naperville, despite all its noisy, Watch Us
Grow boosterism, was still a small town, and Lori,
for all her by now accustomed daze of loss, was
keen enough yet to recognize she had been elevated
to instant celebrity status, inspiring curious glances
and whispered appraisals whenever she ventured
outside the house. Which anymore was rarely. And
with good cause. Once, in a supermarket, a corpulent
woman, utterly unknown to her, came waddling over
to exclaim, "Oh, Mrs. Quinn, I want you to know
we're all praying for you. We feel your pain." As
though that pious sentiment, by the simple act of ut-
terance, somehow ennobled its speaker. Pain? What
could that lardy, churchy face comprehend of pain?
And what were prayers, those monotone mumblings
flung at an insentient sky, worth? Less than nothing
was the power of prayer, a revelation akin to blas-

phemy for Lori Quinn, herself a preacher's daughter, but illuminating all the same, a liberation from the cruel jest of hope. So in response to that unwelcome gush of condolence she had merely turned her back on the woman and, without a word, walked away. And after that she left the grocery shopping to Marsh (what there was remained of it, the consumption of food a spiritless obligation anymore, an annoyance, near to abandoned, the way their lovemaking had been, gross appetites both, emptied of relevance in the wreckage of their lives).

Doctor received her in his consultation office, an austere, windowless room reserved exclusively for the delivery of medical tidings, whether bad, good, or inconclusive. He was seated at an imposing mahogany desk, his framed diplomas and certificates of achievement suspended like halos on the lime green wall behind him, testament to a prescience that, even as with God, canceled the need for article tacked to his title. Grace by grammar. Smiling, professionally cheery, he motioned her to a chair and inquired, "And how's Lori today?"

"About the same," she answered truthfully, thinking how cavalierly they appropriate your given name, how insolently. Craig was his. Craig Horton, M.D., a fiftyish man, studiedly avuncular, ruddy and fit himself, presumably as role model for his charges: do as I say *and* as I do. Same physician who had ministered to her that first terrible night, generously (or perhaps calculatedly, to maintain and reinforce his connection with the college, passport to

Naperville's select fraternity of intellectual elite) responded to anachronistic house call.

"Appetite improving?"

"A bit," she said, not quite so forthcoming.

"Are we sleeping any better?"

She wondered why they had to do that, doctors, affect the plural as though they'd somehow insinuated themselves under your skin, shared your symptoms and experienced your miseries. She wondered, but she said, back in truthful mode, "Seems that's all I'm capable of anymore, sleep."

"Still no pep?"

"No," she replied coldly, put off by his slangy vernacular, conjuring as it did images of some adolescent cheerleader tragically drained of vigor on the eve of the homecoming game. "No pep."

"Could be the medication," he conceded. "Tranquilizers can have that side effect, you know."

"Perhaps I should discontinue them."

"I don't believe that's indicated," he said, frowning slightly at the presumption of a patient tolerably well educated, yes, but certainly a far distance from the Everest of his own omniscience. "Not at this time."

"Then what do you recommend?"

Doctor cleared his throat in diagnostic preface. "Well," he allowed, tapping a file on the desk, "the results of your tests are in, and I'm happy to report everything looks remarkably good. Blood work, X rays—all top drawer. Physically we're in excellent shape, Lori."

"Fit as the proverbial fiddle, am I?" Years of living with Marsh and associating with prickly academicians had honed her capacity for irony.

Wasted on him, it appeared, for he replied soberly, "That would be fair to say."

"So it really is all in my head?"

"This, ah, lassitude you're experiencing is not of any organic origin. None, that is, we've been able to isolate."

You had to admire it, the way they sidestepped, hedged their bets. Reminded her of her father, nimbly glossing over all the world's unprovoked and unpunished evil in a twenty-minute sermon. Job's mystery resolved in a finger snap. Too bad he was gone now, dead less than a year; she'd be interested to hear just how that sanctimonious sophistry explained away the absence of a cherished grandson. To this healer of the flesh she said, "Then I take it there is no remedy."

Doctor delivered up an indulgent little chuckle. "Well, I shouldn't think our condition is all that bad. Medically speaking."

"Then what do you advise?"

He leaned back in the cushioned chair, fixed her with a vaguely benevolent gaze, signal, she supposed, of some thoughtful counsel about to issue from those pursed, bloodless lips. "Tell me, Lori, have you, ah, consulted with Dr. Weiss, as I suggested?"

It had the ring of a trick question, and so she answered evasively, "I saw him."

"But only once, I understand."

"You've spoken with him?"

"We keep in touch. Professionally."

"And what did he tell you? Professionally?"

"Only that he hadn't seen you again. After your initial session."

"That's true."

"May I ask why you've chosen not to follow up with him? Dr. Weiss is a very capable man."

That single "session" returned to her now like an aftertaste of swallowed soured cream, a repugnant memory consciously suppressed. Dr. Aaron Weiss (string out the surname vowels and you got *wise*: wise Weiss), mender of bruised phyches. So smooth he was, so—what was the word?—oleaginous, this owl-eyed, buttery-voiced shaman, tugging wisely (Weissly?) at a recessive goateed chin, poor man's Freud, inviting her to disburden herself of distant traumas that conceivably bore on this present one ("The key to all our current woes—" Weiss liked the plural too—"is invariably to be discovered in the past"), concluding unremarkably and after fifty minutes' wandering exploration of her childhood she had indeed "suffered a personal disaster of truly catastrophic proportions." That's how he talked, Dr. Weiss. Semitic throwback to her father, glib abstractors, both of them, of other people's pain. As if she needed his particular brand of voodoo to tell her that which she already knew. As if any of these doctors, with their magic elixirs and their hollow words, could miraculously materialize a vanished child, undo what was done. She felt a sudden urgent need, near to panic, to be somewhere else. Anywhere but here. "I don't think he's what I need just now," she said. "So if we're finished . . ."

"Surely you realize, Lori, there's no stigma attached to consulting a psychiatrist," Doctor gently persisted. "Dr. Weiss could be of considerable help in this time of, ah, emotional distress."

"If you don't mind, I'd rather not discuss it any further."

"As you wish," he said, hale features settled into an attitude of resignation, the mournful look of prophet scorned. He scribbled a renewal of her prescription, fresh supply of the soporific capsules, time-released tickets to a numbed forgetfulness. "Let's stay with these for another couple of weeks," he advised. "See how we're feeling then."

Still infirm was how, she could have predicted for him but didn't, feeble as an octogenarian, limp as a narcoleptic, consumed by an ache that defied simile and for which there was no vocabulary (a self-diagnosis with a pronounced whine to it, she recognized, she who had never, in that other life, untouched by serious ailment, been given to whimpery complaint). The way she felt now, exhausted by brief dialogue with Dr. Craig (never knew a Craig, it occurred to her whimsically, who wasn't something of a prig, this one not excepted—must be the name), worn out by short walk from clinic to blessed silent sanctuary of home (she who had once, another person altogether, thought nothing of a mile-long swim or an hour's sweaty aerobic jiggle). *Home* was a misnomer, though, no longer accurate. Call it house, or walled enclosure, empty anymore of the familiar resonances of home.

Such reflections came to her unbidden, sagging in

a chair in house's living room (also misnamed) darkened against the sun's slanting light by drawn drapes. First thing on arrival she'd gone straight to the kitchen and swallowed two of the red Nirvana pellets. Only then did she realize Marsh was nowhere in evidence. Just as well. Spared her the effort of speech. Probably still off on his noble quest, Sherlockian pursuit of his fugitive clue. Worse than futile, all that manic scheming, frantic scurrying, doubtless a product of the same guilt that was knotting him, behind all that nervous energy, into a shape twisted and grotesque. The hunchback of guilt. Better to have listened to that policeman who, she had come to believe, had it right the first time: enough spite in this world, enough motiveless malice, for the whole episode on the highway to be nothing more than the wicked prank it surely was.

She had no stamina for it, playing listless Watson to his intense, inept Holmes. Not tonight. Too long a day, crowded with too many faces and voices (well, only one actually, crowd enough anymore). Tomorrow maybe she'd unearth a reserve of buried strength to encourage him on his hopeless mission, be a better helpmate. Maybe tomorrow. But for now she was aware only of a comforting drowsiness settling in, the pills taking hold, slackening her limbs and scrambling her vagrant thoughts, floating her off in the transient charity of sleep.

Marshall, sweltering in his immobile box of a Volvo, its air conditioner undependable in these conditions, cursed loudly and ineffectually and with all the creative flair of a blasphemer new to the art, all restraints waived, all stops out. He had lingered too long (he realized now, too late) on the grass outside the planetarium, lulled by the rhythmic lap of waves on the shore and the gentle touch of a breeze lifting off the lake and the procession of fanciful reveries that tranquil setting evoked, almost a kind of forgotten peace, as though time and trouble were somehow eclipsed, exacted no reckoning. Or arrested by his own baffled impotence, bottled inertia. Whatever the cause, he was paying the price now, stalled on an expressway in a snarl of Friday night rush-hour traffic brought to a dead halt by some collision signaled by whirl of crimson lights in the far distance.

Eventually, wearying of inventive vilification of mischance and bad judgment and worse luck hurled at the muggy, monoxidal air, he switched on the radio and swept the dial through a dissonance of rock music (quaint oxymoron) till he found a traffic report, chirpy female voice announcing a "serious accident on the Eisenhower at Mannheim." Yeah yeah yeah, tell us something we don't already know, bitch. She obliged: "Sorry about that, folks, but that's Chicago for ya. Try not to let it or the weather—gonna be another scorcher, we're told—spoil your weekend. And now—"

Marshall cut her off mid-chirp and settled in to wait it out. He glanced absently at the figures behind the wheels, either side of him. To his right a scowling, fashionably tailored fellow, executive on the rise, no doubt, or brilliant young attorney, piloting success statement of a BMW; to the left of a power-

dressed, pinch-browed woman irritably drumming
the dash of a flashy Corvette. Both of them looked to
be about his own age, both clearly take-charge types,
overachievers, fuming at a circumstance outside
their manipulation zones. Tough fucking titty, Marshall thought sourly, wedged in tacky Volvo wagon
between these two masters of their destinies. Served
them right, traffic tie-ups being fate's great leveler in
this anthill of a city spinning in its dizzying dance of
predation. Welcome to fortune's randomly dispensed
ambushes, however trifling in their respective cases
(late for the chic cocktail party or the carnal tryst?—
horrors!—the world topples!). You want adversity,
vicissitude, upended programs, and swamped
dreams, ask me, Marshall Quinn, professor of personal cataclysm.

Better yet, ask those dazed, bloodied victims they
passed, forty-five minutes later, funneled by flagging
cop (another take-charger) into a single lane opposite two collapsed, steaming husks of metal penned
in by bustling squads of medics and mechanics and
police, methodical salvagers of order. Ask them.
Like himself, they were the ones, those glassy-eyed
walking wounded, could interpret the mystery of
plans shattered as suddenly and effortlessly as glass
or steel or bone. Go on, ask.

But squeezed one by one through the bottleneck
of someone else's annoying catastrophe, nobody
stopped and nobody asked, and once emerged, the
stream of vehicles fanned out into three lanes and
accelerated like sprinters at the crack of a starting
gun, Corvette and BMW soon out of sight, in a hurry

to get somewhere. Not so Marshall, who, after the prolonged delay, had lost all sense of urgency. What was there, really, to get to but empty house and invalided mate. And what could he do for her, finally, but make the polite, feeble inquiries one makes of the chronically unwell, listen to a litany of woes for which neither he nor a spectrum of learned healers had any solutions. Anyway, he'd alerted her to the possibility he could be late, hoping, in his naivete, to return from the Wilcox meeting with the sort of inspiring news that might have proven to be more salutary, more animating, than all those stupeficant pills she popped. Instead of empty-handed, as he was, squashed again.

No, he was in no great hurry to get home. And so he slid over into the dawdler (by expressway velocities) lane and let the swarm of agitated tardy travelers barrel on by to their monumentally critical destinations. And when at last he arrived at his exit, an impulse seized him (a memory, actually, of a time not so far removed when he, achiever once himself, had harbored petty ambitions, aspired after recognition and success as measured by the academic yardstick of publication in the drab journals of his profession), and he steered the Volvo through quiet Naperville streets, pointed in the direction of the campus. God knows why. A place to go.

The building that housed his office was deserted at this hour. Fine with him. He was not in a humor for any idle collegial chatter or, more likely in his case, obligatory condolences dutifully delivered and stiffly received. On those few occasions since Jeff's disappearance he'd stopped by here, to pick up a paltry but badly needed summer check or glance through an accumulation of mail, communiqués from the serene country of the past—on each of those rare appearances he was acutely aware of the increasingly dampening effect his mere presence produced, as though he had become an unfortunate burden to be shouldered, tolerated, his colleagues' sympathy spans as meager as the media's had been. Yesterday's calamity. His sorrowed, stricken face and endless crisis deserving of pity, to be sure, but grown a trifle wearisome. An annoyance, finally, rather like those auto-wreck victims on the highway back there, regrettable, certainly, but better avoided whenever possible. Fuck them all. Their chilling pity, fuck that too. Who needs it?

He came down the dark corridor leading to his office. The jangle of his keys excited a startled throaty voice from the other side of its locked door. "Who's there?"

Marshall said his name.

"Oh, Marsh, hold on, can you? Only be a second."

"Sure."

He waited. The promised second lengthened, its oppressive silence broken by quick rustling sounds from within, subdued whispers. And then his office mate appeared in the swung-open door, square Scandinavian face assembled in jittery grin, greeting hand extended. "Hey, good to see you again, man."

Marshall accepted the offered hand. It felt unnaturally hot. "You too, Chip," he said.

"Been awhile."

"Well, I've been . . . occupied."

The grip tightened, grin dissolved into suitably dolorous attitude. Behind him, partially hidden by the door, stood a rather stout girl, swag of yellow hair slightly disheveled and a look somewhat sheepish on her forgettably plain face. Charlie "Chip" Magnuson, associate professor, married, three kids, downslope of forty, incurable lecher. At it again. His pick of coeds evidently, if this one was representative, shrinking in inverse proportion to his mounting tally of years.

Marshall recovered his hand. "Look, I just stopped by to pick up some materials," he lied. "If I'm—"

"Absolutely not. Come on in. It's your cell too." *Cell* was a flippant reference, not altogether inaccurate, to their cramped shared quarters. His ironic little joke. "This is Kimberly Cross," he added, mindful of the amenities. "Student of mine. Kim, Marshall Quinn."

Marshall nodded at her.

"Pleased to meetcha, Mr. Quinn."

"That's *Dr.* Quinn," Chip corrected. Perennial ABD himself (All But Dissertation, in the hierarchal argot of academe), he was always careful to observe the professional niceties of rank, though always with a lilt of irony in his voice that said Titles prove nothing. Sour envy of the man who'd long since traded in his dreams for the pleasured rush of multiple sexual adventures.

"Quinn, is it?" the girl asked.

"That's right," Marshall said.

A flickering recognition lit her otherwise dull,

sated features. He could pretty much guess what was coming next.

"I'm awful sorry about what happened to your son."

"Yeah. Thanks."

An awkward silence opened.

To put something into it, Chip said, "Kim's doing a paper for me. We've been going over some of her research."

Marshall elevated a brow. "Paper? Term's over, isn't it?"

"It's an independent study project."

"I see." So that's what he's calling it now. Independent study. Sly euphemism. Be a bit more exact, though, to label it yoked or fused study. Or better yet coupled.

"Well, guess we're all finished up here," Chip announced jauntily. He laid a familiar hand on the not-so-small of Kimberly's back, guided her to the door. "Find your way out, Kim?"

"Oh, yeah. No problem."

"See you in a couple of weeks, then."

"Thanks so much for all your, uh, advice," she said, inept actress playing along with the transparent charade. With a shifty glance at Marshall she added, in redundant afterthought, "Real nice to meetcha, Dr. Quinn."

"Same here."

Her footsteps receded down the hall. The two professors settled into swivel chairs at their respective desks set at opposite ends of the small room.

"Bright girl," Chip felt impelled to remark.

"I'm sure."

"Interesting study she's doing. It's an integrative model of collegiate friendship and dating practices."

And teacher balling, Marshall thought but said only, "Really."

"Of course, it's amateurish stuff. Undergraduate level. But she's got potential."

For whatever reason, Chip (absurd name for a man his age—any age—but it was the one he insisted on: "Call me Chip") persisted in the elaborate masquerade of innocence, the dedicated mentor tirelessly giving of himself, shaping, molding, and opening young minds (not to speak of bodies, with those hot, nimble hands of his). Marshall, unwilling to buy in to it tonight, supply the reinforcement he seemed to need, made a show of going through a stack of papers on his desk. Among them were the notes for an article he'd intended to write this summer, its topic all but forgotten, lost in the chaotic swirl of events unanticipated, unforeseen. Looking at them now, those puzzling hieroglyphs from a distant season in his life, he was reminded for a moment of that time when he had routinely juggled the challenges of work, marriage, family, fatherhood. An exemplary citizen, armored in worthy ambition and moral rectitude, immunized to the temptations of easy classroom pecadillos (opportunities of which were plentiful enough) by an inherent sense of fidelity and commitment. Or maybe it was merely a constitutional need for order. Or drilled-in habit. And what had it all come to? Maybe the Chips of this corrupt world, duplicitous seizers of the day, had

the right idea after all. Maybe all along he was the
one played the fool.

This particular Chip, after a thoughtful pause,
ventured, "Look, Marsh, I know your life's a mess
right now, and the last thing I want to do is intrude,
but if there's anything I can do, anything at all . . ."
trailing into a silence that bespoke its own earnest-
ness.

Marshall lifted his gaze from the scribbled notes,
unintelligible to him now anyway. "I appreciate
that," he said, and in an odd way he did too, for it
seemed to be a genuine invitation to open up, share
his demons. Curious, coming from this aging,
crotch-driven girlizer (look at him there: thinning
hair discreetly tinted and artfully arranged over a
widening tract of forehead; once boyish face thick-
ening under the weight of years; perceptible sag of
flesh beneath the chin; softening pouch of tummy—
talk about pitiable!). But though neither quite ap-
proved of the other, their three years of shared space
had gradually evolved from accommodation to tolerance to slender bond, approaching even an unlikely
friendship.

"How about you?" Chip asked him.

"What do you mean?"

"How are you holding up?"

"Well enough."

"Lori?"

"She's another story."

"Sorry to hear that."

Marshall shrugged.

"Police have any leads?"

"Police," Marshall sneered. "Police are worthless. Let me give you a word of advice: if anything like this ever happens to you, forget the police."

"What about a private investigator?"

"Couldn't afford one."

"Have you been able to, uh, offer a reward?"

"Same problem. No way could I raise the kind of money that would interest a kidnapper. Or change the habits of a pedophile."

"Jesus, that's a terrible thought."

"Don't I know."

He hesitated an instant, Chip, his face working through a battery of expressions, all of them pained, the turmoil of some intense inner conflict. "You know," he said, "I've got a little put away. I could loan you some. Wouldn't be much."

"That's very generous of you, but I doubt it would make a difference."

"Maybe some other faculty would kick in. I could ask around."

"Take up a collection, you mean?" Marshall said in a flare of bitterness. "Departmental fund-raisers? Faculty car wash?"

"Just trying to help, Marsh."

Probably true. Chip was one of those sociologists who fancied himself a crypto-therapist, ready with the wise counsel and sympathetic ear, a pose so much a part of his seduction strategy it was worn like a second skin. And, strangely, Marshall found he was seduced by it now. "The only wisp of hope I have left," he said, "turns on a license plate and a bumper sticker I can't for the life of me remember," and he went on to spill out the story of the incident on the highway.

When it was finished, Chip stroked his prow of a jaw and, choosing his words cautiously, said, "You're certain this, uh, encounter was not, well, somebody's idea of a malicious joke?"

"Godammit, it was no joke!" Marshall exploded. "I saw the look on that woman's face! I was there!" But what the fuck was he doing here, confiding in this oaf? The measure of his lonely desperation.

Chip put up a placatory palm. "Okay, okay. I'm not the villain here, Marsh."

"I understand that. It's just that no one seems to want to believe me. Or do a goddamn thing."

"You were able to get only one number off the plate?"

"Two, I think."

"But not enough for the police to trace the car?"

"So they say."

"Okay, let's talk about the bumper sticker. You say there was some kind of symbol on it. Any ideas at all? Associations?"

"None I can recall. If I could just see it again, or even one close to it, something might come back to me."

"How about the library?"

"Library?"

"Everything can be found in the library," Chip declared, voice deepened to pedantic pitch. "That's what I always tell my students. Who knows? Maybe there's a listing of company logos or slogans somewhere. Listing, pamphlet, book—whatever. Can't hurt to look."

"It might work," Marshall conceded, wondering why it had never occurred to him.

"Worth a try."

"You may be right. I'll go over there in the morning."

"Don't bother. Our library's closed on weekends. Between-term hours, austerity and all that. You remember how it goes."

"No, I don't remember," Marshall said, crestfallen, stalled again.

"Listen, you've got your hands full right now, and I've got nothing but time. Let me poke around a little, see what I can turn up in the way of a reference source. Get to it first thing Monday."

"You'd do that?"

"What's a cellie for?" Chip said, arms outspread and with a grin of such charming insouciance Marshall could see how the unsuspecting coeds were snared. A quick glance at his watch erased the grin. "Uh-oh. Running late. Gonna have some heavy explaining to do."

"You might try the truth."

Chip gave him the look of a mischievous child caught with his hand in the jam jar.

"Say you were with me," Marshall clarified.

"There's an idea."

Now a look of quiet collusion passed between them. Simultaneously they came to their feet. "Great talking with you again," Chip said, making hurriedly for the door. "I'll be in touch on the library business."

"Chip?"

"Yes?"

"Sorry about that little outburst of mine. It was nothing personal."

"Hey, I understand perfectly. Don't give it another thought."

He did, though, in the stillness of the moment that followed his office mate's hasty departure, a reflection not so much on the flash of temper as the whole purgative conversation and the scrap of hope Chip's suggestion had inspired. Last person you'd expect it from, but help, like hope, was where you found it. Nail down the maddeningly elusive bumper sticker and maybe, just maybe, the rest of the puzzle pieces would fall into place: logo to company to car to driver to woman, and from there to what he knew they had to know. Pry it out of them some way, he thought grimly, by some kind of force, if it came to that.

Driving home, Marshall felt restless, charged, impatient to get on with it. He wasn't about to wait for Chip, who, well intentioned or not, could be sidetracked by a passing glimpse of girlish thigh. No, tomorrow he'd go directly to the local public library and scour its stacks, his natural province, the scholar detective back on familiar turf. Small and sparsely stocked, it was still a place to begin. And news other than utterly bleak to impart to his wife tonight. Not exactly the sort he'd hoped to bring, but better than nothing.

He found her slumped in a living room chair. Escaped into a drugged sleep. Gently, solicitously, but with no small share of his own charge irretrievably lost, Marshall led her off to bed, steering her like the night walker she had become.

An hour or so after Buck and Waz left the Norseman Lounge, the crowd around Jimmie began to thin out, and with all the orders carefully recorded and tallied, he tucked his notebook in a hip pocket and leaned back on the bar stool, not a little pleased with himself. Tally pushing up near a hundred and a half already, and another full week yet to go. Wait till he dropped them numbers on Dingo. Just wait. In his mind he could see it now: come struttin' up to him, whip out his book, run his eyes down the columns and say, real casual-like, real cool, like it was baby food, what he done, "Look like we'll be needin' three hundred them Rolies" (for the total would surely be that, this time next week, Rolies being the hot commodity they were and him being the cool mover he was). Of course, it was easy for Jimmie to picture himself strutting, since he was a man capable of a strut lying down, strutted in his sleep. Not so easy to get a fix on in his head was the import of an altogether unexpected and vaguely disturbing message intruding on this sunny vision and delivered just that moment by Nick, who waddled over, swiped a rag nasty as his apron across the bar, bent in close and in a growly guttural voice, whole of Hellas in it, said, "Dingo want talk to you."

"Dingo's here?" said a thoroughly baffled Jimmie.

Though in the past they'd done some business with The Greek, supplying him cheap booze to hash his stock, that was the extent of Dingo's connection with the Norseman Lounge. Not his kind of place.

"Out back."

"Fuck's he doin' here?"

Nick shrugged.

"He say when?"

"Say right now." The tar black eyes angled off to the left, fell on Lester, two stools down. "That one too."

"Lester? He wants to talk to *him*?"

"That what he say."

"Uh-oh."

Nick lumbered away, distancing himself from whatever was going on here.

Jimmie moved his head sadly, side to side. But then, optionless, he switched on his greeter smile, swiveled about on the stool, and said, "Yo, Lester, how they goin' down, boy?"

Lester, having exhausted the tolerance of everyone around him with his limitless store of bizarre adventures, sat by himself, blinking at his fuzzy image in the mirror behind the bar. Surprised and flattered by a crumb of attention from anyone so prominent as Jimmie, he turned to him, a kind of stiff, slow-motion wheeling of head and neck and chubby shoulders, and slurred, "Slicker'n cat shit, Jimmie. That's how."

His eyes seemed to be lit by a low-banked fire deep within that vacant skull. A tiny ball of spittle perched on the corner of his underlip, poised to trickle onto his chin. Plainly sozzled. Which was maybe for the best, was Jimmie's consoling thought, if what was going to happen next was what he feared might happen. He said, counterfeit hearty, "Good times rollin', huh."

"Hey, Friday's a honk-a-doodle-doo night."

"That's the ticket. Listen, Lester, got a fella wants to meet you."

"Me? Meet me?"

"Am I lyin'?"

"Who'd that be?"

"He's my supplier. Real important dude, standup guy. You'll like him. He's right out back."

"Yeah, sure, that'd be good, soon's I finish my doctor here," Lester said affably, referencing the current shot and beer in front of him, latest in a night-long procession of them.

"That's okay, man. It'll keep."

Jimmie slipped off his stool and came over and wrapped an arm around Lester's shoulders. He steered him to the back door, and with a waiterly flourish ushered him through it, out into a deserted alley behind the paint-blistered frame building. A pair of lidless trash cans, overflowing with assorted muck and haloed with flies, bracketed the door. Jimmie pulled it shut, hushing the worst of the racket from inside the bar. The light shift of early evening cast a lovely rosy glow over the alley and seemed to pinken the face of a man leaning nonchalantly against the fender of a black Lincoln Town Car parked a few yards away. Seeing him, Jimmie flashed his smile, guided Lester over, and said,

"Lester Caulkins, want you to shake hands with Odell DeCruz."

"Pleased to meetcha, Mr. DeCruz," Lester said, palm extended, grinning extravagantly. Wasn't often he got introduced to somebody important, especially by Jimmie. More like never.

Dingo didn't move from the fender. Didn't move his arms either, which were folded over his chest, over the silk sports shirt he wore, ice green, to match the color of his eyes. "Call me Dingo," he said, also smiling, but with lips unparted. A trio of smilers.

Lester let his hand float in the air a moment, then lowered it and said puzzledly, "Dingo?"

"Yes. Dingo."

"Funny name."

"You find it funny?" Dingo asked, soft-toned and mild, less a challenge than an expression of genuine curiosity.

"Ain't that what they call them dogs? Y'know, ones run loose? Over in Africa?"

"Australia, I believe it is."

"Yeah, one a them places over there. Saw it in a movie once, or on the TV."

Now Dingo pushed off the fender and approached him, staring dead-on into the inflamed eyes. "So you're Lester."

"That's me," he confirmed, witless grin still all over his face.

"You know who I am, Lester?"

"Just what Jimmie Jack tol' me." He turned, only to discover Jimmie had backed away, several feet behind him. "What'd you call him, Jimmie?"

"Supplier," Jimmie mumbled, inspecting the gravel at his feet.

"Supplier," Dingo repeated thoughtfully. "Yes, I suppose that's accurate. You see, Lester, I'm the one supplies you with all those redbirds, peaches, yellow jackets. All that product you depend on to get you through the day."

"No kiddin'. Here I figured it was Jimmie."

"No, I'm the one," Dingo said, speaking very slowly, very patiently, all the while maintaining steady eye contact, as though inviting Lester to join him in deliberating over a proper choice of words. "That's my business, you see. And as a businessman, Lester, I have to keep a set of books for all my business transactions. Same as Jimmie."

Dingo paused, tilted his head slightly, gathering his thoughts. "It's what you call double-entry bookkeeping," he explained, though he wasn't absolutely sure he had the term right, the management book being less than clear on that topic. This company, it didn't matter. "Jimmie enters them in his books," he went on, "and I in mine."

"S'pose that's how y'gotta do it, in business," Lester said, unfailingly good-humored even though he didn't have the dimmest idea what the fuck this guy was woofin' about.

"And mine say your account is well over three months . . ." Dingo considered plugging in his *in arrears,* but looking at this imbecile, he rejected it in favor of "past due." He glanced over at Jimmie, standing now, fittingly, by one of the trash cans, spine pressed to the wall. "What do yours say, Jimmie?"

"Says the same thing, Dingo. 'Course, I told him he got till Sunday. That week you was talkin'."

"My week ends on Friday. Today."

"Think he's good for it, though," Jimmie said hopefully. "Right, Lester?"

Lester looked back and forth between them. It was finally penetrating, like a distant alarm sounding in a remote chamber of his fogged head, what this tri-cornered conference was all about. "Oh—yeah—right," he stammered. "I'm good for it. Bet your ass."

"Well, that may be," Dingo allowed charitably. "I sincerely hope so. But a man gets that far behind on his payments, you've got to wonder if he's running a swindle."

"Huh?"

"Looking to stiff you," Dingo explained, eminently reasonable.

"Oh, no," Lester said quickly, "it sure ain't nothin' like that. Just I had lot a expenses lately. Transmission went out on the car, some other things." He turned over his hands, a palms-up apology.

"Shame," was all Dingo said.

Another illustration of his financial woes, this one more graphic and specific, came to Lester. "Then there was that stash I lost. Jimmie tell ya 'bout that one?"

"No."

"See, what I do is hide it in the back a the oven, in a baggie-like, 'case the law ever come by, toss the place."

"Very cunning of you."

"Yeah, ain't nobody gonna look in there, oven. Anyway, what happen was I come home one night, got a little load on, and I'm hungry, right? So I pull me a TV dinner outta the fridge—maybe it was one a them pot pies—forget—whatever, either one y'gotta heat up the oven first, before y'put it in. Know what happen?"

"Would it be you forgot the product?"

"How'd you know?"

"Wild guess."

"Bingo. Ain't that somethin'. Melt down a whole month's worth a stash. That one set me back little."

"Most unfortunate," Dingo said, but there didn't seem to be much sympathy in it and not much patience anymore, and his stare had hardened, eyes narrowed to needle points.

So Lester said, "That don't mean I forgot what I owe."

"That's good. You remembering, I mean. That part's good."

"Viking shits next Friday. I'll get your money to ya Friday, for sure."

"That's what I like to hear, Lester. I can respect a man who owns up to his obligations. Makes commitments."

"Hey, no prol'um. I say Friday, it'll be Friday. You got my word."

As if to seal that pledge, he put one of the apology palms in the air, an oath-taking gesture. Dingo was silent a moment. Seemed to be pondering. He looked over by the trash cans, inquired, "What do you think, Jimmie?"

"Lester'll step up," Jimmie said, thinking maybe the flash point was past, hoping the fuck it was. But just in case, just to cover his own ass, he added, " 'Course, it's your call, Dingo."

Dingo didn't bother to acknowledge his associate's opinion. Instead, and without a word, he walked over to the door of the Lincoln, opened it, took an object off the front seat, and returned.

"Whaddya got there?" Lester asked.

"It's a light bulb, Lester. Forty watts."

"What's it for?"

"Illumination. You know how people will say a bulb went off in somebody's head, meaning the person in question understands something? Suddenly?"

"Yeah, I heard that."

"Well, before I leave I want to be absolutely certain you understand your obligations. That's only fair, isn't it?"

"Sound fair to me."

"Good. So what I'd like you to do is put this bulb in your mouth," Dingo said, handing it to him.

"In my mouth? Why'd I wanta do that?"

"Just do it for me, please."

"What for?"

"For that illumination I was speaking of."

"It's too big."

"Open wide. It'll fit."

Lester looked at the bulb in his hand. He giggled, the high, nervous whinny of someone who doesn't quite get a joke, one that's maybe on him, but then he stretched open his mouth and, very gingerly, inserted the bulb and stood there, cheeks chipmunk-puffed, waiting for the punch line; and then his eyes went buggy as Dingo's arms shot up and out and back in, flattened palms clapping those swollen cheeks violently; and Lester sank to his knees and from there to an all-fours stance, spitting blood and slivers of glass, gagging, pinching off a scream.

Dingo took a step back, gazed at him clemently. "It gives me no pleasure, this sort of thing," he said. "But perhaps now you see the light, Lester." He lifted the gaze and locked it on Jimmie, back fused to the wall, face gone chalky. "Collections are your responsibility, Jimmie, not mine," he said, but whereas with Lester his voice had been gentle, forbearant, now it was freighted with an ugly menace. "Be here Monday night. With the money."

Without waiting for a reply he got in the car and backed out of the alley and sped away. Jimmie, however, was careful to wait till he was sure Dingo was gone, and then he came over and helped Lester to his feet. "C'mon," he said, "we'll get ya cold rag or somethin', your mouth there. Get ya some 'ludes. It'll be okay." Somebody got to be doing some p.r. around here.

"Why'd he do that?" Lester whimpered, still hacking up blood-soaked flakes of glass.

"Did it 'cuz he's straight outta the twitch house," Jimmie said disgustedly. "That's why."

Marshall came bolting up out of a sleep riddled with feverish, fantastic dreams. His father was in them somewhere, and of course his son, and some shadowy figure, featureless, who might have been himself, might not. But the man who was himself sprang into wakefulness possessed of a kind of divine revelation. It was the shape of a person on that bumper sticker. Not an aminal, not a bird, not a machine. A person. That much was certain; that much the oracle of night conceded him, and not a thing more. Beyond it, everything remained blurry as before.

The scarlet digits of the nightstand clock read 3:17. He lay there awhile, watching their glacial progress. Time numbering the night. Lori tossed fitfully beside him. At 3:33 he slipped out of bed and tiptoed across the room and down the hall to his study. He switched on the desk lamp, dropped into the chair, got out a fresh pad, and began tracing the outline of a human figure: androgynous, for he had no conception of its gender; faceless, for the tantalizing vision had blotted its face. But queerly magnified, larger than life, and distorted somehow, the way a caricature will bend an aspect of face or form to insinuate a quality or a virtue or flaw. Also outlandishly costumed, this murky figure, and hefting some curious appurtenance.

He examined his sketch. No, that wasn't right. He did another. Still not it. He filled a sheet with variations on this elusive fixation of a theme. His hand moved quickly and by pure instinct, independent of any conscious command, like spirit drawing. At times he seemed almost on the cusp of a breakthrough; other times he left a figure deliberately unfinished, as though informed in advance of its misdirection. When the sheet was fully covered, he put down the pen and studied his collection of crude representations. None of them was right. If indeed there was a right, if the whole thing was nothing more than airy fancy, chimerical as the disjointed dream that had birthed it. Another feeble grasping after hope.

He gazed through the window above the desk, out into a black, humid night. Here and there a firefly winked, like some taunting specter come cloaked in darkness to remind him of his dreadful loss, terrible guilt. Abruptly, he was aware of another presence in the room, a real one, and he spun around and discovered his wife standing in the doorway.

"What are you doing, Marsh?"

Her face bore the blank expression of a somnambulist, and her voice was flat and toneless as the soft bleat of an owl. "You shouldn't be up," he said, a gentle remonstrance. "It's the middle of the night."

She came padding into the room, slow and sleep-heavy, and stood over him, staring perplexedly at his sheet filled with sketchings. "But what is it you're doing?"

"I'm trying to remember that damned symbol—logo—whatever it was. On the bumper sticker. Trying to reconstruct it."

"How will you ever do that, Marsh."

It was not a question, and it was delivered now in a wistful, condoling pitch that conveyed a hopelessness that trampled the tiniest scintilla of hope. "I don't know," he said. "All I know is it's there."

"Where?"

"In my eye. Like a shadow in the corner of my eye. If I can just coax it around, center it, get it in focus . . . I *know* it's there."

"Did you speak to the police today?"

"Yes."

"That sergeant?"

"Wilcox. Yes."

"What did he say?"

"Nothing. Nothing of any use. They're no help."

"Nobody can help."

"That's right," he snapped, and then he took in a long breath, to contain the force of the abstract, sweeping vexation that had got hold of him. "What you're saying is right. Which is why it's up to me. Us."

"Don't be angry, Marsh," she said plaintively.

"I'm not. I'm sorry."

He watched her. Watched her eyes drift languidly over the sheet, bathed in a pool of yellow light cast by the lamp. Saw what he thought was something come into them. "What is it? Do you recognize anything?"

"It's that one," she said.

"What? Which one? Which?"

She laid a finger on a rough drawing of a figure holding some object, flat and irregular in shape, unidentifiable, across its chest. "It was something like that."

"How do you know?"

"Come along. I'll show you."

She led him down the stairs and into the kitchen. Marshall got the overhead light, and she went directly to a drawer by the sink, pulled it open, and removed a box of aluminum foil. "This," she said, holding it up and pointing at the logo stamped on its side, an exaggeratedly muscular male in shaggy buskins, animal-hide skirt, horned helmet, bearing spear in one hand, shield with the embossed letters NA in the other, a proud, fierce glare on the lantern-jawed Nordic face, oddly reminiscent of his philandering office mate. The Norse Aluminum Viking.

Marshall gaped at it. "Jesus, you're right. That's it!"

From another drawer he yanked out a phone directory and slapped it on the counter and began thumbing through the yellow pages, stooping over the fat book and breathing fast now, chewing on his lower lip, the veins in his temples pulsing. "Cicero!" he exclaimed, stabbing a finger at an entry on a page. "They've got a plant right over in Cicero!" He turned and faced her, made two fists, and shook them jubilantly in the air. "You *did* it!"

"Did I help you?"

"Help me? You just maybe saved the day."

She stood there forlornly, a box of aluminum foil in her hands, unable to share his moment of exultant stasis. Her eyes misted over, mouth trembled, and the look she gave him was imploring, needful. "Can you hold me, Marsh? Just hold me? I feel so empty. So lost."

He came over and wrapped her in his arms. "I know," he said, "I know. But we've got something to go on now. Something tangible. We'll find him."

The words seemed to rise out of some dark place

inside him, a place he didn't know about yet, didn't quite understand. But uttering them, he believed, perhaps for the first time, there was a chance they might be true.

PART
FOUR

The congregation gathered for Sunday worship in the First Methodist Church was restless and frazzled and itchy to get out of there, those of them not yet nodding through a sermon of great sedative power, something about the still, small voice of God. But even the man-engineered marvel of central air was feeble in the face of God's blistering, sticky heat, laid over the land these past forty-eight hours like a divinely ordered test, a lesson in humility. And so when the closing hymn was finally, mercifully called, everyone was relieved to rise and warble, more or less in tune with the golden-robed choir and pealing organ: "Our God, our help in ages past, our hope in years to come . . ." Buck not least among them, belting out the lyrics in a deep baritone, but catching himself thinking, Yeah right, where was all that good help when Sara was suffering, and where is it now, with this latest shadow cast over their hopes for another run at happiness. Some help, all this loving God drone he'd been hearing the last sixty-plus minutes.

Nevertheless, he sang right along, a little off-key maybe, but doing his best, for Norma's sake, doing a kind of penance for letting her down Friday night, coming home late and beery and agitated over Waz's disturbing revelation. They shared a hymnal held above the boy wedged between them and clinging tightly to her free hand, his puzzled eyes barely clearing the pew. And later, at the obligatory post-service palms pumping, Buck was careful to be civil to the pastor, who greeted them with mushy, rigged-out Sunday smile, gurgling, "Norma, Dale, so happy to see you both." Heavy and meaningful on that *both*.

"It's always good to be here," Norma said.

Buck seconded that sentiment with a quick jerk of the head and simultaneous recovery of his hand.

"Dale," said the pastor, gently chiding, "it's been awhile." He was a well-fed man, fiftyish, but with a full head of silvery hair and a smooth pink face, not a worry line anywhere in it.

"Yeah, well, been puttin' in a lot of overtime," Buck mumbled.

"There's always men's Bible study. Wednesday evenings. We'd love to have you join us."

"I'll sure think about it."

"I hope you will," the pastor said, and then he stooped slightly and chucked the boy under the chin. "And how's this young man today?"

"Can you say good morning to pastor?" Norma prompted.

Evidently not, for he shrank back, eyes lowered and lips squeezed shut. Pastor smiled tolerantly and restored the grace of his attention to the parents. "Everything, uh, going fine for you folks?"

"Real good," Buck said tersely, leaving it to Norma to expand on an answer to the pointed question. "Just fine," she affirmed, beaming. "Davie's made us so happy. He's a part of the family now."

"I can't tell you how pleased I am," Pastor gushed. "For all of you. There's nothing quite like family." And with that benedictory bromide he dispatched them on their way.

Driving out of the lot, Buck grumbled, "He sure knows how to shove the needle in."

"What do you mean?" Norma said.

"That 'been awhile' business."

She knew how he felt about religion, after Sara, and she never pressed him. For herself it was a comfort of sorts, a grounding, ritual of connection, and she wanted them all to share it, all three of them now. And so it was encouraging when he'd volunteered to come along this morning, particularly since he'd been so moody and glum all weekend, his conversation, what there was of it, falling between long, dour silences.

"Men's Bible study," he went on, a contemptuous snort.

"He just wants to see you back in church," she said neutrally.

"Easy for him. Works an hour a week, you wanta call that work, gassin' about the voice of God like he got a hotline to heaven."

Norma was quiet for a moment. She had resolved never to argue in front of Davie, who sat in the backseat staring through the window of the year-old Chevy Caprice, what they called jokingly their dress-up car. Dress-up car, dress-up clothes, Sunday services, big Sunday dinner coming up, served on the dining room table with the good silver and china—what should have been a fine family day, one of those connections she prized. So when she did speak, it was pitched softly and with genuine concern, not the barest hint of irritation. "What's bothering you, Dale?"

"Nothin'," he said, a little too quickly. "It's nothin'."

"Is something wrong? You upset about something?"

"Just a lot comin' down out to the plant. Heat, the job—you get tired, is all. Knocked out."

"I know," she said. "It's got to be awful for you in there, this time of year."

She put a tentative hand on his arm, and a look of instant regret crossed his face. "It'll be okay," he said and, forcing a jaunty grin, "Nothin' a Viking he-person can't handle."

At home, they changed into casual clothes, and Norma set immediately to preparing dinner. Davie followed her into the kitchen. She poured him a glass of Kool-Aid, and he climbed onto a chair and watched her flutter about the room. When the glass was empty, she said, "You like the Kool-Aid, honey?"

He shook his head affirmatively.

"Want some more?"

Again he nodded.

She got the pitcher out of the refrigerator and filled the glass. "When you want something," she said, "all you have to do is ask Mom. Whatever you want. This is your home now too. Okay?"

He said nothing.

"Davie? Okay?"

" 'Kay," he repeated dutifully, and in a burst of tenderness she bent over and held him against her, nuzzled his neck. He hugged back. The sun poured through the window above the sink, and the aromas of food filled the room, and for the first time in longer than she could remember the kitchen seemed to take on a lived-in look, the comforting furniture of home.

After a while Buck came through the door, looking himself infinitely more comfortable in jeans and T-shirt, though no less jumpy. He stepped over by Norma, who was slicing carrots into a roasting pan on the stove. He popped one into his mouth, and she gave him a mock scolding slap on the hand. "Dale!"

"How long you figure it's gonna be?"

"Another hour. At least. Can't you find something to do?"

"Like what?"

"The paper's in the living room."

"Paper's fulla bad news. I don't wanta read the paper."

"Isn't there a game on TV today?"

"Maybe me'n the boy run down to the park," he said and, turning to him, "Whaddya say, big guy?"

The child gazed at him over the rim of the glass, his expression wide-eyed and hopeful but a little startled too, a little wary. He shifted the gaze onto Norma, as though looking for her permission.

"Would you like to go to the park with Daddy?" she asked him.

His head bobbed eagerly.

"All right. But don't eat anything, either of you. I don't want you spoiling your dinner."

"Hey," Buck said, "you can count on us."

A half hour later, they were sitting on a bench by the grassy banks of a large, kidney-shaped pond, each holding a big bucket of popcorn from which they fed a flock of noisily quacking ducks, though each was putting away his own share too. Buck's reliable old Pontiac was parked in a lot near the playground equipment they'd headed for first thing on arriving, Buck pumping the swing for him, sending him soaring, cheering him down the fearsome cyclone slide and helping him negotiate the formidable monkey bars, elevating him on a teeter-totter with the simple balance weight of his two hands. From there they'd strolled along the walk by the pond and, catching sight of the ducks, gone over to a concession pavilion set back in a stand of trees, bought the popcorn, and brought it down to the water's edge. The minute it was gone, the fickle ducks waddled away.

"Can never trust a duck," Buck said. He was out of practice, talking to kids. Six years out of practice. But he was trying.

"Why not?"

"Y'got me. Just the way they are, I guess, ducks."

"I 'member ducks."

"You mean from them other times we been here?"

"Unh-uh."

"When, then?"

"Before."

Buck flinched at the sound of the word, abruptly jolted out of the serenity of the park and all the safety it seemed to promise. But led by a fascination larger than his dread, he asked, "Before you, uh, come to live with us?"

"Uh-huh."

"You remember where 'bouts you seen these ducks?"

"Big place," the boy said, arms held aloft and spread in a child's demonstration of immense size. "Was bears too. And lions."

"Like a zoo, was it?"

"Zoo?"

"Where they got all the animals runnin' around," Buck explained. Made a kind of sense. Even a bad mother maybe take her kid to see the zoo.

"No. These were quiet. Stood still. Didn't run."

"You sure? All animals got to run."

"These ones didn't," he insisted.

Buck looked at him quizzically, a cautious squint. "You, uh, remember anything else? From before?"

" 'Member stars."

"Got to see the stars, did you? Like late at night?" Probably kept him up all hours, that mother of his, was why he'd remember stars.

"Mouse and a cat mad at each other. Fighting. Then I got real sleepy."

Buck couldn't follow it, all this corkscrew kid talk, weird blur of memories. Wasn't sure he wanted to. To turn it another direction he said, "Well, corn's all gone. Now what?"

The reply came phrased as timid question. "Go swimming?"

" 'Fraid not. See, they don't let you swim in here. Water's too mucky."

The boy looked clearly disappointed, but he made no plea or objection or complaint. Nothing. Not the way Sara would have done, put up an argument, demanded more of an explanation than that. Whole different kind of kid, this one, like someone drained all the spunk out of him. Sad thing to see.

Even with the scorching midday heat the park was filling with people, families mostly, a few couples here and there. From across the widest part of the pond the tinsel music of a carousel started up, drifted their way. "Could go for a little gallop," Buck suggested.

"Ride the merry-go-round?"

"Look like they got 'er goin'. Whaddya think?"

He moved his head up and down vigorously. First show of spirit Buck had seen all day, and he took him by the hand and said, "Let's do it."

They walked around the pond, past another thick grove of trees, and up a small rise to the ticket booth, where a line had already formed. Gradually it moved forward. Buck laid some bills on the counter, got a supply of tickets, and led the boy through the gate. He hoisted him onto the back of the grinning mount of his choice, locked the tiny hands around the pole, said, "Hold on tight, now," and stepped off the platform and stood leaning against the guard rail, watching, the music brassy in his ears.

The carousel began to spin, slowly at first, then picking up speed, the garishly painted horses rising and falling fluidly, their riders squealing joyously, even Davie displaying a ghost of a delighted smile. And watching him, this solemn mini-man, come to them like a miraculous gift, a belated blessing, Buck felt something dense and roped inside him. Something peculiar. Something like the fear of a man who knows, none better, his worst fears have a habit of routinely coming true.

The sun hung in the sky like a huge burnished coin. Its blazing light glanced off the surface of the pond, stung his eyes. A voice, not his own, seemed to rise around the perimeters of his troubled reverie, and a thought tumbled into place, more conviction than thought. And though all the confusion and nagging doubts of these past two days were still with him, all the fear, he knew suddenly what had to be done. He felt stronger for the knowing, and he found himself wondering about the source of the voice and thinking maybe there was something to this God business after all.

Lester, at that same visionary moment for Buck, was explaining to Victor Diaz the baffling mysteries of chance, as gleaned from an "Ask the Doctor" column he'd read in yesterday's newspaper. More accurately was he explaining to a skinny, coveralls-clad ass riding high over the elevated hood of a Ford Taurus, the head and torso lost to sight from where he sat in the shade of a weeping willow, nursing a beer and watching the beaner work. "What he's sayin', doctor there," Lester was saying, "is that each little drop a jizzum different. One you come from's different than the one right before it or after it. Y'follow me?"

When Victor was occupied with the more tangible mysteries of an ailing automotive engine, he could be laconic to a fault, and now he merely grunted.

Lester took that as a signal to continue. "Which means then if your old man had put the pipe to your old lady five minutes before when he actual' did— fuck, wouldn't even have to be that long—half a second do, point I'm makin' here—but if he had, there'd be a whole different Vic Diaz boppin' around. Look different, talk different, act different, think different. Ain't that somethin'?"

The single word "shit" echoed up out of the bowels of the motor.

"Listen," Lester insisted, "I'm tellin' ya. That's in science. You can read it for yourself, paper there."

Victor boosted himself up and came over and dropped onto the grass beside Lester. His narrow brown face was sweat-streaked, his hair glittered with oils natural and applied. "Ain't talkin' about that," he said.

"What then?"

"Goddam engine. Way they make 'em now-days, can't get right goddam angle on it."

"Angle a your dangle direct proportion to the heat a your meat," Lester said with an accompanying grin that was of necessity abridged, since it still hurt to stretch his lips too wide. "That's all the geometry I ever learned."

Victor gave him a sideways glance. "How come you talkin' funny?"

"Bit down on my tongue other day. Y'know. How y'do sometimes."

Actually, the lacerations inside his mouth were coming along nicely, though he was still passing tiny slivers of glass. At twenty-eight his body healed quickly, and his mind and spirit, with the time horizons of a cheery moppet, even more rapidly. He bore no grudges. You owe somebody, you don't come to the window, sooner or later they gonna lay on the hurts. That's just how it was.

"So you sayin' could be hundred different me's?" Victor asked.

Apparently he'd been listening after all. Lester was pleased. Surprised but pleased. "Million," he said. "More'n that even, all the come man's got, his life. Think about it. Fill a couple dozen whiskey kegs, easy. An' it's just that one special little dribble that one special minute makes you who you are. Ain't just you either. Same for everybody. Same for me."

Thinking about it, he wondered what variations on Lester Caulkins might have been, had the random chance he was trying to get across to Vic here not produced the one he was. No way he'd ever even get to guess, seeing he had no idea who his folks was, orphanage and a bunch of foster homes where they beat on you all he ever knew as a kid. He didn't much like to think about those times, though, so he seldom did.

"Aah, that don't make no sense," Victor said.

"Tellin' ya what I read. It's in the paper."

"Paper fulla shit."

Lester shrugged. No talkin' to a spic, 'less it was about cars, or stealin' 'em. Which was what this one done, kikein' him down to four long and some loose change for his pickup, brand-new practically. Still, was enough to clear them books that Dingo dude was yappin' about the other night before he got mean, so Lester figured he couldn't bitch too much. Only trouble was, here he's out in Aurora, deal done, and no way to get home till Vic finish up the Taurus there and give him a lift, like he promised. Also no way into work tomorrow, but he'd worry about that later. For now, he said, "How's that motor comin'?"

"Gettin' there."

"How long y'think it gonna take?"

"Why? You in a sweat, spend that loot?"

"Just askin', Vic."

"Not long."

Four hours and nine beers later, Victor dropped him off at the corner of Ogden and Cass, and Lester hoofed it the three blocks down to Chicago Avenue. He stopped off at the White Hen and picked himself up a sixer and a jar of Cheez Whiz (the chips and salsa he preferred still too prickly on the mouth) and carried them up the two flights to his apartment next door, you want to call a one room not-so-efficient efficiency an apartment, place no bigger than a single-stall garage and about as gritty. He found a spoon in the pile of unwashed dishes in the sink, took it over and sank onto the unmade, unhidden hide-a-bed, scooped up some Whiz, popped back a couple brews, and fell asleep.

When he woke, it was dark outside. He shuffled into the closet-sized can and took a leak. He felt like day-old dog flop. Looked like it too, the reflection in the smeary glass above the basin staring back at him with eyes like a matched pair of red marbles stuck in a bleached and shapeless lump of dough. On closer examination he thought he detected tiny flaps of loose flesh alongside either ear. An "Ask the Doctor" column he'd once read said that was a sure sign of a coming heart attack, and for a flicker of an instant he experienced a twinge of fear. Could be it was maybe just fat, though. Fuck, don't matter anyhow. Everybody got to croak sometime.

Which stoic thought reminded him there was something he was supposed to do yet tonight, couldn't quite remember what. Something important. He stood there awhile longer, peering into the mirror, and finally it came to him. No place like the head, get your head right, haw haw.

So he was feeling a little better when, a moment later, he said into the phone, "Hey, Jimmie, got some boss news tell ya."

Jimmie's voice came back measured and distant and cool: "That wouldn't be about some foldin' billies, that news?"

"There y'go."

"Was hopin' that's what I'd hear. You get it all?"

"Whole bundle."

"Good boy, Lester."

"Get it to ya first thing in the morning."

"Let's be sure it's first thing. You know I gotta get it to that Dingo fella tomorrow, no later. You know that, Lester."

"Yeah, I know."

"No hard feelings, by the way, 'bout the other night?"

"I ain't got none, Jimmie."

"Just business, is all. Wasn't my idea."

"I know. Listen, you wanna hear how I raised it? Cush, I mean?"

"Sure, you wanta tell me."

"Hocked my wheels. Sold 'em to Vic the Spic."

Lester waited expectantly, but instead of the hoped-for offer of a ride into work, all he got was a beat of stone silence followed by a noncommittal "Oh" followed by, "Look, Lester, gotta run. Catch ya in the morning." Followed by the buzz of the dial tone. No help there.

Lester put down the phone and searched his head for a solution to his transportation problem. Twenty-six hundred grunts out to the plant, oughta be somebody he could hit up for a lift. What're we talkin' here?—few days, couple weeks, outside, till he got his shit together, got something worked out, wheels-wise. Wasn't a whole lot to ask. Except no names occurred to him. Lots of boozin' buddies, no friends.

The room he called home seemed suddenly very quiet, very lonely. Maybe a man better off his ticker just up an' quit on him. Better off wormfood. Or not bein' born, first place. Or born somebody else. But

since none of those things happened or seemed
likely to happen, and since tomorrow was coming on
fast for this still living version of all the possible mu-
tations on the person of Lester Caulkins, he gave it
some more thought, settled finally and by process of
elimination on Waz. Took awhile to turn up the
phone directory, mess the place was in, but once he
did, he flipped through the pages to the W's, got the
number, and tapped it out on the phone, thinking,
Good old Wazo, he'll come through.

Good old Waz was not, however, of an amiable
humor when the phone jolted him out of a fitful
sleep. He'd already taken one call earlier that night,
and it was troubling enough. Came from Buck, that
first one, which was kind of peculiar right there,
Sunday and all, and Buck never big on chitchat anyway, especially on the horn. He starts in offhand
like, like he's just calling to shoot the shit: "Waz,
how's she goin'?"

"Goin' good. You?"

"Pretty good. Watch the game today?"

"Yeah, I seen it."

"I missed it. Heard the score, though."

"Don't mean dick. Bears still ain't worth diddly
squat."

"Doin' okay so far."

"Wait'll the season starts. You'll see."

Which seemed to do in the football talk.

"Hot one today, huh," Buck said.

"Real scorcher," Waz agreed.

"Be a bitch in the plant tomorrow."

They're talkin' about the weather, f'chrissake? Something was up. And so that's what Waz said, careful to keep it casual, "So, what's up?"

"Oh, nothin' much."

A silence filled the line, Waz thinking maybe he oughta just ring off, ring him back, start over. Instead he said, "Somethin' on your mind?"

"Matter a fact, there was somethin' I wanted to run by you."

"What'd that be?" Waz asked cautiously.

"You in a place you can talk?"

Waz was standing in a small room cluttered with boxes of Della's unsold Amway products, directly off the kitchen. She was in the living room getting teary over a disease-of-the-week flick on the TV, and both kids were out somewhere. "I can talk," he said.

"Remember that business you was tellin' me about? Out on the tollway there?"

"Sure, I remember."

"I'm thinking maybe you should say something to him."

"Jimmie Jack?"

"Who else we be talkin' about?"

Waz hesitated a moment before replying, "Well, I could do that, Buck. Not exactly sure what I'd say, though."

"Just tell him what you told me. All of it. Ask him flat-out is there any connection."

"You sure you want me to?"

"I'm sure. Somethin' shifty goin' on, I better know now."

"Like I said the other night, pro'ly nothin' to it."

"But if there is I need to know. You can see how that is, Waz. Don't wanta get blindsided."

"Yeah," Waz allowed, "I can see that."

"So you talk to him, okay?"

"Okay. Soon's I get a chance."

"Tomorrow if you can, huh."

"Yeah, if I can."

"An' then you let me know what he says, right?"

"Right."

"Find out the truth. Truth better'n this not knowin'. If it's bad news, I'll take it from there."

"Ain't gonna be bad news," Waz said, but not very confidently.

"We'll see. Oh, an' Waz?"

"Yeah?"

"Wanta thank you, what you're doin' for me here. Everything you done."

"No prol'um, buddy."

But there was a prol'um, big one, and after he put down the phone and joined Della in the other room, that's all Waz could think about, even as the sad story on the screen wound down, the disease lady there spreadin' it on about how death ain't so bad, nothin' to fear, scheize like that, Della sniffin' into a hanky and him wonderin' to himself how you ask a man is he a crook, even when you know he is and he knows you know it. Fuck y'do that, anyhow?

He was sorry he'd ever said anything to Buck. Sorrier still he'd volunteered to talk to Jimmie. Sorriest of all he'd ever got himself tangled in this, ever agreed to act as go-between, first place. Till he remembered it was Buck bailed him out with a loan

ten years ago when he was lookin' bankruptcy
square in the face, his back to the wall, all his good-
time friends faded into the woodwork, relatives too.
Bailed him out no questions asked, no interest on the
money, no pressure to pay it back, even when it took
seven long years. That kinda friend don't come
along every day.

But remembering all this tonight didn't make it
any easier to figure what he was going to do tomorrow, how he'd approach Jimmie, what he'd say. And
so when the weep show was over, he told Della there
was an exhibition game on the ESPN he wanted to
watch awhile, and after she went off to bed he sat
there turning it over in his head so many times and
still coming up zip, it made him irritable and then
drowsy and finally just put him to sleep.

Which is why he was not your happiest camper
when the phone rattled a second time that night. He
rolled off the couch and trudged through the kitchen
and into the Amway room muttering *Yeah yeah yeah*
under his breath and eventually, louder, into the
speaker: "Yeah?"

"How's she goin', Wazzer?"

Waz wondered who the fuck this *she* was, everybody askin' about. "Who's this?" he said.

"Lester. Cock."

Waz glanced sleepily at his watch. "You know
what time it is, Lester?"

"Nope?"

"Half past twelve."

"No kiddin'. That late, is it? Forgot to look at the
clock. Wake ya up?"

"What's your best guess?"

"Sorry, I did."

"How come you talkin' funny?"

Lester, who along with the time had also momentarily forgotten his speech problem, said, "Whaddya mean, funny?"

"Sloshy funny. Like you gotta mouthful a shit. You ain't in the bag, are ya, or stoned? I ain't talkin' to ya if you're stoned."

"Ain't stoned, Waz. Just bit my tongue, other day."

"So what you want?"

"Ask a favor."

Jesus, everybody hittin' on him tonight. Place gettin' to be like your basic parish, him the priest. Father Waz. "What kinda favor?" he said.

"Was wonderin' could you gimme a lift into work, next couple days."

"What's the matter, your vehicle?"

"Had to unload it."

"Sold it? Why'd y'do that?"

"Some money I owed," Lester said vaguely.

That was as much as Waz wanted to know. He could fill in the blanks, the rest. He said, "Yeah, I can do that, Lester."

"Hey, that'd be great. Knew I could count on you in a pinch, Wazzer."

"You're still at that place on Chicago and Cass, right?"

"That's the one. Next to a White Hen."

"Be outside, seven bells."

"I'll be there."

"You know my car?" Waz remembered to ask him. With Lester you had to cover every base.

"Sure, I know it. Bronze Merc, barely holdin' together."

"Don't knock it. It's what's gonna get you into work tomorrow."

"Ain't knockin' it, Waz. Just remember how it gave ya all that grief. Speakin' a which, cars, I ever tell ya 'bout that time I was at the license plate office, what happen to me, that lady there? Ever tell ya that one?"

Fucker was for sure sauced, got another his brainfart stories to tell, middle a the goddam night. "No," Waz said grouchily, "an' I ain't about to listen to it now either."

"Okay," Lester said meekly.

"So I'll see ya in the morning."

"Yeah, morning. Oh, Waz, thanks for helpin' me out. Saved my ass."

"Ain't nothin'."

"I could put in on the gas, you want."

"Forget the fuckin' gas," Waz said, feeling a little guilty in spite of himself, which is how the poor dumb fuck always made you feel, like you got a duty to look out for him. "Glad to help."

Like his father before him, Marshall Quinn was a professor (he recognized now, having gravitated jittery and insomniac to his study late that Sunday night) quite simply because it was a convenient and socially sanctioned way of holding at arm's length a coarse world brash in its arrogance and boorish in its

ignorance. In a curious, pensive way Marshall
wished he could have known him, this phantom figure. Not so much as a father—a conception outside
his grasp—but as a child, the two of them, through
some magic warp of time, growing into youth and
manhood together. In this fantasy they were fast
friends, inseparable companions, the way he'd intended it to be with Jeff, perhaps as compensation
for his own loss. Or atonement for some indefinable
transgression clung to him like a weighted shadow
over the steady advance of years.

But though Marshall had never known the man,
he was all too well acquainted with the myth. Fashioned and nurtured and perpetuated over the years by
his grieving mother and an assortment of worshipful
uncles and aunts, it elevated a bookish, timorous,
and very likely rather ordinary J.—for Jeffrey—War-
ren Quinn, Ph.D., to towering figure of vast learning
and quiet wisdom. His field had been (up until the
day his hand clutched at a spasmed heart during a
classroom exegesis of an Elizabethan sonnet) Re-
naissance literature, professed at an academic
Siberia in the sleepy outpost of Moorhead, Minnesota. Perhaps as small reaction to that fuzzy discipline, Marshall had elected for himself the slightly
more pragmatic and measurable study of sociology,
though like him he had collected his degrees sedu-
lously, married a hometown girl, and settled comfortably into the genteel life of the mind, slipping
easily from one side of the podium to the other without so much as an excursion outside the shelter of
the lecture hall. Exactly as his father had done. Two

timid men unequal to the rigors of an insolent red-
neck world.

These fantasies and reflections and conclusions
came drifting up out of the mists of a past at once remote as the vanished years of his boyhood and near
as the last two days. And seated at his lamplit desk
surrounded by the books of the wise, the corners and
ceiling of the room engulfed in shadows, he was persuaded of the hard, incriminating truth of his self
and, by extension, paternal assessment. How else explain away the bumbling—clownish, even—efforts
of those galling, frustrating forty-eight hours. Had to
lay the blame somewhere, and the pair of them,
ghost and man, were handiest.

The morning after that inspiriting revelation of the
bumper sticker's symbol (that would be only yesterday—seemed an eon ago) he had taken pains to for-
mulate a careful strategy. He'd never been near an
industrial plant in his life, much less inside one, but
he suspected you didn't just stroll in off the street
and start making pointed inquiries. Doubtless the
proper procedure would be first to contact some
ranking official, secure an audience, produce one of
the missing-child leaflets, and explain his request
calmly and rationally. In that way would he, in this
thoughtful plan, surely be granted authorization to
conduct a thorough and management-endorsed investigation: that is to say, search the plant, find the
man from the happenstance tollway encounter, confront him and wring the truth from him by whatever
means necessary. As strategy, it seemed eminently
practical, eminently workable.

Accordingly, he waited till nine a.m. and then placed a call to the general—the only—listing for Norse Aluminum. After a seemingly interminable number of rings a female voice announced in the staccato intonation of an electronically ejaculated message, "Norse Aluminum can you hold please," no upward inflection whatsoever, and followed instantly by syrupy elevator music, an acquiescent Yes left hanging unuttered on his tongue. Another lengthy wait. At last the voice severed the strains of a melancholy tune ("Feelings," it was) with "Thank you for holding, how may I direct your call?"

This one at least was put as a question, to which Marshall replied quickly, "I wonder if I could speak with someone in public relations." Seemed to him the logical place to start.

"Management offices closed on weekends."

"All of them?"

"That's correct."

This wasn't the way his plan was scripted. "You mean there's, uh, no one in a position to . . . well, in charge?" he said, a mounting anxiety manifest in the stammery speech and ill-chosen words.

"There's the supervisors, plant floor."

"Foremen, you mean?"

"Supervisors."

"Maybe I could try one of them."

"Which one? Dozen of 'em on a shift, at least."

"I don't know," he was obliged to admit.

"Got to have a name, sir."

"But I don't have . . . You're sure there's no one else?"

"Like I said, management offices closed till Monday. You could try then."

"I see."

There must have been enough sinking desolation in his voice for her to offer the sighed suggestion, "S'pose you could try security."

"There's someone I could speak with there?"

"Mr. Petrella might be in today. Can't guarantee it."

"Petrella's the name?"

"That's correct. Joe Petrella. You want me to try him?"

"If you would."

"Hold a moment, please."

The moment translated into several bars of "Do You Know the Way to San Jose" and then fourteen, by close count, rings, and Marshall was about to give it up when another voice, bass, brusque, declared, "Security."

"Mr. Petrella, please."

"Speaking."

But not at all patiently and not very civilly either. Marshall said, "Mr. Petrella, I wonder if you could spare me a few minutes of your time if I were to stop by your, uh, facility this morning."

"In regards to what matter?"

"Well, I'd rather discuss it with you in person."

"Better you tell me now. Save yourself the trip."

Tell him now? Tell him what? Where do you begin? How do you explain in twenty-five words or less the disorder and aching sorrow in your life? "I was hoping maybe you could get me a pass to your plant," Marshall said weakly.

"Into the plant?"

"Yes."

"To what end?"

"I'm trying to locate one of your employees."

"Who?"

"Actually, I don't know his name. I'd recognize him, though."

"This an emergency?"

"To me it is."

"How about to this person whose name you don't know?"

"Probably not to him."

"Your name is?"

"Marshall Quinn."

"You're affiliated with?"

"Pardon me?"

"What firm you represent?"

"None. Myself."

"Okay. Twenty-six hundred employees in here, Mr. Quinn. And even if you knew the name of the one you're looking for, which you say you don't, there's no unauthorized personnel ever allowed inside our plant."

"But don't you see, that's what I'm asking for. Authorization. If you'd just—"

"Can't be done. We got propriety interests here to protect."

It was hopeless, all this circular conversation with rude, disembodied voices. Worse than futile. Nevertheless, Marshall tried one last time, desperately

now, all that remained of composure and pride departed in a snivelly plea, "Look, why don't I just
come over there and talk with you? I could explain
why it's vital I get a pass. What all's at stake. It
wouldn't take long."

"Can't today. Tied up."

"Tomorrow, then?"

"Tomorrow's Sunday. Won't be in."

"Monday?"

"Can if you want. Answer be the same."

"Thanks for all your generous help," Marshall
said, heavy with irony.

Lost, it appeared, on this Petrella person, who
merely replied, "Welcome," and rang off.

So much for his good plan.

What he should have done was skip the call altogether, gone there directly, and presented his case.
Any reasonable man, anyone with a speck of empa-
thy, would have listened, bent the iron rules, granted
his simple request. Hindsight's perfect clarity of vision.

So now he was looking down forty-eight long
hours. The first half of them were spent stewing,
roaming the house, watching a clock that seemed to
freeze-frame time. Lori's suggestion that he take the
matter to the police was met with a curt response
that fell just short of a sneer: "Police! Police don't
give a damn."

"You could try that sergeant. He seemed kind."

"You're wrong," he snapped. "He's no more kind
or caring than the rest of them. He thinks it's all a
joke too."

"What if it is, Marsh."

"A joke? You're saying it's a joke?"

"I'm not saying that. I don't know."

"Look," he said, the muscles in his face tightening," I'd rather not talk about this anymore, all right? I'm going to handle it in my own way." Psychiatric nursemaiding was one thing, action another.

But of course there was nothing in the way of action to be taken. His misguided phone call had effectively seen to that. Nothing, that is, till it occurred to him this morning he'd never actually been to Cicero, had only the vaguest notion where it was. Somewhere in the collection of faceless suburbs ringing the city. He got out a map, checked the Norse address, pinpointed it. But given his acknowledged genius for getting lost, an X on a map was no guarantee of a speedy and trouble-free arrival at a destination. Any destination, for him. The thing to do was hop in the car and go over there today. Made good sense. A Sunday, the traffic thin, he could take his time, plot a route, look for landmarks. A reconnaissance of sorts. Trial run against tomorrow morning. Also a productive means of chewing up a few of those glacially moving hours.

Lori wanted to come along, and he didn't argue. Could use some help with the map. She laid it out on her lap, and he steered the trusty wagon north on Washington, then east on Ogden. Looked to him to be the most direct route. Glued-together towns, their boundaries sometimes established by small roadside markers, sometimes not, stretched out ahead of them, baking in the heat. The Volvo chugged along,

passed over the Tri-State into neighborhoods growing increasingly shabbier, the artery that was Ogden
Avenue flanked now by factories, foundries, ware-
houses, auto graveyards. The Sears Tower, backlit by
the sun, shimmered like a mystic vision materializing on the horizon.

They pushed on. Drove by an enormous railyard,
a mile or more of twining tracks, and into a looping
tangle of bridges and over- and underpasses. The
traffic, nowhere near as light as he'd anticipated,
forced him into a sudden decision that brought them
out onto a street lined with taverns, greasy spoons,
pawnshops, dingy markets, crumbling, graffiti-
scarred buildings, and peopled with swaggery-look-
ing toughs, either gender, who eyed them sullenly
and whose complexions seemed to darken with each
passing block.

"Where are we?" Marshall asked peevishly.

"I'm not sure."

"Well, this sure as hell isn't Ogden."

"I know. But I can't seem to find where we are."

"Are we in Cicero?"

She glanced up from the map and squinted at a
street sign barely visible at the intersection ahead.
"Does that say Pulaski?"

"I think so. Yes."

"Then we've passed it."

"How the—" He throttled the obscenity risen to
his lips, started over. "How did this happen?"

"I don't know. But I think you'd better turn left."

"On this Pulaski?"

"Yes."

Too late. Pulaski was behind them. At the next corner he swung left, drove down a narrow street full of soot-grimed apartment buildings that rose, either side, blotted the sun and seemed to hem them in. Worse, it dead-ended at a rail track. And worst of all, as he shifted into reverse, cursing softly, the Volvo stalled, and a pair of tall, rope-muscled blacks came up leisurely off the stoop of a nearby building and sauntered toward them.

"Lock your door," Marshall hissed.

"It is."

He cranked the key in the ignition frantically, succeeded only in grinding the motor. The pair drew nearer, approached his side of the car. They wore T-shirts and those glistening baggy trousers that looked to be almost inflated. Inverted baseball caps perched on their brows. One of them boosted himself onto a front fender; the other bent over and filled the raised window with a broad black face, lips stretched back in display of buckled teeth and livid pink gums. "What's pro'lum here, man? Car won't go?"

"It's just a little overheated," Marshall said, straining to keep his voice level. "It'll start."

"Dunno. Don't sound good to me. What you say, Reggie?"

The one on the fender cupped a hand behind an ear. "Sound bad."

"Maybe you ought pop the hood," the face in the window advised. "Step out here and we all take a look at it. Lady too."

Lori stiffened. Firm as he could pitch it, Marshall said, "I don't think so."

A delighted squawk escaped the lips still parted in menacing facsimile of a smile. "Hear that, Reggie?"

"No. What he say?"

"Say he don't think he want come out."

"Shee-it. Why he say that?"

"Gots me."

"Ax' him."

"Why you say that, man?"

Marshall looked into eyes bugged in mock wonder, gazing at him steadily through a thin sheet of glass. "Look," he said, "I appreciate the offer, but we don't need any help."

"What he say now?" Reggie wanted to know.

"Say he don't need no he'p."

"Evahbody need he'p."

"Bet yo black ass. Why else they be down here, fine white genemum and his sweet lady, 'cept for he'p."

"Maybe lookin' score some sniff, you thinks?" Reggie volunteered. "That kind he'p?"

"Could be that. Or maybe they just come by scope how the colored folks live. Rap with the boogies. That it, boy?"

In a whispery voice, riddled with terror, Lori said, "Marsh, what are we going to do?"

Questions both sides of him. Out of answers, he replied to neither.

Reggie hopped off the fender, and the one at the window took a shuffling step back and said, "Well, heah we is, couple pure blood darkies, at yo service." He made a servile bow and, in that posture, reached down and gripped a rock the size of a fist. "Know what we got heah?" he asked Reggie.

"Look like a rock," said his ready straight man.

"No, suh, ain't no rock. This what you call a ghetto key. Open up mos' any aut-mo-bile. Even fancy one like this heah."

Now Lori shuddered. Marshall felt a thick nausea bubbling up from the lower regions of his viscera. His hands gripped the wheel, trembling, as though the motionless car were in fact zooming down a highway, blinding speed. He looked in the rearview and saw a blue and white vehicle, appearing miraculously at the other end of the street. The two blacks traded glances and took off in a sprint.

An instant later the police car pulled up alongside their Volvo. A thirteenth-hour deliverance. The officer poked his sour bulldog face out the window and demanded, "You people crazy?"

"I'm beginning to wonder," Marshall sighed, too relieved to take offense.

"You lost?"

"Afraid so."

"This ain't your best neighborhood, get lost in."

"I see that."

"What're you lookin' for?"

"A Cicero address."

"Which direction you come from?"

"West. Naperville."

"You overshot. Cicero's mile or so back."

"Could you show us a way out of here?"

"Yeah, I can do that. Your car okay?"

"God, I hope so," Marshall said. He turned the

key again, and this time the engine belched, sputtered, finally kicked over.

The officer watched skeptically. "Okay," he said finally, "follow me up to Cermak, hang a left, take you into Cicero. I was you, though, I'd keep right on rollin' back to Naperville. You don't wanta get stuck around here."

"We'll certainly do that," Marshall assured him, but once he was sure they were inside the Cicero city limits he pulled off at the first gas station, let the engine idle, and took the map from Lori.

"What are you doing, Marsh? Why are we stopped?"

"Looking for that plant."

"But I thought we were going home."

"Not till we find it. Not come this far."

"But you heard that officer. It isn't safe."

"Nothing's safe."

"I'm sorry I got us lost," she said, and her eyes began to tear. "I wanted to help."

"Wasn't you. Was those damned bridges."

"It's so confusing here. So ugly."

"Ugly or not," he said sharply, "we're not going home till we find it."

Eventually they did. Following his own directions this time, Marshall wound through a grim low-rent district and emerged onto a long street fronting the Norse Aluminum plant. And what he saw was a confidence-inspiring not in the least. A high metal fence topped with a glittery frosting of razor wire bounded the entire property. Beyond it was a lake of vehicles, a vast parking lot cleanly split in two by an

entrance drive right-angled off the street and leading
to a security station squat as a pillbox, its gate for-
biddingly lowered. An interior razored fence ran the
length of a structure painted a bilious green and
sprouting a file of gritty smokestacks and of such
immense size it dominated the view, reached to the
distant end of the street. A monument to metal. And
somewhere inside it, somewhere among those
twenty-six hundred employees, was the man who
surely would deliver them from all their grief. If he
could be located. And if he could be identified. And
if he could be made to cooperate. If.

Marshall felt his spirits, already meekened, skid-
ding at the magnitude of the task ahead of him. Nor
were they shored up when, approaching the main entrance, he slowed just enough to read a sign that
warned "This property protected by closed-circuit
TV monitors." Yet towering above the security
building was another sign, much larger, displaying
the heroic figure of a Viking, same figure he was
convinced now he'd seen miniaturized on the
bumper sticker, and his pledge sounded again in his
head, a harsh reprimand to himself.

On the drive home he said, "Couple of real
pathfinders, we are," making a little joke of it, something to put into the heavy silence. A stab at apology
for his acid temper. And for what he'd almost gotten
her into.

No reply.

He tried again. "Well, at least we found it."

Her eyes shifted from the windshield to him.
"Yes," she said dismally. "But at what cost."

"What do you mean?" he asked, understanding quite well what she meant.

"Who knows what might have happened back there?"

"Nothing did, though."

"Not today. What about tomorrow?"

"Who knows about tomorrow?" he said, giving back her own line.

"Don't you see what this is doing to you, Marsh? This obsession?"

"What I see is that this obsession, as you choose to call it, is getting us closer to finding Jeff. Anything it may or may not be doing to me is worth the price."

"You're sure of that?"

"I'm sure."

"Will you do something for me, Marsh?"

"What's that?"

"Before you go back to that terrible place tomorrow, that plant, will you talk to the police? Please? For me?"

He said flatly, "No," and she seemed to shrink into herself and that was the end of it.

And now, waiting in the stillness of night, his elbows planted on the desk, chin cradled in his hands, reflecting on the events of the past two days and contemplating those about to come in a few short hours, turning them over and over in his head and then over again, he sensed this strange new life of his possessed its own bizarre, stutter-step momentum, outside his power to control, and he was led to the conclusion the whole experience was nothing more than a test. Just that, a test, though to what end he couldn't begin to say. Perhaps it was a kind of opaque metaphor (as his wise father would doubtless have put it) for those baffling forces of fate and will and capricious chance slogging blindly through mysteries too dark to ponder. The universal whine: Why me? Once he had believed implicitly that intellect shaped fate, cancelled its authority. Now he was not so sure. Chance, fate's sidebar of sniggery puns (a wrong turn, say, or the sudden appearance of two fierce, felonious clowns), was itself without meaning except when something turned on it, something urgent, critical, and in the face of it intellect, ingenuity, reason, resolve, could be tossed and scattered like the rubble in a swoosh of wind. And he was discovering.

And so he sat there, this studious thinker, this deliberative man, wrestling with unfathomables, incapable of sleep, waiting impatiently for morning.

Which morning broke on an orange blob of sun perched on the horizon, promising another sizzling, sticky day. Waz squinted into it as he gripped the wheel of his Merc and crawled along at the mercy of the back-street traffic, stalled every couple blocks by a goddam light. He was pissed that he was on this street instead of his normal route; that he'd agreed to pick up numbnuts, first place; that it was Monday, day one of five long blistering ass-busting days dead ahead; and most of all, when he thought about it, that he was going to have to find a way to talk to Jimmie

Jack, how, he still didn't have a clue. Generally pissed.

So he was not in a mood for any chin dribble when he spotted Lester standing outside his apartment house, and when he pulled up at the curb and Lester piled in, he was quick to say, "No stories, huh?"

"Wasn't gonna tell no stories, Wazzie. Just gonna thank you, helpin' me out."

"Okay, you done it."

"What's matter? You lookin' trashed already, shift ain't even started."

"Monday's the matter. Fuckin' heat's the matter."

"Wanta bird? Spare you one."

"Get away from me, your birds."

Lester shrugged. "Just tryin' to help."

"That kinda help I don't need."

"I do. Be a real pisser today. Radio said it gonna hit a hundred."

"Add fifty, in there."

"Heard a couple guys conked out Saturday, heat."

"Who tol' ya that?"

"Vic. He was doin' o-t, said he seen it."

"Fuck's that bean dip know," Waz said sourly. Just the thing he wanted to hear. Next be somebody croakin' on the job. Pro'ly him.

"Just tellin' ya what he told me."

"You're fulla good news this morning."

Lester grinned but, given the condition of his mouth, only slightly. Still smarted some and still bent his speech a little, his sibilants voiced on a hint of a lisp. Not enough to keep him from talking, though, and he said, "Good news better'n no news. Or however that goes."

"Goes no news is good news, dickwad. An' how come you still talkin' weird?"

"Whaddya mean weird?"

"Like a fag weird."

"Tol' ya," Lester said, warming up his by now standard answer to the question he expected to be fielding all day long. "Bit down on my tongue, other day. Took a real chunk out of it."

"Y'want tongue, try a deli next time."

Lester chortled in spite of the hurting mouth. "Hey, that's a good one, Wazzer. Try a deli. Speakin' a fags, you hear the one about these two goin' past a funeral house?"

"Missed that one," Wazzer said, regretting instantly he'd bought into this ass gas.

"Wanna hear it? It's short."

"Better be."

"Okay, y'got your two sissy boys floatin' down the street, right? They come up by a stiff parlor, and the one, he squeaks to the other—oh, yeah, it's a real hot day too, sorta like this one—anyway, he goes, 'You wanta stop in for a cold one?' "

Lester giggled delightedly, but Waz merely snorted, growled, "What'd I say 'bout stories?" and they rode the rest of the way in silence.

Came in handy, though, that little fag joke, when, seven hours later, shift damn near done, Waz finally got his balls on and found an excuse to slip out of the tool crib and go searching for Jimmie. Not that he was hard to spot, Mr. King Shit expediter scooting along on the autoette he got to ride around on, looking like a goddam banker on a golf cart. Waz hailed him. The autoette veered over, and Jimmie leaned toward him and said, "Yo, Wazo, what's up?"

"You hear the one about these two fruits swishin' by a funeral parlor?" He had to shout over the boom of the hot mill directly behind them, and when he delivered the punch line Jimmie looked at him blankly and shouted back, "Old one?"

"*Cold* one. Cold. Get it?"

Now Jimmie just looked annoyed. "You call me over here to tell *that*?"

"Well, somethin' else too."

"What'd that be?"

"You got a minute, talk?"

Just then an ingot passed through the mill with a grinding, deafening roar, and a volley of sheared metal scraps came firing into the adjacent dumpster. Jimmie tapped an ear, lifted his scrawny shoulders in a helpless shrug.

"We gotta talk," Waz bellowed.

"Sure. Get on board. Take it someplace we don't got to read lips."

Waz climbed on and off they went.

Jimmie pointed his autoette down the length of the rolling belt, made a series of sharp turns, and came to a stop in a remote wing of the plant. He produced his let's talk business smile and said, "So, Waz my man, what can I do ya for? Wanta put in an order, one a them Rolies?"

"Ain't interested in no watch, Jimmie."

"No? What, then? Don't tell me you're into product. Need some poppers, crank?"

"Not that either."

"So what's on your mind?" Jimmie asked, still smiling but not so patiently now.

Waz hesitated. Sitting this close, he got a good whiff of him. Brut, f'chrissake, or Old Spice, or one a them colognes, musky and sweet. Leave it to him, come off a day's work smelling like he just stepped out of the bandbox, or a cathouse. Himself, he had to stink worse'n a jigaboo's jockstrap, day he put in. Nothin' fair, this dogshit world.

"I'm waitin', man. Ain't like I got all day."

Waz watched his own work-roughened hands playing with the buckle on his belt. "Kinda hard to put in words," he mumbled, "what I got to say."

"Whyn't you just try spittin' it out?"

Also wasn't fair this runt half your size calling all the shots, talking at you like you're a retard. That's what all that weight done, all that gelt. That's just the way it was, though, so Waz said, "You remember that adoptin' deal we done, back last June?"

"Sure, I remember that. Was glad to help out."

Waz shifted his gaze off the buckle and drew in a breath before pushing on to the hard part. He looked at him, level as he could, and said, "I gotta ask you, Jimmie. That deal, was it straight up?"

Jimmie let what he had of a jaw drop. "Whaddya sayin', straight?" he yelped indignantly. " 'Course it was straight. Your buddy Buck there, he got a bitch, you tell him come see me. Talk for himself."

"Ain't him. Not exactly. See, what happen was my

old lady, she seen one a them missin'-kid posters.
Y'know, kind they do when a kid's been snatched?"

"Yeah, so?"

"Well, thing is, she thinks it's maybe the same kid
Buck got out to that place in Elgin. Off them people
you said you juiced with all that cash a his I passed
to you."

"That's what she thinks, your old lady?"

"That's what she says."

"Well, you better fix her up with a seein'-eye
pooch, or a pair binoculars. No way could it be the
same kid."

"So you tellin' me it's a mistake she made?"

"Goddam right, mistake," Jimmie said stoutly.

"Sure hopin' that's all it is. So's Buck."

"You talk to him about this?"

"Yeah, figured I better say something."

"An' what's he say?"

"He's kinda shook."

"Okay," Jimmie said, looking him square in the
eye, voice ringing with sincerity, "listen up here,
what I'm tellin' you. Sure, I do a little tradin' here in
the plant. Ain't no secret. Pick up a few coins
movin' goods. But nothin' heavy. Y'know why?"

"Why?"

" 'Cuz it's the heavy stuff buys you a ticket to
Stateville, one way. Which is a trip I ain't big on
takin'. That's why. Use your head, Waz. Guy like me
in there, my size, gettin' my asshole reamed by all
the stirbirds. Or a shank in the back. Fuck, I'd be
crowbait, week into the bid. You think I'd run that
risk?"

"S'pose you wouldn't," Waz agreed. Made sense to him.

"Fuckin' A dog, wouldn't. An' that's exactly the kinda jolt you'd get, dealin' in snatched kids. I may be stupid, but I ain't crazy. Ain't enough bills in the world, take that chance."

"This the straight of it, Jimmie, what you givin' me here?"

"Hand to fuckin' God," Jimmie swore, elevating one in that general direction. "Whole arrangement's clean, start to finish. You got my word."

"Okay. That's all I wanted to hear."

"So we squared away on this?" Jimmie asked, watching him carefully, hand still in the air.

"Yeah. You better run me back now, before my supe gets case a the chapped ass."

"You got it."

"Oh, an' Jimmie, no offense, huh? Just I had to know. Buck too. You can understand that."

Jimmie made a fist of the pledge hand and laid a grazing little punch along Waz's cheekbone. He gave him a big, no hard feelings smile and said tolerantly, "Nobody offended, Wazzer. You tell your buddy relax, enjoy bein' a daddy. Nothin' to sweat."

Waz had been avoiding Buck all day, but at the sound of the shift whistle an hour later, he went looking for him and finally spotted him in a stream of blue uniforms tramping wearily toward one of the many gates in the interior fence. He took him aside and said, "Got some news I think you gonna want to hear." That news he delivered eagerly, here and there embellishing a bit on the dialogue, putting the best face on it. Buck listened, nodding gravely, uttering not a word till it was finished, and then all he said was, "You believe him?"

The question was framed not so much in doubt as hope, and Waz declared, "Absolutely," and then, appropriating some of Jimmie's own lines, he went on to explain why. "Makes good sense. Five and dimer like that ain't gonna run the risk, doin' a stretch in the can. They'd eat him alive in there. He's a turdball, sure, but he ain't crazy."

"So you think Della was wrong, that poster she seen?"

"What Della needs is one a them dogs they get, lead around your blindeyes."

"I hope you're right, Waz."

" 'Course I'm right. It's over and done with. What you gotta do now is quit thinkin' about it, get on with your life."

Both of them wanted desperately to believe, and so they did.

Marshall was waiting outside another of the many gates in that fence. For well over thirty minutes he had been standing there, a stack of missing-child leaflets tucked under one arm, the hand of the other fashioned into a visor against the sun's drilling, angular light. The heat seemed to swell off the asphalt and swim up into his face, and he swayed slightly, like a man on the fine edge of a faint. He felt tapped, exhausted, all the wire-strung charge of nervous energy that comes off a night robbed of sleep drained right out of him. Nothing at all like he'd felt only six hours before.

He'd timed his arrival precisely at ten a.m., his strategy being to give the management types a couple of hours to settle in after the weekend, then to make his pitch. He came outfitted in conservative summer-weight suit, a smart leather briefcase laid conspicuously on the car seat next to him, creating, he hoped, the impression of one of those "representatives" he'd heard about. Once he connected with someone in authority, someone reasonable, he'd whisk a leaflet out of the otherwise empty briefcase, explain the carefully rehearsed rationale behind his innocuous request, and certainly gain entry to the plant. Seemed to him a shrewd enough plan, and on the drive over this morning he had persuaded himself to believe in it.

That belief was, however, put to the first serious test when he pulled the Volvo up short of the access-barring arm outside the security building and the guard, a crusty old-timer, stuck his head through the window and said, "Help you, sir?"

The tone of the query was not unpleasant, but not particularly accommodating either. Bold as he could, Marshall replied, "I'd like to speak with someone in public relations."

"Who?"

"It doesn't really matter. Whoever has a moment free."

"You got an appointment?"

"No. But as I said, it'll only take a moment. If you could just—"

"Can't go inside 'less you got an appointment with somebody."

It was a name, seemed to be the hurdle here. Or the lack thereof. Any name. "Well, actually I do," Marshall said, reluctantly falling back on the only one he had. "With Mr. Petrella."

The guard looked at him skeptically. "Joe Petrella?"

"That's right."

"Mr. Petrella ain't in public relations."

"I realize that. But we spoke on Saturday—by phone, that is—and he said to come see him today, that he'd, uh, arrange for me to meet someone who is. In public relations, I mean."

"You sayin' he told you to come by today?"

"Yes."

The lie must have been heavy in his face, for now the guard leveled a cold stare on him and drawled, "Funny he'd tell you that, seeing he took the week off."

"Off?" Marshall blurted, incredulous, stunned by the treachery of this man, this Petrella, a voice really, nothing more, promising nothing and delivering just that through his calculatedly unmentioned absence. "But I thought—he said—"

"What's the nature of your business here at Norse?" the guard broke in on the desperate stammering.

"Leaflets," Marshall said helplessly, run out of lies and stratagems, his cunning plan unraveled, tattered.

"Huh?"

"All I wanted to do was pass out some leaflets to your employees."

"What kinda leaflets? You sellin' something?"

Marshall reached behind him, took one off the stack on the floor of the backseat, and handed it to him through the window. "It's a missing child," he said. "I've got reason to believe somebody here might have some information on him. Might be able to help me."

The guard studied the leaflet a moment, his face kinked into a frown. Then he looked up at Marshall and, still a little dubious, asked, "Whose kid?"

"Mine."

"Oh."

Marshall thought he detected just the slightest softening in the wary, seamed face. "Could you let me inside the plant?" he said. "Just to distribute the leaflets. That's all I'm asking."

"Can't do it. Rules. S'pose it wouldn't hurt none, though, you was to come back at shift change and hand 'em out, one a the gates along the fence."

"When is that?" Marshall said, a small ripple of hope stirring the surface of his dismay. "That shift change?"

"Four. You gonna have to park down at the end of the lot, visitors area, you decide to come back."

"Oh, I'll be back. Which gate do you suggest I try?"

"Shit, I dunno. Take your pick. Ones like another. But you ain't gonna get to many people that way, one gate. There's twenty-six hundred employees work here."

"So I heard," Marshall said, sliding the car into reverse. "Thanks anyway. I'll do what I can."

Which for the next five and a half hours amounted to nothing at all. He had no desire to return to Naperville, listen to Lori's querulous whines about police, so he found a grungy eatery in a strip mall a couple of miles away and did in two of those hours sipping what seemed to be a gallon or more of bitter black coffee. Around noon the place began to fill, and the waitress appeared at his booth and asked pointedly, "You plannin' to order anything?" The idea of food, particularly in here, made him vaguely nauseous. He paid his bill, went out to the car and waited, sealed in an oven of torrid heat. Perversely, the rush of caffeine induced a drowsiness. Off and on he dozed, his head braced against the window, sometimes slumping onto his chest, sometimes twitching spasmodically as he drifted in and out of fantastic, feverish dreams.

When he woke from the last of them, his watch read ten past three. Time to get moving. But his mouth felt as if it had been coated with resin and his limbs ached, stomach churned. Also was his bladder filled to bursting. He wobbled stiffly into the café, back to the men's room, relieved himself, splashed his face with tepid water. The streaked mirror above the sink revealed a gaunt man in a rumpled suit, hair damp with sweat, eyes pouchy, skin the color of slate. Some stalwart paladin he was, ready not at all for the joust ahead.

Ready as he'd ever be, though, so he drove back to the plant, parked, as directed, in a remote corner

of the lot designated VISITORS, got his leaflets, and
threaded through the sea of vehicles to the interior
fence. There was a gate every hundred yards or so, a
guard stationed at each of them. Not an inspiring
sight. Worn down by rejection and shrugged indifference, abandoned to the vagaries of chance, he
picked the gate closest at hand. Approaching it, he
was conscious of the guard eyeing him suspiciously,
and he said, "I was given permission to hand these
out at your shift change."

"Yeah, we was told. But y'gotta stay on that side."

Jesus, you might believe they were producing
nerve gas in there instead of kitchen foil, was Marshall's thought, but all he said was, "That's fine."

The guard turned away, evidently uninterested in
him or what he was doing there, certainly in any idle
conversation. Beyond the fence the wall of the plant
loomed steep and sheer as a cliff. Fingers of smoke
coiled out of the file of stacks jutting from the roof.
High above, a jet carved a thin white scar into the
powdery blue sky. An image of all those people up
there, settled back in their seats, sipping cool drinks,
exchanging pleasantries or plotting the steady course
of their lives, took shape in Marshall's head. Scald-
ing down here in the sun, he waited.

Punctually at four a shrill whistle sounded. Soon
after, swarms of men came pouring out the several
exits in the plant, making for the nearest gates. The
guard unlocked this one, swung it open, and Marshall positioned himself directly in the path of the
oncoming throng, impossible to overlook or ignore.
Yet that's exactly what most of them did, either ig-

nored him altogether or looked him over sullenly in passing, barest acknowledgment of his existence. A few accepted his leaflets, glanced at them, and kept on walking. And as their numbers gradually dwindled, Marshall was overtaken by the queer, airless sensation of someone stuck in a bizarre dream, other figures visible and events occurring around him though he's really not there at all.

Among the last to troop through the gate was a scrawny little man with a pitted, sneery face, followed by a younger fellow, round and tubby, sporting a grin big with mischief. Predictably, the first one spurned Marshall's offered leaflet and swaggered on by, but the grinner stopped, took the leaflet, and without so much as a peek at it said, "You runnin' for office?"

"No," Marshall said heavily. "It's about a missing boy."

Now he inspected the sheet in his hand, then looked up at Marshall, the grin ebbing some. "He your kid?"

"Yes."

"Tough break, man."

It was the first expression of genuine pity Marshall had heard all day, and he said quickly, "Actually, there's someone works here who might know where he is. Maybe you could help—"

But that's as far as he got. The scrawny one called over his shoulder, "Lester, you comin' or not?" and this one mumbled, "Sorry, man, gotta scoot. Hope you find him." And then they were both gone, leaving Marshall standing there watching the cars roll out of a lot littered with discarded leaflets. So much for pity. And clever strategies and grand designs. And for noble vows.

The gate clanged shut and a voice behind him said, "What're you hustlin' there, anyways?"

Marshall turned and faced the guard staring at him from across the fence. "I'm trying to find my son," he said, holding up one of his leaflets.

The guard squinted at it, grunted, "No luck, huh."

"No. None."

He was a paunchy, leathery man, this guard, with mean, prying eyes and a thin slice of a mouth, out of which Marshall fully expected next some spiteful jibe. Instead what he heard was, "Y'know, these boys come off shift, day like this one, they ain't in your jolliest mood. You might do better checkin' out some a the bars around here. Lot of 'em'll stop off for a cold one, maybe be little mellower."

"Any particular bar?" Marshall asked, his interest picking up a little, but not much.

The guard shrugged. "Bunch of 'em in the neighborhood you could try."

Aloud Marshall said, "Maybe I'll do that," but to himself, under his breath, "But not tonight." His shirt clung wetly to his skin, head throbbed dangerously. There were limits to endurance, boundaries to pain. Frontiers even to grief.

He started across the lot, slow, shuffling gait. A wisp of a breeze lifted a crumpled leaflet at his feet, sent it tumbling out ahead of him. The sun was behind him, and it seemed as if he were tracking his own lengthening shadow.

* * *

Because Lester had come through with the cush first thing that morning, like he promised, Jimmie, in a spontaneous burst of good fellowship, offered to pop for brewsters after work. Also good business. No percentage munchin' a steady customer, even a bumblefuck like him. And because through the course of his straight eight he'd nailed down thirty-eight solid Rolie orders and nineteen likelys, Jimmie had every reason to feel aces by the time the bustout whistle blew. Except for that little rap with the Wazzer, come outta nowhere, blindside, still naggin' some, not much. Sell that dumb polack a lot on the moon, he had to, so he wasn't gonna let it stress him. Sure as fuck wasn't gonna say nothin' to Dingo. Not with all this other nifty news he got to lay on him.

Jimmie told Lester to meet him down by the cast house exit, but naturally Mr. Dillweed got to take his sweet time showin', leave him hangin' there with his thumb up his ass, wonderin' why he'd bothered to make the offer, first place. Wasn't a total wash, though, seein' he managed to collar some grunts on their way out and get three more probables, bumpin' the Rolie total to 210 if everybody stepped up. Payday Friday, no reason they shouldn't. So while Jimmie waited he entertained himself by doing the numbers in his head, and by extravagant visions of what he'd do with his half of the for sure over thirty extra long take-home, maybe more, he got lucky. Which was to get himself a shiny iron, real crotch rocket, fully dressed, go blazin' down the highway with a piece a nasty scooter trash grippin' onto you by the jingleberries. Livin' large. Score like this one, biggest single hit he'd seen since teamin' with Dingo four years back, it wasn't outta reach.

These sunny visions were displaced by the sight of Lester coming around a furnace, moseying along about a mile-a-month, high gear for him. Figured. Little porker pro'ly cornered some poor schmuck with another one a his dickbrain stories. "Think maybe you could move your ass a little?" he said as Lester ambled up to him.

"What's the rush?"

"Can't speak for you, but I don't wanta spend the night here."

"I was just tellin' Beans about that time I was suppose to meet Sheneequa, that porch monkey bar. You ever hear that one?"

"Couple times. C'mon."

They fell in at the end of a column snaking toward the gate. Lester nudged him, nodded at the man standing on the other side. "Lookit that suit there, tryin' to give out some bungwipe."

"Pro'ly some goddam Bible-thumper, gonna save your soul."

"Or collectin' for Jerry's kids."

"Collect this off me," Jimmie said, clutching his testicles.

"Maybe it's one a them politicians, wanna buy our votes."

"Fuck, price is right, I can be bought. Just slap on the grease when y'roll me over."

"Think I'll pull his chain a minute."

"Better be just that, minute, you ridin' with me."

Jimmie stepped through the gate and brushed away the dude's extended leaflet and kept on moving. But the words "missing boy" trailing after him were enough to freeze him to the spot, and he turned his head slightly, cautiously, and called, "Lester, you comin' or not," and then got out of there fast.

Lester caught up with him by the van, and Jimmie said, elaborately casual, "What's that geek peddlin'?"

"Nothin'. He lost his kid."

"Lemme have a look at that," Jimmie said, indicating the leaflet still in Lester's hand. And as he examined it a visible cloud, more than annoyance, less than panic, passed over his shallow, sunken features.

Lester, watching him, said, "What's matter? You know that kid?"

"Fuck would I know him?"

"I dunno. Just look like you maybe seen him or somethin'."

Jimmie balled the sheet and flipped it away. "Squirrels all look alike to me."

"Too bad for the old man there, all them short eyes you got jackin' around now-days."

"Yeah, well, it's a mean world out there."

A memory, buried by the years, surfaced behind Lester's eyes: one a them foster homes he got dumped in, man a the house climbing into his bed, stinking of sweat and booze, pawing at him . . . Ugly man, ugly memory. He tried to shake it, but it wasn't easy. "Still gotta be tough," he said.

"For you maybe. By me, it's a snore."

"Tell ya the truth, I feel kinda sorry for the guy."

"Ain't our pro'lum. Our pro'lum's gettin' outside a cold one. Which you ain't helpin' here, all your sorry. Get in."

But on the drive over to The Greek's, Jimmie couldn't quit thinking about it, about the goddam limpdick with his goddam leaflets, and about what he heard off Waz, and about how the two a them things happen, same day, it got to be more than coincidence. And for all the smoke he had blown at Waz, he wasn't just bumpin' his gums there, come to doin' slam time, which he never done—knock on timber—and which he knew he couldn't do, didn't have the nuts for it. And the longer he thought about it, the more tweaked he got. Especially at the idea of tellin' Dingo, which, like it or not, now he was gonna have to do.

So when they bellied up, first thing he did was lean across the bar and whisper in Nick's furry ear, "You seen Dingo?" Got a negative grunt. So he sat there brooding over his Bud, half listening to dim bulb whining something about the poor guy lost his kid, and so to get him off that song, which wasn't helping his nerves any, Jimmie asked incuriously, "How's the mouth?"

"Mouth?" Lester repeated, momentarily fuddled by the sudden fork in the conversation, or, more accurately, in his dolorous monologue generated by the brief encounter back at the gate and the dark memories it had sparked.

"Yeah. That little, y'know, accident, other night."

"Oh, that. It's comin' along. Still little raw."

"I noticed. Way you talkin'. Maybe you oughta go

see a quack, make sure it ain't infected. Or a dentist maybe."

"Not my dentist."

"Why not? Company pay for it, your health plan there."

"Yeah, I know that. But I ain't goin' back to that chops bender."

"You gonna say why?" Jimmie said irritably. "Or keep it a secret."

"Well, last time I was there—be couple years now—fucker could barely talk. You think I'm bad, you shoulda heard him. Got a voice like a mouse squeak."

"So? Maybe he's out whoopin' and hollerin' night before, lost it. Dentists gotta go bouncin' too."

"Nah, it's more'n that. See, he's apologizin' all over the place for soundin' how he does. Says he's been to the quacks himself, an' they can't find out what it is."

"So what? Talkin' got nothin' to do with fixin' teeth."

"Yeah, but suppose he got the package."

"Package?"

"Y'know, that AIDS shit they get."

"You're sayin' cuz he can't talk he got AIDS?"

"Ain't sayin' he's for sure got it. Sayin' he could."

Jimmie shook his head slowly. "Y'know somethin', Lester. You oughta see somebody, an' I ain't talkin' dentists here. Quacks either. Talkin' shrink. You need some a that professional help."

"Listen, you think it can't happen, dentist give ya

AIDS? It can happen. Read it in the paper once. 'Ask the Doctor,' think it was."

Jimmie was sorry he ever brought it up, whole fuckin' topic. He ordered another round, and two bottles were unceremoniously plunked down in front of them. "Well, you do what you gotta do, dentist-wise," he said. "Was me, I'd go see one."

" 'Course, could be another reason he goin' dummy like that," Lester said, a trace of a smile working into his lips.

"Yeah? What'd that be?"

"Could be he went down on some lady. Every-body know how dentists always headin' south on their lady patients, goin' after Miss Fuzzy down there. Y'know, after they put 'em under with that an-tiseptic."

"It ain't antiseptic, knob drip. Antiseptic's what y'put on cuts. Word you lookin' for's somethin' else."

"Whatever. You know what I mean, though. That giggle gas they use."

"So what's your point?"

"Point is, he's maybe down in some parsley patch there, chompin' away, an' he gets a wire hair caught in his teeth."

"You find that out on Shineequa?"

"Not yet," Lester grinned. "But I'm hopin' to."

"Your luck, it'll come true."

"You wanna hear the rest of it, this theory I got?"

"You settin' me up here, this pussy hair talk?"

"Hey, I'm just givin' you my thought on the mat-ter, is all."

Jimmie glanced at the fake Rolie on his wrist. Wasn't even five yet. No tellin' when Dingo'd show. "Okay," he said. "Let's hear it."

"So he got this twat hair in his teeth, right?" Lester went on, his grin gradually widening. "Shoulda stopped right there, snip it out. Fuck, he got all the tools, his office there. Don't even have to go to the barbershop, which'd be a switch for ya, dentist goin' to a barber for a haircut 'stead of givin' 'em himself, all your muff divers."

Lester snickered softly and Jimmie, against his will, joined in, saying, "So you *was* settin' me up, huh."

"No, that part just come to me. Rest is serious."

"Better be. I ain't in a comedy mood here."

"See, I'm thinkin' he's all stoked, this dentist, got the lady out, figured he'd keep on lappin' while he still could. Only his mistake is he swallows, gets it— this hair I'm talkin' about—stuck in his windpipe. Too small for one a them X rays catch it, so the quacks got no idea what's wrong, his voice. But that's what's makin' it go out on him, that hair."

Lester laid his hands on the bar, signaling theory's end. Jimmie looked at him sourly. "That's your thought, is it?"

"That's it."

"Know what I think?"

"What?"

"Think it sucks."

At about the same time this somewhat disjointed dialogue was winding down, Dingo was pulling his

Lincoln into the alley behind the Norseman Lounge
and Supper Club. He wore a poplin blazer, cranberry
colored, pale gray silk sports shirt, pleated chinos,
leather Docksiders: the very picture of casual ele-
gance. All things considered, he was feeling good,
alert and expectant, but generally good. A quiet
weekend had cooled his temper after Friday night's
little upset, and he was genuinely hopeful his brain-
less partner had settled that matter satisfactorily, as
per his instructions. Loose ends always annoyed
him. Even less did he care for petty disruptions in
the routine conduct of business. Sadly, another such
would necessarily be the result if the delinquent account in question wasn't cleared. Lightbulbs and
other inventive paraphernalia were, in his experience, the equivalent of collection agency notices,
sometimes effective, often not. Accordingly, he
came strapped with snubnosed Ruger .38 and butterfly knife. Neither, to his thinking, had any connection with intemperate emotions or passion. They
were simply a reliable means of ensuring sound
business procedures.

He stepped out of the car's chill air and into a
blast of lingering late afternoon heat. The Norseman's back door opened onto a supremely disagreeable expanse of a room clogged with sweaty bodies,
clamorous with racket, suffused with a fog of smoke
and reeking of noxious grill odors issuing from the
kitchen portal to his immediate right. What a place
to do business! Nevertheless, it was Dingo's philosophy, acquired at no inconsiderable cost to himself at
the Facility and in the years following his release,

you played the hand dealt you, striving always to improve yourself, elevate your status in this shifty world. Some of the great fortunes in this country sprang, after all, from beginnings even more mean, and he aspired to nothing less.

Ignoring the surly glances of the pool players, he stood in the doorway long enough to command the attention of a slutty-looking waitress and to pass along a directive to her loutish boss. Then he returned to the car, switched on the engine and the air, and occupied himself with thoughts of better days ahead. In a moment the door swung open, and Jimmie, his mouth fitted out in squirmy smile, came hurrying over and climbed into the passenger seat, saying, just a shade too quickly, "Got a shitload a buzz for ya, Dingo. Kind you gonna like to hear."

His persistently toxic breath filled the small space between them, and Dingo had to restrain an impulse to avert his head. "I'll be the judge of that," he said coolly.

Jimmie extracted a banded wad of bills from his shirt pocket, handed them over. "How's Lester comin' through grab ya?"

Dingo counted the money carefully and, satisfied with the total, gave him back his half. Relieved now of the unpleasant burden of enforcement, he allowed, "This is indeed welcome news, Jimmie." He liked that word, *indeed,* the genteel rhythm, it brought to one's speech. But he also added, "If long overdue." You never want to give away too much.

"Yeah, well, least that one's off the books."

"True. Spares us another ugly scene. In the future,

though, there'll be no more credit for that oaf. You understand that, Jimmie?"

"Absolutely," Jimmie said, the resolution in his voice underscored by a sharp dicing motion with the blade of a hand. "Everything strictly cash basis with him, here on out."

"What else?"

Jimmie looked startled. "Huh?"

"I understood you to say there was more good news."

"Oh. Yeah. Gets better."

He produced a sheet of paper which Dingo inspected impassively: a list of routine orders—booze, cigarettes, a few small appliances and the like, supplied through their usual channels. Nothing extraordinary here. "And the Rolex project," Dingo said, "how does that go?"

Now Jimmie's lips opened in a prideful smirk. "Savin' the best for last."

"Which is?"

"How's two-ten sound?"

"Two-ten?" Dingo repeated, most agreeably surprised.

"That's where the figure's at right now. Oughta be even more after I catch the second shift tonight, third in the morning."

"That would be a handsome score indeed," Dingo said, truly impressed. Yet there was something about the breathy delivery (offensive of itself) and calculated escalation of all this sunshine news that set him on guard. He knew Jimmie.

"Hope to shit, handsome," Jimmie echoed, jabbing a finger spiritedly at nothing in particular, air.

Also the jittery gestures and darting eyes and the accelerated speech, a little too bubbly for Dingo's tastes. Not your happiest signals. So what he did was take a small tube of Binaca from a blazer pocket and shoot a sprat of it into his mouth in the wan hope his partner might someday pick up on the broad hint, and, that done, he said very deliberately, "Is there something else you have to tell me, Jimmie?"

Jimmie shrugged in confusion. "Whaddya mean?"

"My impression—correct me if I'm wrong— is that you have more news to report. Not necessarily good."

"Well, matter a fact, was another thing I was meanin' to mention."

"And that is?"

"Could be we got us a little pro'lum."

"Really. What would that be?"

"You remember that deal we worked out with the kid? Couple months back?"

Dingo tilted his head quizzically. "Kid?"

"Yeah, grunt wanted me to see could we fix up his buddy with a regular white kid, adopt? Paid us twenty long for it? Remember?"

"Oh yes, that one. Side action. We didn't realize much profit on it. Cute little boy, though. Actually, it was a break for him. There's a lot worse places he could have ended up."

"Sorta like we done him a favor, huh."

"Favor indeed. So what's the problem?"

"Pro'lum is, grunt who's the go-between, that deal, dumb polack name a—"

Dingo put up a silencing hand. "No names, Jimmie."

"Yeah, right, okay. Anyways, he comes by today, this polack, says his old lady seen one a them missin'-kid posters. Thinks it's the same kid."

"Nothing unusual in that. You'd expect the parents of a lost child to be looking for him."

"Yeah, but see, she's friends with the people who got him, this kid. Which is why the grunt, polack, why he's talkin' to me."

"That's no great problem, Jimmie. All you have to do is tell this polack to tell his wife to keep her mouth shut. A wife has to obey her husband. You'll find that in your Bible."

"That's pretty much what I done. More or less. Tol' him ain't nothin' to sweat, everything legit, 20K was just juice, bought 'em a little special treatment. Poot like that. Said his old lady musta got a wild hair up her ass, that poster she seen."

"There you are. End of problem."

Jimmie lowered his eyes to the floor mat, studied it as though he had found something intensely interesting there. "Except that ain't all of it," he mumbled.

"What's the rest?"

"Well, see, I'm comin' off shift today, an' there's this citizen in the lot handin' out flyers, got a kid's picture on it, name, age, all that shit."

"And you think it's the same child?"

"Wouldn't surprise me none."

"What do you suppose is his agenda, this citizen?"

"Way I see it, he gotta be onto somethin', showin'

up at the plant like that. I'm thinkin' we're maybe sailin' close to the rocks, this one."

Dingo was silent awhile. He stroked his chin thoughtfully. Gazed through the windshield. When finally he spoke, his voice was even, calm, but icy as an Arctic wind. "No," he said, "that's where you're mistaken, Jimmie. Not we. You. *You're* the one with the problem. What goes on inside that plant, that's *your* business." And when he was finished, there was on his pursed lips the faintest expression of scorn, like a seal of malice affixed to the message.

"Sure, Dingo, I know that. Sure. But y'got this citizen sniffin' around, he maybe run into the polack or the one got the kid. That happen . . . well, fuck, I dunno. Could happen."

"We don't seem to be communicating," Dingo said, still addressing the windshield. "You and I, we're independents, run our own program. The people who supplied the child, they're wops. Maybe connected, maybe not. Doesn't matter. All wops are tight. And they don't favor bungling. Neither do I. You see what I'm saying, Jimmie?"

"Hey, I hear ya. Thing of it is, though, these fellas I gotta deal with, they're straight-arrow. Ain't the kind y'can crowd."

Now Dingo faced him. A dangerous glint invaded his eyes, but his mouth was set in a smile, wizard smile, full of secrets and the gift of foreknowledge and the pathology that accompanies that dreadful gift. "You're hearing, but you're not listening. Anybody can be crowded, if it comes to that. Who should know better than yourself? You saw it right here, Friday night. Remember?"

"Yeah, I seen it, all right."

"Put your mind to it, this problem of yours. You'll find there's always a solution."

"Do what I can," Jimmie said dismally.

"Meantime, we have more urgent business to attend to. Let's plan to meet here, say, Wednesday night. You should have the final figure on those Rolex orders by then. And progress to report on this other matter, I trust."

Jimmie nodded, slid toward the door.

"I've got confidence in you, Jimmie," Dingo said in parting. "You're an orderly man."

But driving away he felt not so much confidence as vexation at another of those loose ends dangling, and a peevish irritation at this blundering hemorrhoid of a partner he was obliged to work with. Also a mounting impatience for the time to arrive when he could shuck him like a bad habit, move on to the next plateau in his ascending career. Which time the Rolex transaction would certainly hasten, given those numbers he'd heard, exceeded by far his wildest expectations. So till then he'd simply have to tolerate the alliance. Endure. Maybe bring along an air freshener next time they conferred.

They were seated across from each other in living room chairs. The central air he'd gone into hock for last year supplied a steady hum, backdrop to the heavy silences that fell between them. Also a counterfeit nip in the air, welcome relief from the blistering day he'd endured but chill enough for him to keep the suit coat on, though his tie was loosened and collar button undone. She wore only shorts and sheer mauve blouse with a faint floral pattern in it, looking almost like the summertime Lori he remembered. Except for the color—or want of it—of her exposed thighs, pale, blueish hue of a cadaver, this wife of his who had once so effortlessly turned nut brown under the first wash of sunlight. Slim, elegant legs they were yet, and Marshall wondered idly how long it had been since he'd entertained a sexual thought, never mind an urge. Long. "Are you comfortable in here?" he asked her, to fill one of the silences.

"I'm fine. If it's too warm for you, I can turn the air up."

"I was thinking just the other way around."

"I'll turn it down, then," she offered, starting to rise.

He motioned her back. "No. Leave it. I'm good if you are."

The climate-control issue resolved, another gap opened. Finally she breached it with a murmured "I'm sorry you were disappointed today, Marsh."

"Don't be," he said with bitter flippancy. "Wasn't your fault."

"I know how much you'd hoped to turn up something out at that . . . place."

"Yes, well, man proposes and Norse Aluminum disposes."

"Tell me again how it went."

"You've already heard it."

Which was true. He'd been through it with her earlier, arrived home and slumped dejectedly in this very chair, a full account of his latest failure, exercise in self-flagellation, rich in humiliating particulars. All but the mention of the bars yet to search, a detail he was less than eager to share. He could predict her reaction to that one.

"Tell me anyway," she said.

There was a quiet insistence in her voice, a kind of engagement he'd not detected for some time. Not an altogether bad sign. Therapeutic, maybe, the simple act of speech itself a slender link with reality. Unless it was only a labored effort after a display of concern, the way one will try to draw out a chronic depressive or soothe a fretful child. If the latter, it was a role reversal strange to him, and so he said summarily, "It's like I told you. They refused to let me into their sacred factory. Rules, you know. As if that word explained everything. Justified all."

"But they let you hand out the leaflets?"

"Grudgingly."

"What did you do between?"

"You mean between morning rejection and afternoon futile gesture?"

"Yes."

"Killed time," he said vaguely.

"How, all those hours?"

"Oh, had some lunch. Found a bookstore to wander through." A lie, of course, but a small one, and in this case kinder than the truth. Lying came easier to him these days, and anyway, nothing served by revealing a waning need for the bleakness of these rooms and the desolation of her company.

"You should have come back here. Rested. You'd feel better now if you had. Not so tired."

Trust a woman to focus on the inconsequential. The sure feminine instinct for irrelevancy. "I'm *not* tired," he said irritably. "Frustrated, but not tired."

"Please don't be angry, Marsh."

"I'm not that either. Not with you. It's just that it wears you down after a while. All those slammed doors. Borderline spite. The Germans have a word for it, can't recall what it is."

"Schadenfreude," she volunteered.

"That's the one. Pleased at someone else's misfortune. Spite for own sake."

"I wish there were something I could do to help you."

"Don't worry about it."

"I do, though. I want to help. Believe it or not, I don't enjoy being this burden I've become. I'm trying to get . . . better. Stronger."

Maybe she was. Maybe this stilted conversation, uncharacteristically initiated and sustained by her, signaled a gradual ascent out of miseried darkness. And maybe now was the moment to disclose the next faltering—and probably final—step in his muddle of a plan (if it could even be dignified as such). Had to be done sometime. Better sooner than later. "There is one thing," he said, watching her from the corner of an eye. "Not for you to do but to, well, understand."

"What's that?"

"There was this security guard today. At the gate where I handed out—tried to hand out—the leaflets.

He told me about some bars in the neighborhood.
Where the Norse employees hang out. It was his
thought I might have better luck trying there."

"Bars?"

"Yes."

"Workingmen's bars?"

"A bar's a bar," he said with the false bravado and
shaky authority of the man who seldom frequented
one and who, apart from the occasional social cocktail, drank nothing at all.

"Not that kind."

He made a slack-limbed shrug. "They're all that's
left."

An alarm came into her eyes, first real animation
he'd seen there in a long time. "Surely you're not
thinking of going to them?"

"That's exactly what I'm thinking," he said, but
without much enthusiasm and even less confidence.

"By yourself?"

"Who else would do it?"

"Places like that, you don't belong in them,
Marsh. You could get in terrible trouble."

"Nevertheless, I'm going," he said stubbornly.

"When?"

"Tomorrow night, probably."

The animation he'd seen, or thought he'd seen,
was gone suddenly from her eyes, a faraway drift in
its place. Better that, he supposed, than hysteria, or
more of the pleading to consult the police. He'd been
mistaken to believe all those fine, brave words about
eased burdens and renewed strength, but he wasn't
sorry to have his own brave declaration out in the

open, said. One less conflict to deal with. Enough ahead tomorrow.

The subject evidently dismissed, another silence settled over the room. This time Marshall could think of absolutely nothing to put into it. Fortunately, he didn't have to. After a moment of it the phone jangled, and he came up out of his chair saying, "I'll get it," a needless offer since she remained motionless, gazing blankly at the carpet. In the kitchen he lifted the receiver, said an interrogative "Yes?"

"Marsh? That you?"

"Yes."

"Chip here. How you doing?"

"Okay."

"Hardly recognized your voice. You sound kind of down."

"I'm fine, Chip."

"Listen, wanted to let you know I wasn't able to get to the library today. In-laws popped in unannounced. But I haven't forgotten it, though, that little research project we talked about the other night."

Which was more than Marshall could say of him, his last thought of Chip Magnuson having something to do with a loose resemblance to the Norse Viking. "Doesn't matter," Marshall told him. "I was able to remember it after all."

"Great!" the Chip voice came booming back at him, full of an ebullience underlined by no small relief. "How'd you manage that?"

"It's a long story."

"One I'd really like to hear. What do you say we sneak out for a drink?"

"Now? Tonight?"

"What better time?"

"I don't know if that's such a good idea, Chip."

"Sure it is. Do you good." Voice dipping to confidential zone, he added, "Wouldn't do me any harm either."

On reflection, it didn't seem all that bad, a reasonable excuse for an escape from the constrictive gloom of this house. "Hold on a minute," Marshall said and, covering the phone, he called out into the next room, "Lori, it's Chip Magnuson. He wants me to go out for a drink. Would you mind?"

"Rehearsal for tomorrow night?" was her reply, caustic but spiritless. "Trial run?"

Marshall sighed. "Question is, do you mind?"

"No."

"You sure?"

"I don't mind," she said curtly. "I'm tired anyway. Going to bed."

To Chip, he said, "All right."

"Sensational."

Chip suggested a spot, Marshall agreed, they rang off. He put up the phone and went back into the living room and positioned himself behind her chair, searching for a graceful exiting line. None came to him.

Aware of his presence but addressing the floor, she said in a voice gone limp with a weak blend of exhaustion and contrition, "I'm sorry I snapped at you, Marsh."

"You didn't snap."

"I don't mean to be that way."

"I know you don't. You're not."

"Go ahead, now. I really don't mind. Truly."

"I won't be long," he said, backing toward the door. Didn't quite make it.

"Marsh?"

"Yes."

"Will you do something for me?"

"If I can."

"Will you at least think about it?"

"About what?" he asked, a stalling tactic, the reference for *it* transparent.

"Tomorrow night. Going to those places."

"I'll certainly think about it," he lied. Another of those loving lies you tell, but only half a one this time, for he knew the unpleasant, not to say dreaded, prospect of searching rude bars was not going to be far from his thoughts in the next twenty-four hours.

Ten minutes later, Marshall stood in the entrance of the agreed-upon meeting spot, glancing about with the studied nonchalance of a stranger at a party. Not that there was much of a party going on in here: handful of presentable-looking people sitting quietly at the bar, a few handsome couples in booths, soft lights, softer music. None of the rowdy, raucous commerce you'd associate with a saloon. Who said these places had to be intimidating, or hostile?

A flagging arm hailed him from a booth near the back. As Marshall approached, Chip's fleshy Nordic face opened in a big welcoming grin. "Hey, young man, step into my office."

Marshall slid into the opposite seat, as directed. "How'd you get here so soon?" he asked, genuinely curious, for Chip lived over on the other side of the

country club, spacious new house, sprawling lot, all
of it paid for, it was rumored, with his wife's money.

"Federal Express. Guaranteed instant delivery
from too much family togetherness."

"I can appreciate that."

"No, you can't. You'd have to be there, hear the
old boy rant and puff, do the *Gee, boss, you're great*
number."

"Well, you're out of it for a little while anyway,"
Marshall said, his sympathy for these happy domestic problems wafer thin.

"For which I have you to thank. Owe you a drink.
What's your pleasure?"

"What's that you're having?"

"J.D., rocks."

"Which is?"

"Jack Daniel's over ice. Where you been, boy?"

"Out of touch, I'm afraid," Marshall said ruefully.

Chip did his best impression of earnest solemnity.
"Listen, I understand. All you've been through." He
elevated the signaling arm again, and a cocktail
waitress appeared, pert young girl with a veritable
cascade of blond ringlets framing a face that seemed
mostly mouth, the full moist lips painted a fire engine red. Chip's features, pliant as Silly Putty,
shifted back into an easy grin. "How's about one of
these for my friend here, sweetheart? Maybe do another myself."

"Coming right up, Chip."

Away she sauntered.

"Former student of mine," he offered in explanation of the familiar address.

"Another bright girl?"

"Let's just say she had a firm grasp of the material."

After the drinks were served and sipped, Marshall's cautiously, Chip set down his glass, squared his hands on the table and, assuming his empathetic therapist pose, said, "So tell me what all you've been up to."

Marshall told him, commencing with the purely accidental unraveling of the bumper sticker mystery late Friday night and concluding with the dismal results that solution had produced only a few short hours ago, reconstructing the almost surreal events and encounters and conversations of the three days between in fulsome detail, conscious of his own verbosity, the professional taint again, but powerless to contain the bitter rush of words. Oddly, it seemed to help some, getting them said. Even to an overage satyr. Just as oddly did it occur to him he was not unhappy to be here, uncomfortable not in the least. The mellowing ambiance of a bar. Maybe tomorrow wouldn't be so impossible after all.

"Where'd you say this factory is located?" Chip asked him.

"Cicero."

"Hmm. Not exactly your upscale suburb."

"So I discovered," Marshall said and, stretching the Cicero boundaries a bit in the interest of heightened drama, he added, "We nearly got mugged there. Or worse."

"Those less than friendly blacks yesterday?"

"Yes."

"You were lucky."

"I suppose so. The way I define luck anymore."

"Taking your wife along, that was pretty risky."

"How was I to know?" Marshall said, more defensive than question. "Who ever goes to Cicero?"

"Not me, that's for sure."

"Well, I won't make that mistake again."

"You should give it some thought yourself."

"What are you saying?"

"She may be right, you know. About those bars."

"You're suggesting I don't check them out? Forget about the whole thing?"

"Not the *whole* thing. Just the bars part."

"What other options do I have?"

"There's still the factory. At least it ought to be safe in there."

"I already told you," Marshall said, an edge of exasperation in it, "they won't let me in."

Chip lifted his chin in a deliberative tilt, pinched a cleft into it. "Okay, we're a couple of intelligent people. Let's put our heads together, find an answer to the riddle. There's got to be a way to get you inside this sanctum sanctorum of the aluminum industry."

Interesting, his choice of pronouns: our heads but your person on the block. Riddles are always more diverting when there's nothing at stake, nothing to lose. "And what would that be?" Marshall asked.

"You say there's a fence around the building?"

"Two of them. Both tall, with barbed wire at the top and guards patrolling inside. Climbing it would be out of the question, if that's what you're thinking."

"Okay, strike that one. How about at those shift changes? Mobs of people, right?"

"There were a lot of them, yes."

"All right. What if you were to get yourself outfitted in factory worker duds. Find some at Sears, no doubt, or a Kmart, whatever it is they wear."

"You mean try to pass myself off as one of them? Slip in with a crowd?"

"Why not?"

"Because they go through those gates single-file. Past a security guard. Coming in, they probably have to show some kind of ID. It would never work."

"No," Chip reluctantly agreed, "I expect it wouldn't." He was silent a moment, scratching his scalp puzzledly, though with a care not to disturb its cunning camouflage of sparse hair. And then a spark came into his eyes, and with a Eureka finger snap he declared, "I've got it!"

"So?" Marshall said, softening the skepticism as best he could. At least someone was trying to help, or giving the appearance of trying. More than could be said of anybody else.

"Here's what we do. We tell them you're a researcher. Doing a sociological study."

"What sort of study could I possibly be doing at a factory?"

"Shit, I don't know. Behavioral patterns in the work force. Aspirations and anxieties of the lumpen proletariat. We'll think of something. Put a colon in the title and it'll sound scholarly."

"And who is it we—I—will tell this tale of research to?"

"Executive types. It'll wow 'em. They're always

dazzled by us scholars. Flash your Ph.D. and they'll swoon."

"But that's the problem. I can't seem to get to any of these executive types."

"So we send 'em a letter. Put the college seal on it. Make it look official."

"I don't have that kind of time, Chip."

Chip shook his head slowly. "Fall term coming up in another week or so, guess you don't at that," he said, voice subdued now, all the creative zeal gone out of his eyes. "You ready for that, by the way?"

"What choice is there? Bills have to be paid."

"Leaves only those bars then, right?"

"Looking that way."

"You don't want to talk to the police first?"

"Police think I'm a lunatic."

"You know, I'd offer to go with you," Chip said weakly, eyes lowered and fixed on his glass, "if it weren't for the in-laws and all."

"I understand."

"Marsh?"

"Yes."

"Sorry I couldn't come up with anything."

"That's all right. You tried. You listened."

"I want you to know I admire your, well, courage. Everybody does. You're a helluva lot stronger than I could ever be."

Marshall merely looked at him, said nothing. It was one of those empty benedictions that only serve to confirm your isolation, seal your loneliness, and to which there was no adequate reply.

PART
FIVE

"You're really going?"

"Yes."

"Even after everything you said happened yesterday?"

"Which was nothing. Nothing conclusive, anyway. That's why I'm going."

"Won't you at least consider calling that sergeant . . . I forget his name."

"Wilcox."

"Sergeant Wilcox. Won't you call him? He tried to help us."

"Look, Lori, what you don't seem to understand, what I can't get through to you, is that there *is* no help. Anywhere. Only ourselves."

"I wish you wouldn't do this, Marsh."

"Well, I'm doing it. So there's really nothing more to talk about, is there?"

What he was in fact doing just then was standing hunched over his desk, gathering a fresh pile of leaflets, squaring them busily, meticulously, rehearsing in his head (trying to rehearse, between all these pleading sessions he'd been enduring the better part of the day) the approach he'd take, words he'd use ("I'm looking for a missing boy," he might begin, straightforward, plain-spoken, blunt if need be), bearing he'd try to project (earnest but unflinching, unbegging). He was dressed the way he assumed you'd dress for a working man's bar: polo shirt, faded jeans, scuffed sneakers, but his face wore the pinched expression of a man steeling himself against a most unpleasant task ahead. Or a man stalling.

"But it's not right for you to be going to those awful places," Lori persisted. "It's not safe."

"What can happen in a bar?"

"That's just the point. You said those men ignored you yesterday. You said that. What more do you expect *can* happen?"

Difficult to quarrel with that logic. He hadn't the vaguest idea what to expect. More rejection, probably, more indifference. For a moment he hesitated. Wavered. If there was a way out of this, any way at all, he'd gladly seize it. Leap at it. But try as he might, he couldn't justify it to himself. Not till every possibility, however remote, was exhausted. "I don't know," he said. "Nothing, maybe."

"Then, why are you going?"

"Because it's for certain nothing if I don't try. Look at the calendar. Summer's almost over. Couple of weeks classes begin, I'll have to go back to work. Time's closing in on us, Lori. I've got to make *some-*thing happen, and it's got to be now. Don't you see that?"

She nodded slowly, and in that small acquiescent motion there was a kind of china doll fragility that moved him enough to fold her in his arms, and they clung together like two frightened waifs lost in a haunted, trackless woods. The blinds at the window filtered the still harsh afternoon light, laid flat seams of it in neat geometric patterns across the carpet. Outside, clusters of birds chattered noisily in the abundant shrubbery alongside the house. "You'll be careful?" she said.

"I'll be careful."

The Ogden Avenue eatery known as the Mouth Trap (which ingenious name was graphically symbolized by a sign mounted above its roof depicting a gigantic toothy cavern of a mouth, wide open, and complete with lapping pink tongue) catered to families with its reasonable prices, hearty portions, chipper waitpersons (as they chose to identify themselves: "Hi, I'm Cindy, I'll be your waitperson tonight"), and conspicuous absence of alcoholic beverages from its menu. Buck could have used a beer right about now, but he didn't complain, gulped iced tea instead. It wasn't as though he was worried anymore, not exactly. Waz's account of the talk with scumbucket yesterday made a kind of sense, most of it anyway, and he was doing his best to put the whole business out of his head. Accordingly, he'd insisted the three of them eat out tonight, partly to make up for the other night but as much to find a way into another prickly issue that had to be addressed, settled.

They occupied a booth in the back of the place, Buck on one side, Norma and the boy on the other, feasting on burger, fries, and slaw baskets. A departure from Norma's usual wholesome balanced meals, a little treat. Buck picked at his indifferently, watched her attending to Davie's every need, adjusting his napkin, helping him with his carton of chocolate milk and the tiny packets of ketchup. Not that this kid needed much help. Wherever he'd been before, somebody had taught him table manners, and remembering the dull-eyed, gum-popping woman in Elgin, supposed to be his mother, Buck found himself wondering uneasily who that somebody could have been. With some effort, he pushed the discordant thought away, said, "So whaddya think, boy? Chow any good here?"

The child seemed puzzled by the question, looked to Norma for interpretation.

"Do you like your burger, Davie?" she asked him.

He nodded solemnly around a mouthful of it.

"More than your dad there, from the looks of it," Norma said, indicating Buck's barely touched basket.

"Heat," he said by way of explanation. "Real oven in there today. Wrings the appetite right outta you."

"You've got to eat, though, Dale. Keep up your strength. Seems like you've been awfully tired lately."

Buck didn't want to pursue that topic, so to the boy he said, "How about some dessert? They got pie here. Ice cream sundaes. Whaddya say?"

Again the child nodded.

"Which?"

"Ice cream," he murmured.

"Norma?"

"Same for me."

"Ice cream all around," he said, signaling the waitress, person, whatever you called them anymore. They settled on flavors, and shortly the three desserts were laid in front of them. To forestall any more talk about his lagging appetite, Buck spooned his in dutifully, cleaned it right up. Then, offhandedly, as though it had just occurred to him, he remarked, "Y'know what I been thinkin'?"

"What's that?" Norma asked.

"Remember that trip you was sayin', other night?"

"To the Dells?"

"Yeah. I'm thinkin' that's maybe not such a bad idea after all. I still got a few vacation days. Back 'em up to a weekend and we could have ourselves a nice little getaway."

She gave him a look not quite astonished but full of perplexity. And doubt. For both of them the Dells, site of Sara's last vacation, held a bundle of ambiguous memories, joyous, bittersweet, precious. "Are you sure you want to go back there, Dale?"

"Why not? It's great for kids. Boy'd like it up there."

"I'm sure he would, but—"

"What's a Dells?" Davie broke in.

"It's a place in Wisconsin," Norma told him. "Another state. They have all kinds of fun things to do there."

"What things?"

"Oh, there's the Storybook Gardens. That's where all those stories and rhymes we read in your books, well, come to life. And a little choo-choo train you get to ride on."

"And that petting zoo," Buck joined in, catching the spirit, "where they let you feed the animals. Not just ducks either, like over at the park, but big ones too. Deer. Remember that, Norma?"

"I remember," she said quietly.

The boy's eyes widened. "We go feed the deers now?"

"Well, not tonight," Buck said, and at the instant dismay registered on the child's face he added, "But how's next Saturday sound?"

"Go then?"

"Don't see why not."

"But Saturday's the plant open house," Norma reminded him.

"Yeah, well, my thought was we'd maybe just skip it this year," Buck said, looking into his lap.

"But why would we do that? Everybody will be there. Even Della's going."

Now he lifted his eyes, fixed them on her. "How come you know that? You been talkin' to her?"

"No, she told me that Sunday they were over. Why?"

"No reason. Except, see, that's the reason right there. Be a mob a people in there. An' you seen it before."

"*I* have, but Davie hasn't. I thought he might like to see where his daddy works."

"He'd get too tired. You remember them tours— couple miles walkin', last a couple hours, least—all that noise, heat . . ." Buck had the uncomfortable sense of saying too much, too fast, tangling himself in words, which never came easily to him. All the same, he rushed on: "It's no place for a kid. Even runnin' half shift, like they plannin' to do, gonna be hotter'n holy hell in there."

Norma glanced quickly at Davie. "Dale," she said, mild reproval.

"Okay, okay. Sorry. But you see what I'm sayin'."

"Maybe you're right. It might be too much for him this year."

"There you are. Do it next year."

The boy had been following this conversation intently, looking anxiously back and forth between them. "We don't go feed the deers?" he asked Norma.

Buck answered for her. "Oh yeah, we do. Saturday for sure." And to her he said, "Tomorrow I'll put in for three days. Maybe you can call up there, get us a motel. That one we stayed in before, maybe."

"With the wading pool, and the water slide."

"That's the one. We could sleep in Saturday, get started around noon, have most of the day. Come back Wednesday morning."

"Four days! You'll spoil me, Dale."

"Hey, who got it comin' more'n you?"

Norma tucked back a fluttery wisp of hair fallen across her brow. She smiled at him tenderly. It was his way of saying he loved her. Davie too. Loved them both.

Another threesome, Lester, Waz, and Beans, were also dining out that evening, though in their case beer and other spirits were readily available since, at shift's end, they had made it no farther than the Norseman Lounge. Waz was along not so much for the company but because Tuesday was Della's bingo night, leaving him with the scanty options of here or warmed-over Tuna Helper casserole at home. Here was better. Beans, thrice divorced (once on the grounds of extreme cruelty, a legalistic nicety for his chronic and intolerable flatulence) and currently living alone, had elected to join them because, like Waz, he wasn't interested in cooking something for himself: "Too fuckin' hot," in his phrase (even though the Norseman, its air-conditioning system thoroughly routed by the mass of sweaty bodies, could hardly be characterized as cool). And Lester was there for the unremarkable reason that he rode with Waz and this was as far as they got. He didn't mind. Beat the oppressive silence of his room and what remained of a jar of Cheez Whiz.

After a few stand-up brews at the bar, they secured a booth and ordered South of the Border Platters, which spicy dish had the immediate effect of convulsing Beans' lower visceral tract, resulting in a recurrent series of volcanic eruptions. The latest in that series was of such truly Krakatoan proportions that Waz was finally moved to clothespin his nostrils and remonstrate in nasalized moan, "Jesus, Beans, you got no class at all? I'm tryin' to eat here."

Beans merely shrugged. Helpless shrug.

"Could at least wait'll I'm done. That ain't a whole lot to ask."

"Holdin' back a ripper," Beans observed philosophically, "be like holdin' back the heat in summer, snow in winter. Can't be done."

He was a heavy, earthy man, Beans, beady of eye, saggy of jowl, bulbous of gut. Nobody knew for sure how old he was. Old. Plant legend had it that, years back, one of his fabled back-door emissions detonated too near a cast house furnace, ignited a runaway blaze.

Lester, who worked alongside him in the box shop and who, over time, had grown impervious to the stink, remarked, "That makes eight."

"Eight what?" Beans asked him.

"Farts."

"So?" Beans said, somewhat defensively. "You keepin' count?"

"Matter a fact, I am."

"Any particular reason?"

"Reason is because I was readin', just the other day, it was, how your average person farts thirteen times a day. That's an average, now, y'understand."

"Fuck you read that?" Waz wanted to know.

"In the paper there. Ask the Doctor."

Waz gave a skeptical snort. "That all he got to do, go around clockin' farts?"

"Just tellin' ya what I read."

"You sayin' thirteen a day is average?"

"Ain't me sayin' it. It's a doctor."

"Well, he ever check out Beans here, he gonna get his average tipped."

"Fuckin' truth," Beans allowed through a prideful chuckle. "At thirteen a day I'm already about caught up to next November."

"November?" Waz grunted. "Shit, you somewhere out in the twenty-first century."

"Not that far. Be in stiff city by then."

"You'll still be workin' 'em, stiff or not. They hafta plant you off in a desert someplace. Or at sea. 'Cept that wouldn't work either. Snuff all the fish."

Beans turned over the palms of his hands, a gestured What can I say? and Lester seized the opportunity to leap back into the conversation. "I knew a fella worked in one a them funeral places—y'know, room where they spiff 'em up before they plant 'em—and he tol' me that's exactly what they do, your stiffs."

"Do what?" Waz asked.

"Break wind. He said it's real weird, y'got one laid out on the table, doin' whatever it is they do to 'em, an' all a sudden it cracks a boomer. Stiff does, I mean."

"Nothin' weird about that," Waz declared, taking down the last of a burrito on a current of beer. "They got all that gas bubblin' inside 'em, gotta go somewhere."

"Yeah but how they gonna, y'know, squeeze it out? Bein' dead and all. Ain't like they got any control, their asshole down there."

"Don't have to squeeze. It's what you call a reflex."

"Boy, I tell ya. Never catch me workin' a place like that."

"Ain't so bad. Della use to do it."

"Della!" Lester exclaimed, astonished. "Della

worked in a stiff parlor? C'mon, you shittin' us, Waz?"

"Nobody shittin' ya. Back in her hairdressin' days they'd sometimes call her in, pretty up a stiff for the services."

"Y'mean like give 'em a haircut?"

"Haircut, permanent wave, dye job—you name it. All that stuff they do."

"Della done that?"

"What'd I just say, shitear?"

Lester shook his head slowly. "Jesus, that's gotta be creepy. Workin' on dead people like that."

"Least they don't bitch."

"Don't tip none either," Beans put in.

"Can't have it both ways," Waz drawled.

"Must be somethin', bein' dead," Lester said, awed suddenly by the enormity of the prospect of his own passing.

"No, y'got that wrong," Waz corrected him. "Ain't *some*thing. It's nothin', dead is."

"Nothing," Lester repeated dully, and for a moment he contemplated the drab threads of experience—past, present, those yet to come—that, woven together, made up the colorless fabric of his life. Bad as they'd been, stale as they were right now, joyless as they promised to be, the thought of forfeiting them, marooned forever in the long sleep of death, seemed somehow very real, and immensely saddening. "You ever think about that?" he said. "Nothing?"

"You got a real knack for killin' a conversation, speakin' a dead. Y'know that? Am I right, Beano?"

"Real gift," Beans concurred.

"Look at it this way," Waz said, coming to his feet. "Workin' at Norse, you good as dead already. So it won't be much of a jolt when the real thing comes along."

"Pro'ly won't even know the difference," Beans added, also rising.

Lester, still seated, looked anxiously from one to the other. "Where you guys goin'? You ain't leavin' already?"

"Myself, I'm headed home," Waz said. "You want a ride, this your chance."

"Whyn't you stick around, have another brewster. It's early yet."

"Said I'm leavin'. You comin', or no?"

"Beans?"

"Splittin' too," Beans said.

"C'mon. One more. I ever tell ya 'bout that time I went to get my license plates renewed? Wait'll y'hear it. It's a howl, that one."

Waz screwed his face into an attitude of mock indecision. "I dunno, 'nother Lester story, that's a real temptation. Whadda you think, Beans?"

"Tough call, all right."

Both of them chortled. Not Lester. He managed a grin, but weak, near to morose.

"So," Waz asked him, "you want a ride? Last offer."

"Think I'll hang out awhile."

"How you gonna get home?"

"Somebody here gimme a lift. Jimmie maybe. He's shootin' stick in the back."

"You sure, now?"

"Yeah."

"Pick you up in the morning, then. Okay?"

"Okay."

Waz sighed. Goddam sad apple had a way of making you feel guilty even when you doing him a favor. "You okay?" he said gruffly. "All that stiff talk draggin' on your ass?"

"Me? Nah, I'm good."

He wasn't, though, and left to himself the morbid abstraction of mortality soon translated into vivid, particularized images (there was Della trimming his limp hair, there the stiff parlor guy probing his lifeless naked blueing corpse, batting away its foul escaping fumes) that, unaccountably, crowded in on him like advancing ground fog. To hold them off he attached himself to an assembly of grunts gathered at the bar, contributed a couple of jokes that got some small indulgent laughs and then, as the hours passed and the group scattered, was reduced finally to making conversation with Skinny Nick. Or trying to:

"Hey, Nicker, how's she goin'?"

Unintelligible mutter.

"You makin' any money?"

Negative bob of the hairless skull.

"Maybe you oughta get some dancin' girls in here. Liven the place up little."

Irritable scowl.

"Just tryin' to help."

"You drink, or what?"

Jesus, some talker. "Yeah, sure," Lester said. "Gimme another."

The Greek produced a bottle, held out a sausage-fingered hand in rude demand of payment, and steered his bulge of belly away.

Lester settled onto a stool, sloshed down some suds. Oughta find a fluff, he told himself, shack up. Maybe get spliced, even. Least be somebody around, talk to. Except the face gazing back at him from the mirror behind the bar, round, lardy, vacant as an affable sheep, dispatched the mordant and decidedly unaffable question: Who the fuck gonna wanta marry a sorry lump like you? Deep-six that good thought.

The door swung open and he glanced over and saw a guy standing in the entrance, hesitating an instant, like he was lost, maybe stumbled in by mistake. Nobody from Norse, that's for sure. Tell that by the sissy clothes on him. Seemed dimly familiar, though. Lester looked again, closer. Damned if it wasn't the same dude from out by the gate yesterday. He burst into a big welcoming grin and waved him over, calling, "Hey, man, c'mon in. Buy ya a drink."

The cue ball was stuck on the back cushion, not your best angle on the eight, nestled as it was against a side rail and with a whole lot of green between it and its designated corner pocket. No problem, you're Jimmie Jack Jacoby. He lined up the shot, pumped his stick a couple of times for luck, stroked, and sank it, clean drop. "Whoa, see that?" he gloated. "Took the paint right off it." His opponent groaned, laid a five spot on the table, and racked the balls.

He was an accomplished player, Jimmie was, particularly at last-pocket eight ball, which, being more a game of cunning strategy than skill, was right up his alley. 'Course, even he had to admit the competition tonight—knuckle-dragger name of Vernon Mc-Cord, went by Tiny on account of his godzilla size, fucker big enough to fill a room all by himself—was not exactly what you'd call world-class. Already he'd lifted thirty off him, chump change finally, but any kind of sugar in your pocket spent sweet, was Jimmie's motto.

"Break 'em," Tiny growled.

Jimmie chalked up, positioned the cue ball, took careful aim, and split the rack with a resounding boom. Nothing fell. Not enough punch on his stroke, not enough follow-through. Reason was he was more'n a little feeped out, hustlin' Rolies in here late last night, then back again first thing in the morning, nail both the other shifts, then do his own. Who wouldn't be cashed, all them hours? Worth it, though, watchin' that total climb up past 270. Allow, say, twenty backoffs, you still lookin' at a take oughta put a smile even on Dingo's vinegar face. Put one on his own every time he thought about it, which was often. Except when he remembered that other nagging problem. Still in the glue, that one, and still no idea how to wriggle out. Maybe it'd come to him.

Goddam if it didn't, and without an ounce of effort, his part. Tiny sinks an easy natural, misses his next shot, and Jimmie's stretched out across the table, drawing a bead on the nine ball when he hap-

pens to glance over the top of it and down the length
of the bar and fucked it it ain't the leaflets geek,
same goddam shitheel, right there in his sights.
Turkey shoot. Money from home. Shoulda played
the Lotto today.

He laid down his stick, boosted himself off the
table.

"Fuck y'doin'?" Tiny said. "It's your shot."

Jimmie sauntered over by him, looked up into the
baffled eyes. "Tiny, my man, how'd you like to
make back what you lost here tonight? Whole wad,
with a double saw on top of it. How's that sound?"

"Doin' what?"

"What you do best. See that pussy up at the bar?"

"Where?"

"One talkin' with Lester there."

"Yeah, I see. What about him?"

"Y'want that fifty?"

"Fifty'd be good."

"Okay, listen up. Here's what we're gonna do."

It was the first friendly face he'd seen all night.
Only one. Never mind its indelible simpleton stamp.
For Marshall it was like a breath of purest ether to an
expiring man. Incongruous flower blooming in an
arid waste. Blade of sunlight piercing a leaden slab
of sky. Name your sustaining image: that's how
Lester's warm and altogether unexpected greeting
touched him.

Quite in contrast to the uniformly hostile recep-
tions he'd encountered over the past three hours.
There were a dozen or more taverns in the immedi-

ate vicinity of the Norse plant, and he'd tried them all, starting at a place called Turk's Sportsman's Saloon, where his carefully patched-together air of confidence unraveled the instant he came through the door. He paused there uncertainly, leaflets in hand. Eyes skimmed over him. Voices braided in an urgent festive hum. The smallest action in the baseball game playing on the large-screen television excited a raucous whoop. Dramatic difference from the genteel place he'd been in only twenty-four hours ago. Marshall filled his lungs with the smoke-poisoned air, squared his shoulders, and approached the nearest table. "I'm looking for a missing boy," he said, enunciating very slowly, very deliberately, a leaflet displayed like a visual aid.

One of the three men seated there said through a coil of smoke drifting from the cigarette pasted to his lips, "Yeah? So?"

"I wonder if any of you men could help me."

Another, an aspiring comedian, tilted back in his chair, put up disclaimer palms, and said, "Don't look at me, I ain't lost. You lost, Gordy?"

"Me neither. Last I checked."

"You lookin' for a boy," the comedian smirked, "you in the wrong spot, that kinda action."

Marshall stiffened. "Very funny," he said. "But this is not a joke."

"Yeah, well," the smoker put in, "this ain't your missing persons officer either. This is Turk's."

"You suppose you could at least look at the photo?"

"S'pose you could get the fuck outta the way a the TV? We're tryin' to watch a game here."

Marshall slunk away. Inventive variations on the same theme greeted him at the remaining booths and tables. Ribbons of boorish laughter trailed him out the door. Not an auspicious beginning.

And not much better at the other taverns. Some even worse. All of them almost pridefully grungy and seeming to exude a combative aura of macho bullying and throwaway spite. At each he searched its parking lot in the faint hope of stumbling on the elusive AZ plate. About as much chance of that as catching a fly with a pair of chopsticks. Or hearing a charitable word inside. Nevertheless, he kept on going, stubbornly, one to the next. By the time he arrived at the Norseman Lounge the sun was perched on the rim of the world, about to plunge in a gorgeous violet fanfare, drawing after it all that was left of the mean, malignant day. By then the persistent patterns of rejection and failure had drained the spirit out of him, conditioned him to defeat, and coming through the door he wore his anticipated want of welcome in his face.

And so he was nothing short of stunned to discover a pudgy young man with an open, artless grin, utterly empty of impudence or malice, beckoning unmistakably at no one but him. Offering even to buy him a drink. The first and only place he hadn't been treated like a leper, or the invisible man. He came over and sank onto a bar stool and said, "A drink sounds good about now."

"You the fella lookin' for your kid, right?"

"That's right. How did you know?"

"Seen ya out by the gate yesterday."

"You were there?"

"Yeah. You gimme one a them flyers. You don't remember?"

"Afraid not. Sorry. It's mostly a blur, yesterday."

"That's okay. Was just a minute there, anyways."

"My name's Quinn," Marshall said, extending a hand. "Marshall Quinn."

"Mine's Lester Caulkins."

They gripped palms.

"Thanks for inviting me to join you, Lester. I appreciate it."

"Ain't nothin'. Glad for the company. So what're you drinkin'?"

"I don't know. Whatever you're having."

Lester swiveled on his stool and called, "Hey, Nick, couple brewbies here, huh?"

The squat, swarthy man behind the bar uncapped two bottles, brought them over, and grunted, "Three-seventy."

Marshall reached for his wallet. "Let me get this."

"No way," Lester said, slapping a ten on the bar. "My idea, I'm buyin'."

Marshall took a pull on the beer. Tasted bitter, but not all that bad either. Not after all he'd been through tonight. Which thought reminded him why he was here, and so while change was being made he removed a leaflet from his pocket (long since had he given up trying to hand them out), unfolded it, and slid it under the eyes of the bartender. "I don't suppose you could help me with this," he said.

Those surly eyes darkened. Head shook an emphatic no.

"Well, do you have any objections if I ask around in here?"

"What, you a cop?"

"Cop? Hardly. I'm just trying to find this boy."

"No."

"No, what? No you don't object, or no you don't want me asking?"

"Said no."

"I heard what you said. I don't know what you mean."

"Mean don't want you bother my customers," he muttered, and lumbered away.

Marshall sighed. To Lester he said, "Is he always this friendly?"

"Nick, he ain't exactly famous for nice."

"I noticed."

"So you still lookin'? Your kid, I mean."

"I guess you could call it that."

"In here?"

"Here, and the other bars in the neighborhood."

"Jesus, man, you better be careful. These are kick-ass joints. Don't take kindly to strangers."

"I found that out too."

"Didn't have no luck, huh."

"About like what you just saw."

"Shame. Y'know, what y'oughta do is offer a reward. There was any loot in it, even Nick might be interested."

"If I had the money I would."

Lester pointed at the leaflet. "Lemme have a look, can I?"

Another first: someone actually asking to see one of his leaflets. Marshall pushed it over, and Lester gave it a long, brow-pinching inspection, saying finally, "Nope. Wish I could help ya out, man, but I ain't never seen this kid."

"Thanks anyway."

"For what? Like I said, I ain't seen him."

"For trying."

Lester shrugged. "Least I could do, nice-lookin' boy like that. What happen, anyways? He run away or somethin'?"

"He was abducted."

Lester looked at him blankly.

"Kidnapped."

"No shit. Somebody snatched him?"

"That's what happened. About three months ago."

"Around here?"

"No. In the city."

Again Lester showed a baffled face. "So how come you lookin' around here?"

"I've got reason to believe there may be a connection with someone who works at your plant."

"At Norse?"

"Yes."

"What'd that be? That connection?"

"Connection is a license plate," Marshall said, launching into his story, gazing into the vapid face with the intensity of a man who's corralled at last a receptive audience. No matter how dull-witted. Still someone willing to listen. Possibly even to help.

"You see, I was out on the tollway, my wife and I, East-West, awhile back this was, and a car cut in front of me, and when we got to the next toll booth this car, a Mercury, maybe a Buick, but—" He broke off, conscious of the excess of words spilling out, the superfluous detail. Slow down. Keep it simple. Stay with the point.

He was about to begin again when a figure emerging from the back of the room entered his field of vision. Lester caught the drift in his eyes, turned, and hailed the runtish man sidling toward them: "Hey, Jimmie. How y'doin'?"

"Doin' good, Lester."

"Eight ball droppin' for ya?"

"Went down couple times. How 'bout yourself? Mouth any better?"

"It's comin' along."

He laid a companionable arm on Lester's shoulders, glanced at Marshall. A toothpick projected like a moist needle from between his wormy lips. He shuttled it from one corner of his mouth to the other, said, "Who's your friend?"

"Oh, yeah. Forgot my manners. This is, uh, what'd you say your name was again?"

Marshall said his name.

"An' this here's—"

"Jimmie," Jimmie finished for him, adding quickly, "Pleased to meetcha, Mr. Quinn," and offering a spidery hand and a slick smile.

Marshall shook the hand. "Good to meet you."

"Ain't seen you in here before. This your first time?"

"Yes."

"Quite a place, huh?"

"That it is."

"Mr. Quinn, he's lookin' for his boy," Lester explained to Jimmie. "Was out by the gate yesterday. Remember?"

"Yeah, I remember that, now you mention. What happen to him?"

"He was kidnapped," Marshall said.

Jimmie indicated the leaflet on the bar. "That him?"

"Yes."

He picked up the sheet and studied it for a lengthening moment, his head nodding thoughtfully, the gradually disintegrating pick doing a slow dance in his mouth, both motions implicit with meaning.

"What is it?" Marshall said. "Have you seen him?"

"Well, no. Not exactly."

"But you know something about him?"

"No. Mean not *me,* y'understand. But I might know a fella does."

"Who is he? Can you give me his name?"

"Maybe do better'n that, even."

"Better? How?"

"Put you together with him. Thing is, though, this fella don't wanta get mixed up with no heat."

"Heat?"

"Law."

"But I'm not the police," Marshall protested in a voice gone suddenly near to breathless.

"Yeah, *I* know that. But this fella don't. He thinks people might get the wrong idea, they was to see him rappin' with you. That's just how it is in here. You follow what I'm sayin'?"

"No, I guess I don't. Is this man here?"

"Right out back."

"Will he talk to me?"

"He might, I was to put in a word for ya."

"Now?"

"Whyn't we go out there and see?"

For just a speck of an instant Lester, forgotten in this curious exchange and with nothing to add to it, seemed on the verge of uttering something. Instead he lifted his bottle and took a long swallow. He knew, better than most, what it meant to go out back.

What it meant for Marshall was different only insofar as it was nowhere near so imaginative in conception, though no less startling or painful in execution. He was ushered through the door and out into the alley, this Jimmie person behind him, urging him on. His eyes fluttered, adjusting to the dark; and a towering shape seemed to materialize out of the shadows; and there was a peculiar whooshing sound of some object parting the muggy air, and then the sound of his own astonished grunt as it (what *it* was he couldn't tell: lighter than a bat, heavier than a fist) slammed into his chest, exploding the wind from his lungs. Here it comes again, across the small of the back this time, whipsawing him, buttering his knees. And from across a widening distance he hears the Jimmie voice saying, "Enough with the stick, Tiny"; and in the splinter of a second before he goes down, a hand seizes him by the collar, whirls him about, and flattens his back against a wall. It props him up, that hand, while the other, balled into a fist, delivers a series of short, chopping blows to his head, like a piston pounding, setting his eyes spinning, stars—no, whole galaxies—erupting in gorgeous bursts of light behind them.

"Okay, that'll do," said the Jimmie voice; and the pummeling stopped, but for a final coda of a punch driven with the force of a sledge into his midsection, just beneath the belt line; and he doubled over, gagging, and a blackness seemed to swell up from under his feet and he toppled, face first, onto the gravel's cool stones. A silence filled his punished head. Not for long. From the far side of that blessed silence he heard his name pronounced, upwardly inflected. If he made no attempt at a response, maybe it would go away. A hand grasped a hank of his hair, jerked his head back at a spine-stinging angle. "Mr. Quinn? You hear me? Mr. Quinn?"

Wasn't going away. So he tried to speak, but all his mouth would produce was a foamy drool mingled with the blood leaking from his nose and split lips.

"Mr. Quinn? This your friend Jimmie here. How you feelin'?"

He groaned.

"Not so good, huh."

He was silent.

"See, this little thumpin' you took here, it ain't nothin' like what can happen, you keep pesterin' these boys. So what I'm recommendin' is you take your fuckin' flyers and scoot on outta here. While you still can. You understand what I'm tellin' you?"

Still silent.

The hand tightened, yanked his head into the hollow between his shoulder blades. "Askin' you a question, Mr. Quinn."

Some feeble noises, efforts at words, burbled out of his distended throat.

"Think I heard a yes in there. You hear it, Tiny?"

"Unh-uh," another voice rumbled. "Needs more stompin'."

He tried again, sputtered something approximately the yes they wanted to hear.

"There it is. Sure hope so, anyways. 'Cuz for you it don't get no better'n this, Mr. Quinn. Gets worse. Next time you get your ticket punched."

The grip on his hair was released. His head fell limply. He rolled over onto one side and drew himself into a fetal position. A sound of receding footsteps reached his closing ears.

Lester hung out awhile, finished off his beer, and then when this Quinn fella didn't come back inside, drank his too. No sense lettin' a good brew go to waste. Still a few bucks left outta that ten, buy him another, he showed. Fat fuckin' chance a that. Don't wait up.

Never shoulda been here, first place, fine gentleman like that. Educated. You could tell that right off, way he talked, threads he wore. Don't belong, hooch-hole like this. Fuck, he told him that. That's what he told him.

'Course, what he didn't tell him was what goin' out back can mean, even when he had the chance. So what? No skin off his ass. Ain't his fault. Ain't like he got elected bodyguard to the world, or its conscience. Except the poor fuck come in here lookin' for help, and what he gets is Nick dumpin' on him and then Jimmie shuckin' him there, woofin' like he knows somethin' about the kid, which he already said he didn't. Which was just pure mean, dog ass mean. No call for it. Even that ain't enough, not for Jimmie. He gotta take him out back, God knows why. Maybe just a joke, lead him down the alley, get him turned around. Coulda been that, little joke. Hoped so. But he sure as shit ain't goin' back there, find out. Not this grunt. Once is plenty.

Thirty minutes elapsed. He snuck a couple peeks at the back door. Shut up tighter'n a nun's twat. Nick spotted his empties and came over and demanded, "You goin' drink or hold down that stool?" Lester ordered another. Waited some more. Nobody comin' through that door. Not Jimmie. Not Quinn. Nothin' doin' here, so he sank the last of the brew and hauled himself up and, weaving a little, headed for the other door, front one. Outside, it occurred to him he'd neglected to find a ride home. He was about to go back in, see what he could turn up, when, for reasons he couldn't have explained to himself, he walked instead over to the side of the building, peered into the darkness a moment and then, keeping in the shadows, keeping down, edged his way along the wall, moving cautiously toward the alley out back. And when he came around the corner what he saw—a figure on the ground, rocking a little, moaning softly—impelled him to exclaim, "Ah, Jesus. Look what they done."

From between the fingers laced over his battered face he could see the blurry outlines of a shape looming above him, then stooping toward him, and his first panicked thought was *They're back.* He squeezed himself into a tight ball, shrank from the tentative hand laid on his shoulder. Till a sad, slurry voice whispered, "Just me, man. Lester."

"Lester?" he said, his own voice emerging a sandpaper rasp. "You?"

"Yeah. You okay? Gonna make it?"

"Not sure."

"Anything broke?"

Stiff as an arthritic, Marshall uncoiled his limbs, testing them. Amazingly, they seemed to work. Gingerly, he touched his nose and his cheek and jawbones. "Don't think so," he said.

"Piece a luck. Look like they give you the primo whuppin'."

"Why?"

"That ain't important now. What is, is we get small, both of us, an' before quick. Case they take it in their heads to come back."

"Good idea."

"Think you can get up?"

"Try." He sucked in a wide, dragging breath, but on the exhale a fit of hacking seized him and a froth of blood bubbled to his lips and trickled down his chin.

Lester produced a handkerchief, swiped it away.

"Lemme give ya little boost," he said and slipped his hands under Marshall's arms and tugged him heavily to his feet.

"Thanks. I'll be all right now."

Lester braced him against the wall of the building, took a step back, shook his head doubtfully. "I dunno. You got wheels?"

"What?"

"Car?"

"In front."

"What kind?"

"Volvo. Wagon."

"Gimme the keys."

"Why?"

"I'll go get it. Bring it around back."

Marshall hesitated.

"Just gimme the keys, okay? We gotta move."

He reached into a pocket, handed them over.

"You wait right here, huh? An' hold down the coughin', you can."

"Lester?"

"Yeah?"

"You coming back?"

Over his shoulder Lester said, almost ruefully, "Yeah, I'll be back."

Maybe he would. Had to trust somebody. But as the moments lengthened, Marshall also had to wonder if he'd played the fool again. First his body served up for beating, now his car forfeited. Lori was right. Even Chip was right. He was out of his depth here, should have gone to the police.

He heard gravel crunching. A vehicle, head lamps

out, nosed around the corner of the building and rolled into the alley. He recognized it as his own. Wanted to cheer. It pulled up beside him. The passenger door swung open, and he heaved himself in. "We're outta here, man," Lester said, and he switched on the lights, punched the pedal, and they took off, rubber squealing.

After he'd put enough distance behind them, Lester slowed down, glanced over, and said, "Want me find a, like, hospital? Have 'em take a look at you?"

"No hospitals."

"Where, then?"

"I don't know."

"Could go by my place. Least clean ya up little."

"Whatever."

"That okay with you? Go there?"

"Fine."

They drove awhile in silence, down a maze of back streets, dark and winding. Finally Marshall asked him where they were.

"Almost there. That's Cass up ahead. I'm just couple blocks over, on Chicago."

Cass and Chicago. Lester—last name what?—Caulkins, that was it. Marshall filed these casually dropped bits of intelligence in a corner of his gradually clearing head. Why, he wasn't sure.

They pulled into a parking space outside a grim, stucco-sided three-story. Lester cut the engine, handed Marshall the keys, and announced, "Here we are."

"You live here?"

"This the place. C'mon in."

"Thanks, but I think I'll go on home."

Lester looked at him puzzledly, a trace of hurt in his eyes. "Hey, man, it's safe. I ain't gonna roll ya."

"I didn't mean it that way," Marshall said. "It's just that I'm going to be all right now." He was too. Could feel some of the stiffness easing, even the pain lessening a little, settling into a dull throb.

"You drive okay?"

"I'll make it."

"Sure you don't wanna come in? Wash up, have a beer? Get yourself straight?"

"I'm sure."

Lester shrugged. "Well, guess you the one oughta know."

"What I don't know, Lester, is why they did it."

"What, thrash on you, y'mean?"

"Yes."

"Got me. Like I tol' ya in the bar there, they ain't big on strangers. Remember me tellin' ya that?"

"I remember. But he's got to know something about my son."

"Jimmie, you sayin'?"

"Yes. Why else would he do what he did?"

"Beats shit outta me. But I was you, I'd stay outta his traffic. Dudes he runs with, they don't dick around. I know. Took a trip out back once myself."

"You too?"

"Yeah, me too," Lester said dolefully. "They learned me good. I found out in a hurry, same as you better do." He lowered his eyes, seemed to examine his palms a moment. "Look, I gotta go in now, so—"

"Lester, wait a minute. Please."

"What for?"

"Do you remember the story I was telling you, starting to tell, inside the bar?"

"Which story's that?"

"About the car on the tollway? License plates?"

"Oh, yeah, that one. What about it?"

"Does this Jimmie drive a Mercury, bronze color, AZ in the license?"

"No, Jimmie, he drives a van."

"Van," Marshall said defeatedly.

"Yeah. Bronze Merc, AZ in the plates, that'd be Mike."

Now Marshall gazed at him steadily, all that was left of his spirit gone to his eyes in a tight, searching squint. "Mike?"

"Mike Wazinski. Everybody call him Waz, so he got himself them designer plates on his car. Why?"

Marshall opened the glove compartment, took out the notepad and ballpoint. "Mike Wazinski? That's his name?"

"Yeah, that's it. Why you writin' it down?"

"Because he's the one I'm looking for."

"Mike? Listen, I know Mike. He's cleaner'n a whole pack a Boy Scouts. Sure as hell ain't into baggin' kids."

"That may be. But he, or his wife, girlfriend, some woman—they're involved someway. Know something."

"How come you so sure? Lots a guys drive Mercs out there, Norse."

"But only one with AZ in the license."

"So what's that suppose to mean? I don't get it."

"Doesn't matter, Lester. What I have to do is get to him, this Mike Wazinski. Can you help me?"

"No way, man. Mike ain't no Jimmie, but he ain't no pansy neither."

"All I want to do is talk with him. You say you know him. You could arrange it."

"Can't do it. Sorry."

"But *why* can't you?"

"Why is because I ain't gettin' into this no deeper," Lester declared, his voice lifting agitatedly. "Ain't good for the health. Take tonight. If Jimmie'd seen me with you out behind Nick's there, I'd be in the serious dog poop. I gotta live with these guys."

"I understand," Marshall said resignedly. "You've helped me enough. And I want you to know I appreciate it, Lester. All you've done."

"Forget it. Also my name, you decide to go talkin' to anybody. Forget that too, okay?"

"Okay."

Lester cracked open the door, climbed out of the car, and started away. He paused, turned, and said, "Oh, one other thing."

"What's that?"

"You go sniffin' around anymore, you better cover your back, huh."

"I'll do that," Marshall said.

Her reaction was predictable: paralytic stance, epileptic shudder, skin gone waxen, eyes banjoed in sheer, blank fright, voice—"Oh, God! What have they done to you?"—threaded through with hysteria.

Predictable but understandable, forgivable. A passing glimpse in a hallway mirror revealed a face splotched with purpling bruises and crusted with blood. He shuddered too, but what he said was, "It's not as bad as it looks," and kept on moving, wobbling stiffly toward the kitchen.

She fell in behind, tried to touch him. "Marsh, what happened?"

He waved her away. "Later."

"I'll call Dr. Horton."

"Forget Horton. Don't need a doctor. Need the book."

"Book?"

"Phone book."

He pulled it out of a drawer, slapped it on the counter, flipped to the W's. Mumbling "Wazinski, Wazinski . . . Herman, George, Kenneth," he drew a finger down a column of names, and then, stabbing the page, fairly bawling: "Michael! Wazinski, Michael, Mike Wazinski. That's the one. Got to be him."

"Who? What are you talking about?"

He didn't seem to hear. "Lisle? He lives in Lisle? That's just up the road. They were *that* close? All this time?" He shook his head slowly, truly dumbfounded by the geographic proximity.

"Marsh, please. Talk to me. Please please please please."

He glanced up, saw her standing, forgotten, in the doorway, quivery fists held at her chin, voice trembling now on the edge of tears. "I think I've found them," he said exultantly.

"Found who?"

"That car out on the tollway. Those people."

"You found them?"

"I think so."

"How?"

"Never mind how. I found them. We've got a name now. An address."

"And you?"

"What about me?"

"Look at you. That's what it took to get that name? What they did to you?"

He put a flat palm in the air, a motion of blockage, distancing. "Don't say it, Lori."

"What? Say what?"

"What you're thinking. The P-word. I don't want to hear it. I don't need any police to talk to these people."

Her face began to crumple in that peculiar slow-motion descent into an anguish powerless and vast. A tremor passed through her thin shoulders, followed shortly by the quake of great wrenching sobs.

Marshall sighed. He wasn't up to this. Been enough for one night. Nevertheless, he came over and dutifully took her in his arms. Stroked her hair. Empty of solace and comforting words.

"I can't stand any more of this, Marsh. Jeffie's gone . . . I can't lose you too."

A curious oblique memory surfaced, supplied him with something to say. "Lori, listen to me, now. Listen. Remember when he had that cough, infection, whatever it was? About a year ago?"

She moved her head up and down.

"The doctor said it was nothing, gave him some

medicine. It got worse. Remember? Our helplessness at *his* helplessness?"

"Yes."

"When we got him to Emergency he could barely breathe. They took him into an examination room, told us to wait outside. We did it, we did what they told us to do. And all the time we could hear him screaming behind that door. And when they finally brought him out, remember the look on his face? Accusing, it was. Like we'd abandoned him, betrayed him. The people he loved. Trusted."

She tilted her head back, gazed at him through a wall of tears. "I remember, Marsh."

"Well, he's out there somewhere. Maybe close by. And whenever he thinks about us, that's how he's got to look. Only it's not going to happen again. Not this time. Doctors, police—it's all the same. This time we're not going to abandon him."

But that remembered event, so vivid to him in the telling, was in fact murky as a scene lifted from some long-forgotten film, or a snippet of an overheard story, told by a stranger. And later, lying in bed, overtaken by exhaustion and ache but too wired for sleep, it struck him that an obsession—Lori's term for what had gotten hold of him—may doze awhile but never really sleeps, and that this fanatic search of his had somehow, in a manner too subtle to grasp, become paramount, its object subordinate, and anymore he had trouble even conjuring a clear image of his lost son.

PART
SIX

Punctuality was a virtue prized by Dingo, and so when, punctually at six p.m. the following day, he once again swung his Lincoln into the alley behind the Norseman Lounge and found Jimmie nowhere in sight, a furrow of annoyance creased his smooth brow. He waited, fingers drumming the wheel, engine purring, air in the car tempered to a cool, satiny sheen. Moments passed. No Jimmie. He brought the window down a notch, lit a cigarette, and watched the plumes of smoke drift out into the heat-shimmered light of a dropping sun. To spare himself another trip inside that steamy den of rank sweat and assorted stinks, he'd deliberately phoned ahead, spoken directly with Nick (or as directly as one could speak to a sullen, ignorant Greek), and left explicit instructions for his confederate: six o'clock, out back. Yet the digital clock on the dash read 6:19. Still no Jimmie. He crushed out the cigarette, and a for him uncharacteristic obscenity sprang unbidden to his lips. Six meant six.

And that's exactly what he said to him when, thirteen minutes later, Jimmie came through the back

door (moving, Dingo noticed with no small irritation, at a leisurely pace, a slight forward tilt to his
walk, side-to-side swing built in, the sort of stride
that carries the calculated announcement: Look at
me, I'm cool, I'm bad), strutted over to the car, and
climbed into the front seat, displaying an unapolo-
getic face full of teeth, from which grinning mouth
escaped an odor so noxious Dingo was reminded,
too late, of the air freshener he'd forgotten to pur-
chase: "Six means six, Jimmie."

"Huh?"

"We were to meet at six. Didn't you get the message?"

"Yeah, Nick, he tol' me."

Dingo indicated the dash clock, a wordless rebuke.

"Sorry about that," Jimmie said, but his relentless
grin betrayed little in the way of regret.

"Sorry won't cut it, Jimmie. Not in business. In
business, time equals money."

"Wait'll ya hear why, though. Speakin' a business."

"So tell me."

"Okay," Jimmie told him in a voice quickened by
good news and, sadly for Dingo, dispatched on a
breath so gamy it blighted the air between them,
"reason I'm runnin' little late is because I just wrote
up seven more orders inside there, them Rolies.
Bumps the total to—you ready for this, Dingo?"

"Try me."

"How's a big two-seven-seven crank your engines?"

"Two hundred seventy-seven orders?" Dingo said after him, and only by an effort was he able to contain the elation in his own voice. "You've secured *that* many?"

"That many and countin'. Still got a few grunts left to tap. For sure gonna bust three hundred."

"Three hundred is a nice round number."

"Bet your ass, round. Add it up in your head and you lookin' at the kinda loot we ain't never scored. Not off one hit."

No arguing that. And Dingo needed no prompting to do the mental arithmetic and arrive at a figure so inspiriting, so exhilarating, he had to suppress an impulse almost to cheer. That would be unbecoming, a man of his weight, so what he did instead was reward his partner with a thin smile and some carefully chosen words of praise: "This is splendid work you've done, Jimmie. Most impressive."

Jimmie's ordinarily sallow face seemed to glow from within. Out of Dingo praise was never easy to come by, and he took a moment to bask in its nourishing heat. Only a moment. "That ain't all," he declared pridefully.

"There's more?"

"Oh, yeah. Remember that little pro'lum I was tellin' ya about, other night?"

"Regarding the child?"

"That's the one."

"Indeed I do."

"Well, now y'don't have to. Remember, I'm sayin'. Can scrub it right outta your head."

Dingo looked at him skeptically. "Really. And how exactly is that?"

"That weenie I tol' ya showed up at the plant? One handin' out his missing-squirrel flyers?"

"Yes."

Jimmie gave him a long, ironic wink. "He got his punk card pulled last night. Pulled good. You shoulda seen it, Dingo. You'd've got a hoot outta it."

"I doubt that. I've never much cared for that end of this business."

"Yeah, well, anyways, ain't nothin' to sweat there. He ain't gonna be sniffin' around. Not no more."

"You're sure of that?"

"Hey, bet to it. That one's a cold pack."

Dingo cast an oblique glance at this scruffy, rancid-breathed, street-talking partner of his. A thought, not yet fully formed, was taking shape in a distant chamber of his head. Not a scheme exactly, more of a notion, a fancy. He said generously, "The problem cleared up, three hundred Rolex orders—you've had a productive several days, Jimmie."

"Been some a your better ones," Jimmie agreed, beaming.

"How do you want to take delivery? Any ideas?"

"Yeah, I got some ideas on that," Jimmie allowed, clearly pleased to be in on the planning, for a switch.

"Care to share them?"

"See, we got this plant open house Saturday. Little celebration, like. It's for family and friends, anybody works there, which means just about everybody show up. I'm thinkin' you and me'd meet that morning, say, transfer the goods to my van and—"

"When exactly, and where?" Dingo broke in on him.

"In the lot, visitors' end. I'm gonna be inside awhile, could sneak out, oh, 'bout ten."

"What about distribution?"

"What I'd do is spread the word around they can pick 'em up right there. Get it all done in one shot."

"Is it safe? In the lot there?"

"Watches, they ain't like our other commodities. Be an easy pass outta the van. Look like the toy cops gonna gimme grief, I just bring it down the road a piece."

"Collections? Payment?"

"Strictly cash. Friday's payday, they'll be packin' heavy wallets. Whole thing oughta be wrapped by five bells. You want, we can connect here, split the take."

Dingo considered a moment, could find no flaws in the plan. "Sounds workable, Jimmie."

The arrangements evidently sealed, Jimmie expelled a big, gaseous sigh. "Thirty large each," he said dreamily. "Know what I'm gonna do, mine?"

"What would that be?"

"Get me a bike. Talkin' brand-new Harley here, top a the line. Dressed."

"Dressed? I don't know the term."

"Means all the bells'n whistles," Jimmie explained joyously, and he went on to elaborate in tiresome detail what those accessories included, his bony hand dancing descriptively through the air.

Dingo attended to the raptured recital of this pitiable ambition, but not very closely. That elusive earlier thought—notion, fancy, call it what you will—seemed to be gathering momentum, substance, evolving almost with a will of its own into structure, contour, texture, design.

"So what're you gonna do, yours?" Jimmie asked, the paen to his envisioned cycle run down.

"Uh, what's that?"

"Your half. How you lookin' to spend it?"

"I haven't given it much thought."

"You better. Thirty big dimes, that's a lotta sugar in one lump."

So it was. Though nowhere near the sixty in Dingo's gradually emerging plan. "Maybe I'll invest a part of it in a growth mutual fund," he said.

"That like buyin' them stocks?"

"Something like that."

"Why you wanna do that?"

"To prepare for the future. You should do the same, Jimmie. Plan ahead. Your golden years. Nobody's young forever."

"Not me. Way I look at it, y'never know when the ol' hammer gonna fall. Suck up all the goodies while y'still can, that's my motto. Gonna be a long time dead."

Dingo looked at him appraisingly, a trace of a smile in it, tolerant, mellow, close to charitable and slow to leave his face. "Well," he drawled, "I suppose there's something to be said for that philosophy too."

Marshall was himself operating off something of a plan as, that same evening, he steered his Volvo down a Lisle residential street quieted by the lingering heat, craning his neck and squinting to pick out the numbers posted above the doors of a uniform row of frame ranch houses, borderline shabby, set back from the road by patches of grass scorched a liverish brown. The plan, what there was of it, turned on finding the optimum time and conditions to approach this Mike Wazinski, confront him. Conditions were plain enough: at home ideally, the woman very likely around, children possibly, neighbors, witnesses (last night's lesson not entirely lost on him). Time was trickier. Daylight was essential (another hard lesson learned), and so at first he considered the morning hours, then quickly rejected that notion on the reasonable expectation of a curt rebuff by a grouchy man in a hurry to get somewhere. No, morning wouldn't do. Which left only that narrow window of time between late afternoon and dusk.

And that was the extent of his plan. What to say, how to begin, the words to use, persuasions, he had no idea. Extemporize, he supposed. Wing it. Flimsy plan.

He'd spent the better part of the day in bed, body still stitched with aches but mind racing through a host of fanciful scenarios, faking an exhausted sleep to forestall any more energy-squandering dialogues with his wife. What small energy remained needed conservation, preservation, shelter. None to spare in circular debates.

Mercifully, there'd been none—no arguments, no pleading, no tears—when, a quarter of an hour earlier (the scanty distance between Quinn and Wazin-

ski residences continuing to astonish him), he'd
mumbled a farewell and a vague "Be back soon" on
his way out the door. She merely gazed at him
blankly, eyes sluggish with a resignation hopeless
and final. Said nothing. Retreated, no doubt, to the
sanctuary of a private delirium. He'd have to do
more for her, display more understanding, compas-
sion, generosity of spirit. And he would too. Soon.
Just as soon as this Wazinski matter was settled.

But for now, nerves tingling, anticipation mounting, she was furthest from his thoughts. Absent altogether once he spotted the number he was searching
for. He pulled up at the curb in front of the house.
Surveyed the scene. Plenty of light yet; a neighbor
hosing down a car; across the street a couple of seniors chatting on a porch; thin stream of voices floating from the other side of a screen door at the house
itself; a Ford Escort (though no Mercury) parked in
the driveway. Somebody home for sure, conditions
near to optimal—this was as good as it would get.

He took a leaflet from the stack on the floor,
folded and pocketed it, stepped out of the car, and
approached the door. He peered through the screen,
saw no one. The voices, emanating from somewhere
outside his range of vision, assumed that bogus, studio quality peculiar to television speech. He touched
the bell, waited. Nothing. He hit it again, longer this
time. Over a burst of canned laughter another voice,
breezy, soprano, decidedly non-theatrical, called,
"Hold on a minute, be right with ya."

Faithful to the pledge, a smiley female appeared at
the door a moment later. But the smile instantly col-

lapsed at the sight of his battered face, its flowering bruises ineffectually smudged with talcum powder. She recoiled, said dubiously, "Yeah?"

"Mrs. Wazinski?"

"That's right."

"Your husband is Mike Wazinski?"

"Correct."

"Works at Norse Aluminum?"

"Yeah, he works there. So?"

"Is he home?"

"No, tonight's his—" She broke off, looked at him warily. "Why?"

"I was hoping to speak with him."

"In regards to what? We're not interested in buyin' anything."

"I'm not selling anything."

"So what is it you want?"

Marshall hesitated. Inspected her. Was it the same woman from the toll booth? He couldn't be sure. Time and the net of dust-flecked wire between them blurred his memory of that face. It was roundish, he recalled, like this one, crimson-lipped, brows plucked, eyes hooded in shadow and liner, also like this one. But the hair was silvery blond, close-cropped; this was short, yes, but tawnier, inky at the roots. The neck and shoulders he seemed to remember as pale and soft. Similarly here. The rest of the shape of that other woman was unknown to him, concealed by the car. This one was compact, diminutive, almost stumpy, a vampish abbreviation squeezed into hip-hugging shorts and skimpy halter top, bubble gum pink, revealing an abundance of creamy bosom, slight softening through the middle, thighs that lapped a bit at the knees. The same woman? Impossible to tell.

"You gettin' a good peek?" she said, irritably but with just a shade of coquetry riding the upswing of a heartland twang.

"Sorry," Marshall said. "I didn't mean to stare." And then, come this far, nothing to lose, he added, "But I think we've met before."

"Oh yeah, right."

"Don't you remember me, Mrs. Wazinski?"

"Why should I?" she snapped, all irritation now. "Never laid eyes on you before in my life."

"Yes, you have," he plunged on. "At a toll booth. East-West Tollway. Less than two weeks ago."

" 'Fraid you got me mixed up with some other party. Now, I'm watchin' a show in there, so if you'll—"

Marshall produced the leaflet and flattened it on the screen. "Remember now?"

Her brows lifted. Cheeks paled. A gasp rose to her lips, choked there, inverted itself on a quick gulped breath. She didn't speak. Didn't have to. Her face told it all. She knew.

"This boy is my son. He was ab—he was kidnapped. About three months ago. You or your husband know something about him. You've got to help me."

"Never seen that boy," she declared stoutly. "You either."

"You're not telling me the truth," he said, the words tumbling out in a frantic rush. "You saw me at

that booth. I had this same leaflet, poster-size, in the
window of my car. You looked at it. You recognized
him. You said it. You were there. You're the one."

"You gotta be crazy. Now, I'm sorry about your
kid, but I got nothin' more to say to you."

"Mrs. Wazinski, please, you're the only lead I've
got. If you know something, anything at all, please
tell me."

She glared at him darkly. "What I'm tellin' you,"
she told him, voice hardening, "is to get off this
property. You don't, I'll have to call the police."

"Look," Marshall said, despising the mewling,
beggarly whine creeping into his voice but powerless to erase it, "if you'll help me I promise I'll keep
you and your husband out of it. You won't be impli-
cated in any way. All I want is to get him back, no
questions asked."

"I'm callin' the cops."

She reached over and clicked the latch on the
screen door. The wooden one behind it banged shut,
leaving him standing there, face scored with bewildered indignation. Squashed like an odious bug. He
considered leaning on the bell, or dashing around to
the back, forcing his way inside (shoulder to the
door, the way it was done in the movies), shaking
the truth out of her. But he suspected this was the
sort of woman, spite-struck, deceitful, supremely
malevolent, who might just make good on her threat,
might be summoning the law even as he vacillated.
In the echo chamber of his head he could hear it
now: "This fella shows up at the door, Officer, perfect stranger, talkin' crazy, accusin' me of . . ." Hu-

miliating visions of himself being dragged away, kicking and pleading, frolicked behind his eyes, mocked his forced-entry inspiration. He thought better of it, spun on his heels, crossed the parched lawn in a spring, hopped into the wagon, and gunned it away from the curb.

Where now? He didn't know. Away from here. For the moment. But not home either, not yet. What he needed was solitude, time. Time to digest this stunning new intelligence, deliberate on it, amend his plan. Maybe Lori was right. Now, maybe, was the time to call in Thornton and his vaunted "team." But what, really, did he have? An incriminating expression, was what he had, a swallowed gasp, firm denial. An intuition based on a chance highway encounter that seemed anymore, even to him, as unreal as an hallucination, a dream spawned by a dream, so easily stonewalled, so shot full of evidential holes it crumbled like a castle of sand under a wash of hard, irrefutable fact. No, the police were out. Not till he had something more substantial than this.

He drove aimlessly. Arrived at a street identified as Cass Avenue. A memory surfaced. Cass. Lester somebody. Caulkins. Lester Caulkins. On an impulse he turned north, crawled along watching the signs. At the intersection of Cass and Chicago he swung right. There it was, the Lester building, unmistakable in its squalid, stuccoed grimness. He parked the Volvo in the same space it had occupied last night. Sat there a moment. What he was doing here, he didn't fully understand. Some instinct, mysterious as the symmetrical formations of a flock of birds in flight, unerring as their direction. Something to do with his elastic plan.

He got out of the car, walked to the entrance, checked names and numbers on a file of mailboxes set into a scarred plaster wall just inside the door. Lester Caulkins, 2-C. He climbed stairs covered with a filigree of powdery dust. The banister felt greasy to his touch. He went down the second-floor hallway, narrow, constricted, dark as a tomb, and found 2-C. Silence from behind the door. No bell. He knocked. More of the silence. He tried again. Nothing. Nobody home. Stalled again, though from what, precisely, he couldn't begin to say. He returned to the car. Eventually everyone had to come home, even Lester. He waited, not so much from stubbornness as out of some baffling necessity, contorted and fierce.

The sun departed in a gorgeous fireworks of color. The night advanced. Stars, those violent eruptions of lethal gases traveling across unimaginable distances and eons of time, speckled a gradually blackening sky. Like those counterfeit stars, needles of light projected onto the vaulted dome of a planetarium a thousand years ago, in another life. This present life of his seemed little more than a gauzy mist of nights sliding into days into nights again, the way one borderless dream will flow crazily into the next, and then the one after that. Riddles stacked on riddles, the solution to one the birth of another. A curious numbness seized him, a detachment eclipsing all the remembered sorrows and guilts, and he waited, unconscious of his teeth noisily chattering in spite of the durable heat, rattling the bones in his fevered skull.

The interior of his own skull pitched in inebriate fog, blood-alcohol level skirting perilously near the stupefaction zone, the absent Lester was, just then, reeling through the hump day crowd at the Norseman Lounge, spinning his whimsical tales, theories, opinions, sentiments, philosophies, and antic jests to anyone foolhardy enough to listen. Which supply of audiences was rapidly dwindling when, happily for him, he spied Beans and Vic in the back, and he weaved over and slid uninvited into their booth. "Hey, fartman, cholo. What's up?"

Beans, seated next to him, elevated a cheek and expelled a blast, presumably in wordless welcome. Across the table Vic scowled, muttered cryptically, "Nothin' up. All down."

Lester blinked the dour, mud-brown face into a semblance of focus, nudged Beans. "Nothin' up. All down."

"Ain't his ass got burned," Beans drawled, indicating the bandage-swathed thumb of Vic's right hand.

"Holy shit. What happen, Vic?"

"Like he say. Burn it."

"How?"

"Work."

"I figured that. Askin' how, not where."

"Don't matter. It's done."

"Hurt, does it?"

"Hurt wallet," Vic said sourly.

"Wallet? How's that?"

Vic's bandaged hand brushed the air impatiently.

"He got some vehicles suppose to tune up," Beans explained. "Can't work on 'em till the thumb's okay."

"Tough break," Lester allowed. "Oughta heal up quick, though, 'less he got a dog. You got a dog, Vic?"

"Yeah, got a dog."

"Whatever y'do, don't let him no place near it."

"Near what?"

"Your thumb there."

Vic glowered at him. To Beans he said, "Fuck he talkin' about?"

Beans shrugged.

"Fuck you talkin', man, dogs?"

Lester propped his elbows on the table, laid his chin in the palm of a hand, gazed at Vic as steadily as he was able. "I knew this fella once, done the same thing you done, only to his toe. Burned it, I'm sayin'."

"Oh, Jesus," Beans groaned. "Another goddam story."

"Listen," Lester said earnestly, "this one's important, Vic wants to keep his thumb."

"He burned it, fucknuts. Y'don't lose a thumb off a burn."

"This guy did. His toe, I mean. An' he had a dog too, just like Vic."

"What's dog gotta do with burn?" Vic asked, annoyed but still interested in anything remotely relevant to his painful injury.

"See, he's livin' in a trailer, this fella, one a them tin ones, tiny, everything packed in tight. His dog, it's a big sucker, them kind grow almost pony size, got all that shaggy fur on 'em."

"What breed's that?" Beans wanted to know.

"Forget the name. Them ones they use up in the mountains, carry that little whiskey keg around the neck. Y'know, help out people get lost in a snowstorm."

"That's a Saint something you're thinkin' of. They're big, but they don't grow to no pony size."

"Mine's little," Vic said. "Mutt."

"Size don't matter none. Comes to what I'm gonna tell ya, all dogs the same."

"So tell," Vic growled.

"Okay," Lester began again. "This fella—can't place his name—happen way back, I was just a kid—anyway, he's playin' with his pooch, wrestlin' around in the trailer there, got no shoes or socks on, and damn if he don't burn his big toe on a space heater. It's winter, see, which is why the heater's runnin'"

"Must be hard up for tail," Beans guffawed, "this buddy yours. Wrestlin' a dog."

"Wasn't no buddy. Just a guy I knew. Besides, it was a he-dog."

"Fag maybe. Liked them doggie chocolate speedways. Tight."

"Sound like you talkin' from experience, Beanbag."

"Mine's a she," Vic said.

'He, she," Lester insisted, "still don't matter, point I'm tryin' to make here."

"We waitin' on it. That point."

"Where was I at?"

"Burned toe."

"Yeah, right. Toe. So he puts some goop on it, that ointment they use, and first thing he knows the pooch is lickin' on it. Toe, I mean. Guy swats him, don't think no more about it. But all day long, every chance he gets, dog's lickin' away at that torched toe."

"Too bad he didn't burn his dick," Beans said with a sly wink, beady eyes glittering in their wrinkled nests. "Get that hound trained, wouldn't need no pussy ever again, his whole life."

Lester uncradled his chin, threw up his hands. "Listen, this is serious shit, what I'm sayin' here. Could be the difference Vic got a thumb or don't. You wanna hear it?"

"Yeah yeah yeah."

"Vic? You?"

Out of Vic a brusque affirmative nod.

"Okay," Lester resumed yet again, "guy goes to bed that night, wakes up next mornin', looks down an' sees the dog lappin' on his foot. Also sees blood all over the covers. He's thinkin' somethin' funny goin' on, somethin' ain't right. So he yanks 'em back, covers, an' eyeballs his foot an' it's all bloody too. Looks for his toe and it ain't there, just a stump where it suppose to be."

"Wait a minute," Beans put in. "You sayin' the dog ate his toe?"

"Scarfed it right up," Lester affirmed, and he laid his hands dramatically on the table, signaling a conclusion to the cautionary tale.

"Aah, that's horseshit. Never happen. Dog start eatin' your toe, you'd feel it, sleepin' or not."

"Oh, part I forgot to tell ya, this fella got that disease, that di-beet-eez, where y'don't feel nothin' in your body, like normal. Which is how come he don't wake up when the dog's chewin' on the toe."

"I don't got that," Vic said.

"Got what?"

"That disease you say."

"Yeah, I know y'don't, Vic. But supposin' you was to get blitzed some night. Like tonight here, you been sloshin' up a few. Come home blotto, zonk out, next thing y'know they callin' you nine-finger Victor."

"Had five beers, is all."

"Been more'n that," Beans corrected him.

"There y'are," Lester said ominously. "I was you, I'd lock the mutt up tonight, keep him locked till that thumb's right."

"It's a her."

"Dog's a dog."

Vic's brown jaws ground thoughtfully. He glanced at the full bottle of beer in front of him. Didn't reach for it.

"You don't wanta pay no attention," Beans assured him, "any this horseshit. Dogs don't eat people. Least not your live ones." With a chortling laugh he added, "An' you ain't dead yet, last I looked."

"Listen," Lester declared urgently, "dogs'll eat

anything, 'specially if it's rotted, gives off stink. You ever notice how they always sniffin' around piss, puke, flop? Walk in a room an' where they head for first? Your crotch is where. Bend over, they got their nose in your ass." He paused, fastened a bleary gaze on Beans. A thought seemed to occur to him. "You got a dog?" he asked.

"Me? No. Why?"

"Lucky for you. You did, he'd've chewed you a new asshole, all that poison gas leakin' out it."

"Carve *you* a new one," Beans snorted disgustedly, "you don't quit jackin' your mouth off, worryin' Vic with your dogdick stories."

"Tellin' ya what can happen."

"Only place it happen is that sauced head yours."

"My dog never do that," Vic averred.

Lester rolled over helpless palms, a sotted Cassandra, prophecies forever spurned.

"Gotta go," Vic announced, getting abruptly to his feet.

"Take a whiz go," Lester asked him, "or home?"

"Home."

"You maybe gimme a lift?"

"Far as Cass. Ain't takin' you all the way."

"Cass be good."

"No more dog talk, I do."

"You got 'er, Vic."

"C'mon."

On their way out the door Lester ventured tentatively, "You wanna hear 'bout that time I was at the license plate office?"

"No."

Twenty minutes later, the license plate story still untold, Lester came tottering, stagger-drunk, through the narrow parking lot fronting his apartment building. He seemed to hear a voice calling his name. Real? Imagined? Couldn't tell. He cocked his head, peered into the dark.

"Lester?"

Persuaded it was real, he called back, "Whozat?"

A figure emerged cautiously from a band of shadow. "Me," it said. "Marshall Quinn."

"Who?"

The figure came closer. "Last night. Remember?"

Lester's face burst into a ruddy grin. 'Course he remembered: dude got his melon thumped, over to the Greek's. He lifted a hand in a sloppy salute. "Hey, Mr. Quinn. C'mon up, have a brew."

Buck stood with his buttocks taut, knees pressed together and slightly bent, shoulders bunched, sighting down a ball held high and tight to his flank, a knot of focused concentration, all the intensity squeezed into his eyes. Suddenly he sprang forward, simultaneously arcing his arm back and up, then sweeping it out ahead of him, rocketing the ball down the lane. For a man of his bulk he moved with remarkable speed and a grace near to balletic. Poised there in the shred of a second before the violent collision of ball and pins, balanced on one bent leg, he looked rather like a limber dancer frozen in the execution of some intricate, inventive step. Nine of the pins vanished on an explosive *whap;* the tenth teetered for an instant of unendurable suspense.

When at last it toppled, Buck punched the air and boomed jubilantly, "Aw*right*!"

Waz, seated at the scoring table, made a pained face and grumbled, "Dumb luck."

"Luck got nothin' to do with that one. You see the spin on that ball?"

"Spin on this," Waz said, presenting an extended middle finger.

They were serious bowlers, but good-humored ragging was part of their ritual. To keep their skills honed for the winter leagues they practiced religiously, once a week, at a Westmont alley. It was their night out. Also an excuse to soak up a few cold ones, forget the plant and the grinding labor and the heat and the insistent obligations of the onerous business of living, all of them erased for a wink of time in the mindless rhythms of the game.

Of the two, Buck was the more expert. His average hovered around the low two hundreds, though once, years back, he'd rolled a perfect game. What a night that one was! He remembered it yet, all its particulars, vividly: the unnatural calm come over him as the strikes piled up; the mechanic efficiency of his body, like his joints were lubricated; the sense of, well, supreme harmony. What a night. Easily among the finest in his life.

Buck liked bowling. He liked its subtle angles and fluid motions governed by the iron laws of physics and geometry. Unlike pool, say (at which he was an occasional and indifferent player), it required a certain physical presence, a contained, channeled force. There was a kind of artless simplicity to bowling, a comforting either-or quality, utter absence of cunning or guile. Pool, he decided, slouching now on the spectator bench and draining off the last of his brew, was a game for nimble hustlers, pricks. For the likes of the Jimmie Jerkoffs of this world. Which intrusive thought he shoved from his malt-mellowed consciousness and returned his attention to the game at hand.

Waz was setting up for the final roll of the final frame of the series, a tricky alignment of three pins left standing. His approach was vigorous, but his swing was awkward, follow-through a little stiff. He fired a sidewinder that skimmed off two of the pins, wobbled the third but left it upright, denying him the spare crucial to his score. He thwacked his forehead, groaned miserably.

"Look like you just ain't up to the competition tonight," Buck gloated.

"Ain't the competition, it's my wrist. Sprained it at work today."

"Yeah, right."

"Hey, I'm tellin' ya the facts here."

"Whatever you say, buddy."

"You try it, rollin' off a gimp wrist."

"Sounds like sour owl shit to me."

"Wait'll next time."

They changed shoes and walked over to the counter. Both of them reached for their wallets, but Buck produced his first and handed the attendant some bills. Waz looked puzzled. "Whadda ya doin'? We split it."

"Not this time. I'm buyin'."

"How come?"

"I owe you."

"For what?"

"I dunno. Don't sweat it."

"That ain't right, you payin'. All them lines."

"For bein' a pushover, then. Okay?"

Waz shrugged. "That's how you want it. But I'm poppin' for a road-loosener. No arguments."

"Maybe do one more," Buck agreed.

They took a table in a corner of the bar adjacent to the lanes. A waitress, at Waz's direction, brought over two drafts. For a while they analyzed their games, traded advice and opinion, sniped at each other with easy, waggish jests. Then the talk slackened, ran down. Waz slumped back in his chair, gave his extrusive globe of belly, only tenuously restrained by a ton of belt buckle, a contented thump. "Long day," he allowed, to put something into the lengthening silence.

Buck nodded.

"Wears a man out."

Buck leaned over the table and drew circles in a tiny puddle of unmopped beer. For reasons he could neither comprehend nor, if asked, explain, the image of a pool table, its smooth green surface randomly strewn with balls, came back to him. "Listen," he said, tracking an elusive chain of thought unsealed by that troubling image, "want you to know I appreciate it, what you done."

Waz, caught off balance by this opaque remark, said, "What, buy you a beer?"

A disagreeable figure materialized at the pool

table behind Buck's eyes, chalked his stick, and sank all the balls in a single fantastic shot. "Talkin' to him," Buck said.

"Who?"

"You know who."

"You sayin' Jimmie?"

"Who else?"

"Wasn't nothin'. Glad to help."

"To me it was."

"No, what I mean is, I always figured there was nothin' to it. Just Della blowin' smoke out her ass."

"Still had me plenty worried there."

"Well, it's settled now. You can forget about it."

"Got you to thank for that. All of it. Whole thing. You been with me on this from the start."

Waz studied the swell of his belly. He didn't know where to look. It made him acutely uncomfortable, all this gratitude, praise. Had to wonder how much of it he had coming, if the matter was in fact settled. Hoped to Christ it was. To back away from this prickly topic he asked, "You, uh, change your mind on the open house?"

"No, I'm takin' some time off next week. We're goin' up to the Dells."

"No kiddin'. Well, that'll be good, gettin' yourself outta the oven awhile."

"Be good for Norma and the boy too."

"When you leavin'?"

"Saturday."

"Myself, I'm gonna work that day. Can use the o-t."

"You understand why it is we're skippin' the open

house. Della and all. It's nothin' personal, Waz. I like her, always have. Same with Norma."

" 'Course I understand. Who knows Della better'n me?"

"Maybe next year. Let things cool down a little."

Waz raised his glass in a toast. "Here's to next year. You and Norma and the boy. All the good times ahead."

Buck lifted his. "Here's to friends."

They clinked glasses and drank. And though both of them seemed relaxed in the secure warmth of good fellowship, neither, in his private thoughts, could shake the vaguely alarming sense of something still slightly off-center, unresolved yet, some mischief due.

But for Norma, that evening, there was only the comforting sense of abundance that grocery shopping will sometimes inspire, the warm security of pantry and refrigerator and freezer stocked full, the way the pioneers must have felt after a bountiful harvest, provisions laid in against the long, bleak winter ahead. Wednesday, Dale's bowling night, was her routinely scheduled time for this agreeable duty, and so directly after supper she and Davie drove to the Jewel on Ogden and steered a cart through its aisles, up one and down the next, Norma testing produce with a keen touch and practiced eye, sifting through the calculated dazzle of products carefully, prudently, taking pains to explain the rationale behind her choices, turning their pleasant little outing into a learning experience ("You see, Davie, Grape Nuts don't have any sugar, and they taste just as good as Cap'n Crunch, better even"). Not that he required any convincing or persuasion. Not this child. He never argued, never whined, demanded nothing. It was strange, all that meek obedience, almost eerie, but she tried not to think about it. Time and familiarity and affection would eventually change all that. All he needed was the healing balm of love, and for Norma that was a commodity in plentiful supply.

Later, at home, he helped unload the sacks of groceries, handing over cans and cartons and watching her arrange them neatly on the shelves. As reward, she opened a freezer package of Mr. Cookie Face ice cream sandwiches and removed two, one for each of them. "I think we've earned these, don't you? All that shopping we did?"

He didn't seem to know how to respond to this, so he said nothing.

Norma tried again. "You were really a big help to Mom, you know that? I couldn't have managed without you."

He gave her a small, uncertain smile. A smile was a start.

"Are you tired?"

He shook his head negatively.

"Excited about our trip?" she asked him, a question requiring some sort of reply.

"Trip?"

"To the Dells. Remember? Next Saturday. Just three days away."

He looked puzzled, as though the concept of a

Dells was still foreign to him, outside his capacity to grasp.

Norma hesitated a moment. Considered. They had never spoken to him of Sara. Maybe now was the time. "Would you like to see some pictures of where we're going? All the things we're going to do?"

"Uh-huh."

"Okay, Mr. Cookie Face, finish up your ice cream and I'll show you."

Violet bands of sunset seeped through the window and fell across the living room floor. They sat side by side on the couch, the Dells album laid out on Norma's lap, a thin film of dust on its cover. It was not an album she could bring herself to look at often. But she'd offered and he was waiting—no retreating now. She turned the pages slowly, explaining each photo, locating it in space and time and memory, relating it to their own upcoming adventure. As with all her collections of memories, this one was meticulously ordered, a start-to-finish visual record of a trip taken, it seemed, in another century by travelers masquerading as themselves: someone who appeared to be an exuberantly grinning Dale loading bags into the trunk of what was then their car; a Wisconsin souvenir shop they'd stopped at somewhere along the way, Janesville, it was, if she remembered right, probably still there; a woman who looked remarkably like herself, younger version, standing at the entrance to their motel, also smiling, also free of care, blissfully ignorant of all the terrors gathering just outside the borders of this framed blink of experience.

Davie leaned over, the better to see in the paling light, and at the first appearance of Sara (a shot of her in ruffly green bathing suit at the top of the water slide, secure in her father's strong grip, face crinkled in a compound of expectation and fear and glee, poised for the plunge) he asked with a child's blunt curiosity, "Who's she?"

"That's our little girl," Norma said, unwilling even yet to think of her in the past tense.

"Girl?"

"Yes."

"What's her name?"

"Sara. She's your sister."

He lifted his eyes from the picture, gazed at her baffledly. "She live here?"

"Not anymore," Norma said, a small catch in her voice.

"Where she go?"

"With Jesus."

"Where?"

"Jesus took her to heaven."

Now confusion came into those bewildered eyes, a fear utterly unlike that on the image of Sara's face, not a trace of glee in it. "Is Jesus the mean man?"

"No no no, Jesus is a good man. Kind man."

"Why he take her, then?"

Why? A question she'd struggled with for six long years and for which there was still no adequate answer. "I guess He needed her to be with Him," she said. It was the best she could do.

"He take me?"

She put an arm around his shoulders, this frail,

frightened child of hers, drew him in close, stroked his hair. She felt such a density of conflicting emotions her heart seemed tugged in a thousand directions. Too many feelings, too many directions. "No one's going to take you away from us, Davie. Ever. Not even Jesus."

"Why you cry?" he asked her worriedly.

"Because I'm happy," Norma said, dabbing moist eyes. "Because we're going back to the Dells. Because I've got you."

Curiously enough, another woman in another living room, not that distant, was at that same moment viewing a similar procession of images from the past. Only animated, hers were, flickering across a television screen, images sprung to seeming life, moving, gesturing, speaking, prancing, mugging for the camera. It had seemed such an extravagance then, a camcorder. Extravagance for them, newlyweds, graduate students scraping by on poverty-line fellowships, staring down penny-pinching years of degree collecting. But Marsh had insisted ("A visual history of our lives," was how he justified it, "to prove to our grandchildren we were once capable of youth") and now Lori was not sure she was sorry that he had. Not glad—for what exactly did it prove, these shadowland simulations of themselves?—but not unhappy either. Watching them was like summoning blurred memories of an exotic foreign country visited long ago, but only briefly and only once, traveled through and left behind forever.

She would pick a tape randomly from the stack in

the cabinet by the television, slide it into the VCR's portal, hit a play button and set the players in motion, and when she'd seen enough replace it with another. A disordered panorama, without sequence or chronology. There was their tiny, Goodwill-furnished apartment in a shabby neighborhood appropriately called Dinkytown just off the University of Minnesota campus; and there her husband bent over a desk, cramming for some exam, as he seemed perpetually to be doing in those days. Next came Jeff's birth, the glaring lights of a delivery room, jerky scramble of figures, clash of voices calling instructions and encouragement, her own pained yelps and grunts, an infant's wail, Marsh's spontaneous declaration of boundless love, his camera forgotten in the joy of the moment, focused on the floor. Enough of that.

Skipping backward in time, Marsh again, marching stiffly across a stage, accepting the ribbon-wrapped symbol of his achievement: Dr. Quinn at last. And later, still in black robes, wisecracking to some off-camera voice, "What do you call me now? Oh, call me irresistible." And herself, similarly attired, same occasion, clutching her own certificate of wisdom, face bathed in a glow of pride, eyes innocent and untouched by any experience outside the pages of books. Lori Quinn, Master of Arts. But what art? Contemporary European Literature, the diploma said, but what did all those dusty volumes have to say to her now, and how much mastery had she acquired over the confounding vagaries of life?

Maybe the ghost of her father, petitioned from the

grave, had the answer. She cut off the graduation
tape, its celebrative air suddenly wearisome, and
found another labeled Parents' Visit, July '92. Its
first scene was a crowded O'Hare concourse, the
two aged voyagers emerging through a gate, her
mother with the startled, imploring look of the unseasoned traveler, dissolving in a squeal of relief at
the sight of Jeff toddling toward her, gathering him
up in arms grown round and spongy from a lifetime
of hosting church potluck suppers. Not so her father,
that lank, gray, hollow-chested man, always so conscious of who he was, so sure of a guiding presence
hovering over him: limp hand clasp for Marsh, chilly
formal hug for her, was as much as he could muster
in the way of greeting. Segue into that staple of
home videos, the barbecue scene. There was Marsh
firing up the grill, not without difficulty; herself in
gauzy pink dress dispensing lemonade all around;
Jeff, with a child's instinct for loosened discipline,
performing for his grandparents, his frisky acrobat-
ics and high, piping voice ("Watch this, Grampa,
backward somersault!") raising even a thin, indulgent smile from a man conditioned by the gravity of
his calling seldom to smile.

And watching him now, hearing again the measured rhythms of his pulpit-polished voice, she
seemed to see the world through his stern Calvinist
eyes, a fallen place haunted by sin and beyond any
hope of redemption but for the capricious whims of
an impenetrably remote deity: You're saved, you're
not. Like those death camp wardens determining the
fate of their victims at a casual glance and with an

arbitrary flick of a thumb: left column labor camp,
right gas. "God help you, Father—" she heard herself mumbling aloud, not in prayer or supplication so
much as faintly voiced desire to work her way
around some formidable, oppressive obstacle—
"wherever you are . . . and Jeff . . . and Marsh. . . ."
And having uttered last her husband's name—the
only one of that male threesome real to her anymore—she was struck suddenly by just how much
there was left to lose. And with that stunned recognition it was as if a spell had been lifted only to be displaced by another, darker spell.

She touched the stop button and the screen blackened, all its chimerical players vanished. All of
them. With a peculiar, drug-swamped mix of panic
and serenity and immense fatigue, she pushed herself up out of the chair, crossed the room, and
climbed the stairs. In the bathroom she studied her
mirrored reflection, a face scarcely recognizable, at
once gaunt and puffy, sorrow-etched shadows under
the eyes. A liberating thought came to her, more fanciful notion than decision or resolve. For a moment
she hesitated, vacillated. And then something in her
relaxed, let go of fear and grief, and, mindful of the
substantial cost in palpable pain soon to follow, as
early as the first light of morning, she opened the
cabinet over the sink and removed the pills bottle
and emptied its contents into the stool, a chain of red
beads departing in a watery swirl.

"Place little messy."
"That's all right."

"Gonna have to clean 'er up one a these days. Saturday maybe . . . no, that's open house, gotta work. One a these days."

"Don't worry about it."

"So how you feelin' tonight?"

"Not so good, Lester."

"You oughta go see a doctor. Get that face fixed."

"That's not the problem."

"Don't be so sure. Could get, y'know, infected. Or scarred. Like I was tellin' this fella just now, tonight here, burned his thumb, see, watch out for the dog, I sez, tryin' to tell him, nobody listen . . ." The head began sagging toward the chest, nodding, nodding, the words trailing away in slurry mumble.

"Lester?"

"Huh?"

"Don't fall asleep on me."

"I ain't sleepin'."

"Good. I need to talk to you."

"What about?"

"My son."

They were seated opposite each other, Lester precariously perched, swaying slightly, on the edge of his hide-a-bed, Marshall on a cloth-covered not-so-easy chair, its fabric stained and tattered. A TV tray was set up between them, makeshift dining table bearing two cans of beer, two unwashed knives, a nearly depleted jar of Cheez Whiz, and the pale film of gritty dust that seemed permanently settled over every surface of the cramped room like a shower of volcanic ash.

Lester reached for one of the knives, and with a

decelerated deliberateness scraped the bottom of the jar. He paused, blinked up smilingly. There was a malarial cast to the whites of his eyes, not all that far off the color of the glutinous spread clinging to the blade. "Help yourself," he urged.

"No thanks."

"Gotta eat."

"We have to talk, Lester."

" 'Bout your boy?"

"Yes."

"Still lookin' for him, are ya?"

"Yes."

"How's that goin'? Any luck?"

"Not yet."

Lester brought the cheese-smeared blade to his lips, licked it clean. He chewed thoughtfully. A confusion of images—charred thumbs, dogs, lost kids, toes, beatings—jostled in his head. "Sorry hear that," he said.

"You can help me, Lester."

"Me?"

"You."

"How'm I gonna do that?"

"Do you remember telling me about this friend of yours? Mike Wazinski?"

"Ol' Wazzer. Givin' me ride into work, y'know, till I get me another set a wheels. Good man."

"I'm sure he is. But I went to his house today. Tried to talk to his wife. When she heard what it was about, she slammed the door in my face."

A curtain of alarm fell across the rheumy eyes. "Went to his house? Why'd ya do that? You didn't say I was the one tol' you?"

"No."

"You don't wanna go botherin' Waz. He's straight."

"They know something, Lester. She won't talk to me, and it's plain he's not going to either. Not at his house. But if I could get to him inside the plant, he'd have to listen."

"*In*side the plant? Ain't nobody don't work there can get inside."

"That's where you come in."

"Me? How?"

"You have an ID to get in? Badge?"

"Badge."

"Let me use it."

Lester slapped the air. "Use my badge? No way! They'd bounce me for sure, I was to do that."

"I'll pay you. Whatever I can. All I've got."

"Can't do it."

"I need your help, Marshall pleaded. "You're the only one left."

"Look, man, I know how y'feel, but—"

"No, you don't!" Marshall interposed fiercely. "Even if you could, knowing's not understanding. It's not the same."

"Maybe not. But I know it wasn't Waz touched you up. Was Jimmie. An' if he's in this, I don't wanna be no place in the vicinity. You either. Get crossways with guys like him an' they send you home with your nuts in a paper bag."

"Maybe they will," Marshall conceded, speaking gravely now, patiently, the flash of anger throttled, adapting tone and vernacular to his audience. "But the way I see it, Lester, you do bad things, bad things get done to you. That's all right. For us, it's all right. You and me, Lester, we're grown-ups. We get just about what's coming to us. What we've earned. Maybe that's how it's supposed to be."

Marshall wasn't sure where it was going, this meandering lecture, come to him spontaneously but with a certain detached quality too, the verbal levitation of an actor delivering lines committed to memory, or a shrewd pitchman closing a sale. He pushed on, investing his words with earnest emotion, letting them lead him: "But not kids, Lester. Think about it. They're not like us. Look at them. They've still got a foot in heaven. If there's anything innocent left in this sorry world, it's them."

Lester stared at the frayed carpet. Said nothing.

"Lester?"

"Yeah?"

"Look at me."

Slowly, reluctantly, the eyes lifted. Marshall held them with a level, probing gaze. Finally Lester murmured, "Might be I could help little."

"You'll let me use it? Your badge?"

"Badge won't work. Got my picture on it, an' you'n me don't look nothin' alike."

"How, then?"

"There's this open house Saturday, show off the plant. Just for friends an' family, though, grunts that work there. Gotta have a ticket, get in. Could maybe scare you up one."

"Would you do that?"

"Yeah, I can do that," Lester said and he did, removed a worn, discolored wallet from a hip pocket, fumbled through it, found a ticket, and slid it across the tray. "That'll getcha inside."

"Thank you, Lester."

He gave a limp, doleful shrug. "Got nobody else give it to. Got no family. An' I guess we're sorta like friends now, huh?"

"More than that."

"Waz a friend too. Don't want you givin' him no grief."

"All I'm going to do is talk with him."

"How come you think he knows somethin' 'bout your kid?"

"It has to do with his license plate, Lester. It's a long story."

"I got time."

"Some other time," Marshall said, pocketing the ticket and coming to his feet.

"Speakin' a that, license plates, I ever tell ya what happen, I go to get mine renewed?"

"No, but I have to—"

"C'mon, sit a minute. Won't take long. It's real comical."

Marshall sighed. Sat. Figured he owed him that much.

"See," Lester began, "what happens is I show up at the office there thinkin' to just pay my money, get the plates, get gone. Only it don't work that way. Ain't gonna be that easy. There's this lady behind the counter, mean mother, crabby, real skag too, look like a good fuck croak her. Anyways, she looks at my papers there, sez it's time I gotta take all them tests again. Y'know ones I'm talkin' about? Eyes, them road rules?"

"I know the tests."

"Well, eyes I did good. See around a corner and up a skirt, I wanna look hard enough. It's that other part, rules, I know right off gonna snag me up. Ain't like I studied or nothin'. Take one look at all them trick questions an' I'm thinkin', Holy shit, Lester, you in the hot soup now."

"So what did you do?" Marshall asked, to hurry the story along.

Lester grinned slyly. "What I done was I seen this dude takin' same test, real intelligent-lookin' gentleman, wears a suit. Figured if anybody know the answers, oughta be him, right? So I moseys on over, them stand-up tables they got, where ya do the writin', an' crowds in close, this fella. See, what I'm hopin' is to get just enough right, pass the test, so every chance I can I lift 'em, answers, I'm sayin', off his sheet an' copy 'em down on mine."

"Using your keen vision?" Marshall said, more patronizing and ironic than he'd intended.

"Huh?"

"You mentioned your eyes were good."

"That's right. Tell ya, come in handy too. Saved my ass."

"So you passed the test?"

"Flyin' fuckin' colors. Except while I'm takin' it I peeks up once and catch the lady at the counter there eyeballin' me good, got a look on her face like she got her first taste a dick an' don't like it one little bit. So what? I'm thinkin', can't prove nothin'. I go on over and give her my sheet and she checks it out and goddam if I ain't got 'em all right. Perfect score."

He paused significantly, as though awaiting an endorsement or a round of applause. Marshall looked puzzled. "I seem to be missing the point."

"That's 'cuz I ain't got there yet. Best part's comin' up. She's all hacked, see, knows I nicked the answers but nothin' she can do about it. Know what she sez?"

"What?"

"'Got 'em all right, did ya?'" he mimicked, pitching his voice a strident harpy squawk. "'Mr. Perfect? Okay, perfect, step on over here and put your toes on the line.' She's pointin' at where they take your picture," he explained, "an' way she's hollering everybody in the whole place lookin'. Got a voice on her like a bullhorn, an' by now she so pissed the steam comin' out her ears.

"'Give us a perfect smile,'" he went on, back in harpy timbre now. "'See about perfect, then. You maybe get 'em all right on the test, but you're still a rotten little cheat and you're *still ugly*!' Ain't that somethin'?" he concluded, bursting into a sniggery little laugh that gradually inflated, and he rocked back and forth on the bed, suffocated with mirth, shoulders twitching, face pinking, a wetness welling in his eyes.

Marshall watched him curiously. Waited for it to run down. "What did you do?" he asked.

"Whaddaya mean?"

"Did you call her supervisor? Complain?"

"Why'd I do that?"

"Because you don't have to take that kind of treatment. Not from some spiteful, insolent clerk."

"Why not? She knew I was cheatin'. Had me dead to rights. An' like you just said, do somethin' bad, it gonna come back on ya. Remember sayin' that?"

"I remember," Marshall said. And because it seemed important somehow to know, he asked him, "Why did you decide to help me, Lester?"

"I dunno. Felt bad for ya, s'pose, your kid. I been on that end myself, manner a speakin'. Was a orphan. No folks. Grew up in them homes they dump ya in."

"I see. I'm sorry."

"Wasn't so bad. Worked out okay. I'm doin' just fine now."

A silence opened. Lester grinned meagerly, examined his palms. To Marshall's inspecting eye he looked suddenly smaller and, for all his pudgy roundness, pitifully frail. "I want you to know I appreciate it," he said. "All you've done for me."

"Forget it."

"I'm going to have to leave now, Lester."

"Yeah, gettin' late."

"Maybe I'll see you Saturday."

"Ain't likely. Big plant."

"Well, we'll talk again sometime."

"Sure."

Marshall rose and moved toward the door.

"Mr. Quinn?"

"Yes?"

"You ain't finished your beer. Wanna take it along?"

"You drink it."

"Drive careful now, hear?"

Driving away carefully, as advised, already busily plotting his strategy for the Saturday upcoming, Marshall still found it impossible to erase totally the image of that hapless, witless orphan, alone in a deplorably shabby room, in the world. And it occurred to him, with a twinge of guilt, just how calculated it all had been, his seemingly halting plea for help, almost as though it had been lifted, like Lester's lifted rules of the road, from some yellowing lecture notes, or the pages of the book that recorded the tale of his own vanished childhood, its mourned innocence outlived and irretrievably gone. And though he drove with the confidence inspired by a sense of destination, he was not unmindful of another, more disturbing sense of vast distances yet to cross.

Like Marshall, Dingo was pondering the future that evening, though he too was distracted by a persistent image, unsummoned and unwelcomed, flickering on the outskirts of his consciousness. Curiously, unaccountably, it was a visualization of his partner vexing him, not so much the rodent face and stringy form as the obnoxious swagger, witnessed only a few short hours ago and intruding now on his quiet deliberations. Dingo had seen that ostentatious strut before, in the Facility, many a time, and it stirred other images—stark, vivid, ugly, as feculent to the inner olfactory sense as perfumes of raw sewage to one's exposed nasal portals—skulking at the borders of his memory. Lately he'd caught himself thinking often—far too often— about the Facility and about the sinister complicity of police and prosecutors and wise shrinks and luckless parents (whose incinerated remains somehow reached out from the grave falsely to incriminate him) that put him there. Too much remembering. More than was healthy.

And though he had ample leisure now (comfortably settled in the perfect solitude of his immaculate living room, the lights dimmed, snifter of brandy in hand, lulling plink of a piano floating off the stereo) to entertain all manner of irrelevant reflections, however absurd or infuriating, he pushed them away, resolved to steer clear of memory's treacherous quicksand. To remain on the more elevated, inspiriting plane of aspiration and limitless possibility.

Roomy visions opened behind his eyes: himself striking out on his own, a solo player, unencumbered and (after Saturday) substantially bankrolled, breaking new entreprenurial ground, boldly seizing new opportunities, cementing new contacts (the Rolex source, already fruitful, not least among them), networking with a better class of people. It was only fitting things should fall out that way. Only right. Hadn't he, during and after the Facility years, applied himself, studied diligently, watched and learned, planned carefully and executed those plans flawlessly, mastered his calling? Who was more deserving than Odell DeCruz?

And it was time. Time to move on. The empty procession of events that mark the days that shape the directionless lives of other, lesser men, what they

choose to label, mistakenly and in compensation for
a flaccid will, fate or chance or wicked luck—that
was not for him. Of that he was certain.

The shadows in the room lengthened, deepened.
Dingo sipped his brandy, secure in the certainty of
these splendid visions. And yet, perversely, another
Jimmie thought returned to him, not the walk this
time but the pestilent breath, so tolerantly left unre-
marked on over the lengthy course of their association. His nostrils twitched at the recollection. But he
took a kind of whimsical comfort from the equally
certain knowledge that, after Saturday, there would
no longer be any need to equip his car with an air
freshener.

PART
SEVEN

"**H**o-lee kee-rist!" Waz boomed, stringing out the syllables in a melodic rise and fall of astonished consternation. His shovel jaw dropped, mouth hung open, and as he absorbed and processed the dismaying news, his eyes narrowed dangerously. "Why the fuck didn't you *tell* me?"

Della tucked her robe tight at the bosom, prim gesture of a haughty woman determined to abide no carping censure. Yet her face, pale in its absence of paint at this early hour, wore the pouty look of a child whose fear of punishment is veiled behind a wary impudence. "'Cuz I knew you'd just get all steamed," she shot back. "Sure as hell got that one right."

"Goddam right, steamed. Buck's thinkin' everything straight, nothin' to worry about, and now you come tellin' me some asshole shows up here. Right here at my house. Jeez-us *fuck*!"

"Well, least he never came back."

"Not yet he didn't." Waz shoved his chair back and got up and paced the small kitchen furiously, scowling at its linoleum floor. "This happen when, again?" he demanded.

"Other night," she said vaguely.

"I'm askin' you *which* night."

"It was Wednesday," she sighed.

"And you gotta wait three days to let me know?"

"More like two. I was sleepin' when you got back from bowlin'."

"Two, three—fuck's the difference? You shoulda told me."

"Like I said, I knew you'd get bent outta shape. Especially comes to that subject. And I seen you mad before, Waz."

"You sure it was the same guy from that day out on the road there?"

"I think so."

"What's that mean, *think*?"

"Means his face was all beat up, so it was hard to tell for sure."

"Beat up how?"

"Beat up," she repeated petulantly. "Like somebody punched him out."

"How'd he find us?"

"He didn't say."

"What *did* he say?"

"I already told you."

"Tell me again."

Della's eyes did an exasperated spin. "Okay, first he asks for you. I tell him you're not here, and so he starts in on me. Says he seen us up on the tollway, shows me this flyer, like, got Davie's picture on it. He says it's his boy, somebody kidnapped him, and we know about it, got to help him."

"That picture. Was it Buck's boy?"

"It's the same kid, Waz."

"You didn't tell him that?"

" 'Course I didn't. You said not to say anything about it. Any of it."

Waz came over and flopped onto the chair. His shoulders sagged. He stared glumly into a mug of coffee, fixedly, as if the chilling black liquid somehow held a solution to his mounting miseries. All that it gave him was a warped and shimmery reflection of himself.

Della, with a sure feminine instinct for the advantage pendulum swinging her way, said, "He was actin' crazy, Waz. Lookin' that way too. How was I suppose to know what to do?"

In a voice whittled by anxiety he allowed, "Yeah, well, guess you done the best you could."

"I tried."

"Know you did."

"So what're you gonna do now?"

"Fucked if I know. Gotta think."

"You never should've got mixed up in it, first place."

"C'mon, Dell, don't do that 'I told you so' number on me. Buck's the only real friend I got. Who was it come through that time the bill collectors got my nuts in the wringer? Buck is who."

"Loanin' money's one thing. Snatchin' kids, that's something else."

"*Wasn't* snatched!" he declared fiercely. "Was a legal adoption. Just a private kind, was all."

"You know better than that," Della said, phrasing her words coolly, reasonably, backing off a little from the spurt of anger, but not much. "You can't believe that anymore. You got to quit lyin' to yourself, Waz."

"What I gotta do is get movin'," he said with a jittery glance at his watch. He rose and started for the door, hesitated there a beat and then, over his shoulder, asked, "You, uh, still plannin' on comin' out to the hoopla today?"

"Dunno if I want to now."

"Why not?"

"Why? After all that's happened, you askin' me why?"

"Might as well come. Ain't nothin' can be done about it today anyways."

"Later, maybe."

"Pro'ly see you there then, huh?"

"Waz?"

"Yeah?"

"You be careful now."

"About what?"

"You know what. This is scary stuff, what's comin' down here."

"You know somethin'?"

"What's that?"

"Truth is, it scares me too."

Helluva thing for a man to own up to, especially it's his old lady (Waz was thinking, steering the Merc down back streets blessedly empty of traffic at this hour, on his way to dickhead's place), but there it was, out in the open, said, no duckin' it. Mostly was he scared for Buck and Norma, how it gonna tear 'em up, this news, but also for himself, box it put him in, serious flak he gonna catch, maybe even from the law, it was a real snatch job got pulled on the kid. Maybe not, though. All's he done was say a word to a friend, pass along some buzz, instructions. Wasn't like he actually *done* nothin'. Unless they could nail you for bein' a, like, party to the crime, like you see on the TV. If there even was a crime.

Fuck, he didn't know. Only thing he knew for sure anymore was what he told Dell back there: gotta think about it. Think hard. Be a whole lot easier to do, you didn't have a gasbag ridin' along in the car.

Except when he swung around the corner and pulled up at the curb, Lester, he just climbs in and nods and mumbles something sounds like "Mornin'." Which, come to think of it, he'd been doin' all week, actin' peculiar: no stories, no jokes, no fartin' around, nothin' outta him, just sittin' there starin' out the window like some goddam zombie. Which ordinarily be a relief, only now Waz was looking for any excuse not to have to think, so finally he asked him, "Fuck's eatin' you?"

"Whaddya mean?"

"How come you ain't talkin'?"

"Got a trashed head."

"So what's new about that? Your head always half-swacked."

"It's Saturday."

"So?"

"Saturdays I sleep in. Get, y'know, regrouped."

"Nobody makin' you work today. Open house is all volunteer."

"Ain't sayin' they did."

"So quit bitchin'."

"Who's bitchin'? All's I'm sayin' is my rhythm got broke."

"Rhythm," Waz snorted. "Only rhythm you got is your arm swingin' a bottle to your face."

"Why you raggin' on me, Waz? I ain't done nothin'."

"Nobody raggin' you. Just tellin' how it is. Gonna boil your brains, you don't ease up, all that sauce and spike you on."

Lester put his head between his palms. "Okay," he said wearily, "how 'bout I promise to do that, ease off. Startin' tomorrow, or first thing Monday."

"You better, you wanta see your next birthday."

"I will, it'll get me ten minutes a quiet here. Never mind birthdays."

Waz said nothing. He gripped the wheel and drove the rest of the way in stiff silence. Lester calling for quiet? Lester? Dribble-mouth? Made no sense at all. Weird. Everything gone scatty today. Whole world upside down.

Like Waz and Lester, Buck was up early that morning, partly out of a lifetime of habit, partly an insomnia quite uncharacteristic for him. Also like them was he wrapped in silence, sitting alone in the stillness of the kitchen, a cup of watery instant coffee, carelessly prepared, indifferently sipped, and a newspaper, unread, on the table in front of him. Norma and the boy soundly sleeping yet. The house walled in silence.

It wasn't as though his restlessness sprang from

depression or worry. Nothing to worry about any-more. So it wasn't that, exactly. Was more like one of those trifling annoyances that have a way of tak-ing over your life, dominating it, like a splinter lodged deep beneath the skin, say, or a stubborn itch in the unreachable hollow between the shoulder blades. The same curious imbalance he'd felt at bowling the other night. Same peculiar sense of un-certainty, disharmony. Impossible, for a man not given to introspection, to snare with words.

He gave up trying. Stuck a cigarette in his mouth, put a flame to it and then, remembering his pledge, held the smoke in his lungs till he got to the back porch, where he released it into outdoor air already gluey with heat. Already bathed in buttery morning light. He squinted into it, surveying the small strip of ground that belonged to them, the Buckleys, its shrubs and grass and garden and clumps of flowers withering, for all their best efforts, Norma's mostly, under a relentless dog-days sun. Dispiriting, it was, humbling. He resolved to do better, be a better stew-ard of his allotted parcel of earth, his home, family. To shake all those nagging doubts that hounded him. Bury them forever.

This soon-to-be better man heard the creak of the screen door behind him, felt a timid touch at his thigh. He looked down into a pair of sleep-smudged eyes staring up at him in a glaze of confusion. "Hey, boy," he said, the forced jauntiness of a too sudden transition in his voice. "What're you doin' up?"

"Woke up," he said, confirming the obvious.

"It's early."

"Where's she?"

"Huh?"

"She."

"Who? Mom, y'mean?"

"Uh-huh."

"Must be still in bed."

"I go get her?"

"Nah, let's let her sleep awhile. I got a better idea. You hungry?"

A quick little bob of the head, signifying yes.

"There y'go. Gonna be a Cubbie, you got to eat."

It was a reference to the Chicago Cubs legend on the boy's pajamas, a summer-weight cotton trimmed at the elbows and knees, exposing frail pink limbs. He looked puzzled. "What's a cubbie?"

"Baseball player," Buck said, and he reached down and took his hand and led him back into the kitchen. Boosted him, this miniature player, feather-light, onto a chair. He searched a cupboard for cereal. In among the cartons of vitaminized, fortified flakes Norma routinely fed the boy was a box of Froot Loops. What the hell—kid had a treat coming. "You like Froot Loops?"

Another affirmative nod.

"Froot Loops it is."

He filled a bowl, splashed it with milk, and set it before him. Watched him spoon it in, the tiny hands moving steadily, rhythmically, from bowl to mouth, producing the small slurping sounds a child makes. A faint echo from the past buzzed in Buck's ears, kindled a memory, murky and fleeting, of his daughter at this same table, that very chair. To the boy he said, "Maybe we'll go see a ball game one a these days."

The spoon stopped short of the mouth. Eyes lifted expectantly from the bowl. "Go today?"

"Well, no. Not today."

A gaze solemn, wistful, downcast, but without a trace of protest in it.

"Know why not?" Buck asked quickly.

"Unh-unh."

"Remember what day this is?"

"What?"

"Dells day!" Buck exclaimed, the jubilance in his voice genuine now, unfeigned.

"Where the deers are?"

"You got it. Y'know, they got a merry-go-round up there too, just like in the park. Free one. Ride as long as you want."

The eyes widened. Mouth stretched open in a small, hopeful grin.

And seeing it, that wisp of a smile on the face of this boy sitting where Sara once had sat, eating from what had surely once been her bowl, Buck seemed to see again the other child, vividly this time, and to remember his unphraseable, almost uncontainable love for her. And it was something like that he felt now. Something very close.

What Marshall was feeling, that same moment, seated, even as Buck was, at his kitchen table (though without the sustaining presence of a cereal-spooning, memory-sparking child), was a calm almost preternatural, a serenity unlike anything he'd experienced over these past weeks. Certainly unlike the neurasthenic twitchiness of less than an hour ago, jolting out of a sleep dense with dreams that swayed from remote past to unlived-in future with the nutty, time-loosened illogic of dreams. That man, tottering into the bathroom and catching a glimpse of a face shadowed with bruises deep as wine stains and the wild, twinkly eyes of a lunatic clown—that was the man he'd been. No more. This one, stripped of an illusion, no longer haunted by past guilts or tranced by future fictions, existed in a static present grounded on nothing more substantial than a dark conviction of a crossing in store, just ahead. Same face, different man.

The clock on the stove read 7:07. Much too early to get started. The first tour (he'd determined through a call to the plant) was scheduled for nine a.m. Lori was still sleeping. With any luck he'd be gone before she was up. As before, he had no energy to expend in argument. She knew where he was headed, what it was he intended to do, or try to do. She'd accepted that announcement with a tight-lipped wince but, surprisingly, no protests. If she was capable anymore of objections, they went unvoiced. A break for him. After today—however it came out, whatever direction it took—things would change between them. He'd see to that.

The moments ticked silently by. When he looked again, the hands of the clock had advanced to 7:50. Another ten and he would leave, arrive with time to spare, join the tour, find the man. Simple as that. Beyond it he had no plan. No fanciful scenarios, no re-

hearsed scripts. Whatever needed to be said would
come to him. Whatever was required he would do.

He heard a rustling on the floor above him. Footsteps on the stairs. Luck had failed him. While he
didn't believe in omens or portents, he was nevertheless overtaken by a mild dismay. Words, like energy,
were in short supply. So when she came through the
door, he offered a bland "Good morning" and nothing more.

She nodded, sank into a chair. She was bundled in
ankle-length terry cloth robe, seemingly untouched
by the thermometer's rising red bulb, or touched by
it perversely, the way asylum inmates, beguiled by
their private demons, invert the seasons, shivering in
the heat, sweltering in the cold. He ventured the
banal question, "How are you feeling today?"

"Fine."

Fine. Delivered in the clipped accents of a bored
child responding automatically to some adult
inanity: How was school today? Fine. The picnic?
Fine. The circus? Just fine. Marshall withheld a sigh.
"You're looking better," he said, meaning it, for in
spite of the unseasonable robe and terse reply there
was a subtle difference in her, the planes and angles
of her face almost visible again, some of its narcotic
puffiness subsided.

"Thanks."

"Would you like me to fix you some coffee?"

"Are you having any?"

"No."

"No, then."

"Only because I have to leave soon."

"For that factory," she said flatly, no question implied.

"Yes."

"You're determined to go."

"Yes."

"I suppose there's nothing will change your mind."

"No."

She stared at the floor.

"Lori?"

No response.

Now he released the sigh. This was exactly what he'd hoped to avoid. Betrayed by ten short minutes. By his own inertia. "Look," he said wearily, "it's not as bad as you think. I'll get in there, find this person, talk to him. That's it. Inside a plant, all those people around—nothing can happen."

"That's what you said about those bars."

"That was different. I was naive then."

"And now you're not?"

"No . . . well, maybe a little yet."

"They're going to hurt you again, Marsh."

"Not this time."

"So you say."

"Now is not the time to discuss this," he said, rising, his patience dried up. "I'll be back in a few hours. By noon, probably. If I can't find him or can't get anything from him if I do, then we'll go to the police. I promise you."

He started across the room, got as far as the door.

"Marsh?"

"Yes?"

"There's something I need to tell you."

"What's that?"

She lifted her eyes, gazed at him steadily. "I wanted to find him as much as you," she said, her face, vacant of expression only a moment ago, now a landscape of emotions. Curiously, her words carried something of the tone of a plea but none of its substance, declaration more than appeal, an edge almost of defiance in it.

"I never doubted that."

"There was a time when I was strong. I will be again."

"Of course you will," he assured her gently, and with that said he was gone.

She gave it a moment, to be certain, and then she went over to the phone and tapped out a number. A harsh voice winging down the line announced, "District One."

Evenly, very firmly, she said, "I need to speak with Sergeant Wilcox. It's urgent."

About the time Marshall was leaving for the plant, Dingo was surfacing, unassisted by alarm, from a night of restful slumber. His first waking thoughts were sunny, spirited, expectant, and he got up immediately, showered (humming a lively tune), shaved, gargled with Oral Pure mint mouthwash, and blow-dried his hair, after which he deliberated thoughtfully and at considerable length on his choice of wardrobe, settling finally on his finest outfit, worn only for special occasions. Why not? Certainly this day, with its promise of auspicious new beginnings, qualified as special.

Once dressed, he stepped in front of the door mirror and inspected himself critically, head to foot. As always, he was agreeably braced by what it gave back to him, the elegant suit, of course, a salmon pink number with matching handkerchief blossoming like a peony from the breast pocket, though no less the man within it, testing a variety of expressions, smiles mainly, on his reflected likeness. Come a long way from the Facility, that man had, with even further yet to travel.

By now it was approaching nine a.m., so a glance at his Rolex (one of the fakes but soon to be replaced with the real thing) apprised him. Still ample time for a light, nutritious breakfast. Most important meal of the day, he'd read somewhere, energy-wise, and this would be a day that required energy in abundance. Accordingly, he prepared and consumed a soft-boiled egg, two slices of whole grain toast, juice, and a multivitamin capsule. Coffee he skipped. Made him jumpy.

After rinsing the plates and glass and stacking them neatly in the dishwasher, he went into the bedroom and removed the first of three goodly sized cartons from a closet shelf. He carried it through the apartment door, down the hall, and out into the lot. He placed it carefully in the trunk of his Lincoln, went back inside, and returned with the second carton. On his third and last trip he saw a neighbor, a fussy bluehead of slight acquaintance, coming toward him from the other end of the corridor. They converged at the entrance, and she croaked a greeting, " 'Mornin', Mr. DeCruz."

Dingo produced one of his mirror-enhanced smiles, affable and tolerant, this version, if quick to dissolve. "Good morning, Mrs. Gratz."

"Hot enough for ya?"

"Indeed."

"Gonna be a scorcher out there today."

"Well, it is August."

"Knowin' that don't make it any easier."

"I suppose it doesn't," Dingo said neutrally. Since he had no desire to encourage this meteorologic whine, he balanced the carton on one arm, got the door for her with the other, and they exited into a fierce sunlight that confirmed her direst predictions, which she was quick to revive: "What'd I say 'bout hot?"

"You're right again, Mrs. Gratz."

Seemed a mannerly enough closure to this circular dialogue. He turned and started for his car, but she fell in with him, trailing behind a bit, moving with the uncertain wobble of age. "Don't tell me you gotta work today," she bawled after him, assuming, evidently, the rest of the population's hearing was as enfeebled as her own.

"Afraid so."

"On a weekend?"

"Business respects no weekends," Dingo said philosophically.

"What line a business you in?"

"Procurement," he told her. It was a word he'd come across recently, had a flowing grace to it that he liked, a dignity, mystery.

"That the same as sales?"

"You might say that."

They had arrived at the Lincoln now. Dingo bent over the trunk and arranged the three cartons meticulously, securing them against any unforeseen potholes or road ruts. Sixty thousand bones—strike that, sixty thousand *dollars*—sealed in those boxes, can't be too cautious. When he lowered the lid of the trunk, she was still there. Worse than that, she had closed in on him, the nasty old woman smell of her, a pungent confection of dusting powders, gathering sweat, ineffectual deodorizers applied to armpits and assorted body cavities, and some vile stinkwater cologne, defiling the narrow band of ozone between them. Worst of all was that face, its drooly eyes, curdled flesh, liver lips stretched in a snarly grimace (intended, presumably, as a smile) over teeth the color of tarnished brass, thrust almost belligerently into his. The proximity of it all was dizzying. He was reminded, distastefully, of his own mother, she who had birthed him late in life, she who had taken pleasure in trotting him out for the delectation of company (a helpless child on display, like some bauble brought back from a journey, a novelty, curious, amusing, but of no great value), cackling, "Here he is, our little afterthought," which witticism excited a hog-calling laugh from his coarse and equally fossilized father. He wondered, idly but with some small satisfaction, what their final terrified thoughts had been, departing this world in a billow of smoke and inferno of flames. Whoosh!—here one minute, vanished the next. Goodbye, Mom. So long, Dad. Godspeed.

But all that was in the distant past, no longer of any consequence, and he was aware of this present fossil rudely demanding something of him.

"Y'year what I just said?"

"Ah, no. Afraid I missed that."

"Daydreamin', are ya?"

"I hope not, Mrs. Gratz."

"Better not. Can't make no money with your head off in the clouds someplace."

"I'll be sure to keep that in mind."

"What I said was I got a niece in sales."

"Really."

"Dora Gratz her name. My husband's brother's girl. Both of 'em passed on now. The men, I mean, not Dora."

"Sorry to hear that."

"Avon."

Dingo looked at her puzzledly. "I beg your pardon?"

"That's what she sells, Dora. Avon. Goes door to door."

"Dora to door," Dingo said, making a little joke.

"What's that?"

"Nothing."

"That how you do it? Door to door?"

"Not exactly."

"Hard way to make a livin', hear her tell it."

"Perhaps more so for some than others," Dingo drawled, backing away, his endurance exhausted. "You'll have to excuse me now, Mrs. Gratz."

"Gotta leave, do ya?"

"Yes."

"Go do your sellin'?"

"Something like that."

"Well, good luck."

"Thanks."

"You try'n have yourself a nice day anyway. Even if it is hot."

"I'll certainly do my best," Dingo pledged, but the whole loopy conversation, unsolicited and interminable, the uncanny maternal resemblance and the toxic memories it generated—all of it, in concert, seemed to have cast a pall over the promise of the day, soured its niceness in advance.

Marshall was experiencing similar difficulties with a querulous oldster, male in his case, a sallow, shrunken gnome of a man, animate bone bucket come teetering over to examine him up close through eyes moist, myopic and sly, and to demand with the brash presumption that is the prerogative of age, "Hell happen, your face?"

"A little accident," Marshall told him.

"Accident?"

"Yes."

"Huh," the old man snorted skeptically, Adam's apple bobbling like a walnut in the slack-skinned throat, "don't look like no accident to me. Look like somebody whap you upside the head."

"No, it was an accident."

"Gonna leave scars, y'think? This accident?"

"I hope not."

"Could. I knew a fella once, got a banged-up face 'bout like the one you wearin' there, never did heal up. 'Course, it was a thumpin' he took. Wasn't no accident."

"Maybe I'll be luckier."

"Maybe. Wouldn't bet on it."

They were standing in among a flock of people assembled just inside the security building gate, waiting none too patiently for the tour, already well behind schedule, to get underway. Mostly the crowd consisted of women, along with a scattering of children and a handful of geezers in about the same general age bracket of the one accosting Marshall now. To steer the conversation away from his battered visage, he invoked the bland and socially legitimate (particularly given the brutal sun pounding down on them, oozing heat out of a cloudless white sky) topic of weather, remarking, "Hot day."

"Think this is bad, wait'll y'get inside," the old man retorted in yet another of those sour franchises of age, the self-assured forecast of worse to come.

"You've been on these tours before?" Marshall asked, his interest in this grizzled windbag picking up a bit.

"Every one of 'em. Ever since they started doin' 'em back in, oh, '85, think it was."

"You have a relative works here, gets you a pass?"

"Better'n that. I put in thirty-seven years with this company. They gotta let me in."

"You must have made a lot of friends here, that many years."

"Made my share."

"So you come back every year to see them?"

"Who?"

"Your friends."

"Nope," he said, tossing his hairless skull in the direction of a cluster of picnic tables and coolers and portable grills set up outside one of the plant's many entrances. "Myself, I come for the free eats y'get after. They put on a pretty good feed."

"I'm sure they do, but—"

"All y'can eat. Burgers, dogs, salads, pie, pop—you name it. All free too."

"That's very generous of them," Marshall said, and to forestall another interruption he put in quickly, "But about your friends, when you were working here did you happen to know a Mike Wazinski?"

"Wazinski," he repeated, skull in memory-ran-sacking tilt now, "Wazinski. Nope, can't place that name. Couple thousand people workin' here."

"So I've heard," Marshall sighed.

"Why?"

"Why what?"

"Why you ask? You know him, this Wazinski?"

"Not exactly," Marshall improvised. "I know somebody who does, said to say hello. If I should happen to run into him, that is."

"Lotsa luck. It's a big plant."

"I see that."

"This your first time through?"

"Yes."

"What kinda work you do for a livin'?"

"I'm a teacher."

"Schoolteacher?"

"College," Marshall clarified.

The old man looked at him puzzledly, struggling, it seemed, with a concept alien to his experience. "I was a pipe fitter," he declared proudly, "my workin' days."

Marshall was getting mightily sick of all this meandering wheeze. In the hope monosyllables would discourage it he said only, "Oh."

"Lemma tell ya, you gonna learn things today you won't never teachin' school."

"No doubt."

"It's somethin' to see, your first time inside there."

So much for monosyllables. "It will be if we ever get started," Marshall grouched.

"Time's it now?"

"Nine-thirty."

"That's Norse for ya. Always late. Cocksuckers like to make y'sweat for your eats."

As if in divine answer to their shared complaint, a pair of ancient school buses appeared on the other side of the gate, which lifted at a guard's signal and the vehicles rolled through and lurched to a stop. The crowd surged toward them, buzzing like a cloud of agitated flies. A man in a blue twill uniform starched to a regimental stiffness hopped out of the lead bus and put up restraining arms. "Okay, folks, let's just take it easy now," he directed crisply. "Sorry about the delay, but we're finally gonna get this show on the road. Want you to form a couple orderly lines here, board these buses. Take your time, plenty room for everybody."

For Marshall that promised plenty translated ultimately into a small standing space in the aisle of the second bus. All right with him. Anything to escape the chatter of the old man, who had been quick to elbow his way onto the first one. Both vehicles went rattling down the length of the plant, turned a corner, drove another quarter mile, and pulled up at an entrance where two more of the blue twills smilingly waited. The passengers poured out and gathered in a loose semicircle around the uniformed pair, one of whom took a step forward and announced, "Welcome to the annual Norse Aluminum Open House, folks. My name's Chet Skoglund and this fella here is Cliff Bates. He's gonna be your guide this morning. You got any questions, just ask him and—" he gave it a theatrical beat, grinned broadly—"he'll tell you he don't know."

A ripple of laughter passed through the group.

"Plant's runnin' about half capacity today," he continued, grin still locked in place, "just enough so you can get an idea of the process, see where all that kitchen foil an' other fine aluminum products come from. Your tour's gonna take you all through the building. We're talkin' an easy couple hours here, and a good two and a half miles. So I hope you got your walkin' shoes on."

Another pause. Some nervous tittering from his audience.

"Now," he said, voice lowered to sober pitch, "like any industrial facility, there's some serious

safety hazards in here, and last thing we want is anybody get hurt. So for your own protection we ask
you to stay with Cliff and don't go wanderin' off on
your own. Everybody squared away on that point?"

Dutifully nodding heads (Marshall's not among
them) signified they were squared away.

"Any questions before you get started?"

No questions.

"Okay, Cliff," he said with a maestro flourish,
"they're all yours."

Cliff beckoned and they fell in behind him and
filed through the door. Marshall, last in line, batted
his eyes at the sudden transition from brilliant daylight to the sunless world of the plant. The few small
bars of dust-filtered light from the ceiling windows
cast prodigious shadows and played fantastic games
with his vision, reducing him to elfin size in the
sheer immensity of the place, its Brobdingnagian
scale and proportions, towering walls and great
yawning depths. A pygmy he was, stranded in the
kingdom of giants, confused, rattled, deafened by the
thunderous symphony of enormous machines booming, clanging, grinding, chugging, whirring. As-
saulted by the funny stench of scalded metal. And
stricken, finally, by a despair desolate and vast, and
by a chastened awe at the arrogance that first had
impelled him on this impossible search, the prepos-
terous vanity persuading him, in the cool security of
his home, an inspiration would surely arrive, produce the man he sought, carry the day. Blinded, he
was, by a smug faith in his own rectitude, no less

convinced of his own infallibility than that doddering old fool pestering him outside the plant.

Whose bony hand now reached out of the shadows and clutched his arm, and whose raspy voice bawled in his ear, "That Wazinski fella you was askin' about, seems to me I do remember him. Waz we called him."

To which Marshall, astounded by the freakish workings of chance, replied humbly, "Could you tell me how to find him?"

"Works a tool crib, I remember right. In the machine shop. S'pose I could point ya that way."

Which he did, supplying the directions with a conspiratorial smirk.

Marshall offered up a silent prayer for senior citizens, all of them, everywhere. He waited till Cliff was occupied with a long-winded explanation of the function of a soaking furnace, and then he edged to the back of the group and, when the moment presented itself, slipped away.

In marked contrast to the infernal din of the Norse Aluminum plant, the Quinn home was soundless as a sealed crypt. Lori still remained at the kitchen table, watching a phone that stubbornly declined to ring. She felt a peculiar sense of otherness, sitting there, not entirely unpleasant, a paradoxical mix of disjunction and linkage, the way a spirit, some say, will hover over a room in the instant following death, dispassionate witness to the bittersweet world it's soon to leave behind.

This floating self spent her waiting moments re-

constructing the phone conversation of an hour (or
perhaps more, time held equally in airy suspension)
ago, the callous voice informing her, "Wilcox not on
duty today."

"Could you tell me where I could reach him?"

"Home pro'ly."

"Do you have his number?"

"Yeah."

"Well?"

"Not authorized to give out an officer's home
number."

"Is he listed?"

"Not Glenn. He knows better."

"Would you contact him for me? Ask him to call
Lori Quinn. In Naperville. Tell him it's an emergency. Would you do that for me?"

"You talkin' about a police emergency?"

"No. Personal."

There had been a small hesitation, not long.
"S'pose I could maybe give him a jingle," the voice
grudgingly allowed.

"Thank you."

"Can't make no guarantees he'll get back to you."

"I don't expect any."

It was the quiet force of her own voice, remarkably steady, unpleading, absent anymore of fear or
doubt, that had softened him. Of that she was convinced. Through the simple act of picking up an in-
strument of connection with that other world awash
in stormy passions, her departed strength was magically restored, but in curious form, not so much
strength now as engagement without attachment.

Appetite without craving. Desire without will. Fatalism's odd fusion of sinewy resolution and sustaining calm.

She waited. Eventually the phone would ring. Eventually it did. She rose unhurriedly and lifted it out of its cradle. Murmured a greeting.

"Mrs. Quinn?"

"This would be Sergeant Wilcox."

"That's right."

"Thank you for returning my call."

"Station said it was an emergency."

"It is."

"And what's the, ah, nature of this emergency?" he asked, a sober neutrality in his voice.

"My husband is in danger."

"What kind of danger?"

She told him, abridging the story, keeping it manageable, succinct, clear. When it was finished he groaned heavily. "Aah, I tried to tell him stay out of this."

"So did I."

"Why you callin' me, Mrs. Quinn? I'm not on the case."

"You're the only one who cares."

He chose not to remark on that.

"Will you help me?"

"What is it you think I can do?"

"Stop him."

"How'm I gonna do that? I got no authority out there. Not in my jurisdiction."

"You could talk to him. He might listen to you."

"Don't seem likely. Hasn't yet, what you're tellin' me here."

"Will you try?"

"Mrs. Quinn, I'm off today. I got plans."

"Will you break them?" she asked, a petition blunt in its directness, artless in its simplicity.

A silence filled the line. She put nothing into it. Waited. And finally from the far side of that long silence came first a depleted sigh and then the words, "Okay, I'll break 'em."

"Sergeant?"

"Yeah?"

"I'd like to go with you."

"Don't think that's such a good idea."

"Maybe not. But I want to go."

"You sure?"

"Yes."

"Well, s'pose it can't hurt. All we're gonna do is talk."

"Yes, talk."

"You gotta gimme your address, directions. Been awhile since I got out that way."

She gave him both.

"Pick you up in about an hour."

"I'll be waiting."

Jimmie was scooting about importantly on his autoette, now and then favoring a coworker with a wave, occasionally pulling over to remind one of them of the Rolie pickup at the end of the shift, languidly scornful of their plodding grunt lives but much too shrewd to let it show, his own head full of

buoyant visions of the thirty-long bonanza and the
good times it was going to buy, just around the figu-
rative corner and dead ahead. But when he turned a
real corner near the five-stand hot mill and spotted
the weenie slinking along by the rolling belt, eyes
darting busily, taking in everything (everything but
him, spinning the vehicle in sharp U-turn, nick a
fuckin' time too, thank the fuckin' Lord for small fa-
vors) his heart sank, jaw with it, and he exclaimed
out loud, "Holy fuck," the words swallowed up in
the thunk of the machines.

Jimmie had recognized him easily. Instantly. How
you gonna mistake that chopped-liver face? No mis-
takin' your own work, all the good it done him,
shitheel still here and lookin' like he knew exactly
where he was headed, comin' on like a bad case a
the crotch itch, won't go away you scratch it with a
rake. Still gummin' things up. Why the fuck me?
Why now? Knockin' on the door of the biggest single pot a loot in your whole workin' life. Sometimes
a man feel like just throwin' in the towel.

Except there be no towel throwin' today, not with
Mr. Bughouse waitin' in the lot (which thought sent
a shudder of fear through him, it bein' already ten
bells and countin'). He wheeled over to the closest
exit, parked the autoette, and hurried outside. The
sun glanced off the asphalt and stung his eyes, ham-
mered at his head. He squinted into it, made out a
jam of people gathering by the security building
gate. More a the fuckin' gawkers, waitin' for their
turn inside. He stopped suddenly. In among them
was a twat all figged up in pink hot pants and halter

top, pink-rimmed shades, flashy butch haircut, looked like a hooker on the prowl. Only it wasn't no hooker, that much he knew. Was Waz's old lady, cunt who opened up this worm can, first place. And now they both here, her and the weenie both. Run into each other and the whole thing gone straight down the Chinese pisser. Might as well put a stamp on the Jimmie Jack Jacoby ass, address it Stateville, and kiss it goodbye.

His skull throbbed. Headache every place you turn. In the plant, out here, every place. Sun scorchin' you, even the sky got to get in the act. Fuckin' headache from heaven.

No time for headaches. He skirted the edge of the crowd, flicked a salute at the guard (who let him pass without a word: least his jacket for bein' somebody you don't dick with, somebody carries some weight around here, least that still stood up), ducked under the gate and sprinted through the lot. His van was parked in the visitors section, way they'd arranged. Next to it was the black Lincoln. Black as night. Called to mind a hearse, undertaker inside, measuring you with his eyes. He slowed down, pulled in some quick, shallow breaths. Came around to the passenger's side and climbed in. Mumbled a greeting.

"You're late, Jimmie."

"Yeah, I know. But we got us a little snag in there."

Dingo's brows went up, then tightened in a frown. "What kind of snag this time?"

"Remember that goddam citizen I told ya about, one with the flyers, got the kid's picture on it?" Jimmie said, not pausing for answer, speaking very rapidly, as though he was bent on getting through a jumble of thoughts, spilling them out, afraid of losing even a single one to interruption. "He's inside the plant right now. Nosin' around. I seen him. He gets to that polack—or his wife, polack's I'm sayin', she's here too—he gets to either of 'em and we're ass deep in crocodiles."

"That would be alligators," Dingo said quietly.

"Huh?"

"The word is alligators. For the *A* sound. Ass deep in alligators."

"Okay, alligators. Either way, could be bad news for us."

"Bad news is not what I wanted to hear this morning, Jimmie."

"Hey, take a number. Don't exactly mellow me out, tellin' ya."

"My understanding was that you had this problem—what you choose to call a 'little snag'—resolved."

"I *did*!" Jimmie protested. "Least I thought I did. Figured no way this wimp gonna show up again. Not after the thumpin' he took."

"Evidently you were mistaken."

"How'm I suppose to—"

"Be still, Jimmie. I need a moment to think."

Dingo made a meditative steeple of his hands, peered through it, through the windshield, past the assemblage of vehicles glittering under a blaze of sun, and off into the urban rot on the horizon. His face was utterly without expression. His thoughtful moment lengthened. At last he said, "In business, Jimmie, there will always be obstacles that arise unexpectedly. In business you have to learn to be flexible. To treat them as challenges, accommodate them. Fold them into your plan, so to speak. These obstacles, I mean."

"So what're you thinkin' to do, this one?" Jimmie asked fretfully. Clock's tickin' and he's gettin' a goddam business lesson.

Dingo reached over and flipped open the glove compartment. "There's our solution to this particular obstacle," he said.

Jimmie's eyes went buggy. Snubbie in there, couple butterfly knives. Some sensational solution. "You ain't talkin' an icein' here?"

"What else?"

"Jesus, I dunno, Dingo. Tuneup's one thing. But I ain't never zapped nobody before. You know that."

"Actually, I didn't."

"Well, I ain't."

"Always a first time for everything, Jimmie."

"But you can't take a piece inside there. Too many people around."

"I expect you're right," Dingo said. "For a change. We'll use the knives."

He removed them from the compartment, dropped one in Jimmie's lap, and slipped the other under his belt. Jimmie didn't move. He stared at the knife, petrified. Didn't trust himself to speak. All he could think of was the *we* he'd heard in there.

"Pick it up, Jimmie."

"Look, Dingo, this ain't my line. I just don't—"

Dingo laid a gentle finger on his partner's lips. Gentle shushing gesture. "Not to worry," he said, winter in his voice, sleet in his eyes. "I'll show you how it's done. And when it's finished we'll have a chat, you and I."

" 'Bout what?"

"Your breath, among other things. Come along, now. Time is short."

Astonishingly, no one challenged him. A few of the workers glanced up from their stations as he passed, ran incurious eyes over him, and turned away. Maybe it was the general racket, or the heat. Dumb luck, maybe. Whatever the reason, Marshall was not of a mind to explore it. If the directions were right, he was almost there. He kept moving.

Everything about the place summoned an impression of weight, tonnage, a blackened, ugly burden laid on the back of the fragile green earth. Everything ponderous, bulky, larger than life, and noisier. And dangerous, it seemed, as the abundance of signs mounted on the soot-stained walls attested, relaying such redundant alerts as: MAKE EVERY MOVE A SAFE ONE. LET YOUR BRAIN KEEP YOUR HEAD FROM INJURY. THINK SAFETY. EXPECT THE UNEXPECTED. Messages to live by. Even the machines were massive and daunting, fashioned, to his wonderstruck eye, in shapes weird, surreal. Look at that one up ahead: a brace of rockets poised for liftoff, burping steam, issuing a sustained roar; or a gigantic onion peeler, maybe, straddling the crawling belt and skinning the slabs of metal that rolled beneath it. That would be the hot mill, if the old man told true. To the left of it should be an entrance opening onto another wing of the plant. And there it was. The machine shop, stretching back a full fifty yards or more.

He took a cautious step inside. The din was of a different quality and pitch in here, its predominant sound a shrill, grating screak, some background clanking to it, hammering. Odors of oil and grease slicked the air. Along one wall a column of welders, showered in sparks, bent like surgeons over skeletal husks of metal. And on the other, in the corner just off the entrance, stood a boxy, windowless shed.

Marshall approached it. A sign on the door identified it as the Tool Crib and warned all unauthorized personnel to keep out. Authorized only by the justice of his mission, its lawful rightness, authority in plenty for him, he burst through that door unannounced either by knock or query.

And discovered a man of formidable size slouched on a stool, thick shoulders hunched, chin supported by a palm, gaze blankly fixed on the stone floor. The Thinker in blue twill. Meditating under the pale yellow light of an unshaded bulb dangling from the ceiling. Flanked on two sides by steel shelves stacked with the mechanical gadgetry of labor and backed by a wooden workbench strewn with tools. Startled by this sudden intrusion on his private precinct, he demanded, "Fuck're you doin' in here?"

"Looking for you."

"Me?"

"Yes. You."

"And who'd you be?"

"You know who I am."

"What I know is you're somebody who's in a place he ain't suppose to be. This area's off limits to visitors."

Marshall pulled the door shut behind him. "You're Mike Wazinski," he said, a flat assertion of fact.

"Yeah, so?"

"They call you Waz."

"That's right. Still waitin' to hear what you're doin' here."

"I want you to tell me where my son is."

"Dunno what the fuck you talkin' about," Waz declared, but the inward turn of his eyes gave him away, stamped the lie on his face.

"Yes, you do."

"You ain't wrapped too tight, are ya? Now get the—"

"Just tell me, Mr. Wazinski."

Waz got to his feet and crossed the narrow space between them. He stood with his hands planted on his hips, jaw belligerently outthrust. Hostility pooled in his eyes. "What I'm tellin' you," he growled, "is to shag your ass outta here. Before I call security."

"I don't think you're going to do that," Marshall said, looking steadily at this man looming over him, half again his size, bristling with toughness and latent force. He was conscious of his own hands going again, clasping and unclasping, as if to pump courage from the air. "I don't think you're going to call anyone. Not security. Not the police. No one."

"You don't think so, huh?"

"No."

"Why's that?"

"Because you know why I'm here."

"See that phone over there?" Waz said, indicating a beige half shell tacked to the wall above the bench.

"I see it."

"All's I gotta do is pick it up and you're in the deep shit."

"Go ahead. Pick it up."

Waz hesitated. Glared at him. "Aah, you're fuckin' sick in the head. I ain't gonna talk to you no more."

"Yes, you are," Marshall said. He took a quick sideways hop. Blocked the door.

"You gonna get outta my way there?"

"No."

The last brawl Marshall could recall being in (apart from the beating he'd taken the other night, which hardly qualified as a fight) had occurred some two decades ago, some truculent bully goading him into a playground tussle that commenced with an exchange of insults, advanced to threats, erupted in cuffing fists, and culminated in a sprawled tangle of legs and wildly flailing arms, disentangled finally (fortunately for him, his stamina and will draining fast) by some officious schoolmarm. Except for the absence of a scolding angel of deliverance and an expanse of grass and blue sky, this one was not much different. This bully seized him by the shoulders, spun him around, laid a flat hand in his tender face, and sent him reeling into one of the shelving units, from which he pushed off, lunged, wrapped his arms around the broad torso, and tugged it away from the door. They grappled, lurching this way and that, now forward, now back, into the shelves, into the bench, locked in furious embrace, like some goofy, twittery dance choreographed by a drunk. Into the stool it took them, this staggery waltz, toppled them to the floor, tumbling across the stone, Waz, by virtue of his vastly superior strength, emerging on top, pinning him with his bulk, pummeling him with his fists.

Marshall could feel blood squirting from his nostrils and mouth. He thrust a forearm over his face, feeble effort to deflect the heavy blows. He flung the other arm out to one side, grasping for something to serve as a weapon. Anything would do. His hand clutched some object, indistinguishable but weighty, and he swung it in a wide looping arc, the apex of which was the Wazinski skull, the impact sufficient to terminate the pounding and to wrench a chugging grunt from his antagonist, followed by a stiffening, followed by a loose-limbed slump.

Marshall squirmed out from under him. He sucked in some hawking breaths, blinked the fog from his eyes. The object was still in his hand. He recognized it as an ordinary cordless power drill, but it looked curiously like some futuristic raygun, its plastic trigger crimson as the blood leaking from his face, its black barrel spectacularly elongated, its gold-tipped titanium bit a miniature bayonet. He looked at this Mike Wazinski, this bully, on his back now and groaning. Momentarily stunned. *A moment is all that's required,* a voice as remote from his own as the voice of a visitor from a distant galaxy whispered in his ear. He scrambled over and straddled the mound of belly and lowered the spiraled tip of his raygun to the Wazinski throat, snarling toughly, "Goddam you, now you're going to tell me."

Waz glared up the length of the barrel. "Tell you shit."

"Now! Or I'll drill you right into this floor."

"Fuck you."

Marshall slid the bit over onto the rope of muscle sloping from neck to shoulder. He squeezed the trigger, and fragments of ragged flesh and shreds of blue cotton, perhaps a bone chip or two in there as well, rose on a geyser of blood. Waz's scream spiked the air like a flashbulb burst. Marshall released the trigger and covered the widening twist of mouth with his free hand and rode the bucking torso till it was perfectly still, its spasms stopped, the scream run down. *The eyes,* the voice advised him, and that's about what he said: "Tell me where he is or your eyes are next."

"Buck," he gasped.

"What? Speak up."

"Buck's got him."

"Who's Buck?"

"Dale Buckley."

"Where is he? Is he here?"

Waz shook his head no.

Marshall elevated the drill, held it over him, and gave the trigger a quick warning squeeze.

"Westmont. He lives in Westmont."

"Is he there now?"

"I think so."

"You got a phone book here?"

"Yeah."

"Where?"

"Under the bench."

Marshall stood, backed warily over to the bench, stooped down, and produced the directory. "There better be a Dale Buckley in Westmont," he said.

There was. He ripped out the page and tucked it carefully in the pocket of his shirt. The trusty raygun he laid on the bench. Clearly no need for it anymore from the looks of his bloodied opponent, who lay there cringing, glazed with shock, clutching his lacerated shoulder.

About that Marshall was wrong. He started for the door, but it swung open just ahead of him and two men stepped inside. Both of them stood squarely in his path. Both carried wicked-looking knives. One he recognized, the ambusher from the bar, splinter thin, crafting an attitude of menace compounded of scowl and sneer. The other, unknown to him, nattily suited, the glitter in his frosted green eyes softened by an expression of faint, almost charitable, amusement on his lips, shook his head slowly. "Well," he said mildly, "appears to have been a little altercation here."

Marshall said nothing.

"Is this the gentleman, Jimmie?"

"That's him. Figured he'd come here."

"Get the door."

Beans had elected not to work today, which left

Lester alone in a corner of the box shop, listlessly
nailing crates for the packing line and wishing there
was somebody around to sling the shit with. The
quiet he sought, or had claimed to Waz he sought,
was welcome at first but soon enough grew oppressive. Little quiet go a long ways. Especially when
you got a yantsy thought stowed in the back of your
head, keeps creeping up front, won't butt out no
mater how you shoo it away.

Wasn't actually a thought so much as a nagging,
vaguely guilty sensation of something undone, un-
said. He tried to penetrate it, frame it with words.
Okay, you got a friend, been one a long time, years.
Then you got this Quinn fella, barely know him.
Sure, you can feel sorry for a guy like that, kid
bagged and all, but you also got to ask yourself
where your loyalties lie. Trouble was, he pretty
much knew the answer, but he didn't like it. Was like
either way somebody got to eat the hurtburger, and
both of 'em decent guys too.

What he wished now was he'd never run into this
Quinn, first place, never gone back behind the bar
there to help him out, never said nothin' to him
about Waz, never give him a pass to the open house.
Wished he had a redbird, get his head unswizzled.
Wished he'd stayed home today. Wished he'd been
born somebody else. Yeah, right, and if horse turds
was doughnuts we'd eat till we died, or however that
old saying went. Something about wishes and
horses, forgot how the doughnuts got in there.
Maybe because it was comin' up on break time. Dr
Pepper and a sinker go good about now.

He put down his hammer and went out onto the plant floor, pointed for the vending machines. And as he ambled along, a notion gradually insinuated itself in his miseried head, evolved into a decision and resolved the conflict in there. If he hustled he could still get to Waz first, get square with him. The right thing to do? Fuck, he didn't know no more. Least it might scrub away them smudges of guilt. Some of 'em anyways.

He walked faster, broke into a trot. A grunt he passed called, "Hey, Cock, where's the fire?" Lester ignored him. He came down the passageway along the rolling belt, turned into the machine shop, and hurried over to the crib. He paused for an instant, caught his breath, gathered his words. And then he came through the door, saying, "Hey, Wazzer, something I gotta—" And that was as far as he got.

Jimmie whirled around and barked, "Lester, what the fuck you doin' here?"

Lester, goggle-eyed at what he saw—Waz on the floor, moaning; Mr. Quinn backed up to a shelf, bleeding, boxed in by Jimmie and that Dingo dude, both of 'em packin' shanks—mumbled, "Uh, just stopped by to see Waz."

"Nice sense a timing you got."

Frowns and incongruous grins chased each other across Lester's extravagantly startled face. "Yeah, well, I'll be leavin' now," he volunteered apologetically, more accurate than he could have known. Never could he have imagined that the terrible moment of his death had arrived at last. Nor guessed the manner of the death he was about to die. Dingo said

to Jimmie, "Cover him," meaning Quinn; and then
he stepped over to Lester and drew the blade across
his throat, a clean gash, ear to ear; and Lester, sporting the fatal wound like a scarlet secondary grin,
slumped to the floor and died much the same way he
had lived, without protest or fuss or bother.

Like all deaths, Lester's palliated life for someone
else, Marshall in this instance. More even than palliated—salvaged, in fact.

They had exchanged quick facial signals, advanced cautiously, circled him. The skinny one hung
back a bit, his spindly shoulders tight, knife hand extended rigidly, as though in stiff formal greeting. Not
so the other, who moved with the supple grace of a
dancer, blade weaving like the head of a coiled ser-
pent. A slow, expectant smile worked its way into
his face. His eyes seemed to shimmer and spark.

A dry terror constricted Marshall's throat, shel-
lacked his tongue. His arms felt leaden, his feet sta-
pled to the floor. The raygun, abandoned in the
presumptuous arrogance of a self-assured certainty,
lay on the bench, tauntingly out of reach. Paralyzed,
he watched them close in on him. The dancer's blade
split the air, speed of a laser, and opened a diagonal
fissure from Marshall's collarbone to his waist. Half
of an X. He felt a stinging sensation, more prickly
than painful. Warm emergent blood seeped around
the edges of his ripped shirt.

"That's called a slice and dice," the dancer informed him. "Know what a splatter platter is?"

Marshall found enough voice to say simply, "No," though he suspected he knew.

"That's what happens next."

Undoubtedly it would have too, had it not been for Lester's sudden appearance, untimely for him, fortuitous for Marshall, who seized the subsequent instant of Lester's grisly passing to lunge for the drill and to touch its trigger, flattening the skinny one against a shelf with a jabbing motion, clearly understood, as though Marshall possessed the power to discharge the whirring bit like some lethal minimissile, which instead he drove into the flank of the dancer, spinning too late to dodge it, though in the violence of his convulsive shudder wrenching it from Marshall's grip and sending it clattering across the floor, spitting rashers of torn flesh. His knees buckled. A squawk, guttural, croaky, but remarkably restrained considering the pain he must have felt, echoed off the walls and ceiling of the shed. Marshall bolted for the door, made it through, but not before he heard rising on the sustained squawk the bawled commands, "Get him! Kill him!"

He came out shouting, his voice a frantic yip lost in the dissonant, unrhythmic clash of sounds. He glanced to his right, his left, searching desperately for help. Welders busily welded, machinists machined. Nobody took notice. No help here. The scrawny one stumbled through the door. Scrawny, yes, puny even, but empowered by deadly knife and emboldened by vengeful purpose.

He took off running. Less was it a run, this flight, than ambulant twitch, part hobble, part skitter, the

comic wiggly motion of a windup toy, its mecha-
nisms defective, corroded. He got to the entrance,
looked over his shoulder and discovered, as in some
cataclysmic vision, his pursuer narrowing the gap
between them. About to fall on him.

He swiveled. Backpedaled toward the rolling belt.
Some unyielding object stalled his retreat. A Dumpster, by the feel of it, redolent of freshly shaved
metal. He stiffened himself against it. No help anywhere. Nowhere left to run.

Like some runtish agent of ruin, the knife wielder
pressed in on him. Slowed. Stopped short of him by
a couple of feet. His eyes were wild. Mouth a ven-
omous slit. His blade hand made quick pecking
thrusts. Over the boom of the hot mill thundering up
behind them, he bellowed, "What'd I tell you, suck-
wad? What'd I say? Now you gonna feel the heavy
hurts."

Marshall reached over the top of the Dumpster,
grasped a jagged sheet of scrap metal, sidestepped
and raked the makeshift weapon across the eyes of
the charging figure. Who screamed. Dropped the
knife. Caromed off the Dumpster, reeled about
blindly, a spastic dance. Marshall plowed into him,
driving him back, sprawling him face first onto the
belt. A great silvery ingot bore down on him like the
prow of a massive dreadnought.

Marshall's senses registered, in concert, a dazzling
blue: deep rumble, hiss of oil, splash of scalded
water, howls of unendurable agony, acrid stink of
grinding metal, sour tang of shredding tissue; peculiar seepage at his chest; savor of varnish in his

mouth; flashes of bone and gristle and butchered meat, tomatoey red, crawling up the small lateral conveyor belt and firing into the Dumpster. He allowed himself an ironic coda to this extraordinary sensory spectacle: "Your turn for the hurts."

He set out again, retracing the route that had brought him to the machine shop. His step was steadier now, surer. Along the way he passed his tour group. The guide spotted him, called, "Sir, sir." Marshall responded with a dismissive swatting at air, kept on moving in the direction of an exit just ahead. Never looked back.

Which was a mistake. For if he had he might have seen the other one, the dancer, not so nimble now, not so agile, but still stumbling on doggedly, gaining on him.

The sight of them out there, Dale and Davie, her two men, advancing across the lawn, taking turns with the hose, conscientiously, if belatedly, drenching the parched grass and hopeless garden, filled her with such joy she felt almost weightless, anchored only by a heart grown too big for her chest. Almost sanctified she felt, blessed by this gentle, good man, and by the solemn, sweet child miraculously plucked from life's bewildering grab bag, its surprises sometimes exquisite (Sara, for instance), often cruel (again, Sara), always mysterious.

Norma stood at the kitchen window, shaking off the torpor that comes with the unaccustomed luxury of a late sleep. Unobserved herself and watching them this way, thinking these thoughts, she experienced a curious scattering of emotions. There was the joy, of course, and the pleasured anticipation of a family outing about to begin. But also, sprung from nowhere, an odd sensation of misgiving, of a reckoning yet to come, and, odder still, the shadowy guilt of the eavesdropper or the stealthy witness to a loved one's slumber, the familiar face sealed with secrets, weirdly distanced behind the impenetrable mask of sleep.

A trilling of the phone released her from these bizarre and unwelcome reflections. She said her hello into it and got back a breathy voice telegraphic in its message: "Gotta talk to Buck."

"Waz? Is that you?"

"Yeah, me."

"Is something wrong?"

"No. He there, Buck?"

"Yes."

"Put him on, can you?"

"Just a minute. I'll get him."

She fluttered over to the screen door and called, "Dale, telephone for you." He handed Davie the hose, directed him by gesture to a particularly arid patch of lawn, and walked leisurely toward the house. As he neared the porch she said, "It's Waz. He sounds awfully strange."

"Whadda you mean, strange?"

"Not like himself."

His face darkened. He speeded up. Came through the door and crossed the room and lifted the phone to his ear. "Waz," he said. "What's up?"

"He's comin'."

"Who is?"

"The old man."

"Who you talkin' about?"

"Davie's old man."

It was strange, all right, his friend's voice, clotted and thick and full of the squeezed accents of pain. Also was Buck conscious of the sounds of water running in the sink behind him, drawers opening and shutting. Norma elaborately busying herself, but listening, surely listening. Had to keep cool, steady. Had to choose his words carefully. "How you know that?" he asked.

"He was here."

"At the plant there?"

"Yeah."

"You talk to him?"

"Yeah."

"How'd he find you?"

"Dunno."

"You, uh, told him?"

"I hadda, Buck. He jumped me. Cut me up bad. Woulda killed me."

"You okay?"

"Yeah. Lester, though, he's dead."

"Lester? How'd he get in it?"

"Bad luck."

"He did it?"

"Who?"

"That fella you said."

"No."

"Who, then?"

"Jimmie in on it. Some other guy. Don't matter now."

"And you say he's comin'?"

"Yeah."

"When?"

"Now."

Buck felt a sudden sickness of the heart. Though he couldn't have known it, all the color was drained from his face. "All right," he said formally. "Thanks for lettin' me know."

"Buck?"

"What?"

"Listen, I'm sorry."

"That's okay, man. You done what you could."

"You watch out for yourself, now."

"Yeah, I'll do that."

He put up the phone. Braced himself against the wall. Against the tidal waves of shock washing over him, numbing him. Against the lynch mob world tightening in on him.

"Dale, what is it? What's wrong?"

That would be Norma addressing him, her features crimped in an attitude of wifely concern. Had to speak to Norma. Tell her something. Buy some time. "Been an accident out to the plant," he told her. Wasn't all that far off the truth.

"An accident? What happened?"

"Uh, boiler blew," he improvised. "Somethin' like that. Ain't exactly clear."

"Was Waz hurt?"

"No, he's okay."

"Thank God for that."

"But Lester was."

"Lester?"

"Lester Caulkins. You remember him? Chubby little guy, all the time tellin' crazy stories?"

"I remember him. Was he hurt bad?"

"Got killed."

"Oh, Dale, that's just terrible. I'm so sorry."

Everybody sorry today, but nobody got any answers, directions, solutions. Him included. "Yeah, well, that's how it goes sometimes," he said, for a thing to say.

"But Waz is all right?"

"He's fine."

"Do you want to go over there?"

For a moment he didn't reply. Something unusual was happening inside his head. Half of it was attending to this time squandering conversation, supplying him words absent and empty of substance, while the other half sorted through a tumbling rush of crafty plots, schemes, tactics, visions of flight, exotic destinations, safe harbors, all of them out of reach, as phantasmal as those shimmery fragments of dreams that nudge the borders of sleep.

"Dale?"

"Huh?"

"Do you think you should go out to the plant?"

Out of desperation's negative reduction he arrived finally at the only sanctuary he knew. He said, "No, nothin' I can do there. Gonna go over to the park awhile. Take the boy."

Norma looked puzzled. "But why would you go there?"

"Just I need some time to, y'know, think about this. What happened and all. We'll get started later, Dells."

"We don't have to go today, Dale. Not if you're upset."

"Said we will," he snapped, and because now she looked hurt he added quickly, "just little later, is all."

"I understand. Are you sure you want Davie along?"

"I'm sure."

He was too, sure as he was of anything anymore. Park was safe. Park was a place you could run to. Get your head straight. Get a plan together. Something solid, workable, made some sense. He'd come up with one. Time was all he needed. Little quiet, and time.

Except there was Norma here, and the guy, the father—*maybe* father—coming, on his way right now. What about Norma? Bring her along? Leave her here? He didn't know. Everything snarled, disordered. Everything a riot of confusion. And instantaneous choices to be made. "Look," he said, "if anybody comes by, don't tell 'em where we at."

"Why not?"

"Because I'm askin' you, is why. Better yet, don't talk to nobody. Lock the doors and stay inside."

A gathering alarm clouded her face, and the concern he'd seen before was rapidly shading over into apprehension, and from there to dread. "There's more to this, isn't there? More than you're telling me."

"Just do it, okay? Do it for me. We'll be back real soon."

He sprinted out into the yard and scooped up the boy and carried him around the house to the Pontiac parked in the drive, mumbling something about the park, the ducks, the merry-go-round. Something incoherent. The child, half bewildered by this abrupt change of plan, half delighted, said nothing, but he waved a vigorous goodbye to Norma, standing at the front door, watching them with stricken eyes. She returned the wave limply.

Buck backed the car into the street and streaked away. He was still mumbling, but his gaze was fixed on the road. Had he looked in the mirror above the dash he'd have seen a boxy Volvo just then rounding a corner a few blocks behind them, and picking up speed.

Except for the wardrobe, Glenn Wilcox off duty was, by training and instinct and a lifetime of jaded experience, not a whole lot different from when he was on the clock: stolid, unflappable, leery, alert behind the curtain of perpetual fatigue. He'd been on enough domestics, his day, to know enough to come strapped, and from what he could get out of her on the drive to Cicero (which wasn't much beyond the bare-bones account he'd heard over the phone), this one was shaping up a possible domestic. Or worse. Near as he could tell, what you got here is a loose cannon hub playing at gumshoe, raising sand with some very tough citizens, sinking himself deeper in the doo by the ticking minute. Add to that a wife spaced on one kind of helper or another, trying to throw him a line he don't want.

Stir them ingredients together and you got a bag of first-class fireworks waiting to go off. Fourth of July in August.

Accordingly, he'd brought along a throwdown piece (discreetly hip-holstered under his loose-fitting jacket) and a pair of cuffs (slid under the front seat of his ancient Dodge), just in case. Even though his capacity here was strictly unofficial, like some poor schmuck neighbor or a distant relation unwillingly dragged in to referee a family dispute, never hurt to pack some policy. Come this close to hanging it up for good, last thing he needed was a blindside zap off a good-deed errand gone bad. Stranger things been known to happen. Your luck, could happen to you. So you better be alert.

'Course, it was his own fucking fault, being here, first place. Never learned. Was always a mark for a fluff in distress (though this one, sitting there with her hands folded in her lap, absent look on her face, seemed more resigned than distressed, aloof from it all, a pretty lady on her way to a party she'd rather not attend). Still was booting himself in the ass for caving in. Putting himself between a rock and another one just as hard. Doing the eagle scout number, a role he never liked, was never really suited for, and not very good at either.

He liked it even less when he turned the Norse Aluminum corner and came down the road leading to the security building and saw what he'd hoped not to see: couple of Cicero P.D. cars, their dome lights whirling, an ambulance, also sparking, and a jam of people swarming around an entrance to the plant. He stole a quick peek at her, expecting a panicked yelp or instant waterworks. Got neither. Instead all she said, quietly and with her hands still in her lap, was, "I knew this would happen."

"We don't know what 'this' is yet, Mrs. Quinn. You don't wanta go leapin' to conclusions."

"It's him."

"Whyn't we find out first?"

"It's him."

A flash of his shield got them by the gate. He pulled up behind one of the Cicero cars, cut the engine, loosened the knot in the tie he wished now he hadn't worn. "You better wait here," he said.

"No, I'll come along."

"Think you oughta wait till I see what's shakin' down."

"No."

There was a firmness in it that drew his eyes to her face. Years on the force had inoculated him against the contagion of pity, but all that proximity to corruption and cynicism never quite rubbed off. Never quite took. And looking at that serene, stubborn, reconciled face, looking through it, past it, into the pools of darkness of her disaster-struck life, he seemed to see, telescoped there, a time-crumbled album of all the faces of all the victims of all the world's pitiless crimes, and he felt as though he'd stumbled, quite by chance, upon something in himself long ago mislaid, long forgotten. "Okay," he said, "but you got to do exactly what I tell you."

"I will, Sergeant."

"Start by stickin' close."

"Whatever you say."

"Let me do the talkin'."

"Of course."

"I say you go back, you go."

"Well, we'll see."

"Mrs. Quinn?"

"Yes."

"Could be nothin' here. With your husband, I mean."

"We'll see."

He elbowed a path for them through the buzzing crowd, sidled up to a Cicero badge, a squat, doughy man planted like a roadblock at the front of the ambulance. Wilcox presented his ID. The officer gave it a thorough inspection, fastened an insolent stare on him, and drawled, "Kinda off your turf, ain't you, Sergeant?" The suburban cop's natural resentment of a downtowner.

"Was in the neighborhood," Wilcox said. "Thought you could maybe use some help." Might as well start off diplomatic.

"Takin' in the Cicero sights, was you?"

"Something like that."

"Sure do appreciate the offer, but we're gettin' it secured. More cars on the way."

"What went down?"

"Looks like a couple waxings. Maybe more."

"Any witnesses?"

"Why you ask?"

"Because I'm lookin' for a fella might of been involved."

"So you moonlightin' today?"

"How about you just tell me?" Wilcox growled, putting some squad room steel in his voice. Enough with the diplomacy.

It got results. "Was one," the badge said. "Got cut up pretty bad. They're workin' on him right now." A thumb wag at the ambulance specified where.

"He in a condition to talk?"

"Was when they brought him out."

"You got any objection, me havin' a word with him? Got any pro'lum with that?"

The officer grudged him a lippy smile just short of a sneer. "S'pose it couldn't hurt," he allowed, adding with a meaningful glance at the woman standing there, taking it all in, "long as it's just yourself."

"She's with me," Wilcox told him, to spare her any hassling, but to her he said, "Here's where you wait."

She responded wordlessly, a small compliant nod.

He strode to the back of the vehicle. Its door was wide open, a flurry of activity going on in its cramped interior: scurrying medics, sobbing female stooped over an ashen-faced vic laid out on a stretcher, wicked gouge in him. But he wasn't who Wilcox fully expected to see. Wasn't Marshall Quinn.

He identified himself, climbed in, and knelt by the stretcher. A medic scowled at him. "This man's in shock, Officer."

"Just a couple quick questions here."

"This is *not* a good time."

Wilcox tuned him out. To the vic he said, very gently, "Sir, can you tell me what happened?"

Got only a hollow-eyed gaze for reply.

"I'll tell ya who done this to him," the woman wailed, her voice full of the hysteric music of anger and grief.

Another voice, faint, slurry, rose from the stretcher. "Shut up, Della."

"Goddamned if I'll shut up. Not this time. 'Bout time somebody said something."

"You his wife?" Wilcox asked.

"Yeah, I'm his wife. He'd've listened to me, none of this would've happened."

Beneath her the husband groaned miserably.

"Whyn't you tell it to me?" Wilcox suggested.

"You bet I'll tell ya. Was the same crazy bastard come to our house other night. Lookin' for his kid."

"You sure about that?"

"Goddam right I'm sure."

"How's that?"

" 'Cuz he just told me. When they was bringin' him out here."

"He say where this person is now?"

"On his way to the Buckleys."

"An' who'd they be, these Buckleys?"

"Ones got the kid."

"You got an address?"

She did. She gave it to him, along with the instructions to find the son bitch, lock him up, and throw away the key.

"See what I can do," Wilcox said noncommittally, and he hopped out onto the asphalt and hurried to the

front of the ambulance. Mrs. Quinn saw him coming. She started to say something, but he cut her off
with a staying motion, a quick fanning of air.

"You get anything?" the badge wanted to know.

"Nah, was a false alarm."

"False alarm," he repeated doubtfully.

"That's right."

"Detectives oughta be here any minute now.
Maybe you should be talkin' to them."

"Good thought," Wilcox said, but his movements
said something else. He took Mrs. Quinn by the arm,
turned her around, and led her away, whispering in
her ear, "Wasn't him."

"But where—"

Wilcox made his fanning gesture again.

"Where you goin'?" the badge called after them.

Over his shoulder, in parting shot, Wilcox called
back, "Wanna thank you for your cooperation. You
burb boys really know how to treat a brother officer."

In the car he said, "Your husband's walkin' a high
wire in a windstorm."

She looked at him baffledly.

"He's gettin' himself in serious trouble," he translated for her.

"Has he been hurt?"

"Not as far as I know. Ain't in the meat wagon
back there."

"Do you know where he is?"

"Maybe," was all he volunteered. About the kid
he said nothing. Better to leave that one alone for
now. Got enough to keep him occupied.

Not the least of which was locating the address. Fuck did he know about the geography out here? Dick is what he knew. So he took Ogden west till he saw a sign said Westmont, then swung south and wound through some residential streets till he came across the one he was looking for. He turned onto it and went two blocks, checking the ascending house numbers. Wrong fucking direction. He made a sudden bootleg and headed the other way. Finally found it.

He parked along the curb opposite the house, gave the scene a quick visual sweep. No vehicles in the drive, none on the street. Place looked quiet. No signs of trouble. Maybe he got lucky, beat the trailblazer professor over here. About time for some luck.

"Are you going to tell me what we're doing here?" she asked calmly.

"What I'm gonna tell you is to stay put. No arguments, okay?"

"Is Marsh here?"

"I dunno."

"Is my son?"

Already she put it together. Quick lady. Whole lot different from the way he remembered her, them couple times at the station. How, exactly, he wasn't sure. "Dunno that either," he said truthfully. "But if you wait here like I'm tellin' you, I'll find out."

She deliberated a moment, not long. "I trust you," she said. "I'll wait."

It was the calm, was different, and the total absence of fear or hope, either one. Was almost spooky, all that calm. All that control. Like she was putting her trust in the hands of the Lord. Him being the Lord. Some Lord.

He hurried up the walk, climbed the porch steps, and laid a thumb on the bell. Nobody came to the door, no sounds from inside. He went around to the back, saw a hose snaked out across the grass, pumping water. Didn't much like the looks of that. Maybe got here late instead of early. Not so lucky after all.

He gazed at the house, pondering his dwindling store of moves. A shadow of a figure flitted past a window. He approached the door, pounded on it, and kept on pounding till a shaky female voice behind it said, "Who's there?"

"Police. Open up."

The door pulled back a notch. He stuck his shield in it. "Mrs. Buckley?"

"Yes?"

"Glenn Wilcox, Chicago P.D. Like to speak with your husband if I could."

"He's not here now."

"You tell me where I can find him?"

"Why? What's wrong?"

"Nothin' wrong," he lied. "Just I need to talk to him."

"What about? Maybe I can help you."

"I do appreciate that, but it's him I gotta talk to."

"It's about Davie, isn't it?"

"Davie's your boy?"

"Yes."

"He here with you?"

"No, he's with Dale."

"That's your husband, Dale?"

"Yes."

"You had any other, uh, visitors this morning?"

"No. Please tell me what's happening. Please."

There were tears in her voice now. Kindly as he could, Wilcox said, "Be better if you tell me where it is your husband's at."

Where he was just then was not, in measurable distance, all that far removed, under a mile, in fact, though if it were measured in the manic accelerating confusion in his head, he could as easily have been on the dark side of the moon. With the boy clutched tightly to his chest, he raced through the park, past the playground, around the pond, and up the slight grade to the carousel. The sun stood high in a white, luminous sky. Bars of light penetrated the branches in the thick stand of trees, seemed to sprint along with him as he ran. A towering oak, home to a chittering choir of birds, seemed to warble a medley of jeers. Everything seemed queerly slanted, warped, askew.

Nevertheless, he kept running. Arrived at last at the refuge of the ticket booth. Set the boy down, leaned over the counter, and demanded simply, "Tickets."

"We ain't open yet," said a sour-looking old man, his eyes droopy-lidded, skin the bleached yellow of a withering tobacco leaf.

"Start it up. He's gonna ride."

"You deaf? Said we ain't open."

Buck thrust out a hand and seized him by the collar. "What *I* said was start it up."

The lids lifted, mouth twisted into an effort at accommodating mercantile smile. "Okay, okay. Guess we can get 'er rollin' little early. You wanna let go my shirt here?"

Buck released him, yanked out his wallet, and emptied all its bills on the counter.

"How many tickets you want, anyways?"

"Many as that'll buy."

"How long you plannin' for him to ride?"

"Long as he wants. All day, he wants."

The old man stepped out the back of the booth, muttering something about loony fucks. He went over to the squat box of an engine and hit some switches. The carousel seemed to erupt in a dazzle of flashing lights and a strident blast of tinny music.

Buck hoisted Davie onto one of the smirky mounts. "What'd I tell ya?" he said triumphantly. "I say we was gonna ride?" His voice was cracked and trembling. Sweat dampened his shirt, slicked his brow.

The child looked at him doubtfully, as though uncertain if this was a question to be responded to or merely a statement of accomplished fact. He interpreted it as the latter and remained silent.

Buck signaled the old man, who pulled a lever and set the horses prancing and spinning in their closed circle. After a couple of turns Buck leaped off the platform and positioned himself, sentinel-like, at the gate in the guard rail, his feet spaced wide, fists balled, jaw rigid, eyes relentlessly shifting, scanning

the park, the trees, the pond, the small clusters of
people beginning to appear. Out of which he picked
a figure coming up the slope, moving in a slow, for-
ward-stooping lurch, leaving a trail of blood in the
laggard shadow he tugged along behind him.

A blind spot, by ophthalmological definition, is
the small area, insensitive to light, where the optic
nerve enters the retina of the eye. In commonplace
usage, particularly among drivers, it is that zone,
also small, where one's vision is blocked or ob-
scured. Kierkegaard, with the philosopher's heavily
portentous assertion of the obvious, defines it simply
as that which you cannot see.

By no stretch of these definitions could the black
Lincoln Town Car be described as veiled in a blind
spot. A quick glance in the rearview mirror would
have revealed it behind him, initially little more than
a smudge on the receding horizon, gradually enlarg-
ing, taking shape, shrinking the margin between
them, tenacious as a whirlwind, reliable as death.
But Marshall's attention and vision were narrowed
in on another vehicle, the one pulling away from the
very house he was searching for, and out ahead of
him now by several blocks, a man at the wheel and,
unmistakably, a child in the passenger's seat. Jeff?
He couldn't be sure.

He drove wildly, reckless of caution, squealing
around corners, bolting stop signs, zooming past intruding cars, his horn a sustained rude bray. Still
couldn't seem to gain on them. Not until they turned
into the lot of what appeared to be a large suburban

park. He brought the Volvo to a gear-grinding stop. Through the windshield he could see the man dashing toward—of all unlikely destinations—a merry-go-round situated on a little welt of a hill on the other side of a wide pond. The child in his arms was clearly a boy. Jeff? Still too much distance to tell. He set out after them. Soon enough he'd know.

Amazing to himself was his vigor, his stamina. He felt feathery, almost buoyant, as though the ground had slid away beneath him and he were treading on a cushion of air, impervious anymore to pain, indifferent to ooze of blood. To his left was a clump of trees so dense they seemed to have embalmed the night in a shroud of branches; to his right the surface of the pond caught the light and glistened like a mirror of polished green glass; up ahead the carousel's music, piping, shrill, allegro, floated toward him, an aural beacon, guiding him on.

Slight as it was, the incline slowed him, restored his feet ploddingly to earth. The muscles in his legs trembled. Air escaped his lungs in ragged gasps. He trudged up the hill. Like scaling a mountain of wet cement. At the summit of which stood a man whose body, square and thick, bunchy with muscle, seemed charged with energy, all its strength squeezed into a tight, belligerent knot. And who took a step toward him, scowlingly demanding, "What do you want?"

Marshall looked at him, then past him, to the cantering troop of horses, riderless but for one. And that one he recognized as his son. "Him," he said.

"Who are you?"

"His father."

"*I'm* his father! I adopted him. Legal, fair. You're nobody. Leave us alone."

"No. He was kidnapped. I'm taking him back."

"You want him, you gotta come through me."

"Then I will."

"How you gonna do that? Look at you. I could break you in two."

"I don't know how. Find a way."

But as it turned out he didn't have to, for at just that moment the miniature rider passed behind them, and his eyes fell on Marshall. "Dad?" he called, an astonished lift in his voice. His shoulders twisted, neck craned, and on the next pass he scrambled off his mount and hopped off the spinning platform and came running toward Marshall, the shouted "Dad" transformed into a whoop of joy, no longer any question in it.

Marshall gathered him up. The child studied him guardedly. "You come back," he said.

"Yes. I came back."

"To stay?"

"To stay."

The man watched them, stunned, beaten, his face twisted in an anguish of loss, as though he had just crossed the border into the bitter country of truth. Marshall considered him defiantly. "Now what do you say?"

No reply. No more threats. No remonstrances. Nothing. And in the stony vault of his heart, Marshall felt something peculiar, only dimly remembered, something approaching pity for this sorrowed man who claimed to be the father, probably nothing

more than another pawn in this ugly game, remorse-
lessly toppled. "I guess . . . well . . . I guess I'm
sorry," he stammered.

Maybe he was too. It was possible. But not sorry
enough to keep him from turning away and starting
down the hill, retracing his path along the trees and
around the pond, wobbling a bit under the weight of
his son. Who gingerly touched his bruised face and
said, "You cut yourself, Dad."

"That's right."

"It hurt?"

"How about if I say only when I laugh."

"Huh?"

"No, it doesn't hurt."

"You tore your shirt," the boy persisted.

"So I did."

"Mom be mad."

"We won't tell her," Marshall said, and they
grinned at each other in the unuttered conspiracy of
love.

But another voice, drifting toward them from behind the trees, flat as an echo ascending from the
bottom of a deep well, declared, "Could be somebody else is mad, though."

Dingo had pulled in next to the Volvo and followed him with his eyes, this meddling, soon-to-be-
wormfood citizen limping and staggering through
the park, barely on his feet. It had given him a certain grim, if incomplete, satisfaction, helped a little
to soothe his own pain, which was like a siren gone
off inside him, wailing down every boulevard and

back alley of his punished body, thrumming its far-
thest outskirts. Raising a godawful racket. To muffle
it, get centered again, focused, he allowed himself a
moment's respite. Little intermission before the last
act.

Cigarette might help. There was time. He tapped
himself (taking care to avoid the damp, pulpy hole in
his side) till he found a pack in a breast pocket of his
jacket, irreparably ruined now, its fabric shredded
and hopelessly stained. His best suit too. Another
good reason why some payback was in order. And
Odell DeCruz, damaged goods or not, was just the
man to deliver it. Express mail.

Curiously, the cigarette pack was moist with
blood. Blood flowing upward? Defying gravity?
Couldn't be. Made no sense. He examined his hands,
crimson-stained and sticky. There's your answer.
Every riddle yields to analysis, reason. No mysteries.
Other than the big one: what went wrong?—what
mix of flawed judgment and evil luck combined to
bring him to this sorry and entirely unforeseen condition? For that he had no ready answers. Puzzle it
out later, after this errand was run.

He touched the glowing tip of the dash lighter to
the cigarette dangling from his lips. Inhaled. The
smoke scored his lungs but seemed to steady him
some, hush the siren. Still was a bad habit, smoking,
picked up in the Facility years ago. Have to kick it
one of these days, or cut down. Meantime, though,
he watched, fascinated, as the ash on this one slowly
advanced, relentless as a mud slide engulfing a field
of snow. Called to mind the blight unfairly cast over

this life of his, so meticulously fashioned, created from nothing, woven of soaring visions and burning thirsts, and reduced in an instant, a finger snap, to a cinder heap of fractured illusions and botched plans and broken dreams. Another riddle to be addressed, unraveled.

But not now. Time to get moving now, get properly stationed. At considerable cost in lancing pain, he reached over, opened the glove compartment, removed the snub-nosed Ruger .38, and tucked it under his belt, the ungashed side. No less painful was the walk to the grove of trees, the sun beating on him, light glinting off the water like points of daggers in the eyes, the world seeming to pitch and sway beneath his feet.

He stepped into the grove's merciful shade. Braced himself against the sturdy trunk of a tree. In its branches, high above, a flock of birds twittered and chirped. A singing tree. Better that than the siren wail, starting in on him again, a rising screech, piercing and shrill.

It didn't matter. He could manage, endure. He'd survive. More than survive. Prevail. All he had to do was nurture the slow, silent ferocity building in his head. And wait. Eventually the citizen would have to pass this way.

And at last he did.

"You!"

"Who else? You think I'd forget you? After this hole you put in me?"

Marshall was held mute in an instant of sickened

dismay. It wasn't fair. Come this close, this far—wasn't fair. Yet there he was, the dancer, blanched, bloodied, rocking from side to side like some comical drunk, but coming at them all the same, mouth set in a fierce smile, eyes in cold, unblinking glare, and the weapon in his hand this time a gun. A knife you could dodge maybe, if you were nimble enough, or wrest away, if you were strong enough, or maybe outrun. Not a gun.

He backed toward the pond. Lowered Jeff to the ground and made a little shooing gesture. "Move away now," he said.

The boy looked up at him, baffled and hurt. "Dad? You said—"

"Just get away from here. Go."

"Squirrel stays," the dancer hissed at him.

"What?"

"Kid. He's a part of this too. He stays."

"But you can't mean to—"

"Man holding the piece can do anything he wants."

Inarguably true. And Marshall, motionless as an insect sealed in amber, could only gaze, mesmerized, at the gun leveled on them, at the malevolent figure holding it, and then beyond him, into the space directly behind him, gradually filling with another figure, the aspirant father, coming down the hill in a bullish, legs-pumping charge. And Marshall's eyes, loaded with wonder and perhaps a snippet of hope, gave away something; for the dancer wheeled around and got off a round just as the figure drove into him, slamming them both to the ground.

It was like watching the sluggish motion of under-water action. At the sound of the shot a tree seemed to explode with birds, blackening the sky. The gun seemed to sail through the air. The dancer seemed to be wriggling out from under the inert figure sprawled over him. Marshall heard himself calling, "Run, Jeff, run!" but the child was too terrified to move. So was he. Till the action seemed magically to accelerate, and he saw the dancer scrambling for the gun and, destitute of options, he threw himself on him and they tumbled across the grass, panting, grunting, cursing, limbs twined, bloods mingling, fused like some maddened, thrashing beast, rolling down the bank and plunging into the murky water and under it for what seemed an immensity of time. Till the grip on him loosened, and he came up gagging and sputtering. Till the head bobbed to the surface and, seething with fury, he grasped it by the throat and forced it under again, howling, "Gonna kill us, are you? See who does the killing. See."

Arms and legs flailed and splashed around him. He didn't mind. Nothing to him. Barely conscious of them anyway, for all that remained of his strength was funneled into his hands, and all his rage codified in a single word, chanted over and over again, a lunatic singsong: "Kill kill kill kill. . . ."

"That's enough, Mr. Quinn."

His own voice, counseling mercy? Seemed doubtful. The demon in his head, urging prudence? Even less likely. He turned slightly, enough to detect a new figure, pair of them actually, a male, bear-bulky, baggy-faced, vaguely familiar, and next to him, sheltering Jeff in her arms, a female who appeared to be his wife. He stared at them dazedly.

"Said that's enough. Let him go."

There was, in that sharp command, an authoritative growl Marshall remembered from somewhere. Couldn't quite place where. He released his grip on the throat, and the man waded into the pond, jerked the soggy dancer upright, dragged him roughly onto the bank, flattened him, yanked his arms behind him, and slapped handcuffs on the wrists. It came back to Marshall who he was, this briskly efficient fellow. That cop, Sergeant somebody, forgot the name.

The cop shambled over to the other figure, the fallen one, lying in the grass, mouth ajar, eyes wide open and bulging and fixed on nothing at all. He stooped down and examined him, but only briefly. With a hard glance at Marshall he said, "This one's dead."

"Dead?"

"Yeah, dead."

Marshall, still standing in the water, did his best to assimilate that blunt pronouncement, bald in its simplicity, stark in its finality. But it wasn't easy. Something seemed to be giving way inside him, like a tunnel punched through a wall of granite and out into the wan light of what he remembered of what was commonly called reality. Dead. This man who could have broken him in two but hadn't, rescued them instead. And all the others: Lester dead; the one he'd killed at the plant; the one he might have killed had he refused to speak, drilled him through without a second thought; and the one up on the bank that he surely would have killed had someone not intervened. The lilting strains of the carousel drifted down the hill. Corpses of wasps and dragonflies floated on a scum of moss lapping at his knees. Living, he was surrounded by death.

"How 'bout him?"

The cop again, indicating the cuffed figure twitching like a snared fish on the grass. "What about him?" Marshall said. Question for a question.

"Who is he?"

"I don't know."

A squint of doubt came into the canny, weary eyes. "Lot you don't know, Mr. Quinn."

"He tried to kill us. That much I know."

"Well, you better come outta there. It's over now."

Over, was it? Every fable has a beginning and an ending and events in between, but an ending is not necessarily a resolution, nor a beginning a commencement. The memories of all that had gone before this fable's beginning and the visions of all that would follow its ending came to him now like a dream draped in shadow, its dreamer a stranger to that man he had once been, the two no longer even on nodding terms.

The woman who held his salvaged son and who was certainly his wife regarded him cautiously, as though from across some galactic distance, a melancholy speculation in her eyes. She rewarded him with a faint smile, scarcely more than a flicker, and said, "You did it, Marsh. You found him."

Though it cost him a small stitch of pain and no

little awe over all he had forfeited to arrive at this moment of tarnished triumph, he lifted his shoulders in a lopsided shrug. "Yes, well . . . promise is a promise."